CHANTRY HOUSE

CHARLOTTE M. YONGE

1st WORLD
LIBRARY
Literary Society

Chantry House

Charlotte M. Yonge

© 1st World Library, 2007
PO Box 2211
Fairfield, IA 52556
www.1stworldlibrary.com
First Edition

LCCN: 2007927763

Softcover ISBN: 978-1-4218-4512-8
Hardcover ISBN: 978-1-4218-4428-2
eBook ISBN: 978-1-4218-4596-8

Purchase *"Chantry House"*
as a traditional bound book at:
www.1stWorldLibrary.com/purchase.asp?ISBN=978-1-4218-4512-8

1ˢᵗ World Library Literary Society

Giving Back to the World

"If you want to work on the core problem, it's early school literacy."

- James Barksdale, former CEO of Netscape

"No skill is more crucial to the future of a child, or to a democratic and prosperous society, than literacy."

- Los Angeles Times

"Literacy... means far more than learning how to read and write... The aim is to transmit... knowledge and promote social participation."

- UNESCO

"Literacy is not a luxury, it is a right and a responsibility. If our world is to meet the challenges of the twenty-first century we must harness the energy and creativity of all our citizens."

- President Bill Clinton

"Parents should be encouraged to read to their children, and teachers should be equipped with all available techniques for teaching literacy, so the varying needs and capacities of individual kids can be taken into account."

- Hugh Mackay

CHAPTER I

A NURSERY PROSE

'And if it be the heart of man
Which our existence measures,
Far longer is our childhood's span
Than that of manly pleasures.

'For long each month and year is then,
Their thoughts and days extending,
But months and years pass swift with men
To time's last goal descending.'

ISAAC WILLIAMS.

The united force of the younger generation has been brought upon me to record, with the aid of diaries and letters, the circumstances connected with Chantry House and my two dear elder brothers. Once this could not have been done without more pain than I could brook, but the lapse of time heals wounds, brings compensations, and, when the heart has ceased from aching and yearning, makes the memory of what once filled it a treasure to be brought forward with joy and thankfulness. Nor would it be well that some of those mentioned in the coming narrative should be wholly forgotten, and their place know them no more.

To explain all, I must go back to a time long before the morning when my father astonished us all by exclaiming, 'Poor old James Winslow! So Chantry House is came to us after all!' Previous to that event I do not think we were aware of the existence of that place, far less of its being a possible inheritance, for my parents would never have permitted themselves or their family to be unsettled by the notion of doubtful contingencies.

My father, John Edward Winslow, was a barrister, and held an appointment in the Admiralty Office, which employed him for many hours of the day at Somerset House. My mother, whose maiden name was Mary Griffith, belonged to a naval family. Her father had been lost in a West Indian hurricane at sea, and her uncle, Admiral Sir John Griffith, was the hero of the family, having been at Trafalgar and distinguished himself in cutting out expeditions. My eldest brother bore his name. The second was named after the Duke of Clarence, with whom my mother had once danced at a ball on board ship at Portsmouth, and who had been rather fond of my uncle. Indeed, I believe my father's appointment had been obtained through his interest, just about the time of Clarence's birth.

We three boys had come so fast upon each other's heels in the Novembers of 1809, 10, and 11, that any two of us used to look like twins. There is still extant a feeble water-coloured drawing of the trio, in nankeen frocks, and long white trowsers, with bare necks and arms, the latter twined together, and with the free hands, Griffith holding a bat, Clarence a trap, and I a ball. I remember the emulation we felt at Griffith's privilege of eldest in holding the bat.

Charlotte M. Yonge

The sitting for that picture is the only thing I clearly remember during those earlier days. I have no recollection of the disaster, which, at four years old, altered my life. The catastrophe, as others have described it, was that we three boys were riding cock-horse on the balusters of the second floor of our house in Montagu Place, Russell Square, when we indulged in a general melee, which resulted in all tumbling over into the vestibule below. The others, to whom I served as cushion, were not damaged beyond the power of yelling, and were quite restored in half-an-hour, but I was undermost, and the consequence has been a curved spine, dwarfed stature, an elevated shoulder, and a shortened, nearly useless leg.

What I do remember, is my mother reading to me Miss Edgeworth's Frank and the little do Trusty, as I lay in my crib in her bedroom. I made one of my nieces hunt up the book for me the other day, and the story brought back at once the little crib, or the watered blue moreen canopy of the big four-poster to which I was sometimes lifted for a change; even the scrawly pattern of the paper, which my weary eyes made into purple elves perpetually pursuing crimson ones, the foremost of whom always turned upside down; and the knobs in the Marseilles counterpane with which my fingers used to toy. I have heard my mother tell that whenever I was most languid and suffering I used to whine out, 'O do read Frank and the little dog Trusty,' and never permitted a single word to be varied, in the curious childish love of reiteration with its soothing power.

I am afraid that any true picture of our parents, especially of my mother, will not do them justice in the eyes of the young people of the present day, who are accustomed to a far more indulgent government, and yet seem to me to know little of the loyal veneration and submission with which we have, through life, regarded our father and mother. It would have been reckoned disrespectful to address them by these names; they were through life to us, in private, papa and mamma, and we never presumed to take a liberty with them. I doubt whether the petting, patronising equality of terms on which children now live with their parents be equally wholesome. There was then, however, strong love and self-sacrificing devotion; but not manifested in softness or cultivation of sympathy. Nothing was more dreaded than spoiling, which was viewed as idle and unjustifiable self-gratification at the expense of the objects thereof. There were an unlucky little pair in Russell Square who were said to be 'spoilt children,' and who used to be mentioned in our nursery with bated breath as a kind of monsters or criminals. I believe our mother laboured under a perpetual fear of spoiling Griff as the eldest, Clarence as the beauty, me as the invalid, Emily (two years younger) as the only girl, and Martyn as the after-thought, six years below our sister. She was always performing little acts of conscientiousness, little as we guessed it.

Thus though her unremitting care saved my life, and was such that she finally brought on herself a severe and dangerous illness, she kept me in order all the time, never wailed over me nor weakly pitied me, never permitted resistance to medicine nor rebellion against treatment, enforced little courtesies, insisted on every required exertion, and hardly ever relaxed the rule of Spartan fortitude in herself as in me. It is to this resolution on her part, carried out consistently at whatever present cost to us both, that I owe such powers of locomotion as I possess, and the habits of exertion that have been even more valuable to me.

When at last, after many weeks, nay months, of this watchfulness, she broke down, so that her life was for a time in danger, the lack of her bracing and tender care made my life very trying, after I found myself transported

Charlotte M. Yonge

to the nursery, scarcely understanding why, accused of having by my naughtiness made ray poor mamma so ill, and discovering for the first time that I was a miserable, naughty little fretful being, and with nobody but Clarence and the housemaid to take pity on me.

Nurse Gooch was a masterful, trustworthy woman, and was laid under injunctions not to indulge Master Edward. She certainly did not err in that respect, though she attended faithfully to my material welfare; but woe to me if I gave way to a little moaning; and what I felt still harder, she never said 'good boy' if I contrived to abstain.

I hear of carpets, curtains, and pictures in the existing nurseries. They must be palaces compared with our great bare attic, where nothing was allowed that could gather dust. One bit of drugget by the fireside, where stood a round table at which the maids talked and darned stockings, was all that hid the bare boards; the walls were as plain as those of a workhouse, and when the London sun did shine, it glared into my eyes through the great unshaded windows. There was a deal table for the meals (and very plain meals they were), and two or three big presses painted white for our clothes, and one cupboard for our toys. I must say that Gooch was strictly just, and never permitted little Emily, nor Griff—though he was very decidedly the favourite,—to bear off my beloved woolly dog to be stabled in the houses of wooden bricks which the two were continually constructing for their menagerie of maimed animals.

Griff was deservedly the favourite with every one who was not, like our parents, conscientiously bent on impartiality. He was so bright and winning, he had such curly tight-rolled hair with a tinge of auburn, such merry bold blue eyes, such glowing dimpled cheeks, such a joyous smile all over his face, and such a ringing laugh;

he was so strong, brave, and sturdy, that he was a boy to be proud of, and a perfect king in his own way, making every one do as he pleased. All the maids, and Peter the footman, were his slaves, every one except nurse and mamma, and it was only by a strong effort of principle that they resisted him; while he dragged Clarence about as his devoted though not always happy follower.

Alas! for Clarence! Courage was not in him. The fearless infant boy chiefly dwells in conventional fiction, and valour seldom comes before strength. Moreover, I have come to the opinion that though no one thought of it at the time, his nerves must have had a terrible and lasting shock at the accident and at the sight of my crushed and deathly condition, which occupied every one too much for them to think of soothing or shielding him. At any rate, fear was the misery of his life. Darkness was his horror. He would scream till he brought in some one, though he knew it would be only to scold or slap him. The house-maid's closet on the stairs was to him an abode of wolves. Mrs. Gatty's tale of The Tiger in the Coal-box is a transcript of his feelings, except that no one took the trouble to reassure him; something undefined and horrible was thought to wag in the case of the eight-day clock; and he could not bear to open the play cupboard lest 'something' should jump out on him. The first time he was taken to the Zoological Gardens, the monkeys so terrified him that a bystander insisted on Gooch's carrying him away lest he should go into fits, though Griffith was shouting with ecstasy, and could hardly forgive the curtailment of his enjoyment.

Clarence used to aver that he really did see 'things' in the dark, but as he only shuddered and sobbed instead of describing them, he was punished for 'telling fibs,' though the housemaid used to speak under her breath of his being a 'Sunday child.' And after long penance, tied to his stool in the corner, he would creep up to me and whisper, 'But, Eddy, I really did!'

However, it was only too well established in the nursery that Clarence's veracity was on a par with his courage. When taxed with any misdemeanour, he used to look round scared and bewildered, and utter a flat demur. One scene in particular comes before me. There were strict laws against going into shops or buying dainties without express permission from mamma or nurse; but one day when Clarence had by some chance been sent out alone with the good natured housemaid, his fingers were found sticky.

'Now, Master Clarence, you've been a naughty boy, eating of sweets,' exclaimed stern Justice in a mob cap and frills.

'No—no—' faltered the victim; but, alas! Mrs. Gooch had only to thrust her hand into the little pocket of his monkey suit to convict him on the spot.

The maid was dismissed with a month's wages, and poor Clarence underwent a strange punishment from my mother, who was getting about again by that time, namely, a drop of hot sealing-wax on his tongue, to teach him practically the doom of the false tongue. It might have done him good if there had been sufficient encouragement to him to make him try to win a new character, but it only added a fresh terror to his mind; and nurse grew fond of manifesting her incredulity of his assertions by always referring to Griff or to me, or even to little Emily. What was worse, she used to point him out to her congeners in the Square or the Park as 'such a false child.'

He was a very pretty little fellow, with a delicately rosy face, wistful blue eyes, and soft, light, wavy hair, and perhaps Gooch was jealous of his attracting more notice than Griffith, and thought he posed for admiration, for she used to tell people that no one could guess what a child he was for slyness; so that he could not bear going out with her, and sometimes bemoaned himself to me.

There must be a good deal of sneaking in the undeveloped nature, for in those days I was ashamed of my preference for Clarence, the naughty one. But there was no helping it, he was so much more gentle than Griff, and would always give up any sport that incommoded me, instead of calling me a stupid little ape, and becoming more boisterous after the fashion of Griff. Moreover, he fetched and carried for me unweariedly, and would play at spillekins, help to put up puzzles, and enact little dramas with our wooden animals, such as Griff scorned as only fit for babies. Even nurse allowed Clarence's merits towards me and little Emily, but always with the sigh: 'If he was but as good in other respects, but them quiet ones is always sly.'

Good Nurse Gooch! We all owe much to her staunch fidelity, strong discipline, and unselfish devotion, but nature had not fitted her to deal with a timid, sensitive child, of highly nervous temperament. Indeed, persons of far more insight might have been perplexed by the fact that Clarence was exemplary at church and prayers, family and private,—whenever Griff would let him, that is to say,—and would add private petitions of his own, sometimes of a startling nature. He never scandalised the nursery, like Griff, by unseemly pranks on Sundays, nor by innovations in the habits of Noah's ark, but was as much shocked as nurse when the lion was made to devour the elephant, or the lion and wolf fought in an embrace fatal to their legs. Bible stories and Watt's hymns were more to Clarence than even to me, and he used to ask questions for which Gooch's theology was quite insufficient, and which brought the invariable answers, 'Now, Master Clarry, I never did! Little boys should not ask such questions!' 'What's the use of your pretending, sir! It's all falseness, that's what it is! I hates hypercriting!' 'Don't worrit, Master Clarence; you are a very naughty boy to say such things. I shall put you in the corner!'

Even nurse was scared one night when Clarence had a frightful screaming fit, declaring that he saw 'her—her—all white,' and even while being slapped reiterated, 'HER, Lucy!'

Lucy was a kind elder girl in the Square gardens, a protector of little timid ones. She was known to be at that time very ill with measles, and in fact died that very night. Both my brothers sickened the next day, and Emily and I soon followed their example, but no one had it badly except Clarence, who had high fever, and very much delirium each night, talking to people whom he thought he saw, so as to make nurse regret her severity on the vision of Lucy.

CHAPTER II

SCHOOLROOM DAYS

'In the loom of life-cloth pleasure,
Ere our childish days be told,
With the warp and woof enwoven,
Glitters like a thread of gold.'

JEAN INGELOW.

Looking back, I think my mother was the leading spirit in our household, though she never for a moment suspected it. Indeed, the chess queen must be the most active on the home board, and one of the objects of her life was to give her husband a restful evening when he came home to the six o'clock dinner. She also had to make both ends meet on an income which would seem starvation at the present day; but she was strong, spirited, and managing, and equal to all her tasks till the long attendance upon me, and the consequent illness, forced her to spare herself—a little—a very little.

Previously she had been our only teacher, except that my father read a chapter of the Bible with us every morning before breakfast, and heard the Catechism on a Sunday. For we could all read long before young gentlefolks

Charlotte M. Yonge

nowadays can say their letters. It was well for me, since books with a small quantity of type, and a good deal of frightful illustration, beguiled many of my weary moments. You may see my special favourites, bound up, on the shelf in my bedroom. Crabbe's Tales, Frank, the Parent's Assistant, and later, Croker's Tales from English History, Lamb's Tales from Shakespeare, Tales of a Grandfather, and the Rival Crusoes stand pre-eminent— also Mrs. Leicester's School, with the ghost story cut out.

Fairies and ghosts were prohibited as unwholesome, and not unwisely. The one would have been enervating to me, and the other would have been a definite addition to Clarence's stock of horrors. Indeed, one story had been cut out of Crabbe's Tales, and another out of an Annual presented to Emily, but not before Griff had read the latter, and the version he related to us probably lost nothing in the telling; indeed, to this day I recollect the man, wont to slay the harmless cricket on the hearth, and in a storm at sea pursued by a gigantic cockroach and thrown overboard. The night after hearing this choice legend Clarence was found crouching beside me in bed for fear of the cockroach. I am afraid the vengeance was more than proportioned to the offence!

Even during my illness that brave mother struggled to teach my brothers' daily lessons, and my father heard them a short bit of Latin grammar at his breakfast (five was thought in those days to be the fit age to begin it, and fathers the fit teachers thereof). And he continued to give this morning lesson when, on our return from airing at Ramsgate after our recovery from the measles, my mother found she must submit to transfer us to a daily governess.

Old Miss Newton's attainments could not have been great, for her answers to my inquiries were decidedly funny, and prefaced sotto voce with, 'What a child it is!' But she was a good kindly lady, who had the faculty of teaching, and of forestalling rebellion; and her little thin corkscrew curls, touched with gray, her pale eyes, prim black silk apron, and sandalled shoes, rise before me full of happy associations of tender kindness and patience. She was wise, too, in her own simple way. When nurse would have forewarned her of Clarence's failings in his own hearing, she cut the words short by declaring that she should like never to find out which was the naughty one. And when habit was too strong, and he had denied the ink spot on the atlas, she persuasively wiled out a confession not only to her but to mamma, who hailed the avowal as the beginning of better things, and kissed instead of punishing.

Clarence's queries had been snubbed into reserve, and I doubt whether Miss Newton's theoretic theology was very much more developed than that of Mrs. Gooch, but her practice and devotion were admirable, and she fostered religious sentiment among us, introducing little books which were welcome in the restricted range of Sunday reading. Indeed, Mrs. Sherwood's have some literary merit, and her Fairchild Family indulged in such delicious and eccentric acts of naughtiness as quite atoned for all the religious teaching, and fascinated Griff, though he was apt to be very impatient of certain little affectionate lectures to which Clarence listened meekly. My father and mother were both of the old-fashioned orthodox school, with minds formed on Jeremy Taylor, Blair, South, and Secker, who thought it their duty to go diligently to church twice on Sunday, communicate four times a year (their only opportunities), after grave and serious preparation, read a sermon to their household on Sunday evenings, and watch over their children's religious instruction, though in a reserved undemonstrative manner. My father always read one daily chapter with us every morning, one Psalm at family prayers, and my mother made us repeat a few verses of Scripture before our other studies began; besides which there was special teaching on Sunday, and an abstinence from amusements, such as would now be called Sabbatarian, but a walk in the Park with papa was so much esteemed that it made the day a happy and honoured one to those who could walk.

There was little going into society, comparatively, for people in our station,—solemn dinner-parties from time to time—two a year, did we give, and then the house was turned upside down,—and now and then my father dined out, or brought a friend home to dinner; and there were so-called morning calls in the afternoon, but no tea-drinking. For the most part the heads of the family dined alone at six, and afterwards my father read aloud some book of biography or travels, while we children were expected to employ ourselves quietly, threading beads, drawing, or putting up puzzles, and listen or not as we chose, only not interrupt, as we sat at the big, central, round, mahogany table. To this hour I remember portions of Belzoni's Researches and Franklin's terrible American adventures, and they bring back tones of my father's voice. As an authority 'papa' was seldom invoked, except on very serious occasions, such as Griffith's audacity, Clarence's falsehood, or my obstinacy; and then the affair was formidable, he was judicial and awful, and, though he would graciously forgive on signs of repentance, he never was sympathetic. He had not married young, and there were forty years or more between him and his sons, so that he had left too far behind him the feelings of boyhood to make himself one with us, even if he had thought it right or dignified to do so,—yet I cannot describe the depth of the respect and loyalty he inspired in us nor the delight we felt in a word of commendation or a special attention from him.

The early part of Miss Newton's rule was unusually fertile

in such pleasures, and much might have been spared, could Clarence have been longer under her influence; but Griff grew beyond her management, and was taunted by 'fellows in the Square' into assertions of manliness, such as kicking his heels, stealing her odd little fringed parasol, pitching his books into the area, keeping her in misery with his antics during their walks, and finally leading Clarence off after Punch into the Rookery of St. Giles's, where she could not follow, because Emily was in her charge.

This was the crisis. She had to come home without the boys, and though they arrived long before any of the authorities knew of their absence, she owned with tears that she could not conscientiously be responsible any longer for Griffith,—who not only openly defied her authority, but had found out how little she knew, and laughed at her. I have reason to believe also that my mother had discovered that she frequented the preachings of Rowland Hill and Baptist Noel; and had confiscated some unorthodox tracts presented to the servants, thus being alarmed lest she should implant the seeds of dissent.

Parting with her after four years under her was a real grief. Even Griff was fond of her; when once emancipated, he used to hug her and bring her remarkable presents, and she heartily loved her tormentor. Everybody did. It remained a great pleasure to get her to spend an evening with us while the elders were gone out to dinner; nor do I think she ever did us anything but good, though I am afraid we laughed at 'Old Newton' as we grew older and more conceited. We never had another governess. My mother read and enforced diligence on Emily and me, and we had masters for different studies; the two boys went to school; and when Martyn began to emerge from babyhood, Emily was his teacher.

Charlotte M. Yonge

CHAPTER III

WIN AND SLOW

'The rude will shuffle through with ease enough:
Great schools best suit the sturdy and the rough.'

COWPER.

At school Griffith was very happy, and brilliantly successful, alike in study and sport, though sports were not made prominent in those days, and triumphs in them were regarded by the elders with doubtful pride, lest they should denote a lack of attention to matters of greater importance. All his achievements were, however, poured forth by himself and Clarence to Emily and me, and we felt as proud of them as if they had been our own.

Clarence was industrious, and did not fail in his school work, but when he came home for the holidays there was a cowed look about him, and private revelations were made over my sofa that made my flesh creep. The scars were still visible, caused by having been compelled to grasp the bars of the grate bare-handed; and, what was worse, he had been suspended outside a third story window by the wrists, held by a schoolfellow of thirteen!

'But what was Griff about?' I demanded, with hot tears of indignation.

'Oh, Win!—that's what they call him, and me Slow—he said it would do me good. But I don't think it did, Eddy. It only makes my heart beat fit to choke me whenever I go near the passage window.'

I could only utter a vain wish that I had been there and able to fight for him, and I attacked Griff on the subject on the first opportunity.

'Oh!' was his answer, 'it is only what all fellows have to bear if there's no pluck in them. They tried it on upon me, you know, but I soon showed them it would not do'—with the cock of the nose, the flash of the eyes, the clench of the fist, that were peculiarly Griff's own; and when I pleaded that he might have protected Clarence, he laughed scornfully. 'As to Slow, wretched being, a fellow can't help bullying him. It comes as natural as to a cat with a mouse.' On further and reiterated pleadings, Griff declared, first, that it was the only thing to do Slow any good, or make a man of him; and next, that he heartily wished that Winslow junior had been Miss Clara at once, as the fellows called him—it was really hard on him (Griff) to have such a sneaking little coward tied to him for a junior!

I particularly resented the term Slow, for Clarence had lately been the foremost of us in his studies; but the idea that learning had anything to do with the matter was derided, and as time went on, there was vexation and displeasure at his progress not being commensurate with his abilities. It would have been treason to schoolboy honour to let the elders know that though a strong, high-spirited popular boy like 'Win' might venture to excel big bullying dunces, such fair game as poor 'Slow' could be terrified into not only keeping below them, but into doing their work for them. To him Cowper's 'Tirocinium' had only too much sad truth.

As to his old failing, there were no special complaints, but in those pre-Arnoldian times no lofty code of honour was even ideal among schoolboys, or expected of them by masters; shuffling was thought natural, and allowances made for faults in indolent despair.

My mother thought the Navy the proper element of boyhood, and her uncle the Admiral promised a nomination,—a simple affair in those happy days, involving neither examination nor competition. Griffith was, however, one of those independent boys who take an aversion to whatever is forced on them as their fate. He was ready and successful with his studies, a hero among his comrades, and preferred continuing at school to what he pronounced, on the authority of the nautical tales freely thrown in our way, to be the life of a dog, only fit for the fool of the family; besides, he had once been out in a boat, tasted of sea-sickness, and been laughed at. My father was gratified, thinking his brains too good for a midshipman, and pleased that he should wish to tread in his own steps at Harrow and Oxford, and thus my mother could not openly regret his degeneracy when all the rest of us were crazy over Tom Cringle's Log, and ready to envy Clarence when the offer was passed on to him, and he appeared in the full glory of his naval uniform. Not much choice had been offered to him. My mother would have thought it shameful and ungrateful to have no son available, my father was glad to have the boy's profession fixed, and he himself was rejoiced to escape from the miseries he knew only too well, and ready to believe that uniform and dirk would make a man of him at once, with all his terrors left behind. Perhaps the chief drawback was that the ladies WOULD say, 'What a darling!' affording

Griff endless opportunities for the good-humoured mockery by which he concealed his own secret regrets. Did not even Selina Clarkson, whose red cheeks, dark blue eyes, and jetty profusion of shining curls, were our notion of perfect beauty, select the little naval cadet for her partner at the dancing master's ball?

In the first voyage, a cruise in the Pacific, all went well. The good Admiral had carefully chosen ship and captain; there were an excellent set of officers, a good tone among the midshipmen, and Clarence, who was only twelve years old, was constituted the pet of the cockpit. One lad in especial, Coles by name, attracted by Clarence's pleasant gentleness, and impelled by the generosity that shields the weak, became his guardian friend, and protected him from all the roughnesses in his power. If there were a fault in that excellent Coles, it was that he made too much of a baby of his protege, and did not train him to shift for himself: but wisdom and moderation are not characteristics of early youth. At home we had great enjoyment of his long descriptive letters, which came under cover to our father at the Admiralty, but were chiefly intended for my benefit. All were proud of them, and great was my elation when I heard papa relate some fact out of them with the preface, 'My boy tells me, my boy Clarence, in the Calypso; he writes a capital letter.'

How great was our ecstasy when after three years and a half we had him at home again; handsome, vigorous, well-grown, excellently reported of, fully justifying my mother's assurances that the sea would make a man of him. There was Griffith in the fifth form and a splendid cricketer, but Clarence could stand up to him now, and Harrovian exploits were tame beside stories of sharks and negroes, monkeys and alligators. There was one in particular, about a whole boat's crew sitting down on what they thought was a fallen tree, but which suddenly swept

Charlotte M. Yonge

them all over on their faces, and turned out to be a boa-constrictor, and would have embraced one of them if he had not had the sail of the boat coiled round the mast, and palmed off upon him, when he gorged it contentedly, and being found dead on the next landing, his skin was used to cover the captain's sea-chest. Clarence declined to repeat this tale and many others before the elders, and was displeased with Emily for referring to it in public. As to his terrors, he took it for granted that an officer of H.M.S. Calypso, had left them behind, and in fact, he naturally forgot and passed over what he had not been shielded from, while his hereditary love of the sea really made those incidental to his profession much more endurable than the bullying he had undergone at school.

We were very happy that Christmas, and very proud of our boys. One evening we were treated to a box at the pantomime, and even I was able to go to it. We put our young sailor and our sister in the forefront, and believed that every one was as much struck with them as with the wonderful transformations of Goody-Two-Shoes under the wand of Harlequin. Brother-like, we might tease our one girl, and call her an affected little pussy cat, but our private opinion was that she excelled all other damsels with her bright blue eyes and pretty curling hair, which had the same chestnut shine as Griff's—enough to make us correct possible vanity by terming it red, though we were ready to fight any one else who presumed to do so. Indeed Griff had defended its hue in single combat, and his eye was treated for it with beefsteak by Peter in the pantry. We were immensely, though silently, proud of her in her white embroidered cambric frock, red sash and shoes, and coral necklace, almost an heirloom, for it had been brought from Sicily in Nelson's days by my mother's poor young father. How parents and doctors in these days would have shuddered at her neck and arms, bare, not only in the evening, but by day! When she was a little younger she could so shrink up from her clothes that Griff, or little Martyn, in a mischievous mood, would put things down her back, to reappear below her petticoats. Once it was a dead wasp, which descended harmlessly the length of her spine! She was a good-humoured, affectionate, dear sister, my valued companion, submitting patiently to be eclipsed when Clarence was present, and everything to me in his absence. Sturdy little Martyn too, was held by us to be the most promising of small boys. He was a likeness of Clarence, only stouter, hardier, and without the delicate, girlish, wistful look; imitating Griff in everything, and rather a heavy handful to Emily and me when left to our care, though we were all the more proud of his high spirit, and were fast becoming a mutual admiration society.

What then were our feelings when Griff, always fearless, dashed to the rescue of a boy under whom the ice had broken in St. James' Park, and held him up till assistance came? Martyn, who was with him, was sent home to fetch dry clothes and reassure my mother, which he did by dashing upstairs, shouting, 'Where's mamma? Here's Griff been into the water and pulled out a boy, and they don't know if he is drowned; but he looks—oh!'

Even after my mother had elicited that Martyn's HE meant the boy, and not Griff, she could not rest without herself going to see that our eldest was unhurt, greet him, and bring him home. What happy tears stood in her eyes, how my father shook hands with him, how we drank his health after dinner, and how ungrateful I was to think Clarence deserved his name of Slow for having stayed at home to play chess with me because my back was aching, when he might have been winning the like honours! How red and gruff and shy the hero looked, and how he entreated no one to say any more about it!

He would not even look publicly at the paragraph about it in the paper, only vituperating it for having made him into 'a juvenile Etonian,' and hoping no one from Harrow would guess whom it meant.

I found that paragraph the other day in my mother's desk, folded over the case of the medal of the Royal Humane Society, which Griff affected to despise, but which, when he was well out of the way, used to be exhibited on high days and holidays. It seems now like the boundary mark of the golden days of our boyhood, and unmitigated hopes for one another.

CHAPTER IV

UBI LAPSUS, QUID FECI

'Clarence is come—false, fleeting, perjured Clarence.'

KING RICHARD III.

There was much stagnation in the Navy in those days in the reaction after the great war; and though our family had fair interest at the Admiralty, it was seven months before my brother went to sea again. To me they were very happy months, with my helper of helpers, companion of companions, who made possible to me many a little enterprise that could not be attempted without him. My father made him share my studies, and thus they became doubly pleasant. And oh, ye boys! who murmur at the Waverley Novels as a dry holiday task, ye may envy us the zest and enthusiasm with which we devoured them in their freshness. Strangely enough, the last that we read together was the Fair Maid of Perth.

Clarence and his friend Coles longed to sail together again, but Coles was shelved; and when Clarence's appointment came at last, it was to the brig Clotho, Commander Brydone, going out in the Mediterranean Fleet, under Sir Edward Codrington. My mother did not

Charlotte M. Yonge

like brigs, and my father did not like what he heard of the captain; but there had been jealous murmurs about appointments being absorbed by sons of officials—he durst not pick and choose; and the Admiral pronounced that if the lad had been spoilt on board the Calypso, it was time for him to rough it—a dictum whence there was no appeal.

Half a year later the tidings of the victory of Navarino rang through Europe, and were only half welcome to the conquerors; but in our household it is connected with a terrible recollection. Though more than half a century has rolled by, I shrink from dwelling on the shock that fell on us when my father returned from Somerset House with such a countenance that we thought our sailor had fallen; but my mother could brook the fact far less than if her son had died a gallant death. The Clotho was on her way home, and Midshipman William Clarence Winslow was to be tried by court-martial for insubordination, disobedience, and drunkenness. My mother was like one turned to stone. She would hardly go out of doors; she could scarcely bring herself to go to church; she would have had my father give up his situation if there had been any other means of livelihood. She could not talk; only when my father sighed, 'We should never have put him into the Navy,' she hotly replied,

'How was I to suppose that a son of mine would be like that?'

Emily cried all day and all night. Some others would have felt it a relief to have cried too. In more furious language than parents in those days tolerated, Griff wrote to me his utter disbelief, and how he had punched the heads of fellows who presumed to doubt that it was not all a rascally, villainous plot.

When the time came my father went down by the night mail to Portsmouth. He could scarcely bear to face the matter; but, as he said, he could not have it on his conscience if the boy did anything desperate for want of some one to look after him. Besides, there might be some explanation.

'Explanation,' said my mother bitterly. 'That there always is!'

The 'explanation' was this—I have put together what came out in evidence, what my father and the Admiral heard from commiserating officers, and what at different times I learned from Clarence himself. Captain Brydone was one of the rough old description of naval men, good sailors and stern disciplinarians, but wanting in any sense of moral duties towards their ship's company. His lieutenant was of the same class, soured, moreover, by tardy promotion, and prejudiced against a gentleman-like, fair-faced lad, understood to have interest, and bearing a name that implied it. Of the other two midshipmen, one was a dull lad of low stamp, the other a youth of twenty, a born bully, with evil as well as tyrannical propensities;— the crew conforming to severe discipline on board, but otherwise wild and lawless. In such a ship a youth with good habits, sensitive conscience, and lack of moral or physical courage, could not but lead a life of misery, losing every day more of his self-respect and spirit as he was driven to the evil he loathed, dreading the consequences, temporal and eternal, with all his soul, yet without resolution or courage to resist.

As every one knows, the battle of Navarino came on suddenly, almost by mistake; and though it is perhaps no excuse, the hurly-burly and horror burst upon him at unawares. Though the English loss was comparatively very small, the Clotho was a good deal exposed, and two

Charlotte M. Yonge

men were killed—one so close to Clarence that his clothes were splashed with blood. This entirely unnerved him; he did not even know what he did, but he was not to be found when required to carry an order, and was discovered hidden away below, shuddering, in his berth, and then made some shallow excuse about misunderstanding orders. Whether this would have been brought up against him under other circumstances, or whether it would have been remembered that great men, including Charles V. and Henri IV., have had their moment de peur, I cannot tell; but there were other charges. I cannot give date or details. There is no record among the papers before me; and I can only vaguely recall what could hardly be read for the sense of agony, was never discussed, and was driven into the most oblivious recesses of the soul fifty years ago. There was a story about having let a boat's crew, of which he was in charge, get drunk and over-stay their time. One of them deserted; and apparently prevarication ran to the bounds of perjury, if it did not overpass them. (N.B.—Seeing seamen flogged was one of the sickening horrors that haunted Clarence in the Clotho.) Also, when on shore at Malta with the young man whose name I will not record—his evil genius—he was beguiled or bullied into a wine-shop, and while not himself was made the cat's-paw of some insolent practical joke on the lieutenant; and when called to account, was so bewildered and excited as to use unpardonable language.

Whatever it might have been in detail, so much was proved against him that he was dismissed his ship, and his father was recommended to withdraw him from the service, as being disqualified by want of nerve. Also, it was added more privately, that such vicious tendencies needed home restraint. The big bully, his corrupter, bore witness against him, but did not escape scot free, for one of the captains spoke to him in scathing tones of censure.

Whenever my mother was in trouble, she always re-arranged the furniture, and a family crisis was always heralded by a revolution of chairs, tables, and sofas. She could not sit still under suspense, and, during these terrible days the entire house underwent a setting to rights. Emily attended upon her, and I sat and dusted books. No doubt it was much better for us than sitting still. My father's letter came by the morning mail, telling us of the sentence, and that he and our poor culprit, as he said, would come home by the Portsmouth coach in the evening.

One room was already in order when Sir John Griffith kindly came to see whether he could bring any comfort to a spirit which would infinitely have preferred death to dishonour, and was, above all, shocked at the lack of physical courage. Never had I liked our old Admiral so well as when I heard how his chief anger was directed against the general mismanagement, and the cruelty of blighting a poor lad's life when not yet seventeen. His father might have been warned to remove him without the public scandal of a court-martial and dismissal.

'The guilt and shame would have been all the same to us,' said my mother.

'Come, Mary, don't be hard on the poor fellow. In quiet times like these a poor boy can't look over the wall where one might have stolen a horse, ay, or a dozen horses, when there was something else to think about!'

'You would not have forgiven such a thing, sir.'

'It never would have happened under me, or in any decently commanded ship!' he thundered. 'There wasn't a fault to be found with him in the Calypso. What possessed Winslow to let him sail with Brydone? But the service is going,' etc. etc., he ran on—forgetting that it was he himself who had been unwilling, perhaps rightly, to press the Duke of Clarence for an appointment to a crack frigate for his namesake. However, when he took leave he repeated, as he kissed my mother, 'Mind, Mary, don't be set against the lad. That's the way to make 'em desperate, and he is a mere boy, after all.'

Poor mother, it was not so much hardness as a wounded spirit that made her look so rigid. It might have been better if the return could have been delayed so as to make her yearn after her son, but there was nowhere for him to go, and the coach was already on its way. How strange it was to feel the wonted glow at Clarence's return coupled with a frightful sense of disgrace and depression.

The time was far on in October, and it was thus quite dark when the travellers arrived, having walked from Charing Cross, where the coach set them down. My father came in first, and my mother clung to him as if he had been absent for weeks, while all the joy of contact with my brother swept over me, even though his hand hung limp in mine, and was icy cold like his cheeks. My father turned to him with one of the little set speeches of those days. 'Here is our son, Mary, who has promised me to do his utmost to retrieve his character, as far as may be possible, and happily he is still young.'

My mother's embrace was in a sort of mechanical obedience to her husband's gesture, and her voice was not perhaps meant to be so severe as it sounded when she said, 'You are very cold—come and warm yourself.'

They made room for him by the fire, and my father stood up in front of it, giving particulars of the journey. Emily and Martyn were at tea in the nursery, in a certain awe that hindered them from coming down; indeed, Martyn seems to have expected to see some strange transformation in his brother. Indeed, there was alteration in the absence of the blue and gold, and, still more, in the loss of the lightsome, hopeful expression from the young face.

There is a picture of Ary Scheffer's of an old knight, whose son had fled from the battle, cutting the tablecloth in two between himself and the unhappy youth. Like that stern baron's countenance was that with which my mother sat at the head of the dinner-table, and we conversed by jerks about whatever we least cared for, as if we could hide our wretchedness from Peter. When the children appeared each gave Clarence the shyest of kisses, and they sat demurely on their chairs on either side of my father to eat their almonds and raisins, after which we went upstairs, and there was the usual reading. It is curious, but though none of us could have told at the time what it was about, on turning over not long ago a copy of Head's Pampas and Andes, one chapter struck me with an intolerable sense of melancholy, such as the bull chases of South America did not seem adequate to produce, and by and by I remembered that it was the book in course of being read at that unhappy period. My mother went on as diligently as ever with some of those perpetual shirts which seemed to be always in hand except before company, when she used to do tambour work for Emily's frocks. Clarence sat the whole time in a dark corner, never stirring, except that he now and then nodded a little. He had gone through many wakeful, and worse than wakeful, nights of wretched suspense, and now the worst was over.

Family prayers took place, chill good-nights were exchanged, and nobody interfered with his helping me up to my bedroom as usual; but there was something in his face to which I durst not speak, though perhaps I looked, for he exclaimed, 'Don't, Ned!' wrung my hand, and sped away to his own quarters higher up. Then came a sound which made me open my door to listen. Dear little Emily! She had burst out of her own room in her dressing-gown, and flung herself upon her brother as he was plodding wearily upstairs in the dark, clinging round his neck sobbing, 'Dear, dear Clarry! I can't bear it! I don't care. You're my own dear brother, and they are all wicked, horrid people.'

That was all I heard, except hushings on Clarence's part, as if the opening of my door and the thread of light from it warned him that there was risk of interruption. He seemed to be dragging her up to her own room, and I was left with a pang at her being foremost in comforting him.

My father enacted that he should be treated as usual. But how could that be when papa himself did not know how changed were his own ways from his kindly paternal air of confidence? All trust had been undermined, so that Clarence could not cross the threshold without being required to state his object, and, if he overstayed the time calculated, he was cross-examined, and his replies received with a sigh of doubt.

He hung about the house, not caring to do much, except taking me out in my Bath chair or languidly reading the most exciting books he could get;—but there was no great stock of sensation then, except the Byronic, and from time to time one of my parents would exclaim, 'Clarence, I wonder you can find nothing more profitable to occupy yourself with than trash like that!'

He would lay down the book without a word, and take up Smith's Wealth of Nations or Smollett's England—the profitable studies recommended, and speedily become lost in a dejected reverie, with fixed eyes and drooping lips.

CHAPTER V

A HELPING HAND

'Though hawks can prey through storms and winds,
The poor bee in her hive must dwell.'

HENRY VAUGHAN.

In imagination the piteous dejection of our family seems to have lasted for ages, but on comparison of dates it is plain that the first lightening of the burthen came in about a fortnight's time.

The firm of Frith and Castleford was coming to the front in the Chinese trade. The junior partner was an old companion of my father's boyhood; his London abode was near at hand, and he was a kind of semi-godfather to both Clarence and me, having stood proxy for our nominal sponsors. He was as good and open-hearted a man as ever lived, and had always been very kind to us; but he was scarcely welcome when my father, finding that he had come up alone to London to see about some repairs to his house, while his family were still in the country, asked him to dine and sleep—our first guest since our misfortune.

Charlotte M. Yonge

My mother could hardly endure to receive any one, but she seemed glad to see my father become animated and like himself while Roman Catholic Emancipation was vehemently discussed, and the ruin of England hotly predicted. Clarence moped about silently as usual, and tried to avoid notice, and it was not till the next morning—after breakfast, when the two gentlemen were in the dining-room, nearly ready to go their several ways, and I was in the window awaiting my classical tutor—that Mr. Castleford said,

'May I ask, Winslow, if you have any plans for that poor boy?'

'Edward?' said my father, almost wilfully misunderstanding. 'His ambition is to be curator of something in the British Museum, isn't it?'

Mr. Castleford explained that he meant the other, and my father sadly answered that he hardly knew; he supposed the only thing was to send him to a private tutor, but where to find a fit one he did not know and besides, what could be his aim? Sir John Griffith had said he was only fit for the Church, 'But one does not wish to dispose of a tarnished article there.'

'Certainly not,' said Mr. Castleford; and then he spoke words that rejoiced my heart, though they only made my father groan, bidding him remember that it was not so much actual guilt as the accident of Clarence's being in the Navy that had given so serious a character to his delinquencies. If he had been at school, perhaps no one would ever have heard of them, 'Though I don't say,' added the good man, casting a new light on the subject, 'that it would have been better for him in the end.' Then, quite humbly, for he knew my mother especially had a disdain for trade, he asked what my father would think of letting him give Clarence work in the office for the present. 'I know,' he said, 'it is not the line your family might prefer, but it is present occupation; and I do not think you could well send a youth who has seen so much of the world back to schooling. Besides, this would keep him under your own eye.'

My father was greatly touched by the kindness, but he thought it right to set before Mr. Castleford the very worst side of poor Clarence; declaring that he durst not answer for a boy who had never, in spite of pains and punishments, learnt to speak truth at home or abroad, repeating Captain Brydone's dreadful report, and even adding that, what was most grievous of all, there was an affectation of piety about him that could scarcely be anything but self-deceit and hypocrisy. 'Now,' he said, 'my eldest son, Griffith, is just a boy, makes no profession, is not—as I am afraid you have seen—exemplary at church, when Clarence sits as meek as a mouse, but then he is always above-board, frank and straightforward. You know where to have a high-spirited fellow, who will tame down, but you never know what will come next with the other. I sometimes wonder for what error of mine Providence has seen fit to give me such a son.'

Just then an important message came for Mr. Winslow, and he had to hurry away, but Mr. Castleford still remained, and presently said,

'Edward, I should like to know what your eyes have been trying to say all this time.'

'Oh, sir,' I burst out, 'do give him a chance. Indeed he never means to do wrong. The harm is not in him. He would have been the best of us all if he had only been let alone.'

Those were exactly my own foolish words, for which I could have beaten myself afterwards; but Mr. Castleford only gave a slight grave smile, and said, 'You mean that your brother's real defect is in courage, moral and physical.'

'Yes,' I said, with a great effort at expressing myself. 'When he is frightened, or bullied, or browbeaten, he does not know what he is doing or saying. He is quite different when he is his own self; only nobody can understand.'

Strange that though the favoured home son and nearly sixteen years old, it would have been impossible to utter so much to one of our parents. Indeed the last sentence felt so disloyal that the colour burnt in my cheeks as the door opened; but it only admitted Clarence, who, having heard the front door shut, thought the coast was clear, and came in with a load of my books and dictionaries.

'Clarence,' said Mr. Castleford, and the direct address made him start and flush, 'supposing your father consents, should you be willing to turn your mind to a desk in my counting-house?'

He flushed deeper red, and his fingers quivered as he held by the table. 'Thank you, sir. Anything—anything,' he said hesitatingly.

'Well,' said Mr. Castleford, with the kindest of voices, 'let us have it out. What is in your mind? You know, I'm a sort of godfather to you.'

'Sir, if you would only let me have a berth on board one of your vessels, and go right away.'

'Aye, my poor boy, that's what you would like best, I've no doubt; but look at Edward's face there, and think what that would come to at the best!'

'Yes, I know I have no right to choose,' said Clarence, drooping his head as before.

"Tis not that, my dear lad,' said the good man, 'but that packing you off like that, among your inferiors in breeding and everything else, would put an end to all hope of your redeeming the past—outwardly I mean, of course—and lodge you in a position of inequality to your brothers and sister, and all—'

'That's done already,' said Clarence.

'If you were a man grown it might be so,' returned Mr. Castleford, 'but bless me, how old are you?'

'Seventeen next 1st of November,' said Clarence.

'Not a bit too old for a fresh beginning,' said Mr. Castleford cheerily. 'God helping you, you will be a brave and good man yet, my boy—' then as my master rang at the door—'Come with me and look at the old shop.'

Poor Clarence muttered something unintelligible, and I had to own for him that he never went out without accounting for himself. Whereupon our friend caused my mother to be hunted up, and explained to her that he wanted to take Clarence out with him—making some excuse about something they were to see together.

That walk enabled him to say something which came nearer to cheering Clarence than anything that had passed since that sad return, and made him think that to be connected with Mr. Castleford was the best thing that could befall him. Mr. Castleford on his side told my father that he was sure that the boy was good-hearted all the time, and thoroughly repentant; but this had the less effect because plausibility, as my father called it, was one of the qualities that specially annoyed him in Clarence, and made him fear that his friend might be taken in. However, the matter was discussed between the elders, and it was determined that this most friendly offer should be accepted experimentally. It was impressed on Clarence, with unnecessary care, that the line of life was inferior; but that it was his only chance of regaining anything like a position, and that everything depended on his industry and integrity.

'Integrity!' commented Clarence, with a burning spot on his cheek after one of these lectures; 'I believe they think me capable of robbing the office!'

We found out, too, that the senior partner, Mr. Frith, a very crusty old bachelor, did not like the appointment, and that it was made quite against his will. 'You'll be getting your clerks next from Newgate!' was what some amiable friend reported him to have said. However, Mr. Castleford had his way, and Clarence was to begin his work with the New Year, being in the meantime cautioned and lectured on the crime and danger of his evil propensities more than he could well bear. 'Oh!' he groaned, 'it serves me right, I know that very well, but if my father only knew how I hate and abhor all those things—and how I loathed them at the very time I was dragged into them!'

'Why don't you tell him so?' I asked.

'That would make it no better.'

'It is not so bad as if you had gone into it willingly, and for your own pleasure.'

'He would only think that another lie.'

No more could be said, for the idea of Clarence's untruthfulness and depravity had become so deeply rooted in our father's mind that there was little hope of displacing it, and even at the best his manner was full of grave constrained pity. Those few words were Clarence's first approach to confidence with me, but they led to more, and he knew there was one person who did not believe the defect was in the bent of his will so much as in its strength.

All the time the prospect of the counting-house in comparison with the sea was so distasteful to him that I was anxious whenever he went out alone, or even with Griffith, who despised the notion of, as he said, sitting on a high stool, dealing in tea, so much that he was quite capable of aiding and abetting in an escape from it. Two considerations, however, held Clarence back; one, the timidity of nature which shrank from so violent a step, and the other, the strong affections that bound him to his home, though his sojourn there was so painful. He knew the misery his flight would have been to me; indeed I took care to let him see it.

And Griffith's return was like a fresh spring wind dispersing vapours. He had gained an excellent scholar-ship at Brazenose, and came home radiant with triumph, cheering us all up, and making a generous use of his success. He was no letter-writer, and after learning that the disaster and disgrace were all too certain, he ignored the whole, and hailed Clarence on his return as if nothing had happened. As eldest son, and almost a University man, he could argue with our parents in a manner we never presumed on. At least I cannot aver what he actually uttered, but probably it was a revised version of what he thundered forth to me. 'Such nonsense! such a shame to keep the poor beggar going about with that hang dog look, as if he had done for himself for life! Why, I've known fellows do ever so much worse of their own accord, and nothing come of it. If it was found out, there might be a row and a flogging, and there was an end of it. As to going about mourning, and keeping the whole house in doleful dumps, as if there was never to be any good again, it was utter folly, and so I've told Bill, and papa and mamma, both of them!'

How this was administered, or how they took it, there is no knowing, but Griff would neither skate nor go to the theatre, nor to any other diversion, without his brother; and used much kindly force and banter to unearth him from his dismal den in the back drawing-room. He was only let alone when there were engagements with friends, and indeed, when meetings in the streets took place, by tacit agreement, Clarence would shrink off in the crowd as if not belonging to his companion; and these were the moments that stung him into longing to flee to the river, and lose the sense of shame among common sailors: but there was always some good angel to hold him back from desperate measures—chiefly just then, the love between us three brothers, a love that never cooled throughout our lives, and which dear old Griff made much more apparent at this critical time than in the old Win and Slow days of school. That return of his enlivened us all, and removed the terrible constraint from our meals, bringing us back, as it were, to ordinary life and natural intercourse among ourselves and with our neighbours.

CHAPTER VI

THE VALLEY OF HUMILIATION

'But when I lay upon the shore,
Like some poor wounded thing,
I deemed I should not evermore
Refit my wounded wing.
Nailed to the ground and fastened there,
This was the thought of my despair.'

ABP. TRENCH.

Clarence's debut at the office was not wholly unsuccessful. He wrote a good hand, and had a good deal of method and regularity in his nature, together with a real sense of gratitude to Mr. Castleford; and this bore him through the weariness of his new employment, and, what was worse, the cold reception he met with from the other clerks. He was too quiet and reserved for the wilder spirits, too much of a gentleman for others, and in the eyes of the managers, and especially of the senior partner, a disgraced, untrustworthy youth foisted on the office by Mr. Castleford's weak partiality. That old Mr. Frith had, Clarence used to say, a perfectly venomous way of accepting his salute, and seemed always surprised and disappointed if he came in in time, or showed up correct work. Indeed, the old man was disliked and feared by all his subordinates as much as his partner was loved; and while Mr. Castleford, with his good-natured Irish wife and merry family, lived a life as cheerful as it was beneficent, Mr. Frith dwelt entirely alone, in rooms over the office, preserving the habits formed when his income had been narrow, and mistrusting everybody.

At the end of the first month of experiment, Mr. Castleford declared himself contented with Clarence's industry and steadiness, and permanent arrangements were made, to which Clarence submitted with an odd sort of passive gratitude, such as almost angered my father, who little knew how trying the position really was, nor how a certain home-sickness for the seafaring life was tugging at the lad's heart, and making each morning's entrance at the counting-house an effort—each merchant-captain, redolent of the sea, an object of envy. My mother would have sympathised here, but Clarence feared her more than my father, and she was living in continual dread of some explosion, so that her dark curls began to show streaks of gray, and her face to lose its round youthfulness.

Lent brought the question of Confirmation. Under the influence of good Bishop Blomfield, and in the wave of evangelical revival—then at its flood height—Confirmation was becoming a more prominent subject with religious people than it had probably ever been in our Church, and it was recognised that some preparation was desirable beyond the power of repeating the Church Catechism. This was all that had been required of my father at Harrow. My mother's godfather, a dignified clergyman, had simply said, 'I suppose, my dear, you know all about it;' and as for the Admiral, he remarked, 'Confirmed! I never was confirmed anything but a post-captain!'

Our incumbent was more attentive to his duties, or rather recognised more duties, than his predecessor. He preached on the subject, and formed classes, sixteen being then the limit of age,—since the idea of the vow, having become far more prominent than that of the blessing, it was held that full development of the will and under-standing was needful.

I was of the requisite age, and my father spoke to the clergyman, who called, and, as I could not attend the classes, gave me books to read and questions to answer. Clarence read and discussed the questions with me, showing so much more insight into them, and fuller knowledge of Scripture than I possessed, that I exclaimed, 'Why should you not go up for Confirmation too?'

'No,' he answered mournfully. 'I must take no more vows if I can't keep them. It would just be profane.'

I had no more to say; indeed, my parents held the same view. It was good Mr. Castleford who saw things differently. He was a clergyman's son, and had been bred up in the old orthodoxy, which was just beginning to put forth fresh shoots, and, as a quasi-godfather, he held himself bound to take an interest in our religious life, while the sponsors, whose names stood in the family Bible, and whose spoons reposed in the plate-chest, never troubled themselves on the matter. I remember Clarence leaning over me and saying, 'Mr. Castleford thinks I might be confirmed. He says it is not so much the promise we make as of coming to Almighty God for strength to keep what we are bound by already! He is going to speak to papa.'

Perhaps no one except Mr. Castleford could have prevailed over the fear of profanation in the mind of my father, who was, in his old-fashioned way, one of the most reverent of men, and could not bear to think of holy things being approached by one under a stigma, nor of exposing his son to add to his guilt by taking and breaking further pledges. However, he was struck by his friend's arguments, and I heard him telling my mother that when he had wished to wait till there had been time to prove sincerity of repentance by a course of steadiness, the answer had been that it was hard to require strength, while denying the means of grace. My mother was scarcely convinced, but as he had consented she yielded without a protest; and she was really glad that I should have Clarence at my side to help me at the ceremony. The clergyman was applied to, and consented to let Clarence attend the classes, where his knowledge, comprehension, and behaviour were exemplary, so that a letter was written to my father expressive of perfect satisfaction with him. 'There,' said my father, 'I knew it would be so! It is not THAT which I want.'

The Confirmation seemed at the time a very short and perfunctory result of our preparation; and, as things were conducted or misconducted then, involved so much crowding and distress that I recollect very little but clinging to Clarence's arm under a strong sense of my infirmities,—the painful attempt at kneeling, and the big outstretched lawn sleeves while the blessing was pronounced over six heads at once, and then the struggle back to the pew, while the silver-pokered apparitor looked grim at us, as though the maimed and halt had no business to get into the way. Yet this was a great advance upon former Confirmations, and the Bishop met my father afterwards, and inquired most kindly after his lame son.

We were disappointed, and felt that we could not attain to the feelings in the Confirmation poem in the Christian Year—Mr. Castleford's gift to me. Still, I believe that, though encumbered with such a drag as myself, Clarence, more than I did,

'Felt Him how strong, our hearts how frail,
And longed to own Him to the death.'

But the evangelical belief that dejection ought to be followed by a full sense of pardon and assurance of salvation somewhat perplexed and dimmed our Easter Communion. For one short moment, as Clarence turned to help my father lift me up from the altar-rail, I saw his face and eyes radiant with a wonderful rapt look; but it passed only too fast, and the more than ordinary glimpse his spiritual nature had had made him all the more sad afterwards, when he said, 'I would give everything to know that there was any steadfastness in my purpose to lead a new life.'

'But you are leading a new life.'

'Only because there is no one to bully me,' he said. Still, there had been no reproach against him all the time he had been at Frith and Castleford's, when suddenly we had a great shock.

Parties were running very high, and there were scurrilous papers about, which my father perfectly abhorred; and one day at dinner, when declaiming against something he had seen, he laid down strict commands that none should be brought into the house. Then, glancing at Clarence, something possessed him to say, 'You have not been buying any.'

'No, sir,' Clarence answered; but a few minutes later, when we were alone together, the others having left him to help me upstairs, he exclaimed, 'Edward, what is to be done? I didn't buy it; but there is one of those papers in my great-coat pocket. Pollard threw it on my desk; and

Charlotte M. Yonge

there was something in it that I thought would amuse you.'

'Oh! why didn't you say so?'

'There I am again! I simply could not, with his eye on me! Miserable being that I am! Oh, where is the spirit of ghostly strength?'

'Helping you now to take it to papa in the study and explain!' I cried; but the struggle in that tall fellow was as if he had been seven years old instead of seventeen, ere he put his hand over his face and gave me his arm to come out into the hall, fetch the paper, and make his confession. Alas! we were too late. The coat had been moved, the paper had fallen out; and there stood my mother with it in her hand, looking at Clarence with an awful stony face of mute grief and reproach, while he stammered forth what he had said before, and that he was about to give it to my father. She turned away, bitterly, contemptuously indignant and incredulous; and my corroborations only served to give both her and my father a certain dread of Clarence's influence over me, as though I had been either deceived or induced to back him in deceiving them. The unlucky incident plunged him back into the depths, just as he had begun to emerge. Slight as it was, it was no trifle to him, in spite of Griffith's exclamation, 'How absurd! Is a fellow to be bound to give an account of everything he looks at as if he were six years old? Catch me letting my mother pry into my pockets! But you are too meek, Bill; you perfectly invite them to make a row about nothing!'

CHAPTER VII

THE INHERITANCE

'For he that needs five thousand pound to live
Is full as poor as he that needs but five.
But if thy son can make ten pound his measure,
Then all thou addest may be called his treasure.'

GEORGE HERBERT.

It was in the spring of 1829 that my father received a
lawyer's letter announcing the death of James Winslow,
Esquire, of Chantry House, Earlscombe, and inviting him,
as heir-at-law, to be present at the funeral and opening of
the will. The surprise to us all was great. Even my mother
had hardly heard of Chantry House itself, far less as a
possible inheritance; and she had only once seen James
Winslow. He was the last of the elder branch of the
family, a third cousin, and older than my father, who had
known him in times long past. When they had last met,
the Squire of Chantry House was a married man, with
more than one child; my father a young barrister; and as
one lived entirely in the country and the other in town,
without any special congeniality, no intercourse had been
kept up, and it was a surprise to hear that he had left no
surviving children. My father greatly doubted whether

Charlotte M. Yonge

being heir-at-law would prove to avail him anything, since it was likely that so distant a relation would have made a will in favour of some nearer connection on his wife's or mother's side. He was very vague about Chantry House, only knowing that it was supposed to be a fair property, and he would hardly consent to take Griffith with him by the Western Royal Mail, warning him and all the rest of us that our expectations would be disappointed.

Nevertheless we looked out the gentlemen's seats in Paterson's Road Book, and after much research, for Chantry House lay far off from the main road, we came upon—'Chantry House, Earlscombe, the seat of James Winslow, Esquire, once a religious foundation; beautifully situated on a rising ground, commanding an extensive prospect—'

'A religious foundation!' cried Emily. 'It will be a dear delicious old abbey, all Gothic architecture, with cloisters and ruins and ghosts.'

'Ghosts!' said my mother severely, 'what has put such nonsense into your head?'

Nevertheless Emily made up her mind that Chantry House would be another Melrose, and went about repeating the moonlight scene in the Lay of the Last Minstrel whenever she thought no one was there to laugh at her.

My father and Griffith returned with the good news that there was no mistake. Chantry House was really his own, with the estate belonging to it, reckoned at 5000 pounds a year, exclusive of a handsome provision to Miss Selby, the niece of the late Mrs. Winslow, a spinster of a certain age, who had lived with her uncle, and now proposed to remove to Bath. Mr. Winslow had, it appeared, lost his only son as a schoolboy, and his daughters, like their mother, had been consumptive. He had always been resolved that the estate should continue in the family; but reluctance to see any one take his son's place had withheld him from making any advances to my father; and for several years past he had been in broken health with failing faculties.

Of course there was much elation. Griff described as charming the place, perched on the southern slope of a wooded hill, with a broad fertile valley lying spread out before it, and the woods behind affording every promise of sport. The house, my father said, was good, odd and irregular, built at different times, but quite habitable, and with plenty of furniture, though he opined that mamma would think it needed modernising, to which she replied that our present chattels would make a great difference; whereat my father, looking at the effects of more than twenty years of London blacks, gave a little whistle, for she was always the economical one of the pair.

Emily, with glowing cheeks and eager eyes, entreated to know whether it was Gothic, and had a cloister! Papa nipped her hopes of a cloister, but there were Gothic windows and doorway, and a bit of ruin in the garden, a fragment of the old chapel.

My father could not resign his office without notice, and, besides, he wished Miss Selby to have leisure for leaving her home of many years; after which there would be a few needful repairs. The delay was not a great grievance to any of us except little Martyn. We were much more Cockney than almost any one is in these days of railways. We were unusually devoid of kindred on both sides, my father's holidays were short, I was not a very movable commodity, and economy forbade long journeys, so that we had never gone farther than Ramsgate, where we claimed a certain lodging-house as a sort of right every summer.

Real country was as much unknown to us as the backwoods. My father alone had been born and bred to village life and habits, for my mother had spent her youth in a succession of seaport towns, frequented by men-of-war. We heard, too, that Chantry House was very secluded, with only a few cottages near at hand—a mile and a half from the church and village of Earlscombe, three from the tiny country town of Wattlesea, four from the place where the coach passed, connecting it with the civilisation of Bath and Bristol, from each of which places it was about half a day's distance, according to the measures of those times. It was a sort of banishment to people accustomed to the stream of life in London; and though the consequence and importance derived from being raised to the ranks of the Squirearchy were agreeable, they were a dear purchase at the cost of being out of reach of all our friends and acquaintances, as well as of other advantages.

To my father, however, the retirement from his many years of drudgery was really welcome, and he had preserved enough of country tastes to rejoice that it was, as he said, a clear duty to reside on his estate and look after his property. My mother saw his relief in the prospect, and suppressed her sighs at the dislocation of her life-long habits, and the loss of intercourse with the acquaintance whom separation raised to the rank of intimate friends, even her misgivings as to butchers, bakers, and grocers in the wilderness, and still worse, as to doctors for me.

'Humph!' said the Admiral, 'the boy will be all the better without them.'

And so I was; I can't say they were the subject of much

regret, but I was really sorry to leave our big neighbour, the British Museum, where there were good friends who always made me welcome, and encouraged me in studies of coins and heraldry, which were great resources to me, so that I used to spend hours there, and was by no means willing to resign my ambition of obtaining an appointment there, when I heard my father say that he was especially thankful for his good fortune because it enabled him to provide for me. There were lessons, too, from masters in languages, music, and drawing, which Emily and I shared, and which she had just begun to value thoroughly. We had filled whole drawing-books with wriggling twists of foliage in B B B marking pencil, and had just been promoted to water-colours; and she was beginning to sing very prettily. I feared, too, that I should no longer have a chance of rivalling Griffith's university studies. All this, with my sister's girl friends, and those kind people who used to drop in to play chess, and otherwise amuse me, would all be left behind; and, sorest of all, Clarence, who, whatever he was in the eyes of others, had grown to be my mainstay during this last year. He it was who fetched me from the Museum, took me into the gardens, helped me up and down stairs, spared no pains to rout out whatever my fanciful pursuits required from shops in the City, and, in very truth, spoilt me through all his hours that were free from business, besides being my most perfect sympathising and understanding companion.

I feared, too, that he would be terribly lonesome, though of late he had been less haunted by longings for the sea, had made some way with his fellows, and had been commended by the managing clerk; and it was painful to find the elders did not grieve on their own account at parting with him. My mother told the Admiral that she thought it would be good for Mr. Winslow's spirits not to be continually reminded of his trouble; and my father might be heard confiding to Mr. Castleford that the separation might be good for both her and her son, if only the lad could be trusted. To which that good man replied by giving him an excellent character; but was only met by a sigh, and 'Well, we shall see!'

Clarence was to be lodged with Peter, whose devotion would not extend to following us into barbarism, where, as he told us, he understood there was no such thing as a 'harea,' and master would have to kill his own mutton.

Peter had been tranquilly engaged to Gooch for years untold. They were to be transformed into Mr. and Mrs. Robson, with some small appointment about the Law Courts for him, and a lodging-house for her, where Clarence was to abide, my mother feeling secure that neither his health, his morals, nor his shirts could go much astray without her receiving warning thereof.

Meanwhile, by the help of an antiquarian friend of my father, Mr. Stafford, who was great in county history, I hunted up in the Museum library all I could discover about our new possession.

The Chantry of St. Cecily at Earlscombe, in Somersetshire, had, it appeared, been founded and endowed by Dame Isabel d'Oyley, in the year of grace 1434, that constant prayers might be offered for the souls of her husband and son, slain in the French wars. The poor lady's intentions, which to our Protestant minds appeared rather shocking than otherwise, had been frustrated at the break up of such establishments, when the Chantry, and the estate that maintained its clerks and bedesmen, was granted to Sir Harry Power, from whom, through two heiresses, it had come to the Fordyces, the last of whom, by name Margaret, had died childless, leaving the estate to her stepson, Philip Winslow, our ancestor.

Moreover, we learnt that a portion of the building was of ancient date, and that there was an 'interesting fragment' of the old chapel in the grounds, which our good friend promised himself the pleasure of investigating on his first holiday.

To add to our newly-acquired sense of consideration and of high pedigree, the family chariot, after taking Miss Selby to Bath, came up post to London to be touched up at the coachbuilder's, have the escutcheon altered so as to impale the Griffith coat instead of the Selby, and finally to convey us to our new abode, in preparation for which all its boxes came to be packed.

A chariot! You young ones have as little notion of one as of a British war-chariot armed with scythes. Yet people of a certain grade were as sure to keep their chariot as their silver tea-pot; indeed we knew one young couple who started in life with no other habitation, but spent their time as nomads, in visits to their relations and friends, for visits WERE visits then.

The capacities of a chariot were considerable. Within, there was a good-sized seat for the principal occupants, and outside a dickey behind, and a driving box before, though sometimes there was only one of these, and that transferable. The boxes were calculated to hold family luggage on a six months' tour. There they lay on the spare-room floor, ready to be packed, the first earnest of our new possessions—except perhaps the five-pound note my father gave each of us four elder ones, on the day the balance at the bank was made over to him. There was the imperial, a grand roomy receptacle, which was placed on the top of the carriage, and would not always go upstairs in small houses; the capbox, which fitted into a curved place in front of the windows, and could not stand alone, but had a frame to support it; two long narrow boxes with the like infirmity of standing, which fitted in below; square ones under each seat; and a drop box fastened on behind. There were pockets beneath each window, and, curious relic in name and nature of the time when every gentleman carried his weapon, there was the sword case, an excrescence behind the back of the best seat, accessible by lifting a cushion, where weapons used to be carried, but where in our peaceful times travellers bestowed their luncheon and their books.

Our chariot was black above, canary yellow below, beautifully varnished, and with our arms blazoned on each door. It was lined with dark blue leather and cloth, picked out with blue and yellow lace in accordance with our liveries, and was a gorgeous spectacle. I am afraid Emily did not share in Mistress Gilpin's humility when

'The chaise was brought,
But yet was not allowed
To drive up to the door, lest all
Should say that she was proud!'

It was then that Emily and I each started a diary to record the events of our new life. Hers flourished by fits and starts; but I having perforce more leisure than she, mine has gone on with few interruptions till the present time, and is the backbone of this narrative, which I compile and condense from it and other sources before destroying it.

CHAPTER VIII

THE OLD HOUSE

'Your history whither are you spinning?
Can you do nothing but describe?
A house there is, and that's enough!'

GRAY.

How we did enjoy our journey, when the wrench from our old home was once made. We did not even leave Clarence behind, for Mr. Castleford had given him a holiday, so that he might not appear to be kept at a distance, as if under a cloud, and might help me through our travels.

My mother and I occupied the inside of the carriage, with Emily between us at the outset; but when we were off the London stones she was often allowed to make a third on the dickey with Clarence and Martyn, whose ecstatic heels could be endured for the sake of the free air and the view. Of course we posted, and where there were severe hills we indulged in four horses. The varieties of the jackets of our post-boys, blue or yellow, as supposed to indicate the politics of their inns, were interesting to us, as everything was interesting then. Otherwise their equipment was exactly alike—neat drab corduroy breeches and

Charlotte M. Yonge

top-boots, and hats usually white, and they were all boys, though the red faces and grizzled hair of some looked as if they had faced the weather for at least fifty years.

It was a beautiful August, and the harvest fields were a sight perfectly new, filling us with rapture unspeakable. At every hill which offered an excuse, our outsiders were on their feet, thrusting in their heads and hands to us within with exclamations of delight, and all sorts of discoveries—really new to us three younger ones. Ears of corn, bearded barley, graceful oats, poppies, corn-flowers, were all delicious novelties to Emily and me, though Griff and my father laughed at our ecstasies, and my mother occasionally objected to the wonderful accumulation of curiosities thrust into her lap or the door pockets, and tried to persuade Martyn that rooks' wings, dead hedgehogs, sticks and stones of various merits, might be found at Earlscombe, until Clarence, by the judicious purchase of a basket at Salisbury, contrived to satisfy all parties and safely dispose of the treasures. The objects that stand out in my memory on that journey were Salisbury Spire, and a long hill where the hedgebank was one mass of the exquisite rose-bay willow herb—a perfect revelation to our city-bred eyes; but indeed, the whole route was like one panorama to us of L'Allegro and other descriptions on which we had fed. For in those days we were much more devoted to poetry than is the present generation, which has a good deal of false shame on that head.

Even dining and sleeping at an inn formed a pleasing novelty, though we did not exactly sympathise with Martyn when he dashed in at breakfast exulting in having witnessed the killing of a pig. As my father observed, it was too like realising Peter's forebodings of our return to savage life.

Demonstrations were not the fashion of these times, and there was a good deal of dull discontent and disaffection in the air, so that no tokens of welcome were prepared for us—not even a peal of bells; nor indeed should we have heard them if they had been rung, for the church was a mile and a half beyond the house, with a wood between cutting off the sound, except in certain winds. We did not miss a reception, which would rather have embarrassed us. We began to think it was time to arrive, and my father believed we were climbing the last hill, when, just as we had passed a remarkably pretty village and church, Griffith called out to say that we were on our own ground. He had made his researches with the game keeper while my father was busy with the solicitor, and could point to our boundary wall, a little below the top of the hill on the northern side. He informed us that the place we had passed was Hillside—Fordyce property,—but this was Earlscombe, our own. It was a great stony bit of pasture with a few scattered trees, but after the flat summit was past, the southern side was all beechwood, where a gate admitted us into a drive cut out in a slant down the otherwise steep descent, and coming out into an open space. And there we were!

The old house was placed on the widest part of a kind of shelf or natural terrace, of a sort of amphitheatre shape, with wood on either hand, but leaving an interval clear in the midst broad enough for house and gardens, with a gentle green slope behind, and a much steeper one in front, closed in by the beechwoods. The house stood as it were sideways, or had been made to do so by later inhabitants. I know this is very long-winded, but there have been such alterations that without minute description this narrative will be unintelligible.

The aspect was northwards so far as the lie of the ground was concerned, but the house stood across. The main

Charlotte M. Yonge

body was of the big symmetrical Louis XIV. style—or, as it is now the fashion to call it, Queen Anne—brick, with stone quoins, big sash-windows, and a great square hall in the midst, with the chief rooms opening into it. The principal entrance had been on the north, with a huge front door and a flight of stone steps, and just space enough for a gravel coach ring before the rapid grassy descent. Later constitutions, however, must have eschewed that northern front door, and later nerves that narrow verge, and on the eastern front had been added that Gothic porch of which Emily had heard,—and a flagrantly modern Gothic porch it was, flanked by two comical little turrets, with loopholes, from which a thread-paper or Tom Thumb might have defended it. Otherwise it resembled a church porch, except for the formidable points of a sham portcullis; but there was no denying that it greatly increased the comfort of the house, with its two sets of heavy doors, and the seats on either side. The great hall door had been closed up, plastered over within, and rendered inoffensive. Towards the west there was another modern addition of drawing and dining rooms, and handsome bedchambers above, in Gothic taste, i.e. with pointed arches filled up with glass over the sash-windows. The drawing-room was very pretty, with a glass door at the end leading into an old-fashioned greenhouse, and two French windows to the south opening upon the lawn, which soon began to slope upwards, curving, as I said, like an amphitheatre, and was always shady and sheltered, tilting its flower-beds towards the house as if to display them. The dining-room had, in like manner, one west and two north windows, the latter commanding a grand view over the green meadow-land below, dotted with round knolls, and rising into blue hills beyond. We became proud of counting the villages and church towers we could see from thence.

There was a still older portion, more ancient than the

square corps de logis, and built of the cream-coloured stone of the country. It was at the south-eastern angle, where the ground began sloping so near the house that this wing—if it may so be called—containing two good-sized rooms nearly on a level with the upper floor, had nothing below but some open stone vaultings, under which it was only just possible for my tall brothers to stand upright, at the innermost end. These opened into the cellars which, no doubt, belonged to the fifteenth-century structure. There seemed to have once been a door and two or three steps to the ground, which rose very close to the southern end; but this had been walled up. The rooms had deep mullioned windows east and west, and very handsome groined ceilings, and were entered by two steps down from the gallery round the upper part of the hall. There was a very handsome double staircase of polished oak, shaped like a Y, the stem of which began just opposite the original front door—making us wonder if people knew what draughts were in the days of Queen Anne, and remember Madame de Maintenon's complaint that health was sacrificed to symmetry. Not far from this oldest portion were some broken bits of wall and stumps of columns, remnants of the chapel, and prettily wreathed with ivy and clematis. We rejoiced in such a pretty and distinctive ornament to our garden, and never troubled ourselves about the desecration; and certainly ours was one of the most delightful gardens that ever existed, what with green turf, bright flowers, shapely shrubs, and the grand beech-trees enclosing it with their stately white pillars, green foliage, and the russet arcades beneath them. The stillness was wonderful to ears accustomed to the London roar—almost a new sensation. Emily was found, as she said, 'listening to the silence;' and my father declared that no one could guess at the sense of rest that it gave him.

Of space within there was plenty, though so much had

been sacrificed to the hall and staircase; and this was apparently the cause of the modern additions, as the original sitting-rooms, wainscotted and double-doored, were rather small for family requirements. One of these, once the dining-room, became my father's study, where he read and wrote, saw his tenants, and by and by acted as Justice of the Peace. The opposite one, towards the garden, was termed the book-room. Here Martyn was to do his lessons, and Emily and I carry on our studies, and do what she called keeping up her accomplishments. My couch and appurtenances abode there, and it was to be my retreat from company,—or on occasion could be made a supplementary drawing-room, as its fittings showed it had been the parlour. It communicated with another chamber, which became my own—sparing the difficulties that stairs always presented; and beyond lay, niched under the grand staircase, a tiny light closet, a passage-room, where my mother put a bed for a man-servant, not liking to leave me entirely alone on the ground floor. It led to a passage to the garden door, also to my mother's den, dedicated to housewifely cares and stores, and ended at the back stairs, descending to the servants' region. This was very old, handsomely vaulted with stone, and, owing to the fall of the ground, had ample space for light on the north side,— where, beyond the drive, the descent was so rapid as to afford Martyn infinite delight in rolling down, to the horror of all beholders and the detriment of his white duck trowsers.

I don't know much about the upper story, so I spare you that. Emily had a hankering for one of the pretty old mullioned-windowed rooms—the mullion chambers, as she named them; but Griff pounced on them at once, the inner for his repose, the outer for his guns and his studies—not smoking, for young men were never permitted to smoke within doors, nor indeed in any home society. The choice of the son and heir was undisputed, and he proceeded to settle his possessions in his new domains, where they made an imposing appearance.

CHAPTER IX

RATS

'As louder and louder, drawing near,
The gnawing of their teeth he could hear.'

SOUTHEY.

'What a ridiculous old fellow that Chapman is,' said Griff, coming in from a conference with the gaunt old man who acted as keeper to our not very extensive preserves. 'I told him to get some gins for the rats in my rooms, and he shook his absurd head like any mandarin, and said, "There baint no trap as will rid you of them kind of varmint, sir."'

'Of course,' my father said, 'rats are part of the entail of an old house. You may reckon on them.'

'Those rooms of yours are the very place for them,' added my mother. 'I only hope they will not infest the rest of the house.'

To which Griff rejoined that they perpetrated the most extraordinary noises he had ever heard from rats, and told Emily she might be thankful to him for taking those rooms, for she would have been frightened out of her little wits. He meant, he said, to get a little terrier, and have a thorough good rat hunt, at which Martyn capered about in irrepressible ecstasy.

This, however, was deferred by the unwillingness of old Chapman, of whom even Griff was somewhat in awe. His fame as a sportsman had to be made, and he had had only such practice as could be attained by shooting at a mark ever since he had been aware of his coming greatness. So he was desirous of conciliating Chapman, and not getting laughed at as the London young gentleman who could not hit a hay-stack. My father, who had been used to carrying a gun in his younger days, was much amused, in his quiet way, at seeing Griff watch Chapman off on his rounds, and then betake himself to the locality most remote from the keeper's ears to practise on the rook or crow. Martyn always ran after him, having solemnly promised not to touch the gun, and to keep behind. He was too good-natured to send the little fellow back, though he often tried to elude the pursuit, not wishing for a witness to his attempts; and he never invited Clarence, who had had some experience of curious game but never mentioned it.

Clarence devoted himself to Emily and me, tugging my garden-chair along all the paths where it would go without too much jolting, and when I had had enough, exploring those hanging woods, either with her or on his own account. They used to come home with their hands full of flowers, and this resulted in a vehement attack of botany,—a taste that has lasted all our lives, together with the hortus siccus to which we still make additions, though there has been a revolution there as well as everywhere else, and the Linnaean system we learnt so eagerly from Martin's Letters is altogether exploded and antiquated. Still, my sister refuses to own the scientific merits of the natural system, and can point to school-bred and lectured young ladies who have no notion how to discover the name or nature of a live plant.

On the Friday after our arrival the noises had been so fearful that Griff had been exasperated into going off across the hills, accompanied by his constant shadow, Martyn, in search of the professional ratcatcher of the neighbourhood, in spite of Chapman's warning—that Tom Petty was the biggest rascal in the neighbourhood, and a regular out and out poacher; and as to the noises—he couldn't 'tackle the like of they.' After revelling in the beauty of the beechwoods as long as was good for me or for Clarence, I was left in the garden to sketch the ruin, while my two companions started on one of their exploring expeditions.

It was getting late enough to think of going to prepare for the six o'clock dinner when Emily came forth alone from the path between the trees, announcing—'An adventure, Edward! We have had such an adventure.'

'Where's Clarence?'

'Gone for the doctor! Oh, no; Griff hasn't shot anybody. He is gone for the ratcatcher, you know. It is a poor little herdboy, who tumbled out of a tree; and oh! such a sweet, beautiful, young lady—just like a book!'

When Emily became less incoherent, it appeared that on coming out on the bit of common above the wood, as she and Clarence were halting on the brow of the hill to admire the view, they heard a call for help, and hurrying down in the direction whence it proceeded they saw a stunted ash-tree, beneath which were a young lady and a little child bending over a village lad who lay beneath moaning piteously. The girl, whom Emily described as the most beautiful creature she ever saw, explained that the boy, who had been herding the cattle scattered around, had been climbing the tree, a limb of which had broken with him. She had seen the fall from a distance, and hurried up; but she hardly knew what to do, for her little sister was too young to be sent in quest of assistance. Clarence thought one leg seriously injured, and as the young lady seemed to know the boy, offered to carry him home. School officers were yet in the future; children were set to work almost as soon as they could walk, and this little fellow was so light and thin as to shock Clarence when he had been taken up on his back, for he weighed quite a trifle. The young lady showed the way to a wretched little cottage, where a bigger girl had just come in with a sheaf of corn freshly gleaned poised on her head. They sent her to fetch her mother, and Clarence undertook to go for a doctor, but to the surprise and horror of Emily, there was a demur. Something was said of old Molly and her 'ile' and 'yarbs,' or perhaps Madam could step round. When Clarence, on this being translated to him, pronounced the case beyond such treatment, it was explained outside the door that this was a terribly poor family, and the doctor would not come to parish patients for an indefinite time after his summons, besides which, he lived at Wattlesea. 'Indeed mamma does almost all the doctoring with her medicine chest,' said the girl.

On which Clarence declared that he would let the doctor know that he himself would be responsible for the cost of the attendance, and set off for Wattlesea, a kind of town village in the flat below. He could not get back till dinner was half over, and came in alarmed and apologetic; but he had nothing worse to encounter than Griff's unmerciful banter (or, as you would call it, chaff) about his knight errantry, and Emily's lovely heroine in the sweetest of cottage bonnets.

Griff could be slightly tyrannous in his merry mockery, and when he found that on the ensuing day Clarence proposed to go and inquire after the patient, he made such wicked fun of the expectations the pair entertained of hearing the sweet cottage bonnet reading a tract in a silvery voice through the hovel window, that he fairly teased and shamed Clarence out of starting till the renowned Tom Petty arrived and absorbed all the three brothers, and even their father, in delights as mysterious to me as to Emily. How she shrieked when Martyn rushed triumphantly into the room where we were arranging books with the huge patriarch of all the rats dangling by his tail! Three hopeful families were destroyed; rooms, vaults, and cellars examined and cleared; and Petty declared the race to be exterminated, picturesque ruffian that he was, in his shapeless hat, rusty velveteen, long leggings, a live ferret in his pocket, and festoons of dead rats over his shoulder.

Chapman, who regarded him much as the ferret did the rat, declared that the rabbits and hares would suffer from letting 'that there chap' show his face here on any plea; and, moreover, gave a grunt very like a scoff; at the idea of slumbers in the mullion rooms (as they were called) being secured by his good offices.

And Chapman was right. The unaccountable noises broke out again—screaming, wailing, sobbing—sounds scarcely within the power of cat or rat, but possibly the effect of the wind in the old building. At any rate, Griff could not stand them, and declared that sleep was impossible when the wind was in that quarter, so that he must shift his bedroom elsewhere, though he still wished to retain the outer apartment, which he had taken pleasure in adorning with his special possessions. My mother would scarcely have tolerated such fancies in any one else, but Griff had his privileges.

CHAPTER X

OUR TUNEFUL CHOIR

'The church has been whitewashed, but right long ago,
As the cracks and the dinginess amply doth show;
About the same time that a strange petrifaction
Confined the incumbent to mere Sunday action.
So many abuses in this place are rife,
The only church things giving token of life
Are the singing within and the nettles without-
Both equally rampant without any doubt.'

F. R. HAVERGAL.

All Griff's teasing could not diminish—nay, rather
increased—Emily's excitement in the hope of seeing and
identifying the sweet cottage bonnet at church on Sunday.
The distance we had to go was nearly two miles, and my
mother and I drove thither in a donkey chair, which had
been hunted up in London for that purpose because the
'pheeaton' (as the servants insisted on calling it) was too
high for me. My father had an old-fashioned feeling about
the Fourth Commandment, which made him scrupulous as
to using any animal on Sunday; and even when, in bad
weather, or for visitors, the larger carriage was used, he
always walked. He was really angry with Griff that

Charlotte M. Yonge

morning for mischievously maintaining that it was a greater breach of the commandment to work an ass than a horse.

It was a pretty drive on a road slanting gradually through the brushwood that clothed the steep face of the hillside, and passing farms and meadows full of cattle—all things quieter and stiller than ever in their Sunday repose. We knew that the living was in Winslow patronage, but that it was in the hands of one of the Selby connection, who held it, together with it is not safe to say how many benefices, and found it necessary for his health to reside at Bath. The vicarage had long since been turned into a farmhouse, and the curate lived at Wattlesea. All this we knew, but we had not realised that he was likewise assistant curate there, and only favoured Earlscombe with alternate morning and evening services on Sundays.

Still less were we prepared for the interior of the church. It had a picturesque square tower covered with ivy, and a general air of fitness for a sketch; indeed, the photograph of it in its present beautified state will not stand a comparison with our drawings of it, in those days of dilapidation in the middle of the untidy churchyard, with little boys astride on the sloping, sunken lichen-grown headstones, mullein spikes and burdock leaves, more graceful than the trim borders and zinc crosses which are pleasanter to the mental eye.

The London church we had left would be a fearful shock to the present generation, but we were accustomed to decency, order, and reverence; and it was no wonder that my father was walking about the churchyard, muttering that he never saw such a place, while my brothers were full of amusement. Their spruce looks in their tall hats, bright ties, dark coats, and white trowsers strapped tight under their boots, looked incongruous with the rest of the congregation, the most distinguished members of which were farmers in drab coats with huge mother-of-pearl buttons, and long gaiters buttoned up to their knees and strapped up to their gay waistcoats over their white corduroys. Their wives and daughters were in enormous bonnets, fluttering with ribbons; but then what my mother and Emily wore were no trifles. The rest of the congregation were—the male part of it—in white or gray smock-frocks, the elderly women in black bonnets, the younger in straw; but we had not long to make our observations, for Chapman took possession of us. He was parish clerk, and was in great glory in his mourning coat and hat, and his object was to marshal us all into our pew before he had to attend upon the clergyman; and of course I was glad enough to get as soon as possible out of sight of all the eyes not yet accustomed to my figure.

And hidden enough I was when we had been introduced through the little north chancel door into a black-curtained, black-cushioned, black-lined pew, well carpeted, with a table in the midst, and a stove, whose pipe made its exit through the floriated tracery of the window overhead. The chancel arch was to the west of us, blocked up by a wooden parcel-gilt erection, and to the east a decorated window that would have been very handsome if two side-lights had not been obscured by the two Tables of the Law, with the royal arms on the top of the first table, and over the other our own, with the Fordyce in a scutcheon of pretence; for, as an inscription recorded, they had been erected by Margaret, daughter of Christopher Fordyce, Esquire, of Chantry House, and relict of Sir James John Winslow, Kt., sergeant-at-law, A.D. 1700—the last date, I verily believe, at which anything had been done to the church. And on the wall, stopping up the southern chancel window, was a huge marble slab, supported by angels blowing trumpets, with a very long inscription about the Fordyce family, ending with this same Margaret, who had

Charlotte M. Yonge

married the Winslow, lost two or three infants, and died on 1st January 1708, three years later than her husband.

Thus far I could see; but Griff was standing lifting the curtain, and showing by the working of his shoulders his amazement and diversion, so that only the daggers in my mother's eyes kept Martyn from springing up after him. What he beheld was an altar draped in black like a coffin, and on the step up to the rail, boys and girls eating apples and performing antics to beguile the waiting time, while a row of white-smocked old men occupied the bench opposite to our seat, conversing loud enough for us to hear them.

My father and Clarence came in; the bells stopped; there was a sound of steps, and in the fabric in front of us there emerged a grizzled head and the back of a very dirty surplice besprinkled with iron moulds, while Chapman's back appeared above our curtain, his desk (full of dilapidated prayer-books) being wedged in between us and the reading-desk.

The duet that then took place between him and the curate must have been heard to be credible, especially as, being so close behind the old man, we could not fail to be aware of all the remarkable shots at long words which he bawled out at the top of his voice, and I refrain from recording, lest they should haunt others as they have done by me all my life. Now and then Chapman caught up a long switch and dashed out at some obstreperous child to give an audible whack; and towards the close of the litany he stumped out—we heard his tramp the whole length of the church, and by and by his voice issued from an unknown height, proclaiming—'Let us sing to the praise and glory in an anthem taken from the 42d chapter of Genesis.'

There was an outburst of bassoon, clarionet, and fiddle,

and the performance that followed was the most marvellous we had ever heard, especially when the big butcher—fiddling all the time—declared in a mighty solo, 'I am Jo—Jo—Jo—Joseph!' and having reiterated this information four or five times, inquired with equal pertinacity, 'Doth—doth my fa-a-u-ther yet live?' Poor Emily was fairly 'convulsed;' she stuffed her handkerchief into her mouth, and grew so crimson that my mother was quite frightened, and very near putting her out at the little door of excommunication. To our last hour we shall never forget the shock of that first anthem.

The Commandments were read from the desk, Chapman's solitary response coming from the gallery; and while the second singing—four verses from Tate and Brady—was going on, we beheld the surplice stripped off,—like the slough of a May-fly, as Griff said,—when a rusty black gown was revealed, in which the curate ascended the pulpit and was lost to our view before the concluding verse of the psalm, which we had reason to believe was selected in compliment to us, as well as to Earlscombe, -

'My lot is fall'n in that blest land
Where God is truly know,
He fills my cup with liberal hand;
'Tis He—'tis He—'tis He—supports my throne.'

We had great reason to doubt how far the second line could justly be applied to the parish! but there was no judging of the sermon, for only detached sentences reached us in a sort of mumble. Griff afterwards declared churchgoing to be as good as a comedy, and we all had to learn to avoid meeting each other's eyes, whatever we might hear. When the scuffle and tramp of the departing congregation had ceased, we came forth from our sable box, and beheld the remnants of a once handsome church, mauled in every possible way, green stains on the walls,

Charlotte M. Yonge

windows bricked up, and a huge singing gallery. Good bits of carved stall work were nailed anyhow into the pews; the floor was uneven; no font was visible; there was a mouldy uncared-for look about everything. The curate in riding-boots came out of the vestry,—a pale, weary-looking man, painfully meek and civil, with gray hair sleeked round his face. He 'louted low,' and seemed hardly to venture on taking the hand my father held out to him. There was some attempt to enter into conversation with him, but he begged to be excused, for he had to hurry back to Wattlesea to a funeral. Poor man! he was as great a pluralist as his vicar, for he kept a boys' school, partially day, partially boarding, and his eyes looked hungrily at Martyn.

If the 'sweet cottage bonnet' had been at church there would have been little chance of discovering her, but we found that we were the only 'quality,' as Chapman called it, or things might not have been so bad. Old James Winslow had been a mere fox-hunting squire till he became a valetudinarian; nor had he ever cared for the church or for the poor, so that the village was in a frightful state of neglect. There was a dissenting chapel, old enough to be overgrown with ivy and not too hideous, erected by the Nonconformists in the reign of the Great Deliverer, but this partook of the general decadence of the parish, and, as we found, the chapel's principal use was to serve as an excuse for not going to church.

My father always went to church twice, so he and Clarence walked to Wattlesea, where appearances were more respectable; but they heard the same sermon over again, and, as my father drily remarked, it was not a composition that would bear repetition.

He was much distressed at the state of things, and intended to write to the incumbent, though, as he said, whatever was done would end by being at his own expense, and the move and other calls left him so little in hand that he sighed over the difficulties, and declared that he was better off in London, except for the honour of the thing. Perhaps my mother was of the same opinion after a dreary afternoon, when Griff and Martyn had been wandering about aimlessly, and were at length betrayed by the barking of a little terrier, purchased the day before from Tom Petty, besieging the stable cat, who stood with swollen tail, glaring eyes, and thunderous growls, on the top of the tallest pillar of the ruins. Emily nearly cried at their cruelty. Martyn was called off by my mother, and set down, half sulky, half ashamed, to Henry and his Bearer; and Griff, vowing that he believed it was that brute who made the row at night, and that she ought to be exterminated, strolled off to converse with Chapman, who was a quaint compound of clerk and keeper—in the one capacity upholding his late master, in the other bemoaning Mr. Mears' unpunctualities, specially as regarded weddings and funerals; one 'corp' having been kept waiting till a messenger had been sent to Wattlesea, who finding both clergy out for the day, had had to go to Hillside, 'where they was always ready, though the old Squire would have been mad with him if he'd a-guessed one of they Fordys had ever set foot in the parish.'

The only school in the place was close to the meeting-house, 'a very dame's school indeed,' as Emily described it after a peep on Monday. Dame Dearlove, the old woman who presided, was a picture of Shenstone's school-mistress,—black bonnet, horn spectacles, fearful birch rod, three-cornered buff 'kerchief, checked apron and all, but on meddling with her, she proved a very dragon, the antipodes of her name. Tattered copies of the Universal Spelling-Book served her aristocracy, ragged Testaments the general herd, whence all appeared to be shouting aloud at once. She looked sour as verjuice when my

Charlotte M. Yonge

mother and Emily entered, and gave them to understand that 'she wasn't used to no strangers in her school, and didn't want 'em.' We found that in Chapman's opinion she 'didn't larn 'em nothing.' She had succeeded her aunt, who had taught him to read 'right off,' but 'her baint to be compared with she.' And now the farmers' children, and the little aristocracy, including his own grand-children,— all indeed who, in his phrase, 'cared for eddication,'— went to Wattlesea.

CHAPTER XI

'THEY FORDYS.'

'Of honourable reckoning are you both,
And pity 'tis, you lived at odds so long.'

SHAKESPEARE.

My father had a good deal of business in hand, and was
glad of Clarence's help in writing and accounts,—a great
pleasure, though it prevented his being Griff's companion
in his exploring and essays at shooting. He had time,
however, to make an expedition with me in the donkey
chair to inquire after the herdboy, Amos Bell, and carry
him some kitchen physic. To our horror we found him
quite alone in the wretched cottage, while everybody was
out harvesting; but he did not seem to pity himself, or
think it otherwise than quite natural, as he lay on a little
bed in the corner, disabled by what Clarence thought a
dislocation. Miss Ellen had brought him a pudding, and
little Miss Anne a picture-book.

He was not so dense and shy as the children of the hamlet
near us, and Emily extracted from him that Miss Ellen
was 'Our passon's young lady.'

Charlotte M. Yonge

'Mr. Mears'!' she exclaimed.

'No: ourn be Passon Fordy.'

It turned out that this place was not in Earlscombe at all, but in Hillside, a different parish; and the boy, Amos, further communicated that there was old Passon Fordy, and Passon Frank, and Madam, what was Mr. Frank's lady. Yes, he could read, he could; he went to Sunday School, and was in Miss Ellen's class; he had been to school worky days, only father was dead, and Farmer Hartop gave him a job.

It was plain that Hillside was under a very different rule from Earlscombe; and Emily was delighted to have discovered that the sweet cottage bonnet's owner was called Ellen, which just then was the pet Christian name of romance, in honour of the Lady of the Lake.

In the midst of her raptures, however, just as we were about to turn in at our own gate into the wood, we heard horses' hoofs, and then came, careering by on ponies, a very pretty girl and a youth of about the same age. Clarence's hand rose to his hat, and he made his eager bow; but the young lady did not vouchsafe the slightest acknowledgment, turned her head away, and urged her pony to speed.

Emily broke out with an angry disappointed exclamation. Clarence's face was scarlet, and he said low and hoarsely, 'That's Lester. He was in the Argus at Portsmouth two years ago;'—and then, as our little sister continued her indignant exclamations, he added, 'Hush! Don't on any account say a word about it. I had better get back to my work. I am only doing you harm by staying here.'

At which Emily shed tears, and together we persuaded

him not to curtail his holiday, which, indeed, he could not have done without assigning the reason to the elders, and this was out of the question. Nor did he venture to hang back when, as our service was to be on Sunday afternoon, my father proposed to walk to Hillside Church in the morning. They came back well pleased. There was care and decency throughout. The psalms were sung to a 'grinder organ'—which was an advanced state of things in those days—and very nicely. Parson Frank read well and impressively, and the old parson, a fine venerable man, had preached an excellent sermon—really admirable, as my father repeated. Our party had been scarcely in time, and had been disposed of in seats close to the door, where Clarence was quite out of sight of the disdainful young lady and her squire, of whom Emily begged to hear no more.

She looked askance at the cards left on the hall table the next day—'The Rev. Christopher Fordyce,' and 'The Rev. F. C. Fordyce,' also 'Mrs. F. C. Fordyce, Hillside Rectory.'

We had found out that Hillside was a family living, and that there was much activity there on the part of the father and son—rector and curate; and that the other clerical folk, ladies especially, who called on us, spoke of Mrs. F. C. Fordyce with a certain tone, as if they were afraid of her, as Sir Horace Lester's sister,—very superior, very active, very strict in her notions,—as if these were so many defects. They were an offshoot of the old Fordyces of Chantry House, but so far back that all recollection of kindred or connection must have worn out. Their property—all in beautiful order—marched with ours, and Chapman was very particular about the boundaries. 'Old master he wouldn't have a bird picked up if it fell over on they Fordys' ground—not he! He couldn't abide passons, couldn't the old Squire—not Miss Hannah More, and all they Cheddar lot, and they Fordys least of all. My son's wife, she was for sending her little maid to Hillside to Madam Fordys' school, but, bless your heart, 'twould have been as much as my place was worth if master had known it.'

The visit was not returned till after Clarence had gone back to his London work. Sore as was the loss of him from my daily life, I could see that the new world and fresh acquaintances were a trial to him, and especially since the encounter with young Lester had driven him back into his shell, so that he would be better where he was already known and had nothing new to overcome. Emily, though not yet sixteen, was emancipated from schoolroom habits, and the dear girl was my devoted slave to an extent that perhaps I abused.

Not being 'come out,' she was left at home on the day when we set out on a regular progress in the chariot with post-horses. The britshka and pair, which were our ambition, were to wait till my father's next rents came in. Morning calls in the country were a solemn and imposing ceremony, and the head of the family had to be taken on the first circuit; nor was there much scruple as to making them in the forenoon, so several were to be disposed of before fulfilling an engagement to luncheon at the farthest point, where some old London friends had borrowed a house for the summer, and had included me in their invitation.

Here alone did I leave the carriage, but I had Cooper's Spy and my sketch-book as companions while waiting at doors where the inhabitants were at home. The last visit was at Hillside Rectory, a house of architecture somewhat similar to our own, but of the soft creamy stone which so well set off the vine with purple clusters, the myrtles and fuchsias, that covered it. I was wishing we had drawn up far enough off for a sketch to be possible, when, from a window close above, I heard the following words in a clear girlish voice-

'No, indeed! I'm not going down. It is only those horrid Earlscombe people. I can't think how they have the face to come near us!'

There was a reply, perhaps that the parents had made the first visit, for the rejoinder was—'Yes; grandpapa said it was a Christian duty to make an advance; but they need not have come so soon. Indeed, I wonder they show themselves at all. I am sure I would not if I had such a dreadful son.' Presently, 'I hate to think of it. That I should have thanked him. Depend upon it, he will never pay the doctor. A coward like that is capable of anything.'

The proverb had been realised, but there could hardly have been a more involuntary or helpless listener. Presently my parents came back, escorted by both the gentlemen of the house, tall fine-looking men, the elder with snowy hair, and the dignity of men of the old school; the younger with a joyous, hearty, out-of-door countenance, more like a squire than a clergyman.

The visit seemed to have been gratifying. Mrs. Fordyce was declared to be of higher stamp than most of the neighbouring ladies; and my father was much pleased with the two clergymen, while as we drove along he kept on admiring the well-ordered fields and fences, and contrasting the pretty cottages and trim gardens with the dreary appearance of our own village. I asked why Amos Bell's home had been neglected, and was answered with some annoyance, as I pointed down the lane, that it was on our land, though in Hillside parish. 'I am glad to have such neighbours!' observed my mother, and I kept to myself the remarks I had heard, though I was still tingling with the sting of them.

We heard no more of 'they Fordys' for some time. The married pair went away to stay with friends, and we only once met the old gentleman, when I was waiting in the street at Wattlesea in the donkey chair, while my mother was trying to match netting silk in the odd little shop that united fancy work, toys, and tracts with the post office. Old Mr. Fordyce met us as we drew up, handed her out with a grand seigneur's courtesy, and stood talking to me so delightfully that I quite forgot it was from Christian duty.

My father corresponded with the old Rector about the state of the parish, and at last went over to Bath for a personal conference, but without much satisfaction. The Earlscombe people were pronounced to be an ungrateful good-for-nothing set, for whom it was of no use to do anything; and indeed my mother made such discoveries in the cottages that she durst not let Emily fulfil her cherished scheme of visiting them. The only resemblance to the favourite heroines of religious tales that could be permitted was assembling a tiny Sunday class in Chapman's lodge; and it must be confessed that her brothers thought she made as much fuss about it as if there had been a hundred scholars.

However, between remonstrances and offers of under-taking a share of the expense, my father managed to get Mr. Mears' services dispensed with from the ensuing Lady Day, and that a resident curate should be appointed, the choice of whom was to rest with himself. It was then and there decided that Martyn should be 'brought up to the Church,' as people then used to term destination to Holy Orders. My father said he should feel justified in building a good house when he could afford it, if it was to be a provision for one of his sons, and he also felt that as he had the charge of the parish as patron, it was right and fitting to train one of his sons up to take care of it. Nor did

Martyn show any distaste to the idea, as indeed there was less in it then than at present to daunt the imagination of an honest, lively boy, not as yet specially thoughtful or devout, but obedient, truthful, and fairly reverent, and ready to grow as he was trained.

CHAPTER XII

MRS. SOPHIA'S FEUD

'O'er all there hung the shadow of a fear,
A sense of mystery the spirit daunted,
And said as plain as whisper in the ear,
The place is haunted.'

HOOD.

We had a houseful at Christmas. The Rev. Charles Henderson, a Fellow of Trinity College, Oxford, lately ordained a deacon, had been recommended to us by our London vicar, and was willing not only to take charge of the parish, but to direct my studies, and to prepare Martyn for school. He came to us for the Christmas vacation to reconnoitre and engage lodgings at a farmhouse. We liked him very much—my mother being all the better satisfied after he had shown her a miniature, and confided to her that the original was waiting till a college living should come to him in the distant future.

Admiral Griffith could not tear himself from his warm rooms and his club, but our antiquarian friend, Mr. Stafford, came with his wife, and revelled in the ceilings of the mullion room, where he would much have liked to sleep, but that its accommodations were only fit for a bachelor.

Our other visitor was Miss Selby, or rather Mrs. Sophia Selby, as she designated herself, according to the becoming fashion of elderly spinsters, which to my mind might be gracefully resumed. It irked my father to think of the good lady's solitary Christmas at Bath, and he asked her to come to us. She travelled half-way in a post-chaise, and then was met by the carriage. A very nice old lady she was, with a meek, delicate babyish face, which could not be spoilt by the cap of the period, one of the most disfiguring articles of head gear ever devised, though nobody thought so then. She was full of kindness; indeed, if she had a fault it was the abundant pity she lavished on me, and her determination to amuse me. The weather was of the kind that only the healthy and hardy could encounter, and when every one else was gone out, and I was just settling in with a new book, or an old crabbed Latin document, that Mr. Stafford had entrusted to me to copy out fairly and translate, she would glide in with her worsted work on a charitable mission to enliven poor Mr. Edward.

However, this was the means of my obtaining some curious enlightenments. A dinner-party was in contemplation, and she was dismayed at the choice of the fashionable London hour of seven, and still more by finding that the Fordyces were to be among the guests. She was too well-bred to manifest her feelings to her hosts, but alone with me, she could not refrain from expressing her astonishment to me, all the more when she heard this was reciprocity for an invitation that it had not been possible to accept. Her poor dear uncle would never hear of intercourse with Hillside. On being asked why, she repeated what Chapman had said, that he could not endure any one connected with Mrs. Hannah More and her canting, humbugging set, as the ungodly old man had chosen to call them, imbuing even this good woman with evil prejudices against their noble work at Cheddar.

'Besides this, Fordyces and Winslows could never be friends, since the Fordyces had taken on themselves to dispute the will, and say it had been improperly obtained.'

'What will?'

'Mrs. Winslow's—Margaret Fordyce that was. She was the heiress, and had every right to dispose of her property.'

'But that was more than a hundred years ago!'

'So it was, my dear; but though the law gave it to us—to my uncle's grandfather (or great-grandfather, was it?)—those Fordyces never could rest content. Why, one of them—a clergyman's son too—shot young Philip Winslow dead in a duel. They have always grudged at us. Does your papa know it, my dear Mr. Edward? He ought to be aware.'

'I do not know,' I said; 'but he would hardly care about what happened in the time of Queen Anne.'

It was curious to see how the gentle little lady espoused the family quarrel, which, after all, was none of hers.

'Well, you are London people, and the other branch, and may not feel as we do down here; but I shall always say that Madam Winslow's husband's son had every right to come before her cousin once removed.'

I asked if we were descended from her, for, having a turn for heraldry and genealogy, I wanted to make out our family tree. Mrs. Sophia was ready to hold up her hands at the ignorance of the 'other branch.' This poor heiress had lost all her children in their infancy, and bequeathed the estate to her stepson, the Fordyce male heir having been endowed by her father with the advowson of Hillside and a handsome estate there, which Mrs. Selby thought ought to have contented him, 'but some people never know when they have enough;' and, on my observing that it might have been a matter of justice, she waxed hotter, declaring that what the Winslows felt so much was the accusation of violence against the poor lady. She spoke as if it were a story of yesterday, and added, 'Indeed, they made the common people have all sorts of superstitious fancies about the room where she died—that old part of the house.' Then she added in a low mysterious voice, 'I hear that your brother Mr. Griffith Winslow could not sleep there;' and when the rats and the wind were mentioned—'Yes, that was what my poor dear uncle used to say. He always called it nonsense; but we never had a servant who would sleep there. You'll not mention it, Mr. Edward, but I could not help asking that very nice housemaid, Jane, whether the room was used, and she said how Mr. Griffith had given it up, and none of the servants could spend a night there when they are sleeping round. Of course I said all in my power to dispel the idea, and told her that there was no accounting for all the noises in old houses; but you never can reason with that class of people.'

'Did you ever hear the noises, Mrs. Selby?'

'Oh, no; I wouldn't sleep there for thousands! Not that I attach any importance to such folly,—my poor dear uncle would never hear of such a thing; but I am such a nervous creature, I should lie awake all night expecting the rats to run over me. I never knew of any one sleeping there, except in the gay times when I was a child, and the house

Charlotte M. Yonge

used to be as full as, or fuller than, it could hold, for the hunt breakfast or a ball, and my poor aunt used to make up ever so many beds in the two rooms, and then we never heard of any disturbance, except what they made themselves.'

This chiefly concerned me, because home cosseting had made me old woman enough to be uneasy about unaired beds; and I knew that my mother meant to consign Clarence to the mullion chamber. So, without betraying Jane, I spoke to her, and was answered, 'Oh, sir, I'll take care of that; I'll light a fire and air the mattresses well. I wish that was all, poor young gentleman!'

To the reply that the rats were slaughtered and the wind stopped out, Jane returned a look of compassion; but the subject was dropped, as it was supposed to be the right thing to hush up, instead of fostering, any popular superstition; but it surprised me that, as all our servants were fresh importations, they should so soon have become imbued with these undefined alarms.

My father was much amused at being successor to this family feud, and said that when he had time he would look up the documents.

Mrs. Sophia was a sight when Mr. Fordyce and his son and daughter-in-law were announced; she was so comically stiff between her deference to her hosts and her allegiance to her poor dear uncle; but her coldness melted before the charms of old Mr. Fordyce, who was one of the most delightful people in the world. She even was his partner at whist, and won the game, and that she DID like.

Parson Frank, as we naughty young ones called him, was all good-nature and geniality—a thorough clergyman after the ideas of the time, and a thorough farmer too; and in each capacity, as well as in politics, he suited my father or Mr. Henderson. His lady, in a blonde cap, exactly like the last equipment my mother had provided herself with in London, and a black satin dress, had much more style than the more gaily-dressed country dames, and far more conversation. Mr. Stafford, who had dreaded the party, pronounced her a sensible, agreeable woman, and she was particularly kind and pleasant to me, coming and talking over the botany of the country, and then speaking of my brother's kindness to poor Amos Bell, who was nearly recovered, but was a weakly child, for whom she dreaded the toil of a ploughboy in thick clay with heavy shoes.

I was sorry when, after Emily's well-studied performance on the piano, Mrs. Fordyce was summoned away from me to sing, but her music and her voice were both of a very different order from ordinary drawing-room music; and when our evening was over, we congratulated ourselves upon our neighbours, and agreed that the Fordyces were the gems of the party.

Only Mrs. Sophia sighed at us as degenerate Winslows, and Emily reserved to herself the right of believing that the daughter was 'a horrid girl.'

CHAPTER XIII

A SCRAPE

'Though bound with weakness' heavy chain
We in the dust of earth remain;
Not all remorseful be our tears,
No agony of shame or fears,
Need pierce its passion's bitter tide.'

VERSES AND SONNETS.

Perhaps it was of set purpose that our dinner. party had been given before Clarence's return. Griffith had been expected in time for it, but he had preferred going by way of London to attend a ball given by the daughter of a barrister friend of my father's. Selina Clarkson was a fine showy girl, with the sort of beauty to inspire boyish admiration, and Griff's had been a standing family joke, even my father condescending to tease him when the young lady married Sir Henry Peacock, a fat vulgar old man who had made his fortune in the commissariat, and purchased a baronetcy. He was allowing his young wife her full swing of fashion and enjoyment. My mother did not think it a desirable acquaintance, and was restless until both the brothers came home together, long after dark on Christmas Eve, having been met by the gig at the corner where the coach stopped. The dinner-hour had been put off till half-past six, and we had to wait for them, the coach having been delayed by setting down Christmas guests and Christmas fare. They were a contrast; Griffith looking very handsome and manly, all in a ruddy glow from the frosty air, and Clarence, though equally tall, well-made, and with more refined features, looked pale and effaced, now that his sailor tan was worn off. The one talked as eagerly as he ate, the other was shy, spiritless, and with little appetite; but as he always shrank into himself among strangers, it was the less wonder that he sat in his drooping way behind my sofa, while Griffith kept us all merry with his account of the humours of the 'Peacock at home;' the lumbering efforts of old Sir Henry to be as young and gay as his wife, in spite of gout and portliness; and the extreme delight of his lady in her new splendours—a gold spotted muslin and white plumes in a diamond agraffe. He mimicked Sir Henry's cockneyisms more than my father's chivalry approved towards his recent host, as he described the complaints he had heard against 'my Lady being refused the hentry at Halmack's, but treated like the wery canal;' and how the devoted husband 'wowed he would get up a still more hexclusive circle, and shut hout these himpertinent fashionables who regarded Halmack's as the seventh 'eaven.'

My mother shook her head at his audacious fun about Paradise and the Peri, but he was so brilliant and good-humoured that no one was ever long displeased with him. At night he followed when Clarence helped me to my room, and carefully shutting the door, Griff began. 'Now, Teddy, you're always as rich as a Jew, and I told Bill you'd help him to set it straight. I'd do it myself, but that I'm cleaned out. I'd give ten times the cash rather than see him with that hang-dog look again for just nothing at all, if he would only believe so and be rational.'

Clarence did look indescribably miserable while it was explained that he had been commissioned to receive about 20 pounds which was owing to my father, and to discharge therewith some small debts to London tradesmen. All except the last, for a little more than four pounds, had been paid, when Clarence met in the street an old messmate, a good-natured rattle-pated youth,—one of those who had thought him harshly treated. There was a cordial greeting, and an invitation to dine at once at a hotel, where they were joined by some other young men, and by and by betook themselves to cards, when my poor brother's besetting enemy prevented him from withdrawing when he found the points were guineas. Thus he lost the remaining amount in his charge, and so much of his own that barely enough was left for his journey. His salary was not due till Lady Day; Mr. Castleford was in the country, and no advances could be asked from Mr. Frith. Thus Griff had found him in utter despair, and had ever since been trying to cheer him and make light of his trouble. If I advanced the amount, which was no serious matter to me, Clarence could easily get Peter to pay the bill, and if my father should demand the receipt too soon, it would be easy to put him off by saying there had been a delay in getting the account sent in.

'I couldn't do that,' said Clarence.

'Well, I should not have thought you would have stuck at that,' returned Griff.

'There must be no untruth,' I broke in; 'but if without THAT, he can avoid getting into a scrape with papa—'

Clarence interrupted in the wavering voice we knew so well, but growing clearer and stronger.

'Thank you, Edward, but—but—no, I can't. There's the

Sacrament to-morrow.'

'Oh—h!' said Griff, in an indescribable tone. But he will never believe you, nor let you go.'

'Better so,' said Clarence, half choked, 'than go profanely—deceiving—or not knowing whether I shall—'

Just then we heard our father wishing the other gentlemen good-night, and to our surprise Clarence opened the door, though he was deadly white and with dew starting on his forehead.

My father turned good-naturedly. 'Boys, boys, you are glad to be together, but mamma won't have you talking here all night, keeping her baby up.'

'Sir,' said Clarence, holding by the rail of the bed, 'I was waiting for you. I have something to tell you—'

The words that followed were incoherent and wrong end foremost; nor had many, indeed, been uttered before my father cut them short with -

'No false excuses, sir; I know you too well to listen. Go. I have ceased to hope for anything better.'

Clarence went without a word, but Griff and I burst out with entreaties to be listened to. Our father thought at first that ours were only the pleadings of partiality, and endeavours to shield the brother we both so heartily loved; but when he understood the circumstances, the real amount of the transgression, and Clarence's rejection of our united advice and assistance to conceal it, he was greatly touched and softened. 'Poor lad! poor fellow!' he muttered, 'he is really doing his best. I need not have cut him so short. I was afraid of more falsehoods if I let him open his mouth. I'll go and see.'

He went off, and we remained in suspense, Griff observing that he had done his best, but poor Bill always would be a fool, and that no one who had not always lived at home like me would have let out that we had been for the suppression policy. As I was rather shocked, he went off to bed, saying he should look in to see what remained of Clarence after the pelting of the pitiless storm he was sure to bring on himself by his ridiculous faltering instead of speaking out like a man.

I longed to have been able to do the same, but my father kindly came back to relieve my mind by telling me that he was better satisfied about Clarence than ever he had been before. When encouraged to speak out, the narrative of the temptation had so entirely agreed with what we had said as to show there had been no prevarication, and this had done more to convince my father that he was on the right track than the having found him on his knees. He had had a patient hearing, and thus was able to command his nerves enough to explain himself, and it had ended in my father giving entire forgiveness for what, as Griff truly said, would have been a mere trifle but for the past. The voluntary confession had much impressed my father, and he could not help adding a word of gentle reproof to me for having joined in aiding him to withhold it, but he accepted my explanation and went away, observing, 'By the by, I don't wonder at what Griffith says of that room; I never heard such strange effects of currents of air.'

Clarence was in my room before I was drest, full of our father's 'wonderful goodness' to him. He had never experienced anything like it, he said. 'Why! he really seemed hopeful about me,' were words uttered with a gladness enough to go to one's heart. 'O Edward, I feel as if there was some chance of "steadfastly purposing" this time.'

It was not the way of the family to say much of religious feeling, and this was much for Clarence to utter. He looked white and tired, but there was an air of rest and peace about him, above all when my mother met him with a very real kiss. Moreover, Mr. Castleford had taken care to brighten our Christmas with a letter expressive of great satisfaction with Clarence for steadiness and intelligence. Even Mr. Frith allowed that he was the most punctual of all those young dogs.

'I do believe,' said my father, 'that his piety is doing him some good after all.'

So our mutual wishes of a happy Christmas were verified, though not much according to the notions of this half of the century. People made their Christmas day either mere merriment, or something little different from the grave Sunday of that date. And ours, except for the Admiral's dining with us, had always been of the latter description, all the more that when celebrations of the Holy Communion were so rare they were treated with an awe and reverence which frequency has perhaps diminished, and a feeling (possibly Puritanical) prevailed which made it appear incongruous to end with festivity a day so begun. That we had a Christmas Day Communion at all at Earlscombe was an innovation only achieved by Mr. Henderson going to assist the old Rector at Wattlesea; and there were no communicants except from our house, besides Chapman, his daughter-in-law, and five old creatures between whom the alms were immediately divided. We afterwards learnt that our best farmer and his wife were much disappointed at the change from Sunday interfering with the family jollification; and Mrs. Sophia Selby was annoyed at the contradiction to her habits under the rule of her poor dear uncle.

Charlotte M. Yonge

Of the irregularities, irreverences, and squalor of the whole I will not speak. They were not then such stumbling-blocks as they would be now, and many passed unperceived by us, buried as we were in our big pew, with our eyes riveted on our books; yet even thus there was enough evident to make my mother rejoice that Mr. Henderson would be with us before Easter. Still this could not mar the thankful gladness that was with us all that day, and which shone in Clarence's eyes. His countenance always had a remarkable expression in church, as if somehow his spirit went farther than ours did, and things unseen were more real to him.

Hillside, as usual, had two services, and my father and his friend were going to walk thither in the afternoon, but it was a raw cold day, threatening snow, and Emily was caught by my mother in the hail and ordered back, as well as Clarence, who had shown symptoms of having caught cold on his dismal journey. Emily coaxed from her permission to have a fire in the bookroom, and there we three had a memorably happy time. We read our psalms and lessons, and our Christian Year, which was more and more the lodestar of our feelings. We compared our favourite passages, and discussed the obscurer ones, and Clarence was led to talk out more of his heart than he had ever shown to us before. Perhaps he had lost some of his reserve through his intercourse with our good old governess, Miss Newton, who was still grinding away at her daily mill, though with somewhat failing eyesight, so that she could do nothing but knit in the long evenings, and was most grateful to her former pupil for coming, as often as he could, to talk or read to her.

She was a most excellent and devout woman, and when Emily, who in youthful gaiete de coeur had got a little tired of her, exclaimed at his taste, and asked if she made him read nothing but Pike's Early Piety, he replied gravely, 'She showed me where to lay my burthen down,' and turned to the two last verses of the poem for 'Good Friday' in the Christian Year, as well as to the one we had just read on the Holy Communion.

My father's kindness had seemed to him the pledge of the Heavenly Father's forgiveness; and he added, perhaps a little childishly, that it had been his impulse to promise never to touch a card again, but that he dreaded the only too familiar reply, 'What availed his promises?'

'Do promise, Clarry!' cried Emily, 'and then you won't have to play with that tiresome old Mrs. Sophia.'

'That would rather deter me,' said Clarence good-humouredly.

'A card-playing old age is despicable,' pronounced Miss Emily, much to our amusement.

After that we got into a bewilderment. We knew nothing of the future question of temperance versus total abstinence; but after it had been extracted that Miss Newton regarded cards as the devil's books, the inconsistent little sister changed sides, and declared it narrow and evangelical to renounce what was innocent. Clarence argued that what might be harmless for others might be dangerous for such as himself, and that his real difficulty in making even a mental vow was that, if broken, there was an additional sin.

'It is not oneself that one trusts,' I said.

'No,' said Clarence emphatically; 'and setting up a vow seems as if it might be sticking up the reed of one's own word, and leaning on THAT—when it breaks, at least mine does. If I could always get the grasp of Him that I felt to-day, there would be no more bewildered heart and failing spirit, which are worse than the actual falls they cause.' And as Emily said she did not understand, he replied in words I wrote down and thought over, 'What we ARE is the point, more than even what we DO. We DO as we ARE; and yet we form ourselves by what we DO.'

'And,' I put in, 'I know somebody who won a victory last night over himself and his two brothers. Surely DOING that is a sign that he IS more than he used to be.'

'If he were, it would not have been an effort at all,' said Clarence, but with his rare sweet smile.

Just then Griff called him away, and Emily sat pondering and impressed. 'It did seem so odd,' she said, 'that Clarry should be so much the best, and yet so much the worst of us.'

I agreed. His insight into spiritual things, and his enjoyment of them, always humiliated us both, yet he fell so much lower in practice,—'But then we had not his temptations.'

'Yes,' said Emily; 'but look at Griff! He goes about like other young men, and keeps all right, and yet he doesn't care about religious things a bit more than he can help.'

It was quite true. Religion was life to the one and an insurance to the other, and this had been a mystery to us all our young lives, as far as we had ever reflected on the contrast between the practical failure and success of each. Our mother, on the other hand, viewed Clarence's tendencies as part of an unreal, self-deceptive nature, and regretted his intimacy with Miss Newton, who, she said, had fostered 'that kind of thing' in his childhood—made him fancy talk, feeling, and preaching were more than truth and honour—and might lead him to run after Irving, Rowland Hill, or Baptist Noel, about whose tenets she was rather confused. It would be an additional misfortune if he became a fanatical Evangelical light, and he was just the character to be worked upon.

My father held that she might be thankful for any good influence or safe resort for a young man in lodgings in London, and he merely bade Clarence never resort to any variety of dissenting preacher. We were of the school called—a little later—high and dry, but were strictly orthodox according to our lights, and held it a prime duty to attend our parish church, whatever it might be; nor, indeed, had Clarence swerved from these traditions.

Poor Mrs. Sophia was baulked of the game at whist, which she viewed as a legitimate part of the Christmas pleasures; and after we had eaten our turkey, we found the evening long, except that Martyn escaped to snapdragon with the servants; and, by and by, Chapman, magnificent in patronage, ushered in the church singers into the hall, and clarionet, bassoon, and fiddle astonished our ears.

CHAPTER XIV

THE MULLION CHAMBER

'A lady with a lamp I see,
Pass through the glimmering gloom,
And flit from room to room.'

LONGFELLOW.

For want of being able to take exercise, the first part of
the night had always been sleepless with me, though my
dear mother thought it wrong to recognise the habit or
allow me a lamp. A fire, however, I had, and by its light,
on the second night after Christmas, I saw my door
noiselessly opened, and Clarence creeping in half-dressed
and barefooted. To my frightened interrogation the
answer came, through chattering teeth, 'It's I—only I—
Ted—no—nothing's the matter, only I can't stand it any
longer!'

His hands were cold as ice when he grasped mine, as if to
get hold of something substantial, and he trembled so as
to shake the bed. 'That room,' he faltered. ''Tis not only
the moans! I've seen her!'

'Whom?'

'I don't know. There she stands with her lamp, crying!' I could scarcely distinguish the words through the clashing of his teeth, and as I threw my arms round him the shudder seemed to pass to me; but I did my best to warm him by drawing the clothes over him, and he began to gather himself together, and speak intelligibly. There had been sounds the first night as of wailing, but he had been too much preoccupied to attend to them till, soon after one o'clock, they ended in a heavy fall and long shriek, after which all was still. Christmas night had been undisturbed, but on this the voices had begun again at eleven, and had a strangely human sound; but as it was windy, sleety weather, and he had learnt at sea to disregard noises in the rigging, he drew the sheet over his head and went to sleep. 'I was dreaming that I was at sea,' he said, 'as I always do on a noisy night, but this was not a dream. I was wakened by a light in the room, and there stood a woman with a lamp, moaning and sobbing. My first notion was that one of the maids had come to call me, and I sat up; but I could not speak, and she gave another awful suppressed cry, and moved towards that walled-up door. Then I saw it was none of the servants, for it was an antique dress like an old picture. So I knew what it must be, and an unbearable horror came over me, and I rushed into the outer room, where there was a little fire left; but I heard her going on still, and I could endure it no longer. I knew you would be awake and would bear with me, so I came down to you.'

Then this was what Chapman and the maids had meant. This was Mrs. Sophia Selby's vulgar superstition! I found that Clarence had heard none of the mysterious whispers afloat, and only knew that Griff had deserted the room after his own return to London. I related what I had learnt from the old lady, and in that midnight hour we agreed that it could be no mere fancy or rumour, but that cruel wrong must have been done in that chamber. Our feeling

Charlotte M. Yonge

was that all ought to be made known, and in that impression we fell asleep, Clarence first.

By and by I found him moving. He had heard the clock strike four, and thought it wiser to repair to his own quarters, where he believed the disturbance was over. Lucifer matches as yet were not, but he had always been a noiseless being, with a sailor's foot, so that, by the help of the moonlight through the hall windows, he regained his room.

And when morning had come, the nocturnal visitation wore such a different aspect to both our minds that we decided to say nothing to our parents, who, said Clarence, would simply disbelieve him; and, indeed, I inclined to suppose it had been an uncommonly vivid dream, produced in that sensitive nature by the uncanny sounds of the wind in the chinks and crannies of the ancient chamber. Had not Scott's Demonology and Witchcraft, which we studied hard on that day, proved all such phantoms to be explicable? The only person we told was Griff, who was amused and incredulous. He had heard the noises—oh yes! and objected to having his sleep broken by them. It was too had to expose Clarence to them—poor Bill—on whom they worked such fancies!

He interrogated Chapman, however, but probably in that bantering way which is apt to produce reserve. Chapman never 'gave heed to them fictious tales,' he said; but, when hard pressed, he allowed that he had 'heerd that a lady do walk o' winter nights,' and that was why the garden door of the old rooms was walled up. Griff asked if this was done for fear she should catch cold, and this somewhat affronted him, so that he averred that he knew nought about it, and gave no thought to such like.

Just then they arrived at the Winslow Arms, and took

each a glass of ale, when Griff, partly to tease Chapman, asked the landlady—an old Chantry House servant—whether she had ever met the ghost. She turned rather pale, which seemed to have impressed him, and demanded if he had seen it. 'It always walked at Christmas time—between then and the New Year.' She had once seen a light in the garden by the ruin in winter-time, and once last spring it came along the passage, but that was just before the old Squire was took for death,—folks said that was always the way before any of the family died—'if you'll excuse it, sir.' Oh no, she thought nothing of such things, but she had heard tell that the noises were such at all times of the year that no one could sleep in the rooms, but the light wasn't to be seen except at Christmas.

Griff with the philosophy of a university man, was certain that all was explained by Clarence having imbibed the impression of the place being haunted; and going to sleep nervous at the noises, his brain had shaped a phantom in accordance. Let Clarence declare as he might that the legends were new to him, Griff only smiled to think how easily people forgot, and he talked earnestly about catching ideas without conscious information.

However, he volunteered to sit up that night to ascertain the exact causes of the strange noises and convince Clarence that they were nothing but the effects of draughts. The fire in his gunroom was surreptitiously kept up to serve for the vigil, which I ardently desired to share. It was an enterprise; it would gratify my curiosity; and besides, though Griffith was good-natured and forbearing in a general way towards Clarence, I detected a spirit of mockery about him which might break out unpleasantly when poor Clarry was convicted of one of his unreasonable panics.

Charlotte M. Yonge

Both brothers were willing to gratify me, the only difficulty being that the tap of my crutches would warn the entire household of the expedition. However, they had—all unknown to my mother—several times carried me about queen's cushion fashion, as, being always much of a size, they could do most handily; and as both were now fine, strong, well-made youths of twenty and nineteen, they had no doubt of easily and silently conveying me up the shallow-stepped staircase when all was quiet for the night.

Emily, with her sharp ears, guessed that something was in hand, but we promised her that she should know all in time. I believe Griff, being a little afraid of her quickness, led her to suppose he was going to hold what he called a symposium in his rooms, and to think it a mystery of college life not intended for young ladies.

He really had prepared a sort of supper for us when, after my father's resounding turn of the key of the drawing-room door, my brothers, in their stocking soles, bore me upstairs, the fun of the achievement for the moment overpowering all sense of eeriness. Griff said he could not receive me in his apartment without doing honour to the occasion, and that Dutch courage was requisite for us both; but I suspect it was more in accordance with Oxford habits that he had provided a bottle of sherry and another of ale, some brandy cherries, bread, cheese, and biscuits, by what means I do not know, for my mother always locked up the wine. He was disappointed that Clarence would touch nothing, and declared that inanition was the preparation for ghost-seeing or imagining. I drank his health in a glass of sherry as I looked round at the curious old room, with its panelled roof, the heraldic devices and badges of the Power family, and the trophy of swords, dirks, daggers, and pistols, chiefly relics of our naval grandfather, but reinforced by the sword, helmet, and spurs of the county Yeomanry which Griff had joined.

Griff proposed cards to drive away fancies, especially as the sounds were beginning; but though we generally yielded to him we COULD not give our attention to anything but these. There was first a low moan. 'No great harm in that,' said Griff; 'it comes through that crack in the wainscot where there is a sham window. Some putty will put a stop to that.'

Then came a more decided wail and sob much nearer to us. Griff hastily swallowed the ale in his tumbler, and, striking a theatrical attitude, exclaimed, 'Angels and ministers of grace defend us!'

Clarence held up his hand in deprecation. The door into his bedroom was open, and Griff, taking up one of the flat candlesticks, pursued his researches, holding the flame to all chinks or cracks in the wainscotting to detect draughts which might cause the dreary sounds, which were much more like suppressed weeping than any senseless gust of wind. Of draughts there were many, and he tried holding his hand against each crevice to endeavour to silence the wails; but these became more human and more distressful. Presently Clarence exclaimed, 'There!' and on his face there was a whiteness and an expression which always recurs to me on reading those words of Eliphaz the Temanite, 'Then a spirit passed before my face, and the hair of my flesh stood up.' Even Griff was awestruck as we cried, 'Where? what?'

'Don't you see her? There! By the press—look!'

'I see a patch of moonlight on the wall,' said Griff.

'Moonlight—her lamp. Edward, don't you see her?'

I could see nothing but a spot of light on the wall. Griff (plainly putting a force on himself) came back and gave him a good-natured shake. 'Dreaming again, old Bill. Wake up and come to your senses.'

'I am as much in my senses as you are,' said Clarence. 'I see her as plainly as I see you.'

Nor could any one doubt either the reality of the awe in his voice and countenance, nor of the light—a kind of hazy ball—nor of the choking sobs.

'What is she like?' I asked, holding his hand, for, though infected by his dread, my fears were chiefly for the effect on him; but he was much calmer and less horror-struck than on the previous night, though still he shuddered as he answered in a low voice, as if loth to describe a lady in her presence, 'A dark cloak with the hood fallen back, a kind of lace headdress loosely fastened, brown hair, thin white face, eyes—oh, poor thing!—staring with fright, dark—oh, how swollen the lids! all red below with crying —black dress with white about it—a widow kind of look —a glove on the arm with the lamp. Is she beckoning— looking at us? Oh, you poor thing, if I could tell what you mean!'

I felt the motion of his muscles in act to rise, and grasped him. Griff held him with a strong hand, hoarsely crying, 'Don't!—don't—don't follow the thing, whatever you do!'

Clarence hid his face. It was very awful and strange. Once the thought of conjuring her to speak by the Holy Name crossed me, but then I saw no figure; and with incredulous Griffith standing by, it would have been like playing, nor perhaps could I have spoken. How long this lasted there is no knowing; but presently the light moved towards the walled-up door and seemed to pass into it.

Clarence raised his head and said she was gone. We breathed freely.

'The farce is over,' said Griff. 'Mr. Edward Winslow's carriage stops the way!'

I was hoisted up, candle in hand, between the two, and had nearly reached the stairs when there came up on the garden side a sound as of tipsy revellers in the garden. 'The scoundrels! how can they have got in?' cried Griff, looking towards the window; but all the windows on that side had peculiarly heavy shutters and bars, with only a tiny heart-shaped aperture very high up, so they somewhat hurried their steps downstairs, intending to rush out on the intruders from the back door. But suddenly, in the middle of the staircase, we heard a terrible heartrending woman's shriek, making us all start and have a general fall. My brothers managed to seat me safely on a step without much damage to themselves, but the candle fell and was extinguished, and we made too heavy a weight to fall without real noise enough to bring the household together before we could pick ourselves up in the dark.

We heard doors opening and hurried calls, and something about pistols, impelling Griff to call out, 'It's nothing, papa; but there are some drunken rascals in the garden.'

A light had come by this time, and we were detected. There was a general sally upon the enemy in the garden before any one thought of me, except a 'You here!' when they nearly fell over me. And there I was left sitting on the stair, helpless without my crutches, till in a few minutes all returned declaring there was nothing—no signs of anything; and then as Clarence ran up to me with my crutches my father demanded the meaning of my being there at that time of night.

'Well, sir,' said Griff, 'it is only that we have been sitting up to investigate the ghost.'

'Ghost! Arrant stuff and nonsense! What induced you to be dragging Edward about in this dangerous way?'

'I wished it,' said I.

'You are all mad together, I think. I won't have the house disturbed for this ridiculous folly. I shall look into it to-morrow!'

CHAPTER XV

RATIONAL THEORIES

'These are the reasons, they are natural.'

JULIUS CAESAR.

If anything could have made our adventure more unpleasant to Mr. and Mrs. Winslow, it would have been the presence of guests. However, inquiry was suppressed at breakfast, in deference to the signs my mother made to enjoin silence before the children, all unaware that Emily was nearly frantic with suppressed curiosity, and Martyn knew more about the popular version of the legend than any of us.

Clarence looked wan and heavy-eyed. His head was aching from a bump against the edge of a step, and his cold was much worse; no wonder, said my mother; but she was always softened by any ailment, and feared that the phantoms were the effect of coming illness. I have always thought that if Clarence could have come home from his court-martial with a brain fever he would have earned immediate forgiveness; but unluckily for him, he was a very healthy person.

Charlotte M. Yonge

All three of us were summoned to the tribunal in the study, where my father and my mother sat in judgment on what they termed 'this preposterous business.' In our morning senses our impressions were much more vague than at midnight, and we betrayed some confusion; but Griff and I had a strong instinct of sheltering Clarence, and we stoutly declared the noises to be beyond the capacities of wind, rats, or cats; that the light was visible and inexplicable; and that though we had seen nothing else, we could not doubt that Clarence did.

'Thought he did,' corrected my father.

'Without discussing the word,' said Griff, 'I mean that the effect on his senses was the same as the actual sight. You could not look at him without being certain.'

'Exactly so,' returned my mother. 'I wish Dr. Fellowes were near.'

Indeed nothing saved Clarence from being consigned to medical treatment but the distance from Bath or Bristol, and the contradictory advice that had been received from our county neighbours as to our family doctor. However, she formed her theory that his nervous imaginings— whether involuntary or acted, she hoped the former, and wished she could be sure—had infected us; and, as she was really uneasy about him, she would not let him sleep in the mullion room, but having nowhere else to bestow him, she turned out the man-servant and put him into the little room beyond mine, and she also forbade any mention of the subject to him that day.

This was a sore prohibition to Emily, who had been discussing it with the other ladies, and was in a mingled state of elation at the romance, and terror at the supernatural, which found vent in excited giggle, and moved Griff to cram her with raw-head and bloody-bone horrors, conventional enough to be suspicious, and send her to me tearfully to entreat to know the truth. If by day she exulted in a haunted chamber, in the evening she paid for it by terrors at walking about the house alone, and, when sent on an errand by my mother, looked piteous enough to be laughed at or scolded on all sides.

The gentlemen had more serious colloquies, and the upshot was a determination to sit up together and discover the origin of the annoyance. Mr. Stafford's antiquarian researches had made him familiar with such mysteries, and enough of them had been explained by natural causes to convince him that there was a key to all the rest. Owls, coiners, and smugglers had all been convicted of simulating ghosts. In one venerable mansion, behind the wainscot, there had been discovered nine skeletons of cats in different stages of decay, having trapped themselves at various intervals of time, and during the gradual extinction of their eighty-one lives having emitted cries enough to establish the ghastly reputation of the place. Perhaps Mr. Henderson was inclined to believe there were more things in heaven and earth than were dreamt of in even an antiquary's philosophy. He owned himself perplexed, but reserved his opinion.

At breakfast Clarence was quite well, except for the remains of his sore throat, and the two seniors were gruff and brief as to their watch. They had heard odd noises, and should discover the cause; the carpenter had already been sent for, and they had seen a light which was certainly due to reflection or refraction. Mr. Henderson committed himself to nothing but that 'it was very extraordinary;' and there was a wicked look of diversion on Griff's face, and an exchange of glances. Afterwards, in our own domain, we extracted a good deal more from them.

Griff told us how the two elders started on politics, and denounced Brougham and O'Connell loud enough to terrify any save the most undaunted ghost, till Henderson said 'Hush!' and they paused at the moan with which the performance always commenced, making Mr. Stafford turn, as Griff said, 'white in the gills,' though he talked of the wind on the stillest of frosty nights. Then came the sobbing and wailing, which certainly overawed them all; Henderson called them 'agonising,' but Griff was in a manner inured to this, and felt as if master of the ceremonies. Let them say what they would by daylight about owls, cats, and rats, they owned the human element then, and were far from comfortable, though they would not compromise their good sense by owning what both their younger companions had perceived—their feeling of some undefinable presence. Vain attempts had been made to account for the light or get rid of it by changing the position of candles or bright objects in the outer room; and Henderson had shut himself into the bedroom with it; but there he still only saw the hazy light—though all was otherwise pitch dark, except the keyhole and the small gray patch of sky at the top of the window-shutters. 'You saw nothing else?' said Griff. 'I thought I heard you break out as Clarence did, just before my father opened the door.'

'Perhaps I did so. I had the sense strongly on me of some being in grievous distress very near me.'

'And you should have power over it,' suggested Emily.

'I am afraid,' he said, 'that more thorough conviction and comprehension are needed before I could address the thing with authority. I should like to have stayed longer and heard the conclusion.'

For Mr. Stafford had grown impatient and weary, and my

father having satisfied himself that there was something to be detected, would not remain to the end, and not only carried his companions off, but locked the doors, perhaps expecting to imprison some agent in a trick, and find him in the morning.

Indeed Clarence had a dim remembrance of having been half wakened by some one looking in on him in the night, when he was sleeping heavily after his cold and the previous night's disturbance, and we suspected, though we would not say, that our father might have wished to ascertain that he had no share in producing these appearances. He was, however, fully acquitted of all wilful deception in the case, and he was not surprised, though he was disappointed, that his vision of the lady was supposed to be the consequence of excited imagination.

'I can't help it,' he said to me in private. 'I have always seen or felt, or whatever you may call it, things that others do not. Don't you remember how nobody would believe that I saw Lucy Brooke?'

'That was in the beginning of the measles.'

'I know; and I will tell you something curious. When I was at Gibraltar I met Mrs. Emmott—'

'Mary Brooke?'

'Yes; I spent a very happy Sunday with her. We talked over old times, and she told me that Lucy had all through her illness been very uneasy about having promised to bring me a macaw's feather the next time we played in the Square gardens. It could not be sent to me for fear of carrying the infection, but the dear girl was too light-headed to understand, and kept on fretting and wandering about breaking her word. I have no doubt the wish carried her spirit to me the moment it was free,' he added, with tears springing to his eyes. He also said that before the court-martial he had, night after night, dreams of sinking and drowning in huge waves, and his friend Coles struggling to come to his aid, but being forcibly withheld; and he had since learnt that Coles had actually endeavoured to come from Plymouth to bear testimony to his previous character, but had been refused leave, and told that he could do no good.

There had been other instances of perception of a presence and of a prescient foreboding. 'It is like a sixth sense,' he said, 'and a very uncomfortable one. I would give much to be rid of it, for it is connected with all that is worst in my life. I had it before Navarino, when no one expected an engagement. It made me believe I should be killed, and drove me to what was much worse—or at least I used to think so.'

'Don't you now?' I asked.

'No,' said Clarence. 'It was a great mercy that I did not die then. There's something to conquer first. But you'll never speak of this, Ted. I have left off telling of such things—it only gives another reason for disbelieving me.'

However, this time his veracity was not called in question,—but he was supposed to be under a hallucination, the creation of the noises acting on his imagination and memory of the persecuted widow, which must have been somewhere dormant in his mind, though he averred that he had never heard of it. It had now, however, made a strong impression on him; he was convinced that some crime or injustice had been perpetrated, and thought it ought to be investigated; but Griffith made us laugh at his championship of this shadow of a shade, and even wrote some mock heroic verses about it,—nor would it have been easy to stir my father to seek for the motives of an apparition which no one in the family save Clarence professed to have seen.

The noises were indisputable, but my mother began to suspect a cause for them. To oblige a former cook we had brought down with us as stable-boy her son, George Sims, an imp accustomed to be the pet and jester of a mews. Martyn was only too fond of his company, and he made no secret of his contempt for the insufferable dulness of the country, enlivening it by various acts of monkey-mischief, in some of which Martyn had been implicated. That very afternoon, as Mrs. Sophia Selby was walking home in the twilight from Chapman's lodge, in company with Mr. Henderson, an eldritch yell proceeding from the vaults beneath the mullion chambers nearly frightened her into fits. Henderson darted in and captured the two boys in the fact. Martyn's asseveration that he had taken the pair for Griff and Emily would have pacified the good-natured clergyman, but Mrs. Sophia was too much agitated, or too spiteful, as we declared, not to make a scene.

Martyn spent the evening alone and in disgrace, and only his unimpeachable character for truth caused the acceptance of his affirmation that the yell was an impromptu fraternal compliment, and that he had nothing to do with the noises in the mullion chamber. He had been supposed to be perfectly unconscious of anything of the kind, and to have never so much as heard of a phantom, so my mother was taken somewhat aback when, in reply to her demand whether he had ever been so naughty as to assist George in making a noise in Clarence's room, he said, 'Why, that's the ghost of the lady that was murdered atop of the steps, and always walks every Christmas!'

'Who told you such ridiculous nonsense?'

Charlotte M. Yonge

The answer 'George' was deemed conclusive that all had been got up by that youth; and there was considerable evidence of his talent for ventriloquism and taste for practical jokes. My mother was certain that, having heard of the popular superstition, he had acted ghost. She appealed to Woodstock to prove the practicability of such feats; and her absolute conviction persuaded the maids (who had given warning en masse) that the enemy was exorcised when George Sims had been sent off on the Royal Mail under Clarence's guardianship.

None of the junior part of the family believed him guilty, but he had hunted the cows round the paddock, mounted on my donkey, had nearly shot the kitchen-maid with Griff's gun, and, if not much maligned, knew the way to the apple-chamber only too well,—so that he richly deserved his doom, rejoiced in it himself, and was unregretted save by Martyn. Clarence viewed him in the light of a victim, and tried to keep an eye on him, but he developed his talent as a ventriloquist, made his fortune, and retired on a public-house.

My mother would fain have had the vaults under the mullion rooms bricked up, but Mr. Stafford cried out on the barbarism of such a proceeding. The mystery was declared to be solved, and was added to Mr. Stafford's good stories of haunted houses.

And at home my father forbade any further mention of such rank folly and deception. The inner mullion chamber was turned into a lumber-room, and as weeks passed by without hearing or seeing any more of lady or of lamp, we began to credit the wonderful freaks of the goblin page.

CHAPTER XVI

CAT LANGUAGE

Soon as she parted thence—the fearful twayne,
That blind old woman and her daughter deare,
Came forth, and finding Kirkrapine there slayne,
For anguish greate they gan to rend their heare
And beate their breasts, and naked flesh to teare;
And when they both had wept and wayled their fill,
Then forth they ran, like two amazed deere,
Half mad through malice and revenging will,
To follow her that was the causer of their ill.'

SPENSER.

The Christmas vacation was not without another breeze about Griffith's expenses at Oxford. He held his head high, and declared that people expected something from the eldest son of a man of property, and my father tried to convince him that a landed estate often left less cash available than did the fixed salary of an office. Griff treated all in his light, good-humoured way, promised to be careful, and came to me to commiserate the poor old gentleman's ignorance of the ways of the new generation.

There ensued some trying weeks of dark days, raw frost,

Charlotte M. Yonge

and black east wind, when the home party cast longing, lingering recollections back to the social intercourse, lamp-lit streets, and ready interchange of books and other amenities we had left behind us. We were not accustomed to have our nearest neighbours separated from us by two miles of dirty lane, or road mended with excruciating stones, nor were they very congenial when we did see them. The Fordyce family might be interesting, but we younger ones could not forget the slight to Clarence, and, besides, the girls seemed to be entirely in the schoolroom, Mrs. Fordyce was delicate and was shut up all the winter, and the only intercourse that took place was when my father met the elder Mr. Fordyce at the magistrates' bench; also there was a conference about Amos Bell, who was preferred to the post left vacant by George Sims, in right of his being our tenant, but more civilised than Earlscombers, a widow's son, and not sufficiently recovered from his accident to be exposed to the severe tasks of a ploughboy in the winter.

Mrs. Fordyce was the manager of a book-club, which circulated volumes covered in white cartridge paper, with a printed list of the subscribers' names. Two volumes at a time might be kept for a month by each member in rotation, novels were excluded, and the manager had a veto on all orders. We found her more liberal than some of our other neighbours, who looked on our wants and wishes with suspicion as savouring of London notions. Happily we could read old books and standard books over again, and we gloated over Blackwood and the Quarterly, enjoying, too, every out-of-door novelty of the coming spring, as each revealed itself. Emily will never forget her first primroses, nor I the first thrush in early morning.

Blankets, broth, and what were uncomfortably termed broken victuals had been given away during the winter, and a bewildering amount of begging women and children used to ask interviews with 'the Lady Winslow,' with stories that crumbled on investigation so as to make us recollect the Rector's character of Earlscombe.

However, Mr. Henderson came in the second week of Lent, and what our steps towards improvement introduced would have seemed almost as shocking to you youngsters, as what they displaced. For instance, a plain crimson cloth covered the altar, instead of the rags in the colours of the Winslow livery, presented, according to the queer old register, by the unfortunate Margaret. There was talk of velvet and the gold monogram, surrounded by rays, alternately straight and wavy, as in our London church, but this was voted 'unfit for a plain village church.' Still, the new hangings of pulpit, desk, and altar were all good in quality and colour, and huge square cushions were provided as essential to each. Moreover, the altar vessels were made somewhat more respectable,—all this being at my father's expense.

He also carried in the Vestry, though not without strong opposition from a dissenting farmer, that new linen and a fresh surplice should be provided by the parish, which surplice would have made at least six of such as are at present worn. The farmers were very jealous of the interference of the Squire in the Vestry—'what he had no call to,' and of church rates applied to any other object than the reward of birdslayers, as thus, in the register -

Hairy Wills, 1 score sprows heds 2d.
Jems Brown, 1 poulcat 6d.
Jarge Bell, 2 howls 6d.

It was several years before this appropriation of the church rates could be abolished. The year 1830, with a brand new squire and parson, was too ticklish a time for many innovations.

Charlotte M. Yonge

Hillside Church was the only one in the neighbourhood where Holy Week or Ascension Day had been observed in the memory of man. When we proposed going to church on the latter day the gardener asked my mother 'if it was her will to keep Thursday holy,' as if he expected its substitution for Sunday. Monthly Communions and Baptisms after the Second Lesson were viewed as 'not fit for a country church,' and every attempt at even more secular improvements was treated with the most disappointing distrust and aversion. When my father laid out the allotment grounds, the labourers suspected some occult design for his own profit, and the farmers objected that the gardens would be used as an excuse for neglecting their work and stealing their potatoes. Coal-club and clothing-club were regarded in like manner, and while a few took advantage of these offers in a grudging manner, the others viewed everything except absolute gifts as 'me-an' on our part, the principle of aid to self-help being an absolute novelty. When I look back to the notes in our journals of that date I see how much has been overcome.

Perhaps we listened more than was strictly wise to the revelations of Amos Bell, when he attended Emily and me on our expeditions with the donkey. Though living over the border of Hillside, he had a family of relations at Earlscombe, and for a time lodged with his grandmother there. When his shyness and lumpishness gave way, he proved so bright that Emily undertook to carry on his education. He soon had a wonderful eye for a wild flower, and would climb after it with the utmost agility; and when once his tongue was loosed, he became almost too communicative, and made us acquainted with the opinions of 'they Earlscoom folk' with a freedom not to be found in an elder or a native.

Moreover, he was the brightest light of the Sunday school

which Mr. Henderson opened at once—for want of a more fitting place—in the disused north transept of the church. It was an uncouth, ill-clad crew which assembled on those dilapidated paving tiles. Their own grandchildren look almost as far removed from them in dress and civilisation as did my sister in her white worked cambric dress, silk scarf, huge Tuscan bonnet, and the little curls beyond the lace quilling round her bright face, far rosier than ever it had been in town. And what would the present generation say to the odd little contrivances in the way of cotton sun-bonnets, check pinafores, list tippets, and print capes, and other wonderful manufactures from the rag-bag, which were then grand prizes and stimulants?

Previous knowledge or intelligence scarcely existed, and then was not due to Dame Dearlove's tuition. Mr. Henderson pronounced an authorised school a necessity. My father had scruples as to vested rights, for the old woman was the last survivor of a family who had had recourse to primer and hornbook after their ejection on 'black Bartholomew's Day;' and when the meeting-house was built after the Revolution, had combined preaching with teaching. Monopoly had promoted degeneracy, and this last of the race was an unfavourable specimen in all save outward picturesqueness. However, much against Henderson's liking, an accommodation was proposed, by which books were to be supplied to her, and the Church Catechism be taught in her school, with the assistance of the curate and Miss Winslow.

The terms were rejected with scorn. No School Board could be more determined against the Catechism, nor against 'passons meddling wi' she;' and as to assistance, 'she had been a governess this thirty year, and didn't want no one trapesing in and out of her school.'

She was warned, but probably did not believe in the

possibility of an opposition school; and really there were children enough in the place to overfill both her room and that which was fitted up after a very humble fashion in one of our cottages. H.M. Inspector would hardly have thought it even worth condemnation any more than the attainments of the mistress, the young widow of a small Bristol skipper. Her qualifications consisted in her piety and conscientiousness, good temper and excellent needle-work, together with her having been a scholar in one of Mrs. Hannah More's schools in the Cheddar district. She could read and teach reading well; but as for the dangerous accomplishments of writing and arithmetic, such as desired to pass beyond the rudiments of them must go to Wattlesea.

So nice did she look in her black that Earlscombe voted her a mere town lady, and even at a penny a week hesitated to send its children to her. Indeed it was currently reported that her school was part of a deep and nefarious scheme of the gentlefolks for reducing the poor-rates by enticing the children, and then shipping them off to foreign parts from Bristol.

But the great crisis was one unlucky summer evening when Emily and I were out with the donkey, and Griffith, just come home from Oxford, was airing the new acqui-sition of a handsome black retriever.

Close by the old chapel, a black cat was leisurely crossing the road. At her dashed Nero, stimulated perhaps by an almost involuntary scss—scss—from his master, if not from Amos and me. The cat flew up a low wall, and stood at bay on the top on tiptoe, with bristling tail, arched back, and fiery eyes, while the dog danced round in agony on his hind legs, barking furiously, and almost reaching her. Female sympathy ever goes to the cat, and Emily screamed out in the fear that he would seize her, or even that Griff might aid him. Perhaps Amos would have done so, if left to himself; but Griff, who saw the cat was safe, could not help egging on his dog's impotent rage, when in the midst, out flew pussy's mistress, Dame Dearlove herself, broomstick in hand, using language as vituperative as the cat's, and more intelligible.

She was about to strike the dog—indeed I fancy she did, for there was a howl, and Griff sprang to his defence with—'Don't hurt my dog, I say! He hasn't touched the brute! She can take care of herself. Here, there's half-a-crown for the fright,' as the cat sprang down within the wall, and Nero slunk behind him. But Dame Dearlove was not so easily appeased. Her blood was up after our long series of offences, and she broke into a regular tirade of abuse.

'That's the way with you fine folk, thinking you can tread down poor people like the dirt under your feet, and insult 'em when you've taken the bread out of the mouths of them that were here before you. Passons and ladies a meddin' where no one ever set a foot before! Ay, ay, but ye'll all be down before long.'

Griff signed to us to go on, and thundered out on her to take care what she was about and not be abusive; but this brought a fresh volley on him, heralded by a derisive laugh. 'Ha! ha! fine talking for the likes of you, Winslows that you are. But there's a curse on you all! The poor lady as was murdered won't let you be! Why, there's one of you, poor humpy object—'

At this savage attack on me, Griff waxed furious, and shouted at her to hold her confounded tongue, but this only diverted the attack on himself. 'And as for you—fine chap as ye think yourself, swaggering and swearing at poor folk, and setting your dog at them—your time's coming. Look out for yourself. It's well known as how the curse is on the first-born. The Lady Margaret don't let none of 'em live to come after his father.'

Griff laughed and said, 'There, we have had enough of this;' and in fact we had already moved on, so that he had to make some long steps to overtake us, muttering, 'So we've started a Meg Merrilies! My father won't keep such a foul-mouthed hag in the parish long!'

To which I had to respond that her cottage belonged to the trustees of the chapel, whereat he whistled. I don't think he knew that we had heard her final denunciation, and we did not like to mention it to him, scarcely to each other, though Emily looked very white and scared.

We talked it over afterwards in private, and with Henderson, who confessed that he had heard of the old woman's saying something of the kind to other persons. We consulted the registers in hopes of confuting it, but did not satisfy ourselves. The last Squire had lost his only son at school. He himself had been originally second in the family, and in the generation before him there had been some child-deaths, after which we came back to a young man, apparently the eldest, who, according to Miss Selby's story, had been killed in a duel by one of the Fordyces. It was not comfortable, till I remembered that our family Bible recorded the birth, baptism, and death of a son who had preceded Griffith, and only borne for a day the name afterwards bestowed on me.

And Henderson, who was so little our elder as to discuss things on fairly equal grounds, had some very interesting talks with us two over ancestral sin and its possible effects, dwelling on the 18th of Ezekiel as a comment on the Second Commandment. Indeed, we agreed that the uncomfortable state of disaffection which, in 1830, was becoming only too manifest in the populace, was the result of neglect in former ages, and that, even in our own parish, the bitterness, distrust, and ingratitude were due to the careless, riotous, and oppressive family whom we represented.

CHAPTER XVII

THE SIEGE OF HILLSIDE

'Ferments arise, imprisoned factions roar,
Represt ambition struggles round the shore;
Till, overwrought, the general system feels
Its motion stop, or frenzy fire the wheels.'

GOLDSMITH.

Griffith had come straight home this year. There were no
Peacock gaieties to tempt him in London, for old Sir
Henry had died suddenly soon after the ball in December;
nor was there much of a season that year, owing to the
illness and death of George IV.

A regiment containing two old schoolmates of his was at
Bristol, and he spent a good deal of time there, and also in
Yeomanry drill. As autumn came on we rejoiced in
having so stalwart a protector, for the agricultural riots
had begun, and the forebodings of another French
Revolution seemed about to be realised. We stayed on at
Chantry House. My father thought his duty lay there as a
magistrate, and my mother would not leave him; nor
indeed was any other place much safer, certainly not
London, whence Clarence wrote accounts of formidable

mobs who were expected to do more harm than they accomplished; though their hatred of the hero of our country filled us with direful prognostications, and made us think of the guillotine, which was linked with revolution in our minds, before we had I beheld the numerous changes that followed upon the thirty years of peace in which we grew up.

The ladies did not much like losing so stalwart a defender when Griff returned to Oxford; and Jane the housemaid went to bed every night with the pepper-pot and a poker, the first wherewith to blind the enemy, the second to charge them with. From our height we could more than once see blazing ricks, and were glad that the home farm was not in our own hands, and that our only stack of hay was a good way from the house. When the onset came at last, it was December, and the enemy only consisted of about thirty dreary-looking men and boys in smock-frocks and chalked or smutted faces, armed only with sticks and an old gun diverted from its purpose of bird-scaring. They shouted for food, money, and arms; but my father spoke to them from the hall steps, told them they had better go home and learn that the public-house was a worse enemy to them than any machine that had ever been invented, and assured them that they would get no help from him in breaking the laws and getting themselves into trouble. A stone or two was picked up, whereupon he went back and had the hall door shut and barred, the heavy shutters of the windows having all been closed already, so that we could have stood a much more severe siege than from these poor fellows. One or two windows were broken, as well as the glass of the conservatory, and the flower beds were trampled; but finding our fortress impregnable they sneaked away before dark. We fared better than our neighbours, some of whom were seriously frightened, and suffered loss of property. Old Mr. Fordyce had for many years past been an active magistrate—that a clergyman

Charlotte M. Yonge

should be on the bench having been quite correct according to the notions of his younger days; and in spite of his beneficence he incurred a good deal of unpopularity for withstanding the lax good-nature which made his brother magistrates give orders for parish relief refused to able-bodied paupers by their own Vestries. This was a mischievous abuse of the old poor-law times, which made people dispose of every one's money save their own. He had also been a keen sportsman; and though his son had given up field sports in deference to higher notions of clerical duty (his wife's, as people said), the old man's feeling prompted him to severity on poachers. Frank Fordyce, while by far the most earnest, hardworking clergyman in the neighbourhood, worked off his super-fluous energy on scientific farming, making the glebe and the hereditary estate as much the model farm as Hillside was the model parish. He had lately set up a threshing-machine worked by horses, which was as much admired by the intelligent as it was vituperated by the ignorant.

Neither paupers nor poachers abounded in Hillside; the natives were chiefly tenants and employed on the property, and, between good management and benefi-cence, there was little real want and much friendly confidence and affection; and thus, in spite of surrounding riots, Hillside seemed likely to be an exception, proving what could he done by rightful care and attention. Nor indeed did the attack come from thence; but the two parsons were bitterly hated by outsiders beyond the reach of their personal influence and benevolence.

It was on a Saturday evening, the day after Griff had come back for the Christmas vacation, that, as Emily was giving Amos his lesson, she saw that the boy was crying, and after examination he let out that 'folk should say that the lads were agoing to break Parson Fordy's machine and fire his ricks that very night;' but he would not give his authority, and when he saw her about to give warning, entreated, 'Now, dont'ze say nothing, Miss Emily—'

'What?' she cried indignantly; 'do you think I could hear of such a thing without trying to stop it?'

'Us says,' he blurted out, 'as how Winslows be always fain of ought as happens to the Fordys—'

'We are not such wicked Winslows as you have heard of,' returned Emily with dignity; and she rushed off in quest of papa and Griff, but when she brought them to the bookroom, Amos had decamped, and was nowhere to be found that night. We afterwards learnt that he lay hidden in the hay-loft, not daring to return to his granny's, lest he should be suspected of being a traitor to his kind; for our lawless, untamed, discontented parish furnished a large quota to the rioters, and he has since told me that though all seemed to know what was about to be done, he did not hear it from any one in particular.

It was no time to make light of a warning, but very difficult to know what to do. Rural police were non-existent; there were no soldiers nearer than Keynsham, and the Yeomanry were all in their own homesteads. However, the captain of Griff's troop, Sir George Eastwood, lived about three miles beyond Wattlesea, and had a good many dependants in the corps, so it was resolved to send him a note by the gardener, good James Ellis, a steady, resolute man, on Emily's fast-trotting pony, while my father and Griff should hasten to Hillside to warn the Fordyces, who were not unlikely to be able to muster trustworthy defenders among their own people, and might send the ladies to take shelter at Chantry House.

My mother's brave spirit disdained to detain an effective man for her own protection, and the groom was to go to

Hillside; he was in the Yeomanry, and, like Griff, put on his uniform, while my father had the Riot Act in his pocket. All the horses were thus absorbed, but Chapman and the man-servant followed on foot.

Never did I feel my incapacity more than on that strange night, when Emily was flying about with Martyn to all the doors and windows in a wild state of excitement, humming to herself -

'When the dawn on the mountain was misty and gray,
My true love has mounted his steed and away.'

My mother was equally restless, prolonging as much as possible the preparation of rooms for possible guests; and when she did come and sit down, she netted her purse with vehement jerks, and scolded Emily for jumping up and leaving doors open.

At last, after an hour according to the clock, but far more by our feelings, wheels were heard in the distance; Emily was off like a shot to reconnoitre, and presently Martyn bounced in with the tidings that a pair of carriage lamps were coming up the drive. My mother hurried out into the hall; I made my best speed after her, and found her hastily undoing the door-chain as she recognised the measured, courteous voice of old Mr. Fordyce. In a moment more they were all in the house, the old gentleman giving his arm to his daughter-in-law, who was quite overcome with distress and alarm; then came his tall, slim granddaughter, carrying her little sister with arms full of dolls, and sundry maid-servants completed the party of fugitives.

'We are taking advantage of Mr. Winslow's goodness,' said the old Rector. 'He assured us that you would be kind enough to receive those who would only be an encumbrance.'

'Oh, but I must go back to Frank now that you and the children are safe,' cried the poor lady. 'Don't send away the carriage; I must go back to Frank.'

'Nonsense, my dear,' returned Mr. Fordyce, 'Frank is in no danger. He will get on much better for knowing you are safe. Mrs. Winslow will tell you so.'

My mother was enforcing this assurance, when the little girl's sobs burst out in spite of her sister, who had been trying to console her. 'It is Celestina Mary,' she cried, pointing to three dolls whom she had carried in clasped to her breast. 'Poor Celestina Mary! She is left behind, and Ellen won't let me go and see if she is in the carriage.'

'My dear, if she is in the carriage, she will be quite safe in the morning.'

'Oh, but she will be so cold. She had nothing on but Rosella's old petticoat.'

The distress was so real that I had my hand on the bell to cause a search to be instituted for the missing damsel, when Mrs. Fordyce begged me to do no such thing, as it was only a doll. The child, while endeavouring to shelter with a shawl the dolls, snatched in their night-gear from their beds, wept so piteously at the rebuff that her grandfather had nearly gone in quest of the lost one, but was stopped by a special entreaty that he would not spoil the child. Martyn, however, who had been standing in open-mouthed wonder at such feeling for a doll, exclaimed, 'Don't cry, don't cry. I'll go and get it for you;' and rushed off to the stable-yard.

This episode had restored Mrs. Fordyce, and while providing some of our guests with wine, and others with tea, we heard the story, only interrupted by Martyn's return from a vain search, and Anne's consequent tears, which, however, were somehow hushed and smothered by fears of being sent to bed, coupled with his promises to search every step of the way to-morrow.

It appeared that while the Fordyce family were at dinner, shouts, howls and yells had startled them. The rabble had surrounded the Rectory, bawling out abuse of the parsons and their machines, and occasionally throwing stones. There was no help to be expected; the only hope was in the strength of the doors and windows, and the knowledge that personal violence was very uncommon; but those were terrible moments, and poor Mrs. Fordyce was nearly dead with suppressed terror when her husband tried haranguing from an upper window, and was received with execrations and a volley of stones, while the glass crashed round him.

At that instant the shouts turned to yells of dismay, 'The so'diers! the so'diers!'

Our party had found everything still and dark in the village, for in truth the men had hidden themselves. They were being too much attached to their masters to join in the attack, but were afraid of being compelled to assist the rioters, and not resolute enough against their own class either to inform against them or oppose them.

Through the midnight-like stillness of the street rose the tumult around the Rectory; and by the light of a few lanterns, and from the upper windows, they could see a mass of old hats, smock-frocked shoulders, and the tops of bludgeons; while at soonest, Sir George Eastwood's troop could not be expected for an hour or more.

'We must get to them somehow,' said my father and Griff to one another; and Griff added, 'These rascals are arrant cowards, and they can't see the number of us.'

Then, before my father knew what he was about—certainly before he could get hold of the Riot Act—he found the stable lantern made over to him, and Griff's sword flashing in light, as, making all possible clatter and jingling with their accoutrements, the two yeomen dashed among the throng, shouting with all their might, and striking with the flat of their swords. The rioters, ill-fed, dull-hearted men for the most part—many dragged out by compulsion, and already terrified—went tumbling over one another and running off headlong, bearing off with them (as we afterwards learnt) their leaders by their weight, taking the blows and pushes they gave one another in their pell-mell rush for those of the soldiery, and falling blindly against the low wall of the enclosure. The only difficulty was in clearing them out at the two gates of the drive.

When Mr. Fordyce opened the door to hail his rescuers he was utterly amazed to behold only three, and asked in a bewildered voice, 'Where are the others?'

There were two prisoners, Petty the ratcatcher, who had attempted some resistance and had been knocked down by Griff's horse, and a young lad in a smock-frock who had fallen off the wall and hurt his knee, and who blubbered piteously, declaring that them chaps had forced him to go with them, or they would duck him in the horse-pond. They were supposed to be given in charge to some one, but were lost sight of, and no wonder! For just then it was discovered that the machine shed was on fire. The rioters had apparently detached one of their number to kindle the flame before assaulting the house. The matter was specially serious, because the stackyard was on a line with the Rectory, at some distance indeed, but on lower ground; and what with barns, hay and wheat ricks, sheds, cowhouses and stables, all thatched, a big wood-pile, and a long old-fashioned greenhouse, there was almost continuous communication. Clouds of smoke and an ominous smell were already perceptible on the wind, generated by the heat, and the loose straw in the centre of the farmyard was beginning to be ignited by the flakes and sparks, carrying the mischief everywhere, and rendering it exceedingly difficult to release the animals and drive them to a place of safety. Water was scarce. There were only two wells, besides the pump in the house, and a shallow pond. The brook was a quarter of a mile off in the valley, and the nearest engine, a poor feeble thing, at Wattlesea. Moreover, the assailants might discover how small was the force of rescuers, and return to the attack. Thus, while Griff, who had given amateur assistance at all the fires he could reach in London; was striving to organise resistance to this new enemy, my father induced the gentlemen to cause the horses to be put to the various vehicles, and employ them in carrying the women and children to Chantry House. The old Rector was persuaded to go to take care of his daughter-in-law, and she only thought of putting her girls in safety. She listened to reason, and indeed was too much exhausted to move when once she was laid on the sofa. She would not hear of going to bed, though her little daughter Anne was sent off with her nurse, grandpapa persuading her that Rosella and the others were very much tired. When she was gone, he declared his fears that he had sat down on Celestina's head, and showed so much compunction that we were much amused at his relief when Martyn assured him of having searched the carriage with a stable lantern, so that whatever had befallen the lady he was not the guilty person. He really seemed more concerned about this than at the loss of all his own barns and stores. And little Anne was certainly as lovely and engaging a little creature as ever I saw; while, as to her elder sister, in all the trouble and anxiety of the night, I could not help enjoying the sight of her beautiful eager face and form. She was tall and very slight, sylph-like, as it was the fashion to call it, but every limb was instinct with grace and animation. Her face was, perhaps, rather too thin for robust health, though this enhanced the idea of her being all spirit, as also did the transparency of complexion, tinted with an exquisite varying carnation. Her eyes were of a clear, bright, rather light brown, and were sparkling with the lustre of excitement, her delicate lips parted, showing the pretty pearly teeth, as she was telling Emily, in a low voice of enthusiasm, scarcely designed for my ears, how glorious a sight our brother had been, riding there in his glancing silver, bearing down all before him with his good sword, like the Captal de Buch dispersing the Jacquerie.

To which Emily responded, 'Oh, don't you love the Captal de Buch?' And their friendship was cemented.

Next I heard, 'And that you should have been so good after all my rudeness. But I thought you were like the old Winslows; and instead of that you have come to the rescue of your enemies. Isn't it beautiful?'

'Oh no, not enemies,' said Emily. 'That was all over a hundred years ago!'

'So my papa and grandpapa say,' returned Miss Fordyce; 'but the last Mr. Winslow was not a very nice man, and never would be civil to us.'

A report was brought that the glare of the fire could be seen over the hill from the top of the house, and off went the two young ladies to the leads, after satisfying themselves that Anne was asleep among her homeless dolls.

Old Mr. Fordyce devoted himself to keeping up the spirits of his daughter-in-law as the night advanced without any tidings, except that the girls, from time to time, rushed down to tell us of fresh outbursts of red flame reflected in the sky, then that the glow was diminishing; by which time they were tired out, and, both sinking into a big armchair, they went to sleep in each other's arms. Indeed I believe we all dozed more or less before any one returned from the scene of action—at about three o'clock.

The struggle with the flames had been very unequal. The long tongues soon reached the roof of the large barn, which was filled with straw, nor could the flakes of burning thatch be kept from the stable, while the water of the pond was soon reduced to mud. Helpers began to flock in, but who could tell which were trustworthy? and all were uncomprehending.

There was so little hope of saving the house that the removal of everything valuable was begun under my father's superintendence. Frank Fordyce was here, there, and everywhere; while Griffith, like a gallant general, fought the foe with very helpless unmanageable forces. Villagers, male and female, had emerged and stood gaping round; but, let him rage and storm as he might, they would not go and collect pails and buckets and form a line to the brook. Still less would they assist in overthrowing and carrying away the faggots of a big wood-pile so as to cut off the communication with the offices. Only Chapman and one other man gave any help in this; and presently the stack caught, and Griff, on the top, was in great peril of the faggots rolling down with him into the middle, and imprisoning him in the blazing pile. 'I never felt so like Dido,' said Griff.

That woodstack gave fearful aliment to the roaring flame, which came on so fast that the destruction of the adjoining buildings quickly followed. The Wattlesea engine had come, but the yard well was unattainable, and all that could be done was to saturate the house with water from its own well, and cover the side with wet blankets; but these reeked with steam, and then shrivelled away in the intense glow of heat.

However, by this time the Eastwood Yeomanry, together with some reasonable men, had arrived. A raid was made on the cottages for buckets, a chain formed to the river, and at last the fire was got under, having made a wreck of everything out-of-doors, and consumed one whole wing of the house, though the older and more esteemed portion was saved.

CHAPTER XVIII

THE PORTRAIT

'When day was gone and night was come,
And all men fast asleep,
There came the spirit of fair Marg'ret
And stood at William's feet.'

SCOTCH BALLAD.

When I emerged from my room the next morning the
phaeton was at the door to take the two clergymen to
reconnoitre their abode before going to church. Miss
Fordyce went with them, and my father was for once
about to leave his parish church to give them his
sympathy, and join in their thanksgiving that neither life
nor limb had been injured. He afterwards said that nothing
could have been more touching than old Mr. Fordyce's
manner of mentioning this special cause for gratitude
before the General Thanksgiving; and Frank Fordyce,
having had all his sermons burnt, gave a short address
extempore (a very rare and almost shocking thing at that
date), reducing half the congregation to tears, for they
really loved 'the fam'ly,' though they had not spirit enough
to defend it; and their passiveness always remained a
subject of pride and pleasure to the Fordyces. It was

against the will of these good people that Petty, the ratcatcher, was arrested, but he had been engaged in other outrages, though this was the only one in which a dwelling-house had suffered. And Chapman observed that 'there was nothing to be done with such chaps but to string 'em up out of the way.'

Griff had toiled that night till he was as stiff as a rheumatic old man when he came down only just in time for luncheon. Mrs. Fordyce did not appear at all. She was a fragile creature, and quite knocked up by the agitations of the night. The gentlemen had visited the desolate rectory, and found that though the fine ancient kitchen had escaped, the pleasant living rooms had been injured by the water, and the place could hardly be made habitable before the spring. They proposed to take a house in Bath, whence Frank Fordyce could go and come for Sunday duty and general superintendence, but my parents were urgent that they should not leave us until after Christmas, and they consented. Their larger possessions were to be stored in the outhouses, their lesser in our house, notably in the inner mullion chamber, which would thus be so blocked that there would be no question of sleeping in it.

Old Mr. Fordyce had ascertained that he might acquit himself of smashing Celestina Mary, for no remains appeared in the carriage; but a miserable trunk was discovered in the ruins, which he identified—though surely no one else save the disconsolate parent could have done so. Poor little Anne's private possessions had suffered most severely of all, for her whole nursery establishment had vanished. Her surviving dolls were left homeless, and devoid of all save their night-clothing, which concerned her much more than the loss of almost all her own garments. For what dolls were to her could never have been guessed by us, who had forced Emily to disdain them; whereas they were children to the maternal heart of this lonely child.

She was quite a new revelation to us. All the Fordyces were handsome; and her chestnut curls and splendid eyes, her pretty colour and unconscious grace, were very charming. Emily was so near our own age that we had never known the winsomeness of a little maid-child amongst us, and she was a perpetual wonder and delight to us.

Indeed, from having always lived with her elders, she was an odd little old-fashioned person, advanced in some ways, and comically simple in others. Her doll-heart was kept in abeyance all Sunday, and it was only on Monday that her anxiety for Celestina manifested itself with considerable vehemence; but her grandfather gravely informed her that the young lady was gone to an excellent doctor, who would soon effect a cure. The which was quite true, for he had sent her to a toy-shop by one of the maids who had gone to restore the ravage on the wardrobes, and who brought her back with a new head and arms, her identity apparently not being thus interfered with. The hoards of scraps were put under requisition to re-clothe the survivors; and I won my first step in Miss Anne's good graces by undertaking a knitted suit for Rosella.

The good little girl had evidently been schooled to repress her dread and repugnance at my unlucky appearance, and was painfully polite, only shutting her eyes when she came to shake hands with me; but after Rosella condescended to adopt me, we became excellent friends. Indeed the following conversation was overheard by Emily, and set down:

'Do you know, Martyn, there's a fairies' ring on

Hillside Down?'

'Mushrooms,' quoth Martyn.

'Yes, don't you know? They are the fairies' tables. They come out and spread them with lily tablecloths at night, and have acorn cups for dishes, with honey in them. And they dance and play there. Well, couldn't Mr. Edward go and sit under the beech-tree at the edge till they come?'

'I don't think he would like it at all,' said Martyn. 'He never goes out at odd times.'

'Oh, but don't you know? when they come they begin to sing -

> '"Sunday and Monday,
> Monday and Tuesday."

And if he was to sing nicely,

> '"Wednesday and Thursday,"

they would be so much pleased that they would make his back straight again in a moment. At least, perhaps Wednesday and Thursday would not do, because the little tailor taught them those; but Friday makes them angry. But suppose he made some nice verse -

> '"Monday and Tuesday
> The fairies are gay,
> Tuesday and Wednesday
> They dance away—"

I think that would do as well, perhaps. Do get him to do so, Martyn. It would be so nice if he was tall and straight.'

Charlotte M. Yonge

Dear little thing! Martyn, who was as much her slave as was her grandfather, absolutely made her shed tears over his history of our accident, and then caressed them off; but I believe he persuaded her that such a case might be beyond the fairies' reach, and that I could hardly get to the spot in secret, which, it seems, is an essential point. He had imagination enough to be almost persuaded of fairyland by her earnestness, and she certainly took him into doll-land. He had a turn for carpentry and contrivance, and he undertook that the Ladies Rosella, etc., should be better housed than ever. A great packing-case was routed out, and much ingenuity was expended, much delight obtained, in the process of converting it into a doll's mansion, and replenishing it with furniture. Some was bought, but Martyn aspired to make whatever he could; I did a good deal, and I believe most of our achievements are still extant. Whatever we could not manage, Clarence was to accomplish when he should come home.

His arrival was, as usual, late in the evening; and, as before, he had the little room within mine. In the morning, as we were crossing the hall to the bright wood fire, around which the family were wont to assemble before prayers, he came to a pause, asking under his breath, 'What's that? Who's that?'

'It is one of the Hillside pictures. You know we have a great many things here from thence.'

'It is SHE,' he said, in a low, awe-stricken voice. No need to say who SHE meant.

I had not paid much attention to the picture. It had come with several more, such as are rife in country houses, and was one of the worst of the lot, a poor imitation of Lely's style, with a certain air common to all the family; but

Clarence's eyes were riveted on it. 'She looks younger,' he said; 'but it is the same. I could swear to the lip and the whole shape of the brow and chin. No—the dress is different.'

For in the portrait, there was nothing on the head, and one long lock of hair fell on the shoulder of the low-cut white-satin dress, done in very heavy gray shading. The three girls came down together, and I asked who the lady was.

'Don't you know? You ought; for that is poor Margaret who married your ancestor.'

No more was said then, for the rest of the world was collecting, and then everybody went out their several ways. Some tin tacks were wanted for the dolls' house, and there were reports that Wattlesea possessed a doll's grate and fire-irons. The children were wild to go in quest of them, but they were not allowed to go alone, and it was pronounced too far and too damp for the elder sister, so that they would have been disappointed, if Clarence—stimulated by Martyn's kicks under the table—had not offered to be their escort. When Mrs. Fordyce demurred, my mother replied, 'You may perfectly trust her with Clarence.'

'Yes; I don't know a safer squire,' rejoined my father.

Commendation was so rare that Clarence quite blushed with pleasure; and the pretty little thing was given into his charge, prancing and dancing with pleasure, and expecting much more from sixpence and from Wattlesea than was likely to be fulfilled.

Griff went out shooting, and the two young ladies and I intended to spend a very rational morning in the book-room, reading aloud Mme. de La Rochejaquelein's

Memoirs by turns. Our occupations were, on Emily's part, completing a reticule, in a mosaic of shaded coloured beads no bigger than pins' heads, for a Christmas gift to mamma—a most wearisome business, of which she had grown extremely tired. Miss Fordyce was elaborately copying our Muller's print of Raffaelle's St. John in pencil on cardboard, so as to be as near as possible a facsimile; and she had trusted me to make a finished water-coloured drawing from a rough sketch of hers of the Hillside barn and farm-buildings, now no more.

In a pause Ellen Fordyce suddenly asked, 'What did you mean about that picture?'

'Only Clarence said it was like—' and here Emily came to a dead stop.

'Grandpapa says it is like me,' said Miss Fordyce. 'What, you don't mean THAT? Oh! oh! oh! is it true? Does she walk? Have you seen her? Mamma calls it all nonsense, and would not have Anne hear of it for anything; but old Aunt Peggy used to tell me, and I am sure grandpapa believes it, just a little. Have you seen her?'

'Only Clarence has, and he knew the picture directly.'

She was much impressed, and on slight persuasion related the story, which she had heard from an elder sister of her grandfather's, and which had perhaps been the more impressed on her by her mother's consternation at 'such folly' having been communicated to her. Aunt Peggy, who was much older than her brother, had died only four years ago, at eighty-eight, having kept her faculties to the last, and handed down many traditions to her great-niece. The old lady's father had been contemporary with the Margaret of ghostly fame, so that the stages had been few through which it had come down from 1708 to 1830.

I wrote it down at once, as it here stands.

Margaret was the only daughter of the elder branch of the Fordyces. Her father had intended her to marry her cousin, the male heir on whom the Hillside estates and the advowson of that living were entailed; but before the contract had been formally made, the father was killed by accident, and through some folly and ambition of her mother's (such seemed to be the Fordyce belief), the poor heiress was married to Sir James Winslow, one of the successful intriguers of the days of the later Stewarts, and with a family nearly as old, if not older, than herself. Her own children died almost at their birth, and she was left a young widow. Being meek and gentle, her step-sons and daughters still ruled over Chantry House. They prevented her Hillside relations from having access to her whilst in a languishing state of health, and when she died unexpectedly, she was found to have bequeathed all her property to her step-son, Philip Winslow, instead of to her blood relations, the Fordyces.

This was certain, but the Fordyce tradition was that she had been kept shut up in the mullion chambers, where she had often been heard weeping bitterly. One night in the winter, when the gentlemen of the family had gone out to a Christmas carousal, she had endeavoured to escape by the steps leading to the garden from the door now bricked up, but had been met by them and dragged back with violence, of which she died in the course of a few days; and, what was very suspicious, she had been entirely attended by her step-daughter and an old nurse, who never would let her own woman come near her.

The Fordyces had thought of a prosecution, but the Winslows had powerful interest at Court in those corrupt times, and contrived to hush up the matter, as well as to win the suit in which the Fordyces attempted to prove that there was no right to will the property away. Bitter enmity remained between the families; they were always opposed in politics, and their animosity was fed by the belief which arose that at the anniversaries of her death the poor lady haunted the rooms, lamp in hand, wailing and lamenting. A duel had been fought on the subject between the heirs of the two families, resulting in the death of the young Winslow.

'And now,' cried Ellen Fordyce, 'the feud is so beautifully ended; the doom must be appeased, now that the head of one hostile line has come to the rescue of the other, and saved all our lives.'

My suggestion that these would hardly have been destroyed, even without our interposition, fell very flat, for romance must have its swing. Ellen told us how, on the news of our kinsman's death and our inheritance, the ancestral story had been discussed, and her grandfather had said he believed there were letters about it in the iron deed-box, and how he hoped to be on better terms with the new heir.

The ghost story had always been hushed up in the family, especially since the duel, and we all knew the resemblance of the picture would be scouted by our elders; but perhaps this gave us the more pleasure in dwelling upon it, while we agreed that poor Margaret ought to be appeased by Griffith's prowess on behalf of the Fordyces.

The two young ladies went off to inspect the mullion chamber, which they found so crammed with Hillside furniture that they could scarcely enter, and returned disappointed, except for having inspected and admired all Griff's weapons, especially what Miss Fordyce called the sword of her rescue.

She had been learning German—rather an unusual study in those days, and she narrated to us most effectively the story of Die Weisse Frau, working herself up to such a pitch that she would have actually volunteered to spend a night in the room, to see whether Margaret would hold any communication with a descendant, after the example of the White Woman and Lady Bertha, if there had been either fire or accommodation, and if the only entrance had not been through Griff's private sitting-room.

CHAPTER XIX

THE WHITE FEATHER

'The white doe's milk is not out of his mouth.'

SCOTT.

Clarence had come home free from all blots. His summer holiday had been prevented by the illness of one of the other clerks, whose place, Mr. Castleford wrote, he had so well supplied that ere long he would be sure to earn his promotion. That kind friend had several times taken him to spend a Sunday in the country, and, as we afterwards had reason to think, would have taken more notice of him but for the rooted belief of Mr. Frith that it was a case of favouritism, and that piety and strictness were assumed to throw dust in the eyes of his patron.

Such distrust had tended to render Clarence more reserved than ever, and it was quite by the accident of finding him studying one of Mrs. Trimmer's Manuals that I discovered that, at the request of his good Rector, he had become a Sunday-school teacher, and was as much interested as the enthusiastic girls; but I was immediately forbidden to utter a word on the subject, even to Emily, lest she should tell any one.

Such reserve was no doubt an outcome of his natural timidity. He had to bear a certain amount of scorn and derision among some of his fellow-clerks for the stricter habits and observances that could not be concealed, and he dreaded any fresh revelation of them, partly because of the cruel imputation of hypocrisy, partly because he feared the bringing a scandal on religion by his weakness and failures.

Nor did our lady visitors' ways reassure him, though they meant to be kind. They could not help being formal and stiff, not as they were with Griff and me. The two gentlemen were thoroughly friendly and hearty; Parson Frank could hardly have helped being so towards any one in the same house with himself; and as to little Anne, she found in the new-comer a carpenter and upholsterer superior even to Martyn; but her candour revealed a great deal which I overheard one afternoon, when the two children were sitting together on the hearth-rug in the bookroom in the twilight.

'I want to see Mr. Clarence's white feather,' observed Anne.

'Griff has a white plume in his Yeomanry helmet,' replied Martyn; 'Clarence hasn't one.'

'Oh, I saw Mr. Griffith's!' she answered; 'but Cousin Horace said Mr. Clarence showed the white feather.'

'Cousin Horace is an ape!' cried Martyn.

'I don't think he is so nice as an ape,' said Anne. 'He is more like a monkey. He tries the dolls by court-martial, and he shot Arabella with a pea-shooter, and broke her eye; only grandpapa made him have it put in again with his own money, and then he said I was a little sneak, and

Charlotte M. Yonge

if I ever did it again he would shoot me.'

'Mind you don't tell Clarence what he said,' said Martyn.

'Oh, no! I think Mr. Clarence very nice indeed; but Horace did tease so about that day when he carried poor Amos Bell home. He said Ellen had gone and made friends with the worst of all the wicked Winslows, who had shown the white feather and disgraced his flag. No; I know you are not wicked. And Mr. Griff came all glittering, like Richard Coeur de Lion, and saved us all that night. But Ellen cried to think what she had done, and mamma said it showed what it was to speak to a strange young man; and she has never let Ellen and me go out of the grounds by ourselves since that day.'

'It is a horrid shame,' exclaimed Martyn, 'that a fellow can't get into a scrape without its being for ever cast up to him.'

'*I* like him,' said Anne. 'He gave Mary Bell a nice pair of boots, and he made a new pair of legs for poor old Arabella, and she can really sit down! Oh, he is VERY nice; but'—in an awful whisper—'does he tell stories? I mean fibs—falsehoods.'

'Who told you that?' exclaimed Martyn.

'Mamma said it. Ellen was telling them something about the picture of the white-satin lady, and mamma said, "Oh, if it is only that young man, no doubt it is a mere mystification;" and papa said, "Poor young fellow, he seems very amiable and well disposed;" and mamma said, "If he can invent such a story it shows that Horace was right, and he is not to be believed." Then they stopped, but I asked Ellen who it was, and she said it was Mr. Clarence, and it was a sad thing for Emily and all of you to have such a brother.'

Martyn began to stammer with indignation, and I thought it time to interfere; so I called the little maid, and gravely explained the facts, adding that poor Clarence's punishment had been terrible, but that he was doing his best to make up for what was past; and that, as to anything he might have told, though he might be mistaken, he never said anything NOW but what he believed to be true. She raised her brown eyes to mine full of gravity, and said, 'I DO like him.' Moreover, I privately made Martyn understand that if he told her what had been said about the white-satin lady, he would never be forgiven; the others would be sure to find it out, and it might shorten their stay.

That was a dreadful idea, for the presence of those two creatures, to say nothing of their parents, was an unspeakable charm and novelty to us all. We all worshipped the elder, and the little one was like a new discovery and toy to us, who had never been used to such a presence. She was not a commonplace child; but even if she had been, she would have been as charming a study as a kitten; and she had all the four of us at her feet, though her mother was constantly protesting against our spoiling her, and really kept up so much wholesome discipline that the little maid never exceeded the bounds of being charming to us. After that explanation there was the same sweet wistful gentleness in her manner towards Clarence as she showed to me; while he, who never dreamt of such a child knowing his history was brighter and freer with her than with any one else, played with her and Martyn, and could be heard laughing merrily with them. Perhaps her mother and sister did not fully like this, but they could not interfere before our faces. And Parson Frank was really kind to him; took him out walking when going to Hillside, and talked to him so as to draw him out; certifying, perhaps, that he would do no harm, although, indeed, the family looked on dear good Frank as a sort of boy, too kind-hearted and genial for his approval to be worth as much as that of the more severe.

These were our only Christmas visitors, for the state of the country did not invite Londoners; but we did not want them. The suppression of Clarence was the only flaw in a singularly happy time; and, after all I believe I felt the pity of it more than he did, who expected nothing, and was accustomed to being in the background.

For instance, one afternoon in the course of one of the grave discussions that used to grow up between Miss Fordyce, Emily, and me, over subjects trite to the better-instructed younger generation, we got quite out of our shallow depths. I think it was on the meaning of the 'Communion of Saints,' for the two girls were both reading in preparation for a Confirmation at Bristol, and Miss Fordyce knew more than we did on these subjects. All the time Clarence had sat in the window, carving a bit of doll's furniture, and quite forgotten; but at night he showed me the exposition copied from Pearson on the Creed, a bit of Hooker, and extracts from one or two sermons. I found these were notes written out in a blank book, which he had had in hand ever since his Confirmation—his logbook as he called it; but he would not hear of their being mentioned even to Emily, and only consented to hunt up the books on condition I would not bring him forward as the finder. It was of no use to urge that it was a deprivation to us all that he should not aid us with his more thorough knowledge and deeper thought. 'He could not do so,' he said, in a quiet decisive manner; 'it was enough for him to watch and listen to Miss Fordyce, when she could forget his presence.'

She often did forget it in her eagerness. She was by nature

one of the most ardent beings that I ever saw, yet with enthusiasm kept in check by the self-control inculcated as a primary duty. It would kindle in those wonderful light brown eyes, glow in the clear delicate cheek, quiver in the voice even when the words were only half adequate to the feeling. She was not what is now called gushing. Oh, no! not in the least! She was too reticent and had too much dignity for anything of the kind. Emily had always been reckoned as our romantic young lady, and teased accordingly, but her enthusiasm beside Ellen's was

'As moonlight is to sunlight, as water is to wine,' -

a mere reflection of the tone of the period, compared with a real element in the character. At least so my sister tells me, though at the time all the difference I saw was that Miss Fordyce had the most originality, and unconsciously became the leader. The bookroom was given up to us, and there in the morning we drew, worked, read, copied and practised music, wrote out extracts, and delivered our youthful minds to one another on all imaginable topics from 'slea silk to predestination.'

Religious subjects occupied us more than might have been held likely. A spirit of reflection and revival was silently working in many a heart. Evangelicalism had stirred old-fashioned orthodoxy, and we felt its action. The Christian Year was Ellen's guiding star—as it was ours, nay, doubly so in proportion to the ardour of her nature. Certain poems are dearer and more eloquent to me still, because the verses recall to me the thrill of her sweet tones as she repeated them. We were all very ignorant alike of Church doctrine and history, but talking out and comparing our discoveries and impressions was as useful as it was pleasant to us.

What the Christian Year was in religion to us Scott was in

history. We read to verify or illustrate him, and we had little raving fits over his characters, and jokes founded on them. Indeed, Ellen saw life almost through that medium; and the siege of Hillside, dispersed by the splendid prowess of Griffith, the champion with silver helm and flashing sword, was precious to her as a renewal of the days of Ivanhoe or Damian de Lacy.

As may be believed, these quiet mornings were those when that true knight was employed in field sports or yeomanry duties, such as the state of the country called for. When he was at home, all was fun and merriment and noise—walks and rides on fine days, battledore and shuttlecock on wet ones, music, singing, paper games, giggling and making giggle, and sometimes dancing in the hall—Mr. Frank Fordyce joining with all his heart and drollery in many of these, like the boy he was.

I could play quadrilles and country dances, and now and then a reel—nobody thought of waltzes—and the three couples changed and counterchanged partners. Clarence had the sailor's foot, and did his part when needed; Emily generally fell to his share, and their silence and gravity contrasted with the mirth of the other pairs. He knew very well he was the pis aller of the party, and only danced when Parson Frank was not dragged out, nothing loth, by his little daughter. With Miss Fordyce, Clarence never had the chance of dancing; she was always claimed by Griff, or pounced upon by Martyn.

Miss Fordyce she always was to us in those days, and those pretty lips scrupulously 'Mistered' and 'Winslowed' us. I don't think she would have been more to us, if we had called her Nell, and had been Griff, Bill, and Ted to her, or if there had not been all the little formalities of avoiding tete a tetes and the like. They were essentials of propriety then—natural, and never viewed as prudish. Nor did it detract from the sweet dignity of maidenhood that there was none of the familiarity which breeds something one would rather not mention in conjunction with a lady.

Altogether there was a sunshine around Miss Fordyce by which we all seemed illuminated, even the least favoured and least demonstrative; we were all her willing slaves, and thought her smile and thanks full reward.

One day, when Griff and Martyn were assisting at the turn out of an isolated barn at Hillside, where Frank Fordyce declared, all the burnt-out rats and mice had taken refuge, the young ladies went out to cater for house decorations for Christmas under Clarence's escort. Nobody but the clerk ever thought of touching the church, where there were holes in all the pews to receive the holly boughs.

The girls came back, telling in eager scared voices how, while gathering butcher's broom in Farmer Hodges' home copse, a savage dog had flown out at them, but had been kept at bay by Mr. Clarence Winslow with an umbrella, while they escaped over the stile.

Clarence had not come into the drawing-room with them, and while my mother, who had a great objection to people standing about in out-door garments, sent them up to doff their bonnets and furs, I repaired to our room, and was horrified to find him on my bed, white and faint.

'Bitten?' I cried in dismay.

'Yes; but not much. Only I'm such a fool. I turned off when I began taking off my boots. No, no—don't! Don't call any one. It is nothing!'

He was springing up to stop me, but was forced to drop back, and I made my way to the drawing-room, where my

Charlotte M. Yonge

mother happened to be alone. She was much alarmed, but a glass of wine restored Clarence; and inspection showed that the thick trowser and winter stocking had so protected him that little blood had been drawn, and there was bruise rather than bite in the calf of the leg, where the brute had caught him as he was getting over the stile as the rear-guard. It was painful, though the faintness was chiefly from tension of nerve, for he had kept behind all the way home, and no one had guessed at the hurt. My mother doctored it tenderly, and he begged that nothing should be said about it; he wanted no fuss about such a trifle. My mother agreed, with the proud feeling of not enhancing the obligations of the Fordyce family; but she absolutely kissed Clarence's forehead as she bade him lie quiet till dinner-time.

We kept silence at table while the girls described the horrors of the monster. 'A tawny creature, with a hideous black muzzle,' said Emily. 'Like a bad dream,' said Miss Fordyce. The two fathers expressed their intention of remonstrating with the farmer, and Griff declared that it would be lucky if he did not shoot it. Miss Fordyce generously took its part, saying the poor dog was doing its duty, and Griff ejaculated, 'If I had been there!'

'It would not have dared to show its teeth, eh?' said my father, when there was a good deal of banter.

My father, however, came at night with mamma to inspect the hurt and ask details, and he ended with, 'Well done, Clarence, boy; I am gratified to see you are acquiring presence of mind, and can act like a man.'

Clarence smiled when they were gone, saying, 'That would have been an insult to any one else.'

Emily perceived that he had not come off unscathed, and

was much aggrieved at being bound to silence. 'Well,' she broke out, 'if the dog goes mad, and Clarence has the hydrophobia, I suppose I may tell.'

'In that pleasing contingency,' said Clarence smiling. 'Don't you see, Emily, it is the worst compliment you can pay me not to treat this as a matter of course?' Still, he was the happier for not having failed. Whatever strengthened his self-respect and gave him trust in himself was a stepping-stone.

As to rivalry or competition with Griff, the idea seemingly never crossed his mind, and envy or jealousy were equally aloof from it. One subject of thankfulness runs through these recollections—namely, that nothing broke the tie of strong affection between us three brothers. Griffith might figure as the 'vary parfite knight,' the St. George of the piece, glittering in the halo shed round him by the bright eyes of the rescued damsel; while Clarence might drag himself along as the poor recreant to be contemned and tolerated, and he would accept the position meekly as only his desert, without a thought of bitterness. Indeed, he himself seemed to have imbibed Nurse Gooch's original opinion, that his genuine love for sacred things was a sort of impertinence and pretension in such as he—a kind of hypocrisy even when they were the realities and helps to which he clung with all his heart. Still, this depression was only shown by reserve, and troubled no one save myself, who knew him best guessed what was lost by his silence, and burned in spirit at seeing him merely endured as one unworthy.

In one of our varieties of Waverley discussions the crystal hardness and inexperienced intolerance of youth made Miss Fordyce declare that had she been Edith Plantagenet, she would never, never have forgiven Sir Kenneth. 'How could she, when he had forsaken the king's banner? Unpardonable!'

Then came a sudden, awful silence, as she recollected her audience, and blushed crimson with the misery of perceiving where her random shaft had struck, nor did either of us know what to say; but to our surprise it was Clarence who first spoke to relieve the desperate embarrassment. 'Is forgiven quite the right word, when the offence was not personal? I know that such things can neither be repaired nor overlooked, and I think that is what Miss Fordyce meant.'

'Oh, Mr. Winslow,' she exclaimed, 'I am very sorry—I don't think I quite meant'—and then, as her eyes for one moment fell on his subdued face, she added, 'No, I said what I ought not. If there is sorrow'—her voice trembled—'and pardon above, no one below has any right to say unpardonable.'

Clarence bowed his head, and his lips framed, but he did not utter, 'Thank you.' Emily nervously began reading aloud the page before her, full of the jingling recurring rhymes about Sir Thomas of Kent; but I saw Ellen surreptitiously wipe away a tear, and from that time she was more kind and friendly with Clarence.

CHAPTER XX

VENI, VIDI, VICI

'None but the brave,
None but the brave,
None but the brave deserve the fair.'

SONG.

Christmas trees were not yet heard of beyond the Fatherland, and both the mothers held that Christmas parties were not good for little children, since Mrs. Winslow's strong common sense had arrived at the same conclusion as Mrs. Fordyce had derived from Hannah More and Richard Lovell Edgeworth. Besides, rick-burning and mobs were far too recent for our neighbours to venture out at night.

But as we were all resolved that little Anne should have a memorable Christmas at Chantry House, we begged an innocent, though iced cake, from the cook, painted a set of characters ourselves, including all the dolls, and bespoke the presence of Frank Fordyce at a feast in the outer mullion room—Griff's apartment, of course. The locality was chosen as allowing more opportunity for high jinks than the bookroom, and also because the swords and

Charlotte M. Yonge

pistols in trophy over the mantelpiece had a great fascination for the two sisters, and to 'drink tea with Mr. Griffith' was always known to be a great ambition of the little queen of the festival. As to the mullion chamber legends, they had nearly gone out of our heads, though Clarence did once observe, 'You remember, it will be the 26th of December;' but we did not think this worthy of consideration, especially as Anne's entertainment, at its latest, could not last beyond nine o'clock; and the ghostly performances—now entirely laid to the account of the departed stable-boy—never began before eleven.

Nor did anything interfere with our merriment. The fun of fifty years ago must be intrinsically exquisite to bear being handed down to another generation, so I will attempt no repetition, though some of those Twelfth Day characters still remain, pasted into my diary. We antici-pated Twelfth Day because our guests meant to go to visit some other friends before the New Year, and we knew Anne would have no chance there of fulfilling her great ambition of drawing for king and queen. These home-made characters were really charming. Mrs. Fordyce had done several of them, and she drew beautifully. A little manipulation contrived that the exquisite Oberon and Titania should fall to Martyn and Anne, for whom crowns and robes had been prepared, worn by her majesty with complacent dignity, but barely tolerated by him! The others took their chance. Parson Frank was Tom Thumb, and convulsed us all the evening by acting as if no bigger than that worthy, keeping us so merry that even Clarence laughed as I had never seen him laugh before.

Cock Robin and Jenny Wren—the best drawn of all—fell to Griff and Miss Fordyce. There was a suspicion of a tint of real carnation on her cheek, as, on his low, highly-delighted bow, she held up her impromptu fan of folded paper; and drollery about currant wine and hopping upon twigs went on more or less all the time, while somehow or other the beauteous glow on her cheeks went on deepening, so that I never saw her look so pretty as when thus playing at Jenny Wren's coyness, though neither she nor Griff had passed the bounds of her gracious precise discretion.

The joyous evening ended at last. With the stroke of nine, Jenny Wren bore away Queen Titania to put her to bed, for the servants were having an entertainment of their own downstairs for all the out-door retainers, etc. Oberon departed, after an interval sufficient to prove his own dignity and advanced age. Emily went down to report the success of the evening to the elders in the drawing-room, but we lingered while Frank Fordyce was telling good stories of Oxford life, and Griff capping them with more recent ones.

We too broke up—I don't remember how; but Clarence was to help me down the stairs, and Mr. Fordyce, frowning with anxiety at the process, was offering assistance, while we had much rather he had gone out of the way; when suddenly, in the gallery round the hall giving access to the bedrooms, there dawned upon us the startled but scarcely displeased figure of Jenny Wren in her white dress, not turning aside that blushing face, while Cock Robin was clasping her hand and pressing it to his lips. The tap of my crutches warned them. She flew back within her door and shut it; Griff strode rapidly on, caught hold of her father's hand, exclaiming, 'Sir, sir, I must speak to you!' and dragged him back into the mullion room leaving Clarence and me to convey ourselves downstairs as best we might.

'Our sister, our sweet sister!'

We were immensely excited. All the three of us were so

Charlotte M. Yonge

far in love with Ellen Fordyce that her presence was an enchantment to us, and at any rate none of us ever saw the woman we could compare to her; and as we both felt ourselves disqualified in different ways from any nearer approach, we were content to bask in the reflected rays of our brother's happiness.

Not that he had gone that length as yet, as we knew before the night was over, when he came down to us. Even with the dear maiden herself, he had only made sure that she was not averse, and that merely by her eyes and lips; and he had extracted nothing from her father but that they were both very young, a great deal too young, and had no business to think of such things yet. It must be talked over, etc. etc.

But just then, Griff told us, Frank Fordyce jumped up and turned round with the sudden exclamation, 'Ellen!' looking towards the door behind him with blank astonishment, as he found it had neither been opened nor shut. He thought his daughter had recollected something left behind, and coming in search of it, had retreated precipitately. He had seen her, he said, in the mirror opposite. Griff told him there was no mirror, and had to carry a candle across to convince him that he had only been looking at the door into the inner room, which though of shining dark oak, could hardly have made a reflection as vivid as he declared that his had been. Indeed, he ascertained that Ellen had never left her own room at all. 'It must have been thinking about the dear child,' he said. 'And after all, it was not quite like her—somehow—she was paler, and had something over her head.' We had no doubt who it was. Griff had not seen her, but he was certain that there had been none of the moaning nor crying, 'In fact, she has come to give her consent,' he said with earnest in his mocking tone.

'Yes,' said Clarence gravely, and with glistening eyes. 'You are happy Griff. It is given to you to right the wrong, and quiet that poor spirit.'

'Happy! The happiest fellow in the world,' said Griff, 'even without that latter clause—if only Madam and the old man will have as much sense as she has!'

The next day was a thoroughly uncomfortable one. Griff was not half so near his goal as he had hoped last night when with kindly Parson Frank.

The commotion was as if a thunderbolt had descended among the elders. What they had been thinking of, I cannot tell, not to have perceived how matters were tending; but their minds were full of the Reform Bill and the state of the country, and, besides, we were all looked on still as mere children. Indeed, Griff was scarcely one-and-twenty, and Ellen wanted a month of seventeen; and the crisis had really been a sudden impulse, as he said, 'She looked so sweet and lovely, he could not help it.'

The first effect was a serious lecture upon maidenliness and propriety to poor Ellen from her mother, who was sure that she must have transgressed the bounds of discretion, or such ill-bred presumption would have been spared her, and bitterly regretted the having trusted her to take care of herself. There were sufficient grains of truth in this to make the poor girl cry herself out of all condition for appearing at breakfast or luncheon, and Emily's report of her despair made us much more angry with Mrs. Fordyce than was perhaps quite due to that good lady.

My parents were at first inclined to take the same line, and be vexed with Griff for an act of impertinence towards a guest. He had a great deal of difficulty in inducing the elders to believe him in earnest, or treat him as a man capable of knowing his own mind; and even thus they felt as if his addresses to Miss Fordyce were, under present circumstances, taking almost an unfair advantage of the other family—at which our youthful spirits felt indignant.

Yet, after all, such a match was as obvious and suitable as if it had been a family compact, and the only objection was the youth of the parties. Mrs. Fordyce would fain have believed her daughter's heart to be not yet awake, and was grieved to find childhood over, and the hero of romance become the lover; and she was anxious that full time should be given to perceive whether her daughter's feelings were only the result of the dazzling aureole which gratitude and excited fancy had cast around the fine, handsome, winning youth. Her husband, however, who had himself married very young, and was greatly taken with Griff, besides being always tender-hearted, did not enter into her scruples; but, as we had already found out, the grand-looking and clever man of thirty-eight was, chiefly from his impulsiveness and good-nature, treated as the boy of the family. His old father, too, was greatly pleased with Griff's spirit, affection, and purpose, as well as with my father's conduct in the matter; and so, after a succession of private interviews, very tantalising to us poor outsiders, it was conceded that though an engagement for the present was preposterous, it might possibly be permitted when Ellen was eighteen if Griff had completed his university life with full credit. He was fervently grateful to have such an object set before him, and my father was warmly thankful for the stimulus.

That last evening was very odd and constrained. We could not help looking on the lovers as new specimens over which some strange transformation had passed, though for the present it had stiffened them in public into the strictest good behaviour. They would have been awkward if it had been possible to either of them, and, save for a certain look in their eyes, comported themselves as perfect strangers.

The three elder gentlemen held discussions in the dining-room, but we were not trusted in our playground adjoining. Mrs. Fordyce nailed Griff down to an interminable game at chess, and my mother kept the two girls playing duets, while Clarence turned over the leaves; and I read over The Lady of the Lake, a study which I always felt, and still feel, as an act of homage to Ellen Fordyce, though there was not much in common between her and the maid of Douglas. Indeed, it was a joke of her father's to tease her by criticising the famous passage about the tears that old Douglas shed over his duteous daughter's head—'What in the world should the man go whining and crying for? He had much better have laughed with her.'

Little did the elders know what was going on in the next room, where there was a grand courtship among the dolls; the hero being a small jointed Dutch one in Swiss costume, about an eighth part of the size of the resuscitated Celestina Mary, but the only available male character in doll-land! Anne was supposed to be completely ignorant of what passed above her head; and her mother would have been aghast had she heard the remarkable discoveries and speculations that she and Martyn communicated to one another.

CHAPTER XXI

THE OUTSIDE OF THE COURTSHIP

'Or framing, as a fair excuse,
The book, the pencil, or the muse;
Something to give, to sing, to say,
Some modern tale, some ancient lay.'

SCOTT.

It seems to me on looking back that I have hardly done
justice to Mrs. Fordyce, and certainly we—as Griffith's
eager partisans—often regarded her in the light of an
enemy and opponent; but after this lapse of time, I can see
that she was no more than a prudent mother, unwilling to
see her fair young daughter suddenly launched into
womanhood, and involved in an attachment to a young
and untried man.

The part of a drag is an invidious one; and this must have
been her part through most of her life. The Fordyces,
father and son, were of good family, gentlemen to their
very backbones, and thoroughly good, religious men; but
she came of a more aristocratic strain, had been in
London society, and brought with her a high-bred air
which, implanted on the Fordyce good looks, made her

daughter especially fascinating. But that air did not recommend Mrs. Fordyce to all her neighbours, any more than did those stronger, stricter, more thorough-going notions of religious obligation which had led her husband to make the very real and painful sacrifice of his sporting tastes, and attend to the parish in a manner only too rare in those days. She was a very well-informed and highly accomplished woman, and had made her daughter the same, keeping her children up in a somewhat exclusive style, away from all gossip or undesirable intimacies, as recommended by Miss Edgeworth and other more religious authorities, and which gave great offence in houses where there were girls of the same age. No one, however, could look at Ellen, and doubt of the success of the system, or of the young girl's entire content and perfect affection for her mother, though her father was her beloved playfellow—yet always with respect. She never took liberties with him, nor called him Pap or any other ridiculous name inconsistent with the fifth Commandment, though she certainly was more entirely at ease with him than ever we had been with our elderly father. When once Mrs. Fordyce found on what terms we were to be, she accepted them frankly and fully. Already Emily had been the first girl, not a relation, whose friendship she had fostered with Ellen; and she had also become thoroughly affectionate and at home with my mother, who suited her perfectly on the conscientious, and likewise on the prudent and sensible, side of her nature.

To me she was always kindness itself, so kind that I never felt, as I did on so many occasions, that she was very pitiful and attentive to the deformed youth; but that she really enjoyed my companionship, and I could help her in her pursuits. I have a whole packet of charming notes of hers about books, botany, drawings, little bits of antiquarianism, written with an arch grace and finish of expression peculiarly her own, and in a very pointed hand, yet too definite to be illegible. I owe her more than I can say for the windows of wholesome hope and ambition she opened to me, giving a fresh motive and zest even to such a life as mine. I can hardly tell which was the most delightful companion, she or her husband. In spite of ill health, she knew every plant, and every bit of fair scenery in the neighbourhood, and had fresh, amusing criticisms to utter on each new book; while he, not neglecting the books, was equally well acquainted with all beasts and birds, and shed his kindly light over everything he approached. He was never melancholy about anything but politics, and even there it was an immense consolation to him to have the owner of Chantry House staunch on the same side, instead of in chronic opposition.

The family party moved to a tall house at Bath, but there still was close intercourse, for the younger clergyman rode over every week for the Sunday duty, and almost always dined and slept at Chantry House. He acted as bearer of long letters, which, in spite of a reticulation of crossings, were too expensive by post for young ladies' pocket-money, often exceeding the regular quarto sheet. It was a favourite joke to ask Emily what Ellen reported about Bath fashions, and to see her look of scorn. For they were a curious mixture, those girlish letters, of village interests, discussion of books, and thoughts beyond their age; Tommy Toogood and Prometheus; or Du Guesclin in the closest juxtaposition with reports of progress in Abercrombie on the Intellectual Powers. It was the desire of Ellen to prove herself not unsettled but improved by love, and to become worthy of her ideal Griffith, never guessing that he would have been equally content with her if she had been as frivolous as the idlest girl who lingered amid the waning glories of Bath.

We all made them a visit there when Martyn was taken to a preparatory school in the place. Mrs. Fordyce took me out for drives on the beautiful hills; and Emily and I had a very delightful time, undisturbed by the engrossing claims of love-making. Very good, too, were our friends, after our departure, in letting Martyn spend Sundays and holidays with them, play with Anne as before, say his Catechism with her to Mrs. Fordyce, and share her little Sunday lessons, which had, he has since told, a force and attractiveness he had never known before, and really did much, young as he was, in preparing the way towards the fulfilment of my father's design for him.

When the Rectory was ready, and the family returned, it was high summer, and there were constant meetings between the households. No doubt there were the usual amount of trivial disappointments and annoyances, but the whole season seems to me to have been bathed in sunlight. The Reform Bill agitations and the London mobs of which Clarence wrote to us were like waves surging beyond an isle of peace. Clarence had some unpleasant walks from the office. Once or twice the shutters had to be put up at Frith and Castleford's to prevent the windows from being broken; and once Clarence actually saw our nation's hero, 'the Duke,' riding quietly and slowly through a yelling, furious mob, who seemed withheld from falling on him by the perfect impassiveness of the eagle face and spare figure. Moreover a pretty little boy, on his pony, suddenly pushed forward and rode by the Duke's side, as if proud and resolute to share his peril.

'If Griffith had been there!' said Ellen and Emily, though they did not exactly know what they expected him to have done.

The chief storms that drifted across our sky were caused by Mrs. Fordyce's resolution that Griffith should enjoy none of the privileges of an accepted suitor before the engagement was an actual fact. Ellen was obedient and conscientious; and would neither transgress nor endure to have her mother railed at by Griff's hasty tongue, and this affronted him, and led to little breezes.

When people overstay their usual time, tempers are apt to get rather difficult. Griffith had kept all his terms at Oxford, and was not to return thither after the long vacation, but was to read with a tutor before taking his degree. Moreover bills began to come from Oxford, not very serious, but vexing my father and raising annoyances and frets, for Griff resented their being complained of, and thought himself ill-used, going off to see his own friends whenever he was put out.

One morning at breakfast, late in October, he announced that Lady Peacock was in lodgings at Clifton, and asked my mother to call on her. But mamma said it was too far for the horse—she visited no one at that distance, and had never thought much of Selina Clarkson before or after her marriage.

'But now that she is a widow, it would be such a kindness,' pleaded Griff.

'Depend upon it, a gay young widow needs no kindness from me, and had better not have it from you,' said my mother, getting up from behind her urn and walking off, followed by my father.

Griff drummed on the table. 'I wonder what good ladies of a certain age do with their charity,' he said.

And while we were still crying out at him, Ellen Fordyce and her father appeared, like mirth bidding good-morrow, at the window. All was well for the time, but Griff wanted Ellen to set out alone with him, and take their leisurely way through the wood-path, and she insisted on waiting for her father, who had got into an endless discussion with mine on the Reform Bill, thrown out in the last Session. Griff tried to wile her on with him, but, though she consented to wander about the lawn before the windows with him, she always resolutely turned at the great beech tree. Emily and I watched them from the window, at first amused, then vexed, as we could see, by his gestures, that he was getting out of temper, and her straw bonnet drooped at one moment, and was raised the next in eager remonstrance or defence. At last he flung angrily away from her, and went off to the stables, leaving her leaning against the gate in tears. Emily, in an access of indignant sympathy, rushed out to her, and they vanished together into the summer-house, until her father called her, and they went home together.

Emily told me that Ellen had struggled hard to keep herself from crying enough to show traces of tears which her father could observe, and that she had excused Griff with all her might on the plea of her own 'tiresomeness.'

We were all the more angry with him for his selfishness and want of consideration, for Ellen, in her torrent of grief, had even disclosed that he had said she did not care for him—no one really in love ever scrupled about a mother's nonsense, etc., etc.

We were resolved, like two sages, to give him a piece of our minds, and convince him that such dutifulness was the pledge of future happiness, and that it was absolute cruelty to the rare creature he had won, to try to draw her in a direction contrary to her conscience.

However, we saw him no more that day; and only learnt that he had left a message at the stables that dinner was not to be kept waiting for him. Such a message from

Clarence would have caused a great commotion; but it was quite natural and a matter of course from him in the eyes of the elders, who knew nothing of his parting with Ellen. However, there was annoyance enough, when bedtime came, family prayers were over, and still there was no sign of him. My father sat up till one o'clock, to let him in, then gave it up, and I heard his step heavily mounting the stairs.

CHAPTER XXII

BRISTOL DIAMONDS

'Stafford. And you that are the King's friends, follow me.

Cade. And you that love the Commons, follow me;
We will not leave one lord, one gentleman,
Spare none but such as go in clouted shoon.'

ACT I. HENRY VI.

The next day was Sunday, and no Griff appeared in the morning. Vexation, perhaps, prevented us from attending as much as we otherwise might have done to Mr. Henderson when he told us that there were rumours of a serious disturbance at Bristol; until Emily recollected that Griff had been talking for some days past of riding over to see his friend in the cavalry regiment there stationed, and we all agreed that it was most likely that he was there; and our wrath began to soften in the belief that he might have been detained to give his aid in the cause of order, though his single arm could not be expected to effect as much as at Hillside.

Long after dark we heard a horse's feet, and in another minute Griff, singed, splashed, and battered, had hurried into the room— 'It has begun!' he said. 'The revolution! I have brought her—Lady Peacock. She was at Clifton, dreadfully alarmed. She is almost at the door now, in her carriage. I'll just take the pony, and ride over to tell Eastwood in case he will call out the Yeomanry.'

The wheels were to be heard, and everybody hastened out to receive Lady Peacock, who was there with her maid, full of gratitude. I heard her broken sentences as she came across the hall, about dreadful scenes—frightful mob— she knew not what would have become of her but for Griffith—the place was in flames when they left it—the military would not act—Griffith had assured her that Mr. and Mrs. Winslow would be so kind—as long as any place was a refuge

We really did believe we were at the outbreak of a revolution or civil war, and, all little frets forgotten, listened appalled to the tidings; how the appearance of Sir Charles Wetherall, the Recorder of Bristol, a strong opponent to the Reform Bill, seemed to have inspired the mob with fury. Griff and his friend the dragoon, while walking in Broad Street, were astonished by a violent rush of riotous men and boys, hooting and throwing stones as the Recorder's carriage tried to make its way to the Guildhall. In the midst a piteous voice exclaimed -

'Oh, Griffith! Mr. Griffith Winslow! Is it you?' and Lady Peacock was seen retreating upon the stone steps of a house either empty, or where the inhabitants were too much alarmed to open the doors. She was terribly frightened, and the two gentlemen stood in front of her till the tumultuary procession had passed by. She was staying in lodgings at Clifton, and had driven in to Bristol to shop, when she thus found herself entangled in the mob. They then escorted her to the place where she was to meet her carriage, and found it for her with some difficulty.

Then, while the officer returned to his quarters, Griff accompanied her far enough on the way to Clifton to see that everything was quiet before her, and then returned to seek out his friend. The court at the Guildhall had had to be adjourned, but the rioters were hunting Sir Charles to the Mansion-House. Griff was met by one of the Town Council, a tradesman with whom we dealt, who, having perhaps heard of his prowess at Hillside, entreated him to remain, offering him a bed, and saying that all friends of order were needed in such a crisis as this. Griff wrote a note to let us know what had become of him, but everything was disorganised, and we did not get it till two days afterwards.

In the evening the mob became more violent, and in the midst of dinner a summons came for Griff's host to attend the Mayor in endeavouring to disperse it. Getting into the Mansion-House by private back ways, they were able to join the Mayor when he came out, amid a shower of brickbats, sticks, and stones, and read the Riot Act three times over, after warning them of the consequences of persisting in their defiance.

'But they were far past caring for that,' said Griff. 'An iron rail from the square was thrown in the midst of it, and if I had not caught it there would have been an end of his Worship.'

The constables, with such help as Griff and a few others could give them, defended the front of the Mansion-House, while the Recorder, for whom they savagely roared, made his escape by the roof to another house. A barricade was made with beds, tables, and chairs, behind which the defenders sheltered themselves, while volleys of stones smashed in the windows, and straw was thrown after them. But at last the tramp of horses' feet was heard, and the Dragoons came up.

'We thought all over then,' said Griff; 'but Colonel Brereton would not have a blow struck, far less a shot fired! He would have it that it was a good-humoured mob! I heard him! When one of his own men was brought up badly hurt with a brickbat, I heard Ludlow, the Town-Clerk, ask him what he thought of their good humour, and he had nothing to say but that it was an accident! And the rogues knew it! He took care they should; he walked about among them and shook hands with them!'

Griff waited at the Mansion-House all night, and helped to board up the smashed windows; but at daylight Colonel Brereton came and insisted on withdrawing the piquet on guard—not, however, sending a relief for them, on the plea that they only collected a crowd. The instant they were withdrawn, down came the mob in fresh force, so desperate that all the defences were torn down, and they swarmed in so that there was nothing for it but to escape over the roofs.

Griffith was sent to rouse the inhabitants of College Green and St. Augustine's Back to come in the King's name to assist the Magistrates, and he had many good stories of the various responses he met with. But the rioters, inflamed by the wine they had found in sacking the Mansion-House, and encouraged by the passiveness of the troops, had become entirely masters of the situation. And Colonel Brereton seems to have imagined that the presence of the soldiers acted as an irritation; for in this crisis he actually sent them out of the city to Keynsham, then came and informed the mob, who cheered him, as well they might.

In the night the Recorder had left the city, and notices were posted to that effect; also that the Riot Act had been read, and any further disturbance would be capital felony. This escape of their victim only had the effect of directing the rage of the populace against Bishop Grey, who had likewise opposed the Reform Bill.

Messages had been sent to advise the Bishop, who was to preach that day at the Cathedral, to stay away and sanction the omission of the service; but his answer to one of his clergy was—'These are times in which it is necessary not to shrink from danger! Our duty is to be at our post.' And he also said, 'Where can I die better than in my own Cathedral?'

Since the bells were ringing, and it was understood that the Bishop was actually going to dare the peril, Griff and others of the defenders decided that it was better to attend the service and fill up the nave so as to hinder outrage. He said it was a most strange and wonderful service. Chants and Psalms and Lessons and prayers going on their course as usual, but every now and then in the pauses of the organ, a howl or yell of the voice of the multitude would break on the ear through the thick walls. Griff listened and hoped for a volley of musketry. He was not tender-hearted! But none came, and by the time the service was over, the mob had been greatly reinforced and had broken into the prisons, set them on fire, and released the prisoners. They were mustering on College Green for an attack on the palace. Griff aided in guarding the entrance to the cloisters till the Bishop and his family had had time to drive away to Almondsbury, four miles off, and then the rush became so strong that they had to give way. There was another great struggle at the door of the palace, but it was forced open with a crowbar, while shouts rang out 'No King and no Bishops!' A fire was made in the dining-room with chairs and tables, and live coals were put into the beds, while the plunder went on.

Griff meantime had made his way to the party headed by the magistrates, and accompanied by the dragoons, and the mob began to flee; but Colonel Brereton had given strict orders that the soldiers should not fire, and the plunderers rallied, made a fire in the Chapter House, and burnt the whole of the library, shouting with the maddest triumph.

They next attacked the Cathedral, intending to burn that likewise, but two brave gentlemen, Mr. Ralph and Mr. Linne, succeeded in saving this last outrage, at the head of the better affected.

Griff had fought hard. He was all over bruises which he really had never felt at the time, scarcely even now, though one side of his face was turning purple, and his clothes were singed. In a sort of council held at the repulse of the attack on the Cathedral, it had been decided that the best thing he could do would be to give notice to Sir George Eastwood, in order that the Yeomanry might be called out, since the troops were so strangely prevented from acting. As he rode through Clifton, he had halted at Lady Peacock's, and found her in extreme alarm. Indeed, no one could guess what the temper of the mob might be the next day, or whether they might not fall upon private houses. The Mansion-House, the prisons, the palace were all burning and were an astounding sight, which terrified her exceedingly, and she was sending out right and left to endeavour to get horses to take her away. In common humanity, and for old acquaintance sake, it was impossible not to help her, and Griff had delayed, to offer any amount of reward in her name for posthorses, which he had at last secured. Her own man-servant, whom she had sent in quest of some, had never returned, and she had to set off without him, Griff acting as outrider; but after the first there was no more difficulty about horses, and she had been able to change them at the next stage.

We all thought the days of civil war were really begun, as

the heads of this account were hastily gathered; but there was not much said, only Mr. Frank Fordyce laid his hand on Griff's shoulder and said, 'Well done, my boy; but you have had enough for to-day. If you'll lend me a horse, Winslow, I'll ride over to Eastwood. That's work for the clergy in these times, eh? Griffith should rest. He may be wanted to-morrow. Only is there any one to take a note home for me, to say where I'm gone;' and then he added with that sweet smile of his, 'Some one will be more the true knight than ever, eh, you Griffith you—'

Griffith coloured a little, and Lady Peacock's eyes looked interrogative. When the horse was announced, Griff followed Mr. Fordyce into the hall, and came back announcing that, unless summoned elsewhere, he should go to breakfast at Hillside, and so hear what was decided on. He longed to be back at the scene of action, but was so tired out that he could not dispense with another night's rest; though he took all precautions for being called up, in case of need.

However, nothing came, and he rode to the Rectory in Yeomanry equipment. Nor could any one doubt that in the ecstasy of meeting such a hero, all the little misunder-standing and grief of the night before was forgotten? Ellen looked as if she trod on air, when she came down with her father to report that Griffith had gone, according to the orders sent, to join the rest of the Yeomanry, who were to advance upon Bristol. They had seen, and tried to turn back, some of the villagers who were starting with bludgeons to share in the spoil, and who looked sullen, as if they were determined not to miss their share.

I do not think we were very much alarmed for Griff's safety or for our own, not even the ladies. My mother had the lion-heart of her naval ancestors, and Ellen was in a state of exaltation. Would that I could put her before other

Charlotte M. Yonge

eyes, as she stood with hands clasped and glowing cheek.

'Oh!—think!—think of having one among us who is as real and true knight as ever watched his armour -

'"For king, for church, for lady fight!" It has all come gloriously true!'

'Should not you like to bind on his spurs?' I asked somewhat mischievously; but she was serious as she said, 'I am sure he has won them.' All the rest of the Fordyces came down afterwards, too anxious to stay at home. Our elders felt the matter more gravely, thinking of what civil war might mean to us all, and what an awful thing it was for Englishmen to be enrolled against each other. Nottingham Castle had just been burnt, and things looked only too like revolution, especially considering the inaction of the dragoons. After Griff had left Bristol, there had been some terrible scenes at the Custom House, where the ringleaders—unhappy men!—were caught in a trap of their own and perished miserably.

However, by the morning, the order sent from Lord Hill, the arrival of Major Beckwith from Gloucester, and the proceedings of the good-humoured mob had put an end to poor Brereton's hesitations; a determined front had been shown; the mob had been fairly broken up; troops from all quarters poured into the city, and by dinner-time Griff came back with the news that all was quiet and there was nothing more to fear. Ellen and Emily both flew out to meet him at the first sound of the horse's feet, and they all came into the drawing-room together—each young lady having hold of one of his hands—and Ellen's face in such a glow, that I rather suspect that he had snatched a reward which certainly would not have been granted save in such a moment of uplifted feeling, and when she was thankful to her hero for forgetting how angry he had been with her two days before.

Minor matters were forgotten in the details of his tidings, as he stood before the fire, shining in his silver lace, and relating the tragedy and the comedy of the scene.

It was curious, as the evening passed on, to see how Ellen and Lady Peacock regarded each other, now that the tension of suspense was over. To Ellen, the guest was primarily a distressed and widowed dame, delivered by Griff, to whom she, as his lady love, was bound to be gracious and kind; nor had they seen much of one another, the elder ladies sitting in the drawing-room, and we in our own regions; but we were all together at dinner and afterwards, and Lady Peacock, who had been in a very limp, nervous, and terrified state all day, began to be the Selina Clarkson we remembered, and 'more too.' She was still in mourning, but she came down to dinner in gray satin sheen, and with her hair in a most astonishing erection of bows and bands, on the very crown of her head, raising her height at least four inches. Emily assures me that it was the mode in use, and that she and Ellen wore their hair in the same style, appealing to portraits to prove it. I can only say that they never astonished my weak mind in the like manner; and that their heads, however dressed, only appeared to me a portion of the general woman, and part of the universal fitness of things. Ellen was likewise amazed, most likely not at the hair, but at the transformation of the disconsolate, frightened widow, into the handsome, fashionable, stylish lady, talking over London acquaintance and London news with my father and Griff whenever they left the endless subject of the Bristol adventures.

The widow had gained a good deal in beauty since her early girlhood, having regular features, eyes of an uncommon deep blue, very black brows, eye-lashes, and hair, and a form of the kind that is better after early youth is over. 'A fine figure of a woman,' Parson Frank pronounced her, and his wife, with the fine edge of her lips replied, 'exactly what she is!'

She looked upon us younger ones as mere children still—indeed she never looked at me at all if she could help it—but she mortally offended Emily by penning her up in a corner, and asking if Griff were engaged to that sentimental little girl.

Emily coloured like a turkey cock between wrath and embarrassment, and hotly protested against the word sentimental.

'Ah yes, I see!' she said in a patronising tone, 'she is your bosom friend, eh? That's the way those things always begin. You need not answer: I see it all. And no doubt it is a capital thing for him; properties joining and all. And she will get a little air and style when he takes her to London.' It was a tremendous offence even to hint that Ellen's style was capable of improvement; perhaps an unprejudiced eye would have said that the difference was between high-bred simplicity and the air of fashion and society.

In our eyes Lady Peacock was the companion of the elders, and as such was appreciated by the gentlemen; but neither of the two mothers was equally delighted with her, nor was mine at all sorry when, on Tuesday, the boxes were packed, posthorses sent for, and my Lady departed, with great expressions of thankfulness to us all.

'A tulip to a jessamine,' muttered Griff as she drove off, and he looked up at his Ellen's sweet refined face.

The unfortunate Colonel Brereton put an end to himself when the court-martial was half over. How Clarence was shocked and how ardent was his pity! But Griffith received the thanks of the Corporation of Bristol for his gallant conduct, when the special assize was held in January. Mrs. Fordyce was almost as proud of him as we were, and there was much less attempt at restraining the terms on which he stood with Ellen—though still the formal engagement was not permitted.

CHAPTER XXIII

QUICKSANDS

'Whither shall I go?
Where shall I hide my forehead and my eyes?'

TENNYSON.

It was in the May of the ensuing year, 1832, that Clarence was sent down to Bristol for a few weeks to take the place of one of the clerks in the office where the cargoes of the incoming vessels of the firm were received and overhauled.

This was a good-natured arrangement of Mr. Castleford's in order to give him change of work and a sight of home, where, by the help of the coach, he could spend his Sundays. That first spring day on his way down was a great delight and even surprise to him, who had never seen our profusion of primroses, cowslips, and bluebells, nor our splendid blossom of trees—apple, lilac, laburnum—all vieing in beauty with one another. Emily conducted him about in great delight, taking him over to Hillside to see Mrs. Fordyce's American garden, blazing with azaleas, and glowing with rhododendrons. He came back with a great bouquet given to him by Ellen, who had been unusually friendly with him, and he was more animated and full of life than for years before.

Next time he came he looked less happy. There was plenty of room in our house, but he used, by preference, the little chamber within mine, and there at night he asked me to lend him a few pounds, since Griffith had written one of his off-hand letters asking him to discharge a little bill or two at Bristol, giving the addresses, but not sending the accounts. This was no wonder, since any enclosure doubled the already heavy postage. One of these bills was for some sporting equipments from the gunsmith's; another, much heavier, from a tavern for breakfasts, or rather luncheons, to parties of gentlemen, mostly bearing date in the summer and autumn of 1830, before the friendship with the Fordyces had begun. On Clarence's defraying the first and applying for the second, two more had come in, one from a jeweller for a pair of drop-earrings, the other from a nurseryman for a bouquet of exotics. Doubting of these two last, Clarence had written to Griff, but had not yet received an answer. The whole amount was so much beyond what he had been led to expect that he had not brought enough money to meet it, and wanted an advance from me, promising repayment, to which latter point I could not assent, as both of us knew, but did not say, we should never see the sum again, and to me it only meant stinting in new books and curiosities. We were anxious to get the matter settled at once, as Griffith spoke of being dunned; and it might be serious, if the tradesmen applied to my father when he was still groaning over revelations of college expenses.

On the ensuing Saturday, Clarence showed me Griff's answer—'I had forgotten these items. The earrings were a wedding present to the pretty little barmaid, who had been very civil. The bouquet was for Lady Peacock; I felt bound to do something to atone for mamma's severe virtue. It is all right, you best of brothers.'

It was consolatory that all the dates were prior to the Hillside fire, except that of the bouquet. As to the earrings, we all knew that Griff could not see a pretty girl without talking nonsense to her. Anyway, if they were a wedding present, there was an end of it; and we were only glad to prevent any hint of them from reaching the ears of the authorities.

Clarence had another trouble to confide to me. He had strong reason to believe that Tooke, the managing clerk at Bristol, was carrying on a course of peculation, and feathering his nest at the expense of the firm. What a grand discovery, thought I, for such a youth to have made. The firm would be infinitely obliged to him, and his fortune would be secured. He shook his head, and said that was all my ignorance; the man, Tooke, was greatly trusted, especially by Mr. Frith the senior partner, and was so clever and experienced that it would be almost impossible to establish anything against him. Indeed he had browbeaten Clarence, and convinced him at the moment that his suspicions and perplexities were only due to the ignorance of a foolish, scrupulous youth, who did not understand the customs and perquisites of an agency. It was only when Clarence was alone, and reflected on the matter by the light of experience gained on a similar expedition to Liverpool, that he had perceived that Mr. Tooke had been throwing dust in his eyes.

'I shall only get into a scrape myself,' said Clarence despondently. 'I have felt it coming ever since I have been at Bristol;' and he pushed his hair back with a weary hopeless gesture.

'But you don't mean to let it alone?' I cried indignantly.

He hesitated in a manner that painfully recalled his failing, and said at last, 'I don't know; I suppose I ought not.'

'Suppose?' I cried.

'It is not so easy as you think,' he answered, 'especially for one who has forfeited the right to be believed. I must wait till I have an opportunity of speaking to Mr. Castleford, and then I can hardly do more than privately give him a hint to be watchful. You don't know how things are in such houses as ours. One may only ruin oneself without doing any good.'

'You cannot write to him?'

'Certainly not. He has taken his family to Mrs. Castleford's home in the north of Ireland for a month or six weeks. I don't know the address, and I cannot run the risk of the letter being opened at the office.'

'Can't you speak to my father?'

'Impossible! it would be a betrayal. He would do things for which I should never be forgiven. And, after all, remember, it is no business of mine. I know of agents at the docks who do such things as a matter of course. It is only that I happen to know that Harris at Liverpool does not. Very possibly old Frith knows all about it. I should only get scored down as a meddlesome prig, worse hypocrite than they think me already.'

He said a good deal more to this effect, and I remember exclaiming, 'Oh, Clarence, the old story!' and then being frightened at the whiteness that came over his face.

Little did I know the suffering to which those words of

Charlotte M. Yonge

mine condemned him. For not only had he to make up his mind to resistance, which to his nature was infinitely worse than it was to Griffith to face a raging mob, but he knew very well that it would almost inevitably produce his own ruin, and renew the disgrace out of which he was beginning to emerge. I did not—even while I prayed that he might do the right—guess at his own agony of supplication, carried on incessantly, day and night, sleeping and waking, that the Holy Spirit of might should brace his will and govern his tongue, and make him say the right thing at the right time, be the consequences what they might. No one, not constituted as he was, can guess at the anguish he endured. I knew no more. Clarence did not come home the next Saturday, to my mother's great vexation; but on Tuesday a small parcel was given to me, brought from our point of contact with the Bristol coach. It contained some pencils I had asked him to get, and a note marked PRIVATE. Here it is -

'DEAR EDWARD—I am summoned to town. Tooke has no doubt forestalled me. We have had some curious interviews, in which he first, as I told you, persuaded me out of my senses that it was all right, and then, finding me still dissatisfied, tried in a delicate fashion to apprise me that I had a claim to a share of the plunder. When I refused to appropriate anything without sanction from headquarters, he threatened me with the consequences of presumptuous interference. It came to bullying at last. I hardly know what I answered, but I don't think I gave in. Now, a sharp letter from old Frith recalls me. Say nothing at home; and whatever you do, do not betray Griff. He has more to lose than I. Help me in the true way, as you know how.—Ever yours, W. C. W.

I need not dwell on the misery of those days. It was well that my father had ruled that our letters should not be family property. Here were all the others discussing a proposed tour in the north of Devon, to be taken conjointly with the Fordyces, as soon as Griff should come home. My mother said it would do me good; she saw I was flagging, but she little guessed at the continual torment of anxiety, and my wonder at the warning about Griff.

At the end of the week came another letter.

'You need not speak yet. Papa and mamma will know soon enough. I brought down 150 pounds in specie, to be paid over to Tooke. He avers that only 130 pounds was received. What is my word worth against his? I am told that if I am not prosecuted it will only be out of respect to my father. I am not dismissed yet, but shall get notice as soon as letters come from Ireland. I have written, but it is not in the nature of things that Mr. Castleford should not accept such proofs as have been sent him. I have no hope, and shall be glad when it is over. The part of black sheep is not a pleasant one. Say not a word, and do not let my father come up. He could do no good, and to see him believing it all would be the last drop in the bucket.

N.B.—In this pass, nothing would be saved by bringing Griff into it, so be silent on your life. Innocence does not seem to be much comfort at present. Maybe it will come in time. I know you will not drop me, dear Ted, wherever I may be.'

Need I tell the distress of those days of suspense and silence, when my only solace was in being left alone, and in writing letters to Clarence which were mostly torn up again.

My horror was lest he should be driven to go off to the sea, which he loved so well, knowing, as nobody else did, the longing that sometimes seized him for it, a hereditary craving that curiously conflicted with the rest of his disposition; and, indeed, his lack was more of moral than of physical courage. It haunted me constantly that his entreaty that my father should not come to London was a bad sign, and that he would never face such another return home. And was I justified in keeping all this to myself, when my father's presence might save him from the flight that would indeed be the surrender of his character, and to the life of a common sailor? Never have I known such leaden days as these, yet the misery was not a tithe of what Clarence was undergoing.

I was right in my forebodings. Prosecution and a second return home in shame and disgrace were alike hideous to Clarence, and the present was almost equally terrible, for nobody at the office had any doubt of his guilt, and the young men who had sneered at his strictness and religious habits regarded him as an unmasked hypocrite, only waiting on sufferance till his greatly deceived patron should write to decide on the steps to be taken with him, while he knew he was thought to be brazening it out in hopes of again deceiving Mr. Castleford.

The sea began to exert its power over him, and he thought with longing of its freedom, as if the sails of the vessels were the wings of a dove to flee away and be at rest. He had no illusions as to the roughness of the life and companionship; but in his present mood, the frank rudeness and profanity of the sailors seemed preferable to his cramped life, and the scowls of his fellows; and he knew himself to have seamanship enough to rise quickly, even if he could not secure a mate's berth at first.

Mr. Castleford could not be heard from till the end of the week. Friday, Saturday came and not a word. That was the climax! When the consignment of cash, hitherto carried by Clarence to the Bank of England, was committed to another clerk, the very office boy sniggered, and the manager demonstratively waited to see him depart.

Unable to bear it any longer, he walked towards Wapping, bought a Southwester, examined the lists of shipping, and entered into conversation with one or two sailors about the vessels making up their crews; intending to go down after dark, to meet the skipper of a craft bound for Lisbon, who, he heard, was so much in want of a mate as perhaps to overlook the lack of testimonials, and at any rate take him on board on Sunday.

Going home to pick up a few necessaries, a book lent to him by Miss Newton came in his way, and he felt drawn to carry it home, and see her face for the last time.

All unconscious of his trouble and of his intentions, the good lady told him of her strong desire to hear a cele-brated preacher at a neighbouring church on the Sunday evening, but said that in her partial blindness and weak-ness, she was afraid to venture, unless he would have the extreme goodness, as she said, to take care of her. He saw that she wished it so much that he had not the heart to refuse, and he recollected likewise that very early on Monday morning would answer his purpose equally well.

It was the 7th of June. The Psalm was the 37th—the supreme lesson of patience. 'Hold thee still in the Lord; and abide patiently on Him; and He shall bring it to pass. He shall make thy righteousness as clear as the light, and thy just dealing as the noonday.'

The awful sense of desolation seemed to pass away under those words, with that gentle woman beside him. And the sermon was on 'Oh tarry thou the Lord's leisure; be

Charlotte M. Yonge

strong, and He shall comfort thine heart; and put thou thy trust in the Lord.'

Clarence remembered nothing but the text. But it was borne in upon him that his purpose of flight was 'the old story,'—cowardice and virtual distrust of the Lord, as well as absolute cruelty to us who loved him.

When he had deposited Miss Newton at her own door, he whispered thanks, and an entreaty for her prayers.

And then he went home, and fought the battle of his life, with his own horrible dread of Mr. Castleford's disappointment; of possible prosecution; of the shame at home; the misery of a life a second time blighted. He fought it out on his knees, many a time persuading himself that flight would not be a sin, then returning to the sense that it was a temptation of his worse self to be overcome. And by morning he knew that it would be a surrender of himself to his lower nature, and the evil spirit behind it; while, by facing the worst that could befall him, he would be falling into the hand of the Lord.

CHAPTER XXIV

AFTER THE TEMPEST

'Nor deem the irrevocable past
As wholly wasted, wholly vain,
If rising on its wrecks at last
To something nobler we attain.'

LONGFELLOW.

All the rest of the family were out, and I was relieved by being alone with my distress, not forced to hide it, when the door opened and 'Mr. Castleford' was announced. After one moment's look at me, one touch of my hand, he must have seen that I was faint with anxiety, and said, 'It is all right, Edward; I see you know all. I am come from Bristol to tell your father that he may be proud of his son Clarence.'

I don't know what I did. Perhaps I sobbed and cried, but the first words I could get out were, 'Does he know? Oh! it may be too late. He may be gone off to sea!' I cried, breaking out with my chief fear. Mr. Castleford looked astounded, then said, 'I trust not. I sent off a special messenger last night, as soon as I saw my way—'

Charlotte M. Yonge

Then I breathed a little more freely, and could understand what he was telling me, namely, that Tooke had accused Clarence of abstracting 20 pounds from the sum in his charge. The fellow accounted for it by explaining that young Winslow had been paying extravagant bills at a tavern, where the barmaid showed his presents, and boasted of her conquest. All this had been written to Mr. Castleford by his partner, and he was told that it was out of deference to himself that his protege was not in custody, nor had received notice of dismissal; but, no doubt, he would give his sanction to immediate measures, and communicate with the family.

The effect had been to make the good man hurry at once from the Giant's Causeway to Bristol, where he had arrived on Sunday, to investigate the books and examine the underlings. In the midst Tooke attempted to abscond, but he was brought back as he was embarking in an American vessel; and he then confessed the whole,—how speculation had led to dishonesty, and following evil customs not uncommon in other firms. Then, when the fugitive found that young Winslow was too acute to be blinded, and that it had been a still greater mistake to try to overcome his integrity, self-defence required his ruin, or at any rate his expulsion, before he could gain Mr. Castleford's ear.

Tooke really believed that the discreditable bills were the young man's own, and proofs of concealed habits of dissipation; but this excellent man had gone into the matter, repaired to the tradesfolk, learnt the date, and whose the accounts really were, and had even hunted up the barmaid, who was not married after all, and had no hesitation in avowing that her beau had been the handsome young Yeomanry lieutenant. Mr. Castleford had spent the greater part of Monday in this painful task, but had not been clear enough till quite late in the evening to despatch an express to his partner, and to Clarence, whom he desired to meet him here.

'He has acted nobly,' said our kind friend. 'His only error seems to have been in being too good a brother.'

This made me implore that nothing should be said about Griffith's bills, showing those injunctions of Clarence's which had so puzzled me, and explaining the circumstances.

Mr. Castleford hummed and hawed, and perhaps wished he had seen my father before me; but I prevailed at last, and when the others came in from their drive, there was nothing to alloy the intelligence that Clarence had shown rare discernment, as well as great uprightness, steadfastness, and moral courage.

My mother, when she had taken in the fact, actually shed tears of joy. Emily stood by me, holding my hand. My father said, 'It is all owing to you, Castleford, and the helping hand you gave the poor boy.'

'Nay,' was the answer, 'it seems to me that it was owing to his having the root of the matter in him to overcome his natural failings.'

Still, in all the rejoicing, my heart failed me lest the express should have come too late, and Clarence should be already on the high seas, for there had been no letter from him on Sunday morning. It was doubtful whether Mr. Castleford's messenger could reach London in time for tidings to come down by the coach—far less did we expect Clarence—and we had nearly finished the first course at dinner, when we heard the front door open, and a voice speaking to the butler. Emily screamed 'It's he! Oh mamma, may I?' and flew out into the hall, dragging in a pale, worn and weary wight, all dust and heat, having travelled down outside the coach on a broiling day, and walked the rest of the way. He looked quite bewildered at the rush at him; my father's 'Well done, Clarence,' and strong clasp; and my mother's fervent kiss, and muttered something about washing his hands.

Formal folks, such as we were, had to sit in our chairs; and when he came back apologising for not dressing, as he had left his portmanteau for the carrier, he looked so white and ill that we were quite shocked, and began to realise what he had suffered. He could not eat the food that was brought back for him, and allowed that his head was aching dreadfully; but, after a glass of wine had been administered, it was extracted that he had met Mr. Frith at the office door, and been gruffly told that Mr. Castleford was satisfied, and he might consider himself acquitted.

'And then I had your letter, sir, thank you,' said Clarence, scarcely restraining his tears.

'The thanks are on our side, my dear boy,' said Mr. Castleford. 'I must talk it over with you, but not till you have had a night's rest. You look as if you had not known one for a good while.'

Clarence gave a sort of trembling smile, not trusting himself to speak. Approbation at home was so new and strange to him that he could scarcely bear it, worn out as he was by nearly a month of doubt, distress, apprehension, and self-debate.

My mother went herself to hasten the preparation of his room, and after she had sent him to bed went again to satisfy herself that he was comfortable and not feverish. She came back wiping away a tear, and saying he had looked up at her just as when she had the three of us in our nursery cribs. In truth these two had seldom been so happy together since those days, though the dear mother, while thankful that he had not failed, was little aware of the conflict his resolution had cost him, and the hot journey and long walk came in for more blame for his exhaustion than they entirely deserved.

My father perhaps understood more of the trial; for when she came back, declaring that all that was needed was sleep, and forbidding me to go to my room before bedtime, he said he must bid the boy good-night.

And he spoke as his reserve would have never let him speak at any other time, telling Clarence how deeply thankful he felt for the manifestation of such truthfulness and moral courage as he said showed that the man had conquered the failings of the boy.

Nevertheless, when I retired for the night, it was to find Clarence asleep indeed, but most uneasily, tossing, moaning, and muttering broken sentences about 'disgracing his pennant,' 'never bearing to see mamma's face'—and the like. I thought it a kindness to wake him, and he started up. 'Ted, is it you? I thought I should never hear your dear old crutch again! Is it really all right'—then, sitting up and passing his hand over his face, 'I always mix it up with the old affair, and think the court-martial is coming again.'

'There's all the difference now.'

'Thank God! yes—He has dragged me through! But it did not seem so in one's sleep, nor waking neither—though sleep is worst, and happily there was not much of that! Sit down, Ted; I want to look at you. I can't believe it is not three weeks since I saw you last.'

We talked it all out, and I came to some perception of the

fearful ordeal it had been—first, in the decision neither to shut his eyes, nor to conceal that they were open; and then in the lack of presence of mind and the sense of confusion that always beset him when browbeaten and talked down, so that, in the critical contest with Tooke, he felt as if his feet were slipping from under him, and what had once been clear to him was becoming dim, so that he had only been assured that he had held his ground by Tooke's redoubled persuasions and increased anger. And for a clerk, whose years were only twenty-one, to oppose a manager, who had been in the service more than the whole of that space, was preposterous insolence, and likely to result in the utter ruin of his own prospects, and the character he had begun to retrieve. It was just after this, the real crisis, that he had the only dream which had not been misery and distress. In it she—she yonder—yes, the lady with the lamp, came and stood by him, and said, 'Be steadfast.'

'It was a dream,' said Clarence. 'She was not as she is in the mullion room, not crying, but with a sweet, sad look, almost like Miss Fordyce—if Miss Fordyce ever looked sad. It was only a dream.'

Yet it had so refreshed and comforted him that we have often since discussed whether the spirit really visited him, or whether this was the manner in which conscience and imagination acted on his brain. Indeed, he always believed that the dream had been either heaven-sent or heaven-permitted.

The die had been cast in that interview when he had let it be seen that he was dangerous, and could not be bought over. The after consequences had been the terrible distress and temptation I have before described, only most inade-quately. 'But that,' said Clarence, half smiling, 'only came of my being such a wretched creature as I am. There, dear old Miss Newton saved me—yes, she did—most unconsciously, dear old soul. Don't you remember how Griff used to say she maundered over the text. Well, she did it all the way home in my ear, as she clung to my arm—"Be strong, and He shall comfort thine heart." And then I knew my despair and determination to leave it all behind were a temptation—"the old story," as you told me, and I prayed God to help me, and just managed to fight it out. Thank God for her!'

If it had not been for that good woman, he would have been out of reach—already out in the river—before Mr. Castleford's messenger had reached London! He might call himself a poor creature—and certainly a man of harder, bolder stuff would not have fared so badly in the strife; but it always seemed to me in after years that much of what he called the poor creature—the old, nervous, timid, diffident self—had been shaken off in that desperate struggle, perhaps because it had really given him more self-reliance, and certainly inspired others with confidence in him.

We talked late enough to have horrified my mother, but I did not leave him till he was sleeping like a child, nor did he wake till I was leaving the room at the sound of the bell. It was alleged that it was the first time in his life that he had been late for prayers. Mr. Castleford said he was very glad, and my mother, looking severely at me, said she knew we had been talking all night, and then went off to satisfy herself whether he ought to be getting up.

There was no doubt on that score, for he was quite himself again, though he was, in looks and in weariness, just as if he had recovered from a bad illness, or, as he put it himself, he felt as tired and bruised as if he had been in a stiff gale. Mr. Castleford was sorry to be obliged to ask him to go through the whole matter with him in the study, and the result was that he was pronounced to have an admirable head for business, as well as the higher qualities that had been put to the test. After that his good friend insisted that he should have a long and complete holiday, at first proposing to take him to Ireland, but giving the notion up on hearing of our projected excursion to the north of Devon. Pending this, Clarence was, for nearly a week, fit for nothing but lying on the grass in the shade, playing with the cats and dogs, or with little Anne, looking over our drawings, listening to Wordsworth, our reigning idol,—and enjoying, with almost touching gratitude, the first approach to petting that had ever fallen to his share.

The only trouble on his mind was the Quarter-Session. Mr. Castleford would hardly have prosecuted an old employe, but Mr. Frith was furious, and resolved to make an example. Tooke had, however, so carefully entrenched himself that nothing could be actually made a subject of prosecution but the abstraction of the 20 pounds of which he had accused Clarence, who had to prove the having received and delivered it.

It was a very painful affair, and Tooke was sentenced to seven years' transportation. I believe he became a very rich and prosperous man in New South Wales, and founded a family. My father received warm compliments upon his sons, and Clarence had the new sensation of being honourably coupled with Griffith, though he laughed at the idea of mere honesty with fierce struggles being placed beside heroism with no struggle at all.

CHAPTER XXV

HOLIDAY-MAKING

'The child upon the mountain side
Plays fearless and at ease,
While the hush of purple evening
Spreads over earth and seas.
The valley lies in shadow,
But the valley lies afar;
And the mountain is a slope of light
Upreaching to a star.'

MENELLA SMEDLEY.

How pleasant it was to hear Griffith's cheery voice, as he swung himself down, out of a cloud of dust, from the top of the coach at the wayside stage-house, whither Clarence and I had driven in the new britshka to meet him. While the four fine coach-horses were led off, and their successors harnessed in almost the twinkling of an eye, Griff was with us; and we did nothing but laugh and poke fun at each other all the way home, without a word of graver matters.

I was resolved, however, that Griff should know how terribly his commission had added to Clarence's danger, and how carefully the secret had been guarded; and the first time I could get him alone, I told him the whole.

The effect was one of his most overwhelming fits of laughter. 'Poor old Bill! To think of his being accused of gallanting about with barmaids!' (an explosion at every pause) 'and revelling with officers! Poor old Bill! it was as bad as Malvolio himself.'

When, indignant at the mirth excited by what had nearly cost us so dear, I observed that these items had nearly turned the scale against our brother, Griff demanded how we could have been such idiots as not to have written to him; I might at least have had the sense to do so. As to its doing him harm at Hillside, Parson Frank was no fool, and knew what men were made of! Griff would have taken the risk, come at once, and thrust the story down the fellow's throat (as indeed he would have done). The idea of Betsy putting up with a pious young man like Bill, whose only flame had ever been old Miss Newton! And he roared again at the incongruous pair. 'Oh, wasn't she married after all, the hussy? She always had a dozen beaux, and professed to be on the point of putting up her banns; so if the earrings were not a wedding present, they might have been, ought to have been, and would be some time or other.'

Then he patted me, and declared there was no occasion for my disgusted looks, for no one knew better than himself that he had the best brace of brothers in existence, wanting in nothing but common sense and knowledge of the world. As to Betsy—faugh! I need not make myself uneasy about her; she knew what a civil word was worth much better than I did.

He showed considerable affection for Clarence after a fashion of his own, which we three perfectly understood, and preferred to anything more conventional. Griff was always delightful, and he was especially so on that vacation, when every one was in high spirits; so that the journey is, as I look back on it, like a spot of brilliant sunshine in the distant landscape.

Mrs. Fordyce kept house with her father-in-law, little Anne, and Martyn, whose holidays began a week after we had started. The two children were allowed to make a desert island and a robbers' cave in the beech wood; and the adventures which their imaginations underwent there completely threw ours into the shade.

The three ladies and I started in the big Hillside open carriage, with my brothers on the box and the two fathers on horseback. Frank Fordyce was a splendid rider, as indeed was the old rector, who had followed the hounds, made a leap over a fearful chasm, still known as the Parson's Stride, and had been an excellent shot. The renunciation of field sports had been a severe sacrifice to Frank Fordyce, and showed of what excellent stuff he was made. He used to say that it was his own fault that he had to give them up; another man would have been less engrossed by them. Though he only read by fits and starts when his enthusiasm was excited, he was thorough, able, and acute, and his intelligence and sympathy were my father's best compensation for the loss of London society.

The two riders were a great contrast. Mr. Winslow had the thoroughly well-appointed, somewhat precise, and highly-polished air of a barrister, and a thin, somewhat worn and colourless face, with grizzled hair and white whiskers; and though he rode well, with full command of his horse, he was old enough to have chosen Chancery for her sterling qualities. Parson Frank, on the other hand, though a thorough gentleman, was as ruddy and weather-browned as any farmer, and—albeit his features were handsome and refined, and his figure well poised and athletic—he lost something of dignity by easiness of gesture and carelessness of dress, except on state occasions, when he discarded his beloved rusty old coat and Oxford mixture trousers, and came out magnificent enough for an arch-deacon, if not an archbishop; while his magnificent horse, Cossack, was an animal that a sporting duke might have envied.

Nothing ever tired that couple, but my father had stipulated for exchanges with Griffith. On these occasions it almost invariably happened that there was a fine view for Ellen to see, so that she was exalted to the box with Griffith to show it to her, and Chancery was consigned to Clarence. Griff was wont to say that Chancery deserved her name, and that he would defy the ninety-ninth part of a tailor to come to harm with her; but Clarence was utterly unpractised in riding, did not like it, was tormented lest Cossack's antics should corrupt Chancery, and was mortally afraid of breaking the knees of the precious mare. Not all Parson Frank's good advice and kindly raillery would induce him to risk riding her on a descent; and as our travels were entirely up and down hill, he was often left leading her far behind, in hot sun or misty rain, and then would come cantering hastily up, reckless of parallels with John Gilpin, and only anxious to be in time to help me out at the halting-place; but more than once only coming in when the beefsteaks were losing their first charm, and then good-humouredly serving as the general butt for his noble horsemanship. Did any one fully comprehend how much pleasanter our journey was through the presence of one person entirely at the service of the others? For my own part, it made an immense difference to have one pair of strong arms and dextrous well-accustomed hands always at my service, enabling me to accomplish what no one else, kind as all were, would have ventured on letting me attempt. Primarily, he was my devoted slave; but he was at the beck and call of every one, making the inquiries, managing the bargains, going off in search of whatever was wanting—taking in fact all the 'must be dones' of the journal. The contemplation of Cossack and Chancery being rubbed down, and devouring their oats was so delightful to Frank Fordyce and Griffith that they seldom wished to shirk it; but if there were any more pleasing occupation, it was a matter of course that Clarence should watch to see that the ostlers did their duty by the animals—an obsolete ceremony, by the bye. He even succeeded in hunting up and hiring a side saddle when the lovers, with the masterfulness of their nature, devised appropriating the horses at all the most beautiful places, in spite of Frank's murmur, 'What will mamma say?' But, as Griff said, it was a real mercy, for Ellen was infinitely more at her ease with Chancery than was Clarence. Then Emily had Clarence to walk up the hills with her, and help her in botany—her special department in our tour. Mine was sketching, Ellen's, keeping the journal, though we all shared in each other's work at times; and Griff, whose line was decidedly love-making, interfered considerably with us all, especially with our chronicler. I spare you the tour, young people; it lies before me on the table, profusely illustrated and written in many hands. As I turn it over, I see noble Dunster on its rock; Clarence leading Chancery down Porlock Hill; Parson Frank in vain pursuit of his favourite ancient hat over that wild and windy waste, the sheep running away from him; a boat tossing at lovely Minehead; a 'native' bargaining over a crab with my mother; the wonderful Valley of Rocks, and many another scene, ludicrous or grand; for, indeed, we were for ever taking the one step between the sublime and the ridiculous! I am inclined to believe it is as well worth reading as many that have rushed into print, and it is full of precious reminiscences to Emily and me; but the younger generation may judge for itself, and it would be an interruption here. The country we saw was of utterly unimagined beauty to the untravelled eyes of most of us. I remember Ellen standing on Hartland Point, with her face to the infinite expanse of the Atlantic, and waving back Griff with 'Oh, don't speak to me.' Yet the sea was a delight above all to my mother and Clarence. To them it was a beloved friend; and magnificent as was Lynmouth, wonderful as was Clovelly, and glorious as was Hartland, I believe they would equally have welcomed the waves if they had been on the flattest of muddy shores! The ripple, plash, and roar were as familiar voices, the salt smell as native air; and my mother never had thawed so entirely towards Clarence as when she found him the only person who could thoroughly participate her feeling.

At Minehead they stayed out, walking up and down together in the summer twilight till long after every one else was tired out, and had gone in; and when at last they appeared she was leaning on Clarence's arm, an unprecedented spectacle!

At Appledore, the only place on that rugged coast where boating tempted them, there was what they called a pretty little breeze, but quite enough to make all the rest of us decline venturing out into Bideford bay. They, however, found a boatman and made a trip, which was evidently such enjoyment to them, that my father, who had been a little restless and uneasy all the time, declared on their return that he felt quite jealous of Neptune, and had never known what a cruelty he was committing in asking a sea-nymph to marry a London lawyer.

Mr. Fordyce told him he was afraid of being like the fisherman who wedded a mermaid, and made Ellen tell the story in her own pretty way; but while we were laughing over it, I saw my mother steal her hand into my father's and give it a strong grasp. Such gestures, which she denominated pawing, when she witnessed them in Emily, were so alien to her in general that no doubt this little action was infinitely expressive to her husband. She was wonderfully softened, and Clarence implied to me that it was the first time she had ever seemed to grieve for him more than she despised him, or to recognise his deprivation more than his disgrace,—implied, I say, for the words he used were little more than—'You can't think how nice she was to me.'

The regaining of esteem and self-respect was lessening Clarence's bashfulness, and bringing out his powers of conversation, so that he began to be appreciated as a pleasant companion, answering Griff's raillery in like fashion, and holding his own in good-natured repartee. Mr. Fordyce got on excellently with him in their tete-a-tetes (who would not with Parson Frank?), and held him in higher estimation than did Ellen. To her, honesty was common, tame, and uninteresting in comparison with heroism; and Griff's vague statement that Clarence was the best brother in the world did not go for much. Emily and I longed to get the two better acquainted, but it did not become possible while Griff absorbed the maiden as his exclusive property.

The engagement was treated as an avowed and settled thing, though I do not know that there had been a formal ratification by the parents; but in truth Mrs. Fordyce must have tacitly yielded her consent when she permitted her daughter to make the journey under the guardianship of Parson Frank. After a walk in the ravine of Lynton, we became aware of a ring upon Ellen's finger; and Emily was allowed at night to hear how and when it had been put on.

Ellen only slightly deepened her lovely carnation tints when her father indulged in a little tender teasing and lamentation over himself. She was thoroughly happy and proud of her hero, and not ashamed of owning it.

There was one evening when she and I were sitting with our sketchbooks in the shade on the beech at Ilfracombe, while the rest had gone, some to bathe, the others to make purchases in the town. We had been condoling with one another over the impossibility of finding anything among our water-colours that would express the wondrous tints before our eyes.

'No, nothing can do it,' I said at last; 'we can only make a sort of blot to assist our memories.'

'Sunshine outside and in!' said Ellen. 'The memory of such days as these can never fade away,—no, nor thankfulness for them, I hope.'

Something then passed about the fact that it was quite possible to go on in complete content in a quiet monotonous life, in an oyster-like way, till suddenly there was an unveiling and opening of unimagined capacities of enjoyment—as by a scene like this before us, by a great poem, an oratorio, or, as I supposed, by Niagara or the Alps. Ellen put it—'Oh! and by feelings for the great and good!' Dear girl, her colour deepened, and I am sure she meant her bliss in her connection with her hero. Presently, however, she passed on to saying how such revelations of unsuspected powers of enjoyment helped one to enter into what was meant by 'Eye hath not seen, nor ear heard, neither hath it entered into the heart of man to conceive, the things that God hath prepared for them that love him.' Then there was a silence, and an inevitable quoting of the Christian Year, the guide to all our best thoughts -

'But patience, there may come a time.'

And then a turning to the 'Ode to Immortality,' for Wordsworth was our second leader, and we carried him on our tour as our one secular book, as Keble was our one religious book. We felt that the principal joy of all this beauty and delight was because there was something beyond. Presently Ellen said, prettily and shyly, 'I am sure all this has opened much more to me than I ever thought of. I always used to be glad that we had no brothers, because our cousins were not always pleasant with us; but now I have learnt what valuable possessions they are,' she added, with the sweetest, prettiest glance of her bright eyes.

I ventured to say that I was glad she said they, and hoped it was a sign that she was finding out Clarence.

'I have found out that I behaved so ill to him that I have been ashamed ever since to look at him or speak to him,' said Ellen; 'I long to ask his pardon, but I believe that would distress him more than anything.'

In which she was right; and I was able to tell her of the excuses there had been for the poor boy, how he had suffered, and how he had striven to conquer his failings; and she replied that the words 'Judge not, that ye be not judged,' always smote her with the remembrance of her disdainfully cantering past him. There was a tear on her eye-lashes, and it drew from me an apology for having brought a painful recollection into our bright day.

'There must be shade to throw up the lights,' she said, with her sparkling look.

Was it shade that we never fell into one of these grave talks when Griffith was present, and that the slightest approach to them was sure to be turned by him into jest?

Charlotte M. Yonge

We made our journey a little longer than we intended, crossing the moors so as to spend a Sunday at Exeter; but Frank Fordyce left us, not liking to give his father the entire duty of a third Sunday.

Emily says she has come to have a superstition that extensions of original plans never turn out well, and certainly some of the charm of our journey departed with the merry, genial Parson Frank. Our mother was more anxious about Ellen, and put more restrictions on the lovers than when the father was present to sanction their doings. Griffith absolutely broke out against her in a way he had never ventured before, when she forbade Ellen's riding with him when he wanted to hire a horse at Lydford and take an excursion on the moor before joining us at Okehampton.

My father looked up, and said, 'Griffith, I am surprised at you.' He was constrained to mutter some apology, and I believe Ellen privately begged my mother's pardon, owning her to have been quite right; but, by the dear girl, the wonderful cascade and narrow gorge were seen through swollen eyes. And poor Clarence must have had a fine time of it when Griffith had to ride off with him faute de mieux.

All was cleared off, however, when we met again, for Griff's storms were very fleeting, and Ellen treated him as if she had to make her own peace with him. She sacrificed her own enjoyment of Exeter Cathedral to go about with him when he had had enough of it, but on Sunday afternoon she altogether declined to walk with him till after the second service. He laughed at her supposed passion for sacred music, and offered to wait with her to hear the anthem from the nave. 'No,' she said, 'that would be amusing ourselves instead of worshipping.'

'We've done our devoir in that way already,' said Griff. 'Paid our dues.'

'One can't,' cried Ellen, with an eager look. 'One longs to do all the more when He has just let us have such a taste of His beautiful things.'

'ONE, perhaps, when one is a little saint,' returned Griff.

'Oh don't, Griff! I'm not THAT; but you know every one wants all the help and blessing that can be got. And then it is so delightful!'

He gave a long whistle. 'Every one to his taste,' he said; 'especially you ladies.'

He did come to the Cathedral with us, but he had more than half spoilt this last Sunday. Did he value her for what was best in her, or was her influence raising him?

CHAPTER XXVI

C. MORBUS, ESQ.

'Forgot were hatred, wrongs, and fears,
The plaintive voice alone she hears,
Sees but the dying man.'

SCOTT.

C. Morbus, Esq. Such was the card that some wicked wag, one of Clarence's fellow-clerks probably, left at his lodgings in the course of the epidemic which was beginning its ravages even while we were upon our pleasant journey—a shade indeed to throw out the light.

In these days, the tidings of a visitation of cholera are heard with compassion for crowded towns, but without special alarm for ourselves or our friends, since its conditions and the mode of combating it have come to be fairly understood.

In 1832, however, it was a disease almost unknown and unprecedented except in its Indian abode, whence it had advanced city by city, seaport by seaport, sweeping down multitudes before it; nor had science yet discovered how to encounter or forestall it. We heard of it in a helpless sort of way, as if it had been the plague or the Black Death, and thought of its victims as doomed.

That terrible German engraving, 'Death as a Foe,' which represents the grisly form as invading a ballroom in Paris, is an expression of the feeling with which the scourge was regarded on that first occasion. Two Years Ago gives some notion of the condition of things in 1849, but by that time there had been some experience, and means of prevention were better understood. On the alarm in that year there was a great inspection of cottages throughout Earlscombe and Hillside, but in 1832 there was no notion of such precautions. Nevertheless, on neither visitation, nor any subsequent one, has the disease come nearer to us than Bristol.

As far as memory serves me, the idea was that wholesome food, regular habits, and cleanliness were some protection, but one locality might be as dangerous as another. There had been cases in London all the spring, but no special anxiety was felt when Clarence returned to his work in the end of July, much refreshed and invigorated by his holiday, and with the understanding that he was to have a rise in position and salary on Mr. Castleford's return from Ireland, where he was still staying with his wife's relations. Clarence was received at the office with a kind of shamefaced cordiality, as if every one would fain forget the way in which he had been treated; and he was struck by finding that all the talk was of the advances of the cholera, chiefly at Rotherhithe. And a great shock awaited him. He went, as soon as business hours were over, to thank good old Miss Newton for the comfort and aid she had unwittingly given him, and to tell her from what she had saved him. Alas! it was the last benefit she was ever to confer on her old pupil. At the door he was told by a weeping, terrified maid that she was very ill with cholera, and that no hope was given. He tried to send up a message, but she was in a state of collapse and insensible; and when he inquired the next morning, the gentle spirit had passed away.

He attended her funeral that same evening. Griff said it was a proof how your timid people will do the most foolhardy things; but Clarence always held that the good woman had really done more for him than any one in actually establishing a contact, so to say, between his spirit and external truth, and he thought no mark of respect beyond her deserts. She was a heavy loss to him, for no one else in town gave him the sense of home kindness; and there was much more to depress him, for several of his Sunday class were dead, and the school had been broken up for the time, while the heats and the fruits of August contributed to raise the mortality.

His return had released a couple more clerks for their holiday; it was a slack time of year, with less business in hand than usual, and the place looked empty. Mr. Frith worked on as usual, but preserved an ungracious attitude, as though he were either still incredulous or, if convinced against his will, resolved that 'that prig of a Winslow' should not presume upon his services. Altogether the poor fellow was quite unhinged, and wrote such dismal bills of mortality, and meek, resigned forebodings that my father was almost angry, declaring that he would frighten himself into the sickness; yet I suppressed a good deal, and never told them of the last will and testament in which he distributed his possessions amongst us. Griff said he had a great mind to go and shake old Bill up and row him well, but he never did.

More than a week passed by, two of Clarence's regular days for writing, but no letter came. My mother grew uneasy, and talked of writing to Mrs. Robson, or, as we still called her, Gooch; but it was doubtful whether the answer would contain much information, and it was quite certain that any ill tidings would be sent to us.

At last we did hear, and found, as we had foreboded, that the letter had not been written for fear of alarming us, or carrying infection, though Clarence underlined the words 'I am perfectly well.'

Having to take a message into the senior partner's room, Clarence had found the old man crouched over the table, writhing in the unmistakable grip of the deadly enemy. No one else was available; Clarence had to collect himself, send for the doctor, and manage the conveyance of the patient to his rooms, which fortunately adjoined the office; for, through all his influx of wealth, Mr. Frith had retained the habits and expenditure of his early struggling days. His old housekeeper and her drudge showed themselves terrified out of their senses, and as incapable as unwilling. Naval experience, and waiting on me, had taught Clarence helpfulness and handiness; and though this was the very thing that had appalled his imagination, he seemed, as he said afterwards, 'to have got beyond his fright' to the use of his commonsense. And when at last the doctor came, and talked of finding a nurse, if possible, for they were scarce articles, the sufferer only entreated between his paroxysms, 'Stay, Winslow! Is Winslow there? Don't go! Don't leave me!'

No nurse was to be found, but to Clarence's amazement Gooch arrived. He had sent by the office boy to explain his absence; and before night the faithful woman descended on him, intending, as in her old days of authority, simply to put Master Clarry out of harm's way, and take the charge upon herself. Then, as he proved unmanageable and would not leave his patient, neither would she leave him, and through the frightful night that ensued, there was quite employment enough for them

Charlotte M. Yonge

both. Gooch fully thought the end would come before morning, and was murmuring something about a clergyman, but was cut short by a sharp prohibition. However, detecting Clarence's lips moving, the old man said, 'Eh! speak it out!' 'And with difficulty, feeling as if I were somebody else,' said Clarence, 'I did get out some short words of prayer. It seemed so awful for him to die without any.'

When the doctor came in early morning, the watchers were astonished to hear that their charge had taken a turn for the better, and might recover if their admirable care were continued. The doctor had brought a nurse; but Mr. Frith would not let her come into the room, and there was plenty of need for her elsewhere.

Several days of unremitting care followed, during which Clarence durst not write to us, so little were the laws of infection understood. Good Mrs. Robson stayed all the time, and probably saved Clarence from falling a victim to his zeal, for she looked after him as anxiously as after the sick man; and with a wondering and thankful heart, he found himself in full health, when both were set free to return home. Clarence had written at the beginning of the illness to the only relations of whose existence or address he was aware, an old sister, Mrs. Stevens, and a young great-nephew in the office at Liverpool; and the consequence was the arrival of a sour-looking, old widow sister, who came to take charge of the convalescence, and, as the indignant Gooch overheard her say, 'to prevent that young Winslow from getting round him.'

There were no signs of such a feat having been performed, when, the panic being past, my father went up to London with Griffith, who was to begin eating his terms at the Temple. He was to share Clarence's lodgings, for the Robsons had plenty of room, and Gooch was delighted to extend her cares to her special favourite, as she already reigned over Clarence's wardrobe and table as entirely as in nursery days; and, to my great exultation, my father said it would be good for Griffith to be with his brother; and, moreover, we should hear of the latter. Nothing could be a greater contrast than his rare notifications or requests, scrawled on a single side of the quarto sheet, with Clarence's regular weekly lines of clerkly manuscript, telling all that could interest any of us, and covering every available flap up to the blank circle left for the trim red seal.

Promotion had come to Clarence in the natural course of seniority, and a small sum, due to him on his coming of age, was invested in the house of business, so that the two brothers could take between them all the Robsons' available rooms. Clarence's post was one of considerable trust; but there were no tokens of special favour, except that Mr. Frith was more civil to my father than usual, and when he heard of the arrangement about the lodgings, he snarled out, 'Hm! Law student indeed! Don't let him spoil his brother!'

Which was so far an expression of gratitude that it showed that he considered that there was something to be spoilt. Mr. Castleford, however, showed real satisfaction in the purchase of a share in the concern for Clarence. His own eldest son inherited a good deal of his mother's Irish nature, and was evidently unfit to be anything but a soldier, and the next was so young that he was glad to have a promising and trustworthy young man, from whom a possible joint head of the firm might be manufactured.

Charlotte M. Yonge

CHAPTER XXVII

PETER'S THUNDERBOLT

If you can separate yourself and your misdemeanours you are welcome to the house; if not, an it would please you to take leave of her, she is very willing to bid you farewell.'

TWELFTH NIGHT.

In the early summer of 1833, we had the opportunity of borrowing a friend's house in Portman Square for six weeks, and we were allowed to take Ellen with us for introduction to the Admiral and other old friends, while we were to make acquaintance with her connections—the family of Sir Horace Lester, M.P.

We were very civil; but there were a good many polite struggles for the exclusive possession of Ellen, whom both parties viewed as their individual right; and her unselfish good-humour and brightness must have carried her over more worries than we guessed at the time.

She had stayed with the Lesters before, but in schoolroom days. They were indolent and uninterested, and had never shown her any of the permanent wonders of London, despising these as only fit for country cousins, whereas we had grown up to think of them with intelligent affection. To me, however, much was as new as to Ellen. Country life had done so much for me that I could venture on what I had never attempted before. The Admiral said it was getting away from doctors and their experiments, but I had also done with the afflictions of attempts at growth in wrong directions. Old friends did not know me, and more than once, as I sat in the carriage, addressed me for one of my brothers—a compliment which, Griff said, turned my head. Happily I was too much accustomed to my own appearance, and people were too kind, for me to have much shyness on that score. Our small dinner parties were great enjoyment to me, and the two girls were very happy in their little gaieties.

Braham and Catalani, Fanny Kemble, and Turner's landscapes at his best, rise in my memory as supreme delights and revelations in their different lines, and awakening trains of thought; and then there was that entertainment which Griffith and Clarence gave us in their rooms, when they regaled us with all the delicacies of the season, and Peter and Gooch looked all pride and hospitality! The dining-parlour, or what served as such, was Griff's property, as any one could see by the pictures of horses, dogs, and ladies, the cups, whips, and boxing-gloves that adorned it; the sitting-room had tokens of other occupation, in Clarence's piano, window-box of flowers, and his one extravagance in engravings from Raffaelle, and a marine water-colour or two, besides all my own attempts at family portraits, with a case of well-bound books. Those two rooms were perfectly redolent of their masters—I say it literally—for the scent of flowers was in Clarence's room, and in Griff's, the odour of cigars had not wholly been destroyed even by much airing. For in those days it was regarded by parents and guardians as an objectionable thing.

Peter was radiant on that occasion; but a few evenings later, when all were gone to an evening party except my father and myself, Mr. Robson was announced as wishing to speak to Mr. Winslow. After the civilities proper to the visit of an old servant had passed, he entered with obvious reluctance on the purpose of his visit, namely, his dissatisfaction with Griff as a lodger. His wife, he said, would not have had him speak, she was THAT attached to Mr. Griffith, it couldn't be more if he was her own son; nor was it for want of liking for the young gentleman on his part, as had known him from a boy, 'but the wife of one's bosom must come first, sir, as stands to reason, and it's for the good of the young gentleman himself, and his family, as some one should speak. I never said one word against it when she would not be satisfied without running the risk of her life after Mr. Clarence; hattending of Mr. Frith in the cholery. That was only her dooty, sir, and I have never a word to say against dooty: but I cannot see her nearly wore out, and for no good to nobody.'

It appeared that Mrs. Robson was 'pretty nigh wore out, a setting up for Mr. Griffith's untimely hours.' 'He laughed and coaxed—what I calls cajoling—did Mr. Griff, to get a latch-key; but we knows our dooty too well for that, and Mrs. Winslow had made us faithfully promise, when Master Clarence first came to us, that he should never have a latch-key,—Mr. Clarence, as had only been five times later than eleven o'clock, and then he was going to dine with Mr. Castleford, or to the theayter, and spoke about it beforehand. If he was not reading to poor Miss Newton, as was gone, or with some of his language-masters, he was setting at home with his books and papers, not giving no trouble to nobody, after he had had his bit of bread and cheese and glass of beer to his supper.'

Ay, Peter knew what young gentlemen was. He did not

expect to see them all like poor Master Clarence, as had had his troubles; the very life knocked out of him in his youth, as one might say. Indeed Peter would be pleased to see him a bit more sprightly, and taking more to society and hamusements of his hage. Nor would there be any objection if the late 'ours was only once a week or so, and things was done in a style fitting the family; but when it came to mostly every night, often to two or three o'clock, it was too much for Mrs. Robson, for she would never go to bed, being mortal afraid of fire, and not always certain that Mr. Griffith was—to say—fit to put out his candle. 'What do you mean, Peter?' thundered my father, whose brow had been getting more and more furrowed every moment. 'Say it out!—Drunk?'

'Well sir, no, no, not to say that exactly, but a little excited, sir, and women is timid. No sir, not to call intoxicated.'

'No, that's to come,' muttered my father. 'Has this often happened?'

Peter did not think that it had been noticed more than three times at the most; but he went on to offer his candid and sensible advice that Mr. Griffith should be placed in a family where there was a gentleman or lady who would have some hauthority, and could not be put aside with his good-'umoured haffability—'You're an old fogy, Peter.' 'Never mind, Nursey, I'll be a good boy next time,' and the like. 'It is a disadvantage you see, sir, to have been in his service, and 'tis for the young gentleman's own good as I speaks; but it would be better if he were somewheres else—unless you would speak to him, sir.'

To the almost needless question whether Clarence had been with his brother on these occasions, there was a most decided negative. He had never gone out with Griffith

220   Charlotte M. Yonge

except once to the theatre, and to dine at the Castlefords, and at first he had sat up for his return, 'but it led to words between the young gentlemen,' said Peter, whose confidences were becoming reckless; and it appeared that when Clarence had found that Gooch would not let him spare her vigil, he had obeyed her orders and ceased to share it.

Peter was thanked for the revelations, which had been a grievous effort to him, and dismissed. My father sat still in great distress and perplexity, asking me whether Clarence had ever told me anything of this, and I had barely time to answer 'No' before Clarence himself came in, from what Peter called his language-master. He was taking lessons in French and Spanish, finding a knowledge of these useful in business. To his extreme distress, my father fell on him at once, demanding what he knew of the way Griffith was spending his time, 'coming home at all sorts of hours in a disreputable condition. No prevarication, sir,' he added, as the only too familiar look of consternation and bewilderment came over Clarence's face. 'You are doing your brother no good by conniving at his conduct. Speak truth, if you can,' he added, with more cruelty than he knew, in his own suffering.

'Sir,' gasped Clarence, 'I know Griff often comes home after I am in bed, but I do not know the exact time, nor anything more.'

'Is this all you can tell me? Really all?'

'All I know—that is—of my own knowledge,' said Clarence, recovering a little, but still unable to answer without hesitation, which vexed my father.

'What do you mean by that? Do you hear nothing?'

'I am afraid,' said Clarence, 'that I do not see as much of him as I had hoped. He is not up till after I have to be at our place, and he does not often spend an evening at home. He is such a popular fellow, and has so many friends and engagements.'

'Ay, and of what sort? Can't you tell? or will you not? I sent him up to you, thinking you a steady fellow who might influence him for good.'

The colour rushed into Clarence's face, as he answered, looking up and speaking low, 'Have I not forfeited all such hopes?'

'Nonsense! You've lived down that old story long ago. You would make your mark, if you only showed a little manliness and force of character. Griffith was always fond of you. Can't you do anything to hinder him from ruining his own life and that sweet girl's happiness?'

'I would—I would give my life to do so!' exclaimed Clarence, in warm, eager tones. 'I have tried, but he says I know nothing about it, and it is very dull at our rooms for him. I have got used to it, but you can't expect a fellow like Griff to stay at home, with no better company than me, and do nothing but read law.'

'Then you DO know,' began my father; but Clarence, with full self-possession, said, 'I think you had better ask me no more questions, papa. I really know nothing, or hardly anything, personally of his proceedings. I went to one supper with him, after going to the play, and did not fancy it; besides, it almost unfitted me for my morning's work; nor does it answer for me to sit up for him—it only vexes him, as if I were watching him.'

'Did you ever see him come home showing traces

of excess?'

'No!' said Clarence, 'I never saw!' and, under a stern, distressed look, 'Once I heard tones that—that startled me, and Mrs. Robson has grumbled a good deal—but I think Peter takes it for more than it is worth.'

'I see,' said my father more gently; 'I will not press you farther. I believe I ought to be glad that these habits are only hearsay to you.'

'As far as I can see,' said Clarence diffidently, but quite restored to himself, 'Griff is only like most of his set, young men who go into society.'

'Oh!' said my father, in a 'that's your opinion' kind of tone; and as at that moment the yell of a newsboy was heard in the street, he exclaimed that he must go and get an evening paper. Clarence made a step to go instead, but was thrust back, as apparently my father merely wanted an excuse for rushing into the open air to recover the shock or to think it over.

Clarence gave a kind of groan, and presently exclaimed, 'If only untruth were not such a sin!' and, on my exclamation of dismay, he added, 'I don't think a blowing up ever does good!'

'But this state of things should not last.'

'It will not. It would have come to an end without Peter's springing this mine. Griff says he can't stand Gooch any longer! And really she does worry him intolerably.'

'Peter professed to come without her knowledge or consent.'

'Exactly so. It will almost break the good old soul's heart for Griff to leave her; but she expects to have him in hand as if he was in the nursery. She is ever so much worse than she was with me, and he is really good-nature itself to laugh off her nagging as he does—about what he chooses to put on, or eating, or smoking, or leaving his room untidy, as well as other things.'

'And those other things? Do you suspect more than you told papa?'

'It amounts to no more. Griff likes amusement, and everybody likes him—that's all. Yes, I know my father read law ten hours a day, but his whole nature and circumstances were different. I don't believe Griff could go on in that way.'

'Not with such a hope before him? You would, Clarence.'

His face and not his tongue answered me, but he added, 'Griff is sure of THAT without so much labour and trouble.'

'And do you see so little of him?'

'I can't help it. I can't keep his hours and do my work. Yes, I know we are drifting apart; I wish I could help it, but being coupled up together makes it rather worse than better. It aggravates him, and he will really get on better without Gooch to worry him, and thrust my droning old ways down his throat,—as if Prince Hal could bear to be twitted with "that sober boy, Lord John of Lancaster." Not,' he added, catching himself up, 'that I meant to compare him to the madcap Prince. He is the finest of fellows, if they only would let him alone.'

And that was all I could get from Clarence.

CHAPTER XXVIII

A SQUIRE OF DAMES

'Spited with a fool-
Spited and angered both.'

CYMBELINE.

This long stay of Ellen's in our family had made our
fraternal relations with her nearer and closer. Familiarity
had been far from lessening our strong feeling for her
goodness and sweetness. Emily, who knew her best, used
to confide to me little instances of the spirit of devotion
and self-discipline that underlay all her sunny gaiety—
how she never failed in her morning's devout readings;
how she learnt a verse or two of Scripture every day, and
persuaded Emily to join with her in repeating it ere they
went downstairs for their evening's pleasure; how she had
set herself a little task of plain work for the poor, which
she did every day in her own room; and the like dutiful
habits, which seemed, as it were, to help her to keep
herself in hand, and not be carried away by what was a
whirl of pleasure to her, though a fashionable young lady
would have despised its mildness.

Indeed Lady Peacock, with whom we exchanged calls,

made no secret of her compassion when she found how many parties the ladies were NOT going to; and Ellen's own relations, the Lesters, would have taken her out almost every night if she had not staunchly held to her promise to her mother not to go out more than three evenings in the week, for Mrs. Fordyce knew her to be delicate, and feared late hours for her. The vexation her cousins manifested made her feel the more bound to give them what time she could, at hours when Griffith was not at liberty. She did not like them to be hurt, and jealous of us, or to feel forsaken, and she tried to put her affection for us on a different footing by averring that 'it was not the same kind of thing—Emily was her sister.'

One day she had gone to luncheon with the Lesters in Cavendish Square, and was to be called for in the carriage by me, on the way to take up the other two ladies, who were shopping in Regent Street.

Ellen came running downstairs, with her cheeks in a glow under the pink satin lining of her pretty bonnet, and her eyes sparkling with indignation, which could not but break forth.

'I don't know how I shall ever go there again!' she exclaimed; 'they have no right to say such things!' Then she explained. Mary and Louisa had been saying horrid things about Griffith—her Griff! It was always their way. Think how Horace had made her treat Clarence! It was their way and habit to tease, and call it fun, and she had never minded it before; but this was too bad. Would not I put it in her power to give a flat contradiction, such as would make them ashamed of themselves?

Contradict what?

Then it appeared that the Misses Lester had laughed at

her, who was so very particular and scrupulous, for having taken up with a regular young man about town. Oh no, THEY did not think much of it—no doubt he was only just like other people; only the funny thing was that it should be Ellen, for whom it was always supposed that no saint in the calendar, no knight in all the Waverley novels, would be good enough! And then, on her hot desire to know what they meant, they quoted John, the brother in the Guards, as having been so droll about poor Ellen's perfect hero, and especially at his straight-laced Aunt Fordyce having been taken in,—but of course it was the convenience of joining the estates, and it was agreeable to see that your very good folk could wink at things like other people in such a case. Then, when Ellen fairly drove her inquiries home, in her absolute trust of confuting all slanders, she was told that Griffith did, what she called 'all sorts of things—billiards and all that.' And even that he was always running after a horrid Lady Peacock, a gay widow.

'They went on in fun,' said Ellen, 'and laughed the more when—yes, I am afraid I did—I lost my temper. No, don't say I well might, I know I ought not; but I told them I knew all about Lady Peacock, and that you were all old friends, even before he rescued her from the Bristol riots and brought her home to Chantry House; and that only made Mary merrier than ever, and say, "What, another distressed damsel? Take care, Ellen; I would not trust such a squire of dames." And then Louisa chimed in, "Oh no, you see this Peacock dame was only conducted, like Princess Micomicona and all the rest of them, to the feet of his peerless Dulcinea!" And then I heard the knock, and I was never so glad in my life!'

'Well!' I could not help remarking, 'I have heard of women's spitefulness, but I never believed it till now.'

'I really don't think it was altogether what you call malice, so much as the Lester idea of fun,' said Ellen, recovering herself after her outpouring. 'A very odd notion I always thought it was; and Mary and Louisa are not really ill-natured, and cannot wish to do the harm they might have done, if I did not know Griff too well.'

Then, after considering a little, she said, blushing, 'I believe I have told you more than I ought, Edward—I couldn't help having it out; but please don't tell any one, especially that shocking way of speaking of mamma, which they could not really mean.'

'No one could who knew her.'

'Of course not. I'll tell you what I mean to do. I will write to Mary when we go in, and tell her that I know she really cares for me enough to be glad that her nonsense has done no mischief, and, though I was so foolish and wrong as to fly into a passion, of course I know it is only her way, and I do not believe one word of it.'

Somehow, as she looked with those radiant eyes full of perfect trust, I could not help longing not to have heard Peter Robson's last night's complaint; but family feeling towards outsiders overcomes many a misgiving, and my wrath against the malignity of the Lesters was quite as strong as if I had been devoid of all doubts whether Griff wore to all other eyes the same halo of pure glory with which Ellen invested him.

Such doubts were very transient. Dear old Griff was too delightful, too bright and too brave, too ardent and too affectionate, not to dispel all clouds by the sunshine he carried about with him. If rest and reliance came with Clarence, zest and animation came with Griffith. He managed to take the initiative by declining to remain any longer with the Robsons, saying they had been spoilt by such a model lodger as Clarence, who would let Gooch feed him on bread and milk and boiled mutton, and put on his clean pinafore if she chose to insist; whereas her indignation, when Griff found fault with the folding of his white ties, amounted to 'Et tu Brute,' and he really feared she would have had a fit when he ordered devilled kidneys for breakfast. He was sure her determination to tuck him up every night and put out his candle was shortening her life; and he had made arrangements to share the chambers of a friend who had gone through school and college with him. There was no objection to the friend, who had stayed at Chantry House and was an agreeable, lively, young man, well reported of, satis-factorily connected, fairly industrious, and in good society, so that Griff was likely to be much less exposed to temptation of the lower kinds than when left to his own devices, or only with Clarence, who had neither time nor disposition to share his amusements.

There was a scene with my father, but in private; and all that came to general knowledge was that Griff felt himself injured by any implication that he was given to violent or excessive dissipation, such as could wreck Ellen's happiness or his own character.

He declared with all his heart that immediate marriage would be the best thing for both, and pleaded earnestly for it; but my father could not have arranged for it even if the Fordyces would have consented, and there were matters of business, as well as other reasons, which made it inexpedient for them to revoke their decision that the wedding should not take place before Ellen was of age and Griffith called to the bar.

So we took our young ladies home, loaded with presents for their beloved school children, of whom Emily said she dreamt, as the time for seeing them again drew near. After all the London enjoyment, it was pretty to see the girls' delight in the fresh country sights and sounds in full summer glory, and how Ellen proved to have been hungering after all her dear ones at home. When we left her at her own door, our last sight of her was in her father's arms, little Anne clinging to her dress, mother and grandfather as close to her as could be—a perfect tableau of a joyous welcome.

Charlotte M. Yonge

CHAPTER XXIX

LOVE AND OBEDIENCE

'Unless he give me all in change
I forfeit all things by him;
The risk is terrible and strange.'

MRS. BROWNING.

You will be weary of my lengthiness; and perhaps I am
lingering too long over the earlier portion of my narrative.
Something is due to the disproportion assumed in our
memories by the first twenty years of existence—something, perhaps, to reluctance to passing from comparative
sunshine to shadow. There was still a period of brightness, but it was so uneventful that I have no excuse for
dwelling on it further than to say that Henderson, our
excellent curate, had already made a great difference in
the parish, and it was beginning to be looked on as almost
equal to Hillside. The children were devoted to Emily,
who was the source of all the amenities of their poor little
lives. The needlework of the school was my mother's
pride; and our church and its services, though you would
shudder at them now, were then thought presumptuously
superior 'for a country parish.' They were a real delight
and blessing to us, as well as to many more of the flock,

who still, in their old age, remember and revere Parson Henderson as a sort of apostle.

The dawning of the new Poor-Law led to investigations which revealed the true conditions of the peasant's life— its destitution, recklessness, and dependence. We tried to mend matters by inducing families to emigrate, but this renewed the distrust which had at first beheld in the schools an attempt to enslave the children. Even accounts, sent home by the exceptionally enterprising who did go to Canada, were, we found, scarcely trusted. Amos Bell, who would have gone, if he had not been growing into my special personal attendant, was letter-writer and reader to all his relations, and revealed to us that it had been agreed that no letter should be considered as genuine unless it bore a certain private mark. To be sure, the accounts of prosperity might well sound fabulous to the toilers and moilers at home. Harriet Martineau's Hamlets, which we lent to many of our neighbours, is a fair picture of the state of things. We much enjoyed those tales, and Emily says they were the only political economy she ever learnt.

The model arrangements of our vestries led to a summons to my father and the younger Mr. Fordyce to London, to be examined on the condition of the pauper, and the working of the old Elizabethan Poor-Law.

They were absent for about a fortnight of early spring, and Emily and I could not help observing that our mother was unusually uncommunicative about my father's letters; and, moreover, there was a tremendous revolution of the furniture, a far more ominous token in our household than any comet.

The truth came on us when the two fathers returned. Mine told me himself that Frank Fordyce was so much displeased with Griffith's conduct that he had declared that the engagement could not continue with his consent.

This from good-natured, tender-hearted Parson Frank!

I cried out hotly that 'those Lesters' had done this. They had always been set against us, and any one could talk over Mr. Frank. My father shook his head. He said Frank Fordyce was not weak, but all the stronger for his gentleness and charity; and, moreover, that he was quite right—to our shame and grief be it spoken—quite right.

It was true that the first information had been given by Sir Horace Lester, Mrs. Fordyce's brother, but it had not been lightly spoken like the daughter's chatter; and my father himself had found it only too true, so that he could not conscientiously call Griffith worthy of such a creature as Ellen Fordyce.

Poor Griff, he had been idle and impracticable over his legal studies, which no persuasion would make him view as otherwise than a sort of nominal training for a country gentleman; nor had he ever believed or acted upon the fact that the Earlscombe property was not an unlimited fortune, such as would permit him to dispense with any profession, and spend time and money like the youths with whom he associated. Still, this might have been condoned as part of the effervescence which had excited him ever since my father had succeeded to the estate, and patience might still have waited for greater wisdom; but there had been graver complaints of irregularities, which were forcing his friend to dissolve partnership with him. There was evidence of gambling, which he not only admitted, but defended; and, moreover, he was known at parties, at races, and at the theatre, as one of the numerous satellites who revolved about that gay and conspicuous young fashionable widow, Lady Peacock.

'Yes, Frank has every right to be angry,' said my father, pacing the room. 'I can't wonder at him. I should do the same; but it is destroying the best hope for my poor boy.'

Then he began to wish Clarence had more—he knew not what to call it—in him; something that might keep his brother straight. For, of course, he had talked to Clarence and discovered how very little the brothers saw of one another. Clarence had been to look for Griff in vain more than once, and they had only really met at a Castleford dinner-party. In fact, Clarence's youthful spirits, and the tastes which would have made him companionable to Griff, had been crushed out of him; and he was what more recent slang calls 'such a muff,' that he had perforce drifted out of our elder brother's daily life, as much as if he had been a grave senior of fifty. It was, as he owned, a heavy penalty of his youthful fall that he could not help his brother more effectually.

It appeared that Frank Fordyce, thoroughly roused, had had it out with Griffith, and had declared that his consent was withdrawn and the engagement annulled. Griff, astounded at the resolute tone of one whom he considered as the most good-natured of men, had answered hotly and proudly that he should accept no dismissal except from Ellen herself, and that he had done no more than was expected of any young man of position and estate. On the other indictment he scorned any defence, and the two had parted in mutual indignation. He had, however, shown himself so much distressed at the threat of being deprived of Ellen, that neither my father nor Clarence had the least doubt of his genuine attachment to her, nor that his attentions to Lady Peacock were more than the effect of old habit and love of amusement, and that they had been much exaggerated. He scouted the bare idea of preferring her to Ellen; and, in his second interview with my father, was ready to make any amount of promises of reformation, provided his engagement were continued.

This was on the last evening before leaving town, and he came to the coach-office looking so pale, jaded, and unhappy that Parson Frank's kind heart was touched; and in answer to a muttered 'I've been ten thousand fools, sir, but if you will overlook it I will try to be worthy of her,' he made some reply that could be construed into, 'If you keep to that, all may yet be well. I'll talk to her mother and grandfather.'

Perhaps this was cruel kindness, for, as we well knew, Mrs. Fordyce was far less likely to be tolerant of a young man's failings than was her husband; and she was, besides, a Lester, and might take the same view.

Abusing the Lesters was our great resource; for we did not believe either the sailor or the guardsman to be immaculate, and we knew them to be jealous. We had to remain in ignorance of what we most wished to know, for Ellen was kept away from us, and my mother would not let Emily go in search of her. Only Anne, who was a high-spirited, independent little person, made a sudden rush upon me as I sat in the garden. She had no business to be so far from home alone; but, said she, 'I don't care, it is all so horrid. Please, Edward, is it true that Griff has been so very wicked? I heard the maids talking, and they said papa had found out that he was a bad lot, and that he was not to marry Ellen; but she would stick to him through thick and thin, like poor Kitty Brown who would marry the man that got transported for seven years.' 'Will he be transported, Edward? and would Ellen go too, like the "nut-brown maid?" Is that what she cries so about? Not by day, but all night. I know she does, for her handkerchief is wet through, and there is a wet place on her pillow always in the morning; but she only says, "Never mind," and nobody WILL tell me. They only say little girls should not think about such things. And I am not so very little. I am eight, and have read the Lay of the Last Minstrel and I know all about people in love. So you might tell me.'

I relieved Anne's mind as to the chances of transportation, and, after considering how many confidences might be honourably exchanged with the child, I explained that her father thought Griff had been idle and careless, and not fit as yet to be trusted with Ellen.

Her parish experience came into play. 'Does papa think he would be like Joe Sparks? But then gentlemen don't beat their wives, nor go to the public-house, nor let their children go about in rags.'

I durst not inquire much, but I gathered that there was a heavy shadow over the house, and that Ellen was striving to do as usual, but breaking down when alone. Just then Parson Frank appeared. Anne had run away from him while on a farming inspection, when the debate over the turnips with the factotum had become wearisome. He looked grave and sorrowful, quite unlike his usual hearty self, and came to me, leaning over my chair, and saying, 'This is sad work, Edward'; and, on an anxious venture of an inquiry for Ellen, 'Poor little maid, it is very sore work with her. She is a good child and obedient—wants to do her duty; but we should never have let it go on so long. We have only ourselves to thank—taking the family character, you see'—and he made a kindly gesture towards me. 'Your father sees how it is, and won't let it make a split between us. I believe that not seeing as much of your sister as usual is one of my poor lassie's troubles, but it may be best—it may be best.'

He lingered talking, unwilling to tear himself away, and ended by disclosing, almost at unawares, that Ellen had held out for a long time, would not understand nor take in

Charlotte M. Yonge

what she was told, accepted nothing on Lester authority, declared she understood all about Lady Peacock, and showed a strength of resistance and independence of view that had quite startled her parents, by proving how far their darling had gone from them in heart. But they still held her by the bonds of obedience; and, by dealing with her conscience, her mother had obtained from her a piteous little note -

'MY DEAR GRIFFITH—I am afraid it is true that you have not always seemed to be doing right, and papa and mamma forbid our going on as we are. You know I cannot be disobedient. It would not bring a blessing on you. So I must break off, though—'

The 'though' could be read through an erasure, followed by the initials, E. M. F.—as if the dismal conclusion had been felt to be only too true—and there followed the postscript, 'Forgive me, and, if we are patient, it may come right.'

This letter was displayed, when, on the ensuing evening, it brought Griff down in towering indignation, and trying to prove the coercion that must have been exercised to extract even thus much from his darling. Over he went headlong to Hillside to insist on seeing her, but to encounter a succession of stormy scenes. Mrs. Fordyce was the most resolute, but was ill for a week after. The old Rector was gentle, and somewhat overawed Griff by his compassion, and by representations that were only too true; and Parson Frank, with his tender heart torn to pieces, showed symptoms of yielding another probation.

The interview with Ellen was granted. She, however, was intrenched in obedience. She had promised submission to the rupture of her engagement, and she kept her word,— though she declared that nothing could hinder her love, and that she would wait patiently till her lover had proved himself, to everybody's satisfaction, as good and noble as she knew him to be. When he told her she did not love him she smiled. She was sure that whatever mistakes there might have been, he would give no further occasion against himself, and then every one would see that all had been mere misunderstanding, and they should be happy again.

Such trust humbled him, and he was ready to make all promises and resolutions; but he could not obtain the renewal of the engagement, nor permission to correspond. Only there was wrung out of Parson Frank a promise that if he could come in two years with a perfectly unstained, unblotted character, the betrothal might be renewed.

We were very thankful for the hope and motive, and Griff had no doubts of himself.

'One can't look at the pretty creature and think of disappointing her,' he said. 'She is altered, you know, Ted; they've bullied her till she is more ethereal than ever, but it only makes her lovelier. I believe if she saw me kill some one on the spot she would think it all my generosity; or, if she could not, she would take and die. Oh no! I'll not fail her. No, I won't; not if I have to spend seven years after the model of old Bill, whose liveliest pastime is a good long sermon, when it is not a ghost.'

CHAPTER XXX

UNA OR DUESSA

'Soone as the Elfin knight in presence came
And false Duessa, seeming ladye fayre,
A gentle husher, Vanitie by name,
Made roome, and passage did for them prepare.'

SPENSER.

The two families were supposed to continue on unbroken terms of friendship, and we men did so; but Mrs. Fordyce told my mother that she had disapproved of the probation, and Mrs. Winslow was hurt. Though the two girls were allowed to be together as usual, it was on condition of silence about Griff; and though, as Emily said, they really had not been always talking about him in former times, the prohibition seemed to weigh upon all they said.

Old Mr. Fordyce had long been talking of a round of visits among relations whom he had not seen for many years; and it was decided to send Ellen with him, chiefly, no doubt, to prevent difficulties about Griffith in the long vacation.

There was no embargo on the correspondence with my

sister, and letters full of description came regularly, but how unlike they were to our journal. They were clear, intelligent, with a certain liveliness, but no ring of youthful joy, no echo of the heart, always as if under restraint. Griff was much disappointed. He had been on his good behaviour for two months, and expected his reward, and I could not here repeat all that he said about her parents when he found she was absent. Yet, after all, he got more pity and sympathy from Parson Frank than from any one else. That good man actually sent a message for him, when Emily was on honour to do no such thing. Poor Emily suffered much in consequence, when she would neither afford Griff a blank corner of her paper, nor write even a veiled message; while as to the letters she received and gave to him, 'what was the use,' he said, 'of giving him what might have been read aloud by the town-crier?'

'You don't understand, Griff; it is all dear Ellen's conscientiousness—'

'Oh, deliver me from such con-sci-en-tious-ness,' he answered, in a tone of bitter mimicry, and flung out of the room leaving Emily in tears.

He could not appreciate the nobleness of Ellen's self-command and the obedience which was the security of future happiness, but was hurt at what he thought weak alienation. One note of sympathy would have done much for Griff just then. I have often thought it over since, and come to the conclusion that Mrs. Fordyce was justified in the entire separation she brought about. No one can judge of the strength with which 'true love' has mastered any individual, nor how far change may be possible; and, on the other hand, unless there were full appreciation of Ellen's character, she might only have been looked on as -

Charlotte M. Yonge

'Puppet to a father's threat,
Servile to a shrewish tongue.'

Yet, after all, Frank Fordyce was very kind to Griff, making himself as much of a medium of communication as he could consistently with his conscience, but of course not satisfying one who believed that the strength of love was to be proved not by obedience but disobedience.

Ellen's letters showed increasing anxiety about her grandfather, who was not favourably affected by the change of habits, consequent on a long journey, and staying in different houses. His return was fixed two or three times, and then delayed by slight attacks of illness, till at last he became anxious to get home, and set off about the end of September; but after sleeping a night at an inn at Warwick, he was too ill to proceed any farther. His old man-servant was with him; but poor Ellen went through a great deal of suspense and responsibility before her parents reached her. The attack was paralysis, and he never recovered the full powers of mind or body, though they managed to bring him back to Hillside—as indeed his restlessness longed for his native home. When once there he became calmer, but did not rally; and a second stroke proved fatal just before Easter. He was mourned alike by rich and poor, 'He WAS a gentleman,' said even Chapman, 'always the same to rich or poor, though he was one of they Fordys.'

My father wrote to summon both his elder sons to the funeral at Hillside, and in due time Clarence appeared by the coach, but alone. He had gone to Griffith's chambers to arrange about coming down together, but found my father's letter lying unopened on the table, and learnt that his brother was supposed to be staying at a villa in Surrey, where there were to be private theatricals. He had forwarded the letter thither, and it would still be possible to arrive in time by the night mail.

So entirely was Griff expected that the gig was sent to meet him at seven o'clock the next morning, but there was no sign of him. My father and Clarence went without him to the gathering, which showed how deeply the good old man was respected and loved.

It was the only funeral Clarence had attended except Miss Newton's hurried one, and his sensitive spirit was greatly affected. He had learnt reserve when amongst others, but I found that he had a strong foreboding of evil; he tossed and muttered in his sleep, and confessed to having had a wretched night of dreams, though he would not describe them otherwise than that he had seen the lady whose face he always looked on as a presage of evil.

Two days later the Morning Post gave a full account of the amateur theatricals at Bella Vista, the seat of Benjamin Bullock, Esquire, and the Lady Louisa Bullock; and in the list of dramatis personae, there figured Griffith Winslow, Esquire, as Captain Absolute, and the fair and accomplished Lady Peacock as Lydia Languish.

Amateur theatricals were much less common in those days than at present, and were held as the ne plus ultra of gaiety. Moreover, the Lady Louisa Bullock was noted for fashionable extravagance of the semi-reputable style; and there would have been vexation enough at Griffith's being her guest, even had not the performance taken place on the very day of the funeral of Ellen's grandfather, so as to be an outrage on decorum.

At the same time, there came a packet franked by a not very satisfactory peer, brother to Lady Louisa. My father threw a note over to Clarence, and proceeded to read a very properly expressed letter full of apologies and condolences for the Fordyces.

'He could not have got the letter in time' was my father's comment. 'When did you forward the letter? How was it addressed? Clarence, I say, didn't you hear?'

Clarence lifted up his face from his letter, so much flushed that my mother broke in—'What's the matter? A mistake in the post-town would account for the delay. Has he had the letter?'

'Oh yes.'

'Not in time—eh?'

'I'm afraid,' and he faltered, 'he did.'

'Did he or did he not?' demanded my mother.

'What does he say?' exclaimed my father.

'Sir' (always an unpropitious beginning for poor Clarence), 'I should prefer not showing you.'

'Nonsense!' exclaimed my mother: 'you do no good by concealing it!'

'Let me see his letter,' said my father, in the voice there was no gainsaying, and absolutely taking it from Clarence. None of us will ever forget the tone in which he read it aloud at the breakfast-table.

> 'DEAR BILL—What possessed you to send a death's-head to the feast? The letter would have bitten no one in my chambers. A nice scrape I shall be in if you let out that your officious precision forwarded it. Of course at the last moment I could not upset the whole

affair and leave Lydia to languish in vain. The whole thing went off magnificently. Keep counsel and no harm is done. You owe me that for sending on the letter.—Yours,

'J. G. W.'

Clarence had not read to the end when the letter was taken from him. Indeed to inclose such a note in a dispatch sure to be opened en famille was one of Griffith's haphazard proceedings, which arose from the present being always much more to him than the absent. Clarence was much shocked at hearing these last sentences, and exclaimed, 'He meant it in confidence, papa; I implore you to treat it as unread!'

My father was always scrupulous about private letters, and said, 'I beg your pardon, Clarence; I should not have forced it from you. I wish I had not seen it.'

My mother gave something between a snort and a sigh. 'It is right for us to know the truth,' she said, 'but that is enough. There is no need that they should know at Hillside what was Griffith's alternative.'

'I would not add a pang to that dear girl's grief,' said my father; 'but I see the Fordyces were right. I shall never do anything to bring these two together again.'

My mother chimed in with something about preferring Lady Peacock and the Bella Vista crew to Ellen and Hillside, which made us rush into the breach with incoherent defence.

'I know how it was,' said Clarence. 'His acting is capital, and of course these people could not spare him, nor understand how much it signified that he should be here.

They make so much of him.'

'Who do?' asked my mother. 'Lady Peacock? How do you know? Have you been with them?'

'I have dined at Mr. Clarkson's,' Clarence avowed; and, on further pressure, it was extracted that Griffith—handsome, and with talents such as tell in society—was a general favourite, and much engrossed by people who found him an enlivenment and ornament to their parties. There had been little or nothing of late of the former noisy, boyish dissipation; but that the more fashionable varieties were getting a hold on him became evident under the cross-questioning to which Clarence had to submit.

My father said he felt like a party to a falsehood when he sent Griff's letter up to Hillside, and he indemnified himself by writing a letter more indignant—not than was just, but than was prudent, especially in the case of one little accustomed to strong censure. Indeed Clarence could not restrain a slight groan when he perceived that our mother was shut up in the study to assist in the composition. Her denunciations always outran my father's, and her pain showed itself in bitterness. 'I ought to have had the presence of mind to refuse to show the letter,' he said; 'Griff will hardly forgive me.'

Ellen looked very thin, and with a transparent delicacy of complexion. She had greatly grieved over her grandfather's illness and the first change in her happy home; and she must have been much disappointed at Griffith's absence. Emily dreaded her mention of the subject when they first met.

'But,' said my sister, 'she said no word of him. All she cared to tell me was of the talks she had with her grandfather, when he made her read his favourite chapters in the Bible; and though he had no memory for outside things, his thoughts were as beautiful as ever. Sometimes his face grew so full of glad contemplation that she felt quite awestruck, as if it were becoming like the face of an angel. It made her realise, she said, "how little the ups and downs of this life matter, if there can be such peace at the last." And, after all, I could not help thinking that it was better perhaps that Griff did not come. Any other sort of talk would have jarred on her just now, and you know he would never stand much of that.'

Much as we loved our Griff, we had come to the perception that Ellen was a treasure he could not esteem properly.

The Lester cousins, never remarkable for good taste, forced on her the knowledge of his employment. Her father could not refrain from telling us that her exclamation had been, 'Poor Griff, how shocked he must be! He was so fond of dear grandpapa. Pray, papa, get Mr. Winslow to let him know that I am not hurt, for I know he could not help it. Or may I ask Emily to tell him so?'

I wish Mrs. Fordyce would have absolved her from the promise not to mention Griff to us. That innocent reliance might have touched him, as Emily would have narrated it; but it only rendered my father more indignant, and more resolved to reserve the message till a repentant apology should come. And, alas! none ever came. Just wrath on a voiceless paper has little effect. There is reason to believe that Griff did not like the air of my father's letter, and never even read it. He diligently avoided Clarence, and the pain and shame his warm heart must have felt only made him keep out of reach.

CHAPTER XXXI

FACILIS DESCENSUS

'The slippery verge her feet beguiled;
She tumbled headlong in.'

GRAY.

One of Griffith's briefest notes in his largest hand
announced that he had accepted various invitations to
country houses, for cricket matches, archery meetings,
and the like; nor did he even make it clear where his
address would be, except that he would be with a friend in
Scotland when grouse-shooting began.

Clarence, however, came home for a brief holiday. He
was startled at the first sight of Ellen. He said she was
indeed lovelier than ever, with an added sweetness in her
clear eyes and the wild rose flush in her delicate cheek;
but that she looked as if she was being refined away to
nothing, and was more than ever like the vision with the
lamp.

Of course the Fordyces had not been going into society,
though Ellen and Emily were as much together as before,
helping one another in practising their school children in

singing, and sharing in one another's studies and pursuits. There had been in the spring a change at Wattlesea; the old incumbent died, and the new one was well reported of as a very earnest hardworking man. He seemed to be provided with a large family, and there was no driving into Wattlesea without seeing members of it scattered about the place.

The Fordyces being anxious to show them attention without a regular dinner-party, decided on inviting all the family to keep Anne's ninth birthday, and Emily and Martyn were of course to come and assist at the entertainment.

It was on the morning of the day fixed that a letter came to me whose contents seemed to burn themselves into my brain. Martyn called across the breakfast-table, 'Look at Edward! Has any one sent you a young basilisk?'

'I wish it was,' I gasped out.

'Don't look so,' entreated Emily. 'Tell us! Is it Griff?'

'Not ill-hurt?' cried my mother. 'Oh no, no. Worse!' and then somehow I articulated that he was married; and Clarence exclaimed, 'Not the Peacock!' and at my gesture my father broke out. 'He has done for himself, the unhappy boy. A disgraceful Scotch marriage. Eh?'

'It was his sense of honour,' I managed to utter.

'Sense of fiddlestick!' said my poor father. 'Don't stop to excuse him. We've had enough of that! Let us hear.'

I cannot give a copy of the letter. It was so painful that it was destroyed; for there was a tone of bravado betraying his uneasiness, but altogether unbecoming. All that it disclosed was, that some one staying in the same house had paid insulting attentions to Lady Peacock; she had thrown herself on our brother's protection, and after interfering on her behalf, he had found that there was no means of sheltering her but by making her his wife. This had been effected by the assistance of the lady of the house where they had been staying; and Griffith had written to me two days later from Edinburgh, declaring that Selina had only to be known to be loved, and to overcome all prejudices.

'Prejudices,' said my father bitterly. 'Prejudices in favour of truth and honour.'

And my mother uttered the worst reproach of all, when in my agitation, I slipped and almost fell in rising—'Oh, my poor Edward! that I should have lived to think yours the least misfortune that has befallen my sons!'

'Nay, mother,' said Clarence, putting Martyn toward her, 'here is one to make up for us all.'

'Clarence,' said my father, 'your mother did not mean anything but that you and Edward are the comfort of our lives. I wish there were a chance of Griffith redeeming the past as you have done; but I see no hope of that. A man is never ruined till he is married.'

At that moment there was a step in the hall, a knock at the door, and there stood Mr. Frank Fordyce. He looked at us and said, 'It is true then.'

'To our shame and sorrow it is,' said my father. 'Fordyce, how can we look you in the face?'

'As my dear good friend, and my father's,' said the kind man, shaking him by the hand heartily. 'Do you think we could blame you for this youth's conduct? Stay'—for we young ones were about to leave the room. 'My poor girl knows nothing yet. Her mother luckily got the letter in her bedroom. We can't put off the Reynoldses, you know, so I came to ask the young people to come up as if nothing had happened, and then Ellen need know nothing till the day is over.'

'If I can,' said Emily.

'You can be capable of self-command, I hope,' said my mother severely, 'or you do not deserve to be called a friend.'

Such speeches might not be pleasant, but they were bracing, and we all withdrew to leave the elders to talk it over together, when, as I believe, kind Parson Frank was chiefly concerned to argue my parents out of their shame and humiliation.

Clarence told us what he knew or guessed; and we afterwards understood the matter to have come about chiefly through poor Griff's weakness of character, and love of amusement and flattery. The boyish flirtation with Selina Clarkson had never entirely died away, though it had been nothing more than the elder woman's bantering patronage and easy acceptance of the youth's equally gay, jesting admiration. It had, however, involved some raillery on his attachment to the little Methodistical country girl, and this gradually grew into jealousy of her—especially as Griff became more of a man, and a brilliant member of society. The detention from the funeral had been a real victory on the widow's part, and the few times when Clarence had seen them together he had been dismayed at the cavaliere serviente terms on which Griff seemed to stand; but his words of warning were laughed down. The rest was easy to gather. He had gone about on the round of visits almost as an appendage to Lady Peacock, till they came to a free and easy house, where her coquetry and love of admiration brought on one of those disputes which rendered his championship needful; and such defence could only have one conclusion, especially in Scotland, where hasty private marriages were still legal. What an exchange! Only had Griff ever comprehended the worth of his treasure?

Emily went as late as she could, that there might be the less chance of a tete-a-tete, in which she might be surprised into a betrayal of her secret: indeed she only started at last when Martyn's impatience had become intolerable.

What was our amazement when, much earlier than we expected, we saw Mr. Fordyce driving up in his phaeton, and heard the story he had to tell.

Emily's delay had succeeded in bringing her only just in time for the luncheon that was to be the children's dinner. There was a keen-looking, active, sallow clergyman, grizzled, and with an air of having seen much service; a pale, worn wife, with a gentle, sensible face; and a bewildering flock of boys and girls, all apparently under the command of a very brisk, effective-looking elder sister of fourteen or fifteen, who seemed to be the readiest authority, and to decide what and how much each might partake of, among delicacies, evidently rare novelties.

The day was late in August. The summer had broken; there had been rain, and, though fine, the temperature was fitter for active sports than anything else. Croquet was not yet invented, and, besides, most of the party were of the age for regular games at play. Ellen and Emily did their part in starting these—finding, however, that the Reynolds boys were rather rough, in spite of the objurgations of their sister, who evidently thought herself quite beyond the age for romps. The sports led them to the great home-field on the opposite slope of the ridge from our own. The new farm-buildings were on the level ground at the bottom to the right, where the declivity was much more gradual than to the left, which was very steep, and ended in furze bushes and low copsewood. It was voted a splendid place for hide-and-seek, and the game was soon in such full career that Ellen, who had had quite running enough, could fall out of it, and with her, the other two elder girls. Emily felt Fanny Reynolds' presence a sort of protection, 'little guessing what she was up to,' to use her own expression. Perhaps the girl had not earlier made out who Emily was, or she had been too much absorbed in her cares; but, as the three sat resting on a stump overlooking the hill, she was prompted by the singular inopportuneness of precocious fourteen to observe, 'I ought to have congratulated you, Miss Winslow.'

Emily gabbled out, 'Thank you, never mind,' hoping thus to put a stop to whatever might be coming; but there was no such good fortune. 'We saw it in the paper. It is your brother, isn't it?'

'What?' asked unsuspicious Ellen, thinking, no doubt, of some fresh glory to Griffith.

And before Emily could utter a word, if there were any she could have uttered, out it came. 'The marriage—John Griffith Winslow, Esquire, eldest son of John Edward Winslow of Chantry House, to Selina, relict of Sir Henry Peacock and daughter of George Clarkson, Esquire, Q.C. I didn't think it could be you at first, because you would have been at the wedding.'

Emily had not even time to meet Ellen's eyes before they

were startled by a shriek that was not the merry 'whoop' and 'I spy' of the game, and, springing up, the girls saw little Anne Fordyce rushing headlong down the very steepest part of the slope, just where it ended in an extremely muddy pool, the watering-place of the cattle. The child was totally unable to stop herself, and so was Martyn, who was dashing after her. Not a word was said, though, perhaps, there was a shriek or two, but the elder sisters flew with one accord towards the pond. They also were some way above it, but at some distance off, so that the descent was not so perpendicular, and they could guard against over-running themselves. Ellen, perhaps from knowing the ground better, was far before the other two; but already poor little Anne had gone straight down, and fallen flat on her face in the water, Martyn after her, perhaps with a little more free will, for, though he too fell, he was already struggling to lift Anne up, and had her head above water, when Ellen arrived and dashed in to assist.

The pond began by being shallow, but the bottom sloped down into a deep hollow, and was besides covered several feet deep with heavy cattle-trodden mire and weeds, in which it was almost impossible to gain a footing, or to move. By the time Emily and Miss Reynolds had come to the brink, Ellen and Martyn were standing up in the water, leaning against one another, and holding poor little Anne's head up—all they could do. Ellen called out, 'Don't! don't come in! Call some one! The farm! We are sinking in! You can't help! Call—'

The danger was really terrible of their sinking in the mud and weeds, and being sucked into the deep part of the pool, and they were too far in to be reached from the bank. Emily perceived this, and ran as she had never run before, happily meeting on the way with the gentlemen, who had been inspecting the new model farm-buildings, and had already taken alarm from the screams.

They found the three still with their heads above water, but no more, for every struggle to get up the slope only plunged them deeper in the horrible mud. Moreover, Fanny Reynolds was up to her ankles in the mud, holding by one of her brothers, but unable to reach Martyn. It seems she had had some idea of forming a chain of hands to pull the others out.

Even now the rescue was not too easy. Mr. Fordyce hurried in, and took Anne in his arms; but, even with his height and strength, he found his feet slipping away under him, and could only hand the little insensible girl to Mr. Reynolds, bidding him carry her at once to the house, while he lifted Martyn up only just in time, and Ellen clung to him. Thus weighted, he could not get out, till the bailiff and another man had brought some faggots and a gate that were happily near at hand, and helped him to drag the two out, perfectly exhausted, and Martyn hardly conscious. They both were carried to the Rectory,—Ellen by her father, Martyn by the foreman,—and they were met at the door by the tidings that little Anne was coming to herself.

Indeed, by the time Mr. Fordyce had put on dry clothes, all three were safe in warm beds, and quite themselves again, so that he trusted that no mischief was done; though he decided upon fetching my mother to satisfy herself about Martyn. However, a ducking was not much to a healthy fellow like Martyn, and my mother found him quite fit to dress himself in the clothes she brought, and to return home with her. Both the girls were asleep, but Ellen had had a shivering fit, and her mother was with her, and was anxious. Emily told her mother of Fanny Reynolds' unfortunate speech, and it was thought right to mention it. Mrs. Fordyce listened kindly, kissed Emily,

Charlotte M. Yonge

and told her not to be distressed, for possibly it might turn out to have been the best thing for Ellen to have learnt the fact at such a moment; and, at any rate, it had spared her parents some doubt and difficulty as to the communication.

CHAPTER XXXII

WALY, WALY

'And am I then forgot, forgot?
It broke the heart of Ellen!'

CAMPBELL

Clarence and Martyn walked over to Hillside the first thing the next morning to inquire for the two sisters. As to one, they were quickly reassured, for Anne was in the porch feeding the doves, and no sooner did she see them than out she flew, and was clinging round Martyn's neck, her hat falling back as she kissed him on both cheeks, with an eagerness that made him, as Clarence reported, turn the colour of a lobster, and look shy, not to say sheepish, while she exclaimed, ' Oh, Martyn! mamma says she never thanked you, for you really and truly did save my life, and I am so glad it was you—

'It was not I, it was Ellen,' gruffly muttered Martyn.

'Oh yes! but papa says I should have been smothered in that horrid mud, before Ellen could get to me if you had not pulled me up directly.'

Charlotte M. Yonge

The elders came out by this time, and Clarence was able to get in his inquiry. Ellen had had a feverish night, and her chest seemed oppressed, but her mother did not think her seriously ill. Once she had asked, 'Is it true, what Fanny Reynolds said?' and on being answered, 'Yes, my dear, I am afraid it is,' she had said no more; and as the Fordyce habit of treating colds was with sedatives, her mother thought her scarcely awake to the full meaning of the tidings, and hoped to prevent her dwelling on them till she had recovered the physical shock. Having answered these inquiries, the two parents turned upon Martyn, who, in an access of shamefacedness, had crept behind Clarence and a great orange-tree, and was thence pulled out by Anne's vigorous efforts. The full story had come to light. The Reynolds' boys had grown boisterous as soon as the restraint of the young ladies' participation had been removed, and had, whether intentionally or not, terrified little Anne in the chases of hide-and-seek. Finally, one of them had probably been unable to withstand the temptation of seeing her timid nervous way of peeping and prying about; and had, without waiting to be properly found, leapt out of his lair with a roar that scared the little girl nearly out of her wits, and sent her flying, she knew not whither. Martyn was a few steps behind, only not holding her hand, because the other children had derided her for clinging to his protection. He had instantly seen where she was going, and shouted to her to stop and take care; but she was past attending to him, and he had no choice but to dart after her, seeing what was inevitable; while George Reynolds had sense to stop in time, and seek a safer descent. Had Martyn not been there to raise the child instantly from the stifling mud, her sister could hardly have been in time to save her.

Mrs. Fordyce tearfully kissed him; her husband called him a little hero, as if in joke, then gravely blessed him; and he looked, Clarence related, as if he had been in the greatest possible disgrace.

It was the second time that one of us had saved a life from drowning, but there was none of the exultation we had felt that time before in London. It was a much graver feeling, where the danger had really been greater, and the rescue had been of one so dear to us. It was tempered likewise by anxiety about our dear Ellen—ours, alas, no longer! She was laid up for several days, and it was thought better that she should not see Emily till she had recovered; but after a week had passed, her father drove over to discuss some plans for the Poor-Law arrangements, and begged my sister to go back in the carriage and spend the day with his daughter.

We brothers could now look forward to some real intelligence; we became restless; and in the afternoon Clarence and I set out with the donkey-chair on the woodland path to meet Emily. We gained more than we had hoped, for as we came round one of the turns in the winding path, up the hanging beech-wood, we came on the two friends— Ellen, a truly Una-like figure, in her white dress with her black scarf making a sable stole. Perhaps we betrayed some confusion, for there was a bright flush on her cheeks as she came towards us, and, standing straight up, said, 'Clarence, Edward, I am so glad you are here; I wanted to see you. I wanted—to say—I know he could not help it. It was his generosity—helping those that need it; and— and—I'm not angry. And though that's all over, you'll always be my brothers, won't you?'

She held her outstretched hands to us both. I could not help it, I drew her down, and kissed her brow; Clarence clasped her other hand and held it to his lips, but neither of us could utter a word.

She turned back and went quietly away through the wood,

Charlotte M. Yonge

while Emily sank down under the beech-tree in a paroxysm of grief. You may see which it was, for Clarence cut out 'E. M. F., 1835' upon the bark. He soothed and caressed poor Emily as in old nursery troubles; and presently she told us that it would be long before we saw that dear one again, for Mrs. Fordyce was going to take her away on the morrow.

Mrs. Fordyce had seen Emily in private, before letting her go to Ellen. There was evidently a great wish to be kind. Mrs. Fordyce said she could never forget what she owed to us all, and could not think of blaming any of us. 'But,' she said, 'you are a sensible girl, Emily,'—'how I hate being called a sensible girl,' observed the poor child, in parenthesis,—'and you must see that it is desirable not to encourage her to indulge in needless discussion after she once understands the facts.' She added that she thought a cessation of present intercourse would be wise till the sore was in some degree healed. She had not been satisfied about her daughter's health for some time, and meant to take her to Bath the next day to consult a physician, and then decide what would be best. 'And, my dear,' she said, 'if there should be a slackening of correspondence, do not take it as unkindness, but as a token that my poor child is recovering her tone. Do not discontinue writing to her, but be guarded, and perhaps less rapid, in replying.'

It was for her friendship that poor Emily wept so bitterly—the first friendship that had been an enthusiasm to her; looking at it as a cruel injustice that Griff's misdoing should separate them. The prediction that all might be lived down and forgotten was too vague and distant to be much consolation; indeed, we were too young to take it in.

We had it all over again in a somewhat grotesque form when, at another turn in the wood, we came upon Martyn and Anne, loaded with treasures from their robbers' cave, some of which were bestowed in my chair, the others carried off between Anne and her not very willing nursery-maid.

Anne kissed us all round, and augured cheerfully that she should lay up a store of shells and rocks by the seaside to make 'a perfect Robinson Crusoe cavern,' she said, 'and then Clarence can come and be the Spaniards and the savages. But that won't be till next summer,' she added, shaking her head. 'I shall get Ellen to tell Emily what shells I find, and then she can tell Martyn; for mamma says girls never write to boys unless they are their brothers! And now Martyn will never be my brother,' she added ruefully.

'You will always be our darling,' I said.

'That's not the same as your sister,' she answered. However, amid auguries of the combination of robbers and Robinson Crusoe, the parting was effected, and Anne borne off by the maid; while we had Martyn on our hands, stamping about and declaring that it was very hard that because Griff chose to be a faithless, inconstant ruffian, all his pleasure and comfort in life should be stopped! He said such outrageous things that, between scolding him and laughing at him, Emily had been somewhat cheered by the time we reached the house.

My father had written to Griffith, in his first displeasure, curt wishes that he might not have reason to repent of the step he had taken, though he had not gone the right way to obtain a blessing. As it was not suitable that a man should be totally dependent on his wife, his allowance should be continued; but under present circumstances he must perceive that he and Lady Peacock could not be received at Chantry House. We were shown the letter, and thought it terribly brief and cold; but my mother said it would be weak to offer forgiveness that was not sought, and my father was specially exasperated at the absence of all contrition as to the treatment of Ellen. All Griff had vouchsafed on that head was—the rupture had been the Fordyces' doing; he was not bound. As to intercourse with him, Clarence and I might act as we saw fit.

'Only,' said my father, as Clarence was leaving home, 'I trust you not to get yourself involved in this set.'

Clarence gave a queer smile, 'They would not take me as a gift, papa.'

And as my father turned from the hall door, he laid his hand on his wife's arm, and said, 'Who would have told us what that young fellow would be to us.'

She sighed, and said, 'He is not twenty-three; he has plenty of money, and is very fond of Griff.'

CHAPTER XXXIII

THE RIVER'S BANK

'And my friend rose up in the shadows,
And turned to me,
"Be of good cheer," I said faintly,
For He called thee.'

B. M.

Mr. Fordyce waited at Hillside till after Sunday, and then went to Bath to hear the verdict of the physician. He returned as much depressed as it was in his sanguine nature to be, for great delicacy of the lungs had been detected; and to prevent the recent chill from leaving permanent injury, Ellen must have a winter abroad, and warm sea or mountain air at once. Whether the disease were constitutional and would have come on at all events no one could tell.

Consumption was much less understood half a century ago; codliver oil was unknown; and stethoscopes were new inventions, only used by the more advanced of the faculty. The only escape poor Parson Frank had from accepting the doom was in disbelieving that a thing like a trumpet could really reveal the condition of the chest.

Charlotte M. Yonge

Moreover, Mrs. Fordyce had had a brother who had, under the famous cowhouse cure, recovered enough to return home, and be killed by the upsetting of a stage coach.

Mrs. Fordyce took her daughter to Lyme, and waited there till her husband had found a curate and made all arrangements. It must have been very inconvenient not to come home; but, no doubt, she wanted to prevent any more partings. Then they went abroad, travelling slowly, and seeing all the sights that came in their way, to distract Ellen's thoughts. She was not allowed to hear what ailed her; but believed her languor and want of interest in everything to be the effect of the blow she had received, struggling to exert herself, and to enter gratefully into the enjoyments provided for her. She was not prevented from writing to Emily; indeed, no one liked to hinder anything she wished, but they were guide-book letters, describing all she saw as a kind of duty, but scarcely concealing the trouble it was to look. Such sentences would slip out as 'This is a nice quiet place, and I am happy to say there is nothing that one ought to see.' Or, 'I sat in the cathedral at Lucerne while the others were going round. The organ was playing, and it was such rest!' Or, again, after a day on the Lago di Como, 'It was glorious, and if you and Edward were here, perhaps the beauty would penetrate my sluggish soul!'

Ellen's sluggish soul!—when we remembered her keen ecstasy at the Valley of Rocks.

Those letters were our chief interest in an autumn which seemed dreary to us, in spite of friendly visitors; for had not our family hope and joy been extinguished? There was no direct communication with Griffith after his unpleasant reply to my father's letter; but Clarence saw the newly married pair on their return to Lady Peacock's house in London, and reported that they were very kind and friendly to him, and gave him more invitations than he could accept. Being cross-examined when he came home for Christmas, he declared his conviction that Lady Peacock had married Griff entirely from affection, and that he had been—well—flattered into it. They seemed very fond of each other now, and were launching out into all sorts of gaieties; but though he did not tell my father, he confided to me that he feared that Griffith had been disappointed in the amount of fortune at his wife's disposal.

It was at that Christmas time, one night, having found an intrusive cat upon my bed, Clarence carried her out at the back door close to his room, and came back in haste and rather pale. 'It is quite true about the lady and the light being seen out of doors,' he said in an awe-stricken voice, 'I have just seen her flit from the mullion room to the ruin.'

We only noted the fact in that ghost-diary of ours—we told nobody, and looked no more. We already believed that these appearances on the lawn must be the cause that every window, up to the attics on the garden side of the house, were so heavily shuttered and barred that there was no opening them without noise. Indeed, those on the ground floor had in addition bells attached to them. No doubt the former inhabitants had done their best to prevent any one from seeing or inquiring into what was unacknowledged and unaccountable. It might be only a coincidence, but we could not help remarking that we had seen and heard nothing of her during the engagement which might have united the two families; though, of course, it would be ridiculous to suppose her cognisant of it, like the White Lady of Avenel, dancing for joy at Mary's marriage with Halbert Glendinning.

Charlotte M. Yonge

The Fordyces had settled at Florence, where they suffered a great deal more from cold than they would have done at Hillside; and there was such a cessation of Ellen's letters that Emily feared that Mrs. Fordyce had attained her wish and separated the friends effectually. However, Frank Fordyce beguiled his enforced leisure with long letters to my father on home business, Austrian misgovernment, and the Italian Church and people, full of shrewd observations and new lights; and one of these ended thus, 'My poor lassie has been in bed for ten days with a severe cold. She begs me to say that she has begun a letter to Emily, and hopes soon to finish it. We had thought her gaining ground, but she is sadly pulled down. Fiat voluntas.'

The letter, which had been begun, never came; but, after three long weeks, there was one from the dear patient herself, mentioning her illness, and declaring that it was so comfortable to be allowed to be tired, and to go nowhere and see nothing except the fragment of beautiful blue sky, and the corner of a campanile, and the flowers Anne brought in daily.

As soon as she could be moved, they took her to Genoa, where she revived enough to believe that she should be well if she were at home again, and to win from her parents a promise to take her to Hillside as soon as the spring winds were over. So anxious was she that, as soon as there was any safety in travelling, the party began moving northwards, going by sea to Marseilles to avoid the Corniche, so early in the year. There were many fluctuations, and it was only her earnest yearning for home and strong resolution that could have made her parents persevere; but at last they were at Hillside, just after Whitsuntide, in the last week of May.

Frank Fordyce walked over to see us on the very evening

after their arrival. He was much altered, his kindly handsome face looked almost as if he had gone through an illness; and, indeed, apart from all his anxiety and sorrow, he had pined in foreign parts for his human flock, as well as his bullocks and his turnips. He had also read, thought, and observed a great deal, and had left his long boyhood behind him, during a space for study and meditation such as he had never had before.

He was quite hopeless of his daughter's recovery, and made no secret of it. In passing through London the best advice had been taken, but only to obtain the verdict that the case was beyond all skill, and that it was only a matter of weeks, when all that could be done was to give as much gratification as possible. The one thing that Ellen did care about was to be at home—to have Emily with her, and once more see her school children, her church, and her garden. Tired as she was she had sprung up in the carriage at the first glimpse of Hillside spire, and had leant forward at the window, nodding and smiling her greetings to all the villagers.

She had been taken at once to her room and her bed, but her father had promised to beg Emily to come up by noon on the morrow. Then he sat talking of local matters, not able to help showing what infinite relief it was to him to be at home, and what music to his ears was the Somersetshire dialect and deep English voice 'after all those thin, shrill, screeching foreigners.'

Poor Emily! It was in mingled grief and gladness that she set off the next day, with the trepidation of one to whom sickness and decay were hitherto unknown. When she returned, it was in a different mood, unable to believe the doctors could be right, and in the delight of having her own bright, sweet Ellen back again, all herself. They had talked, but more of home and village than of foreign experiences; and though Ellen did not herself assist, she had much enjoyed watching the unpacking of the numerous gifts which had cost a perfect fortune at the Custom House. No one seemed forgotten—villagers, children, servants, friends. Some of these tokens are before me still. The Florentine mosaic paper-weight she brought me presses this very sheet; the antique lamp she gave my father is on the mantelpiece; Clarence's engraving of Raffaelle's St. Michael hangs opposite to me on the wall. Most precious in our eyes was the collection of plants, dried and labelled by herself, which she brought to Emily and me—poor mummies now, but redolent of undying affection. Her desire was to bestow all her keepsakes with her own hands, and in most cases she actually did so—a few daily, as her strength served her. The little figures in costume, coloured prints, Swiss carvings, French knicknacks, are preserved in many a Hillside cottage as treasured relics of 'our young lady.' Many years later, Martyn recognised a Hillside native in a back street in London by a little purple-blue picture of Vesuvius, and thereby reached the soft spot in a nearly dried-up heart.

So bright and playful was the dear girl over all her old familiar interests that we inexperienced beings believed not only that the wound to her affections was healed, but that she either did not know or did not realise the sentence that had been pronounced on her; but when this was repeated to her mother, it was met by a sad smile and the reply that we only saw her in her best hours. Still, through the summer, it was impossible to us to accept the truth; she looked so lovely, was so cheerful, and took such delight in all that was about her.

With the first cold, however, she seemed to shrivel up, and the bad nights extended into the days. Emily ascribed the change to the lack of going out into the air, and always found reasons for the increased languor and weakness; till at last there came a day when my poor little sister seemed as if the truth had broken upon her for the first time, when Ellen talked plainly to her of their parting, and had asked us both, 'her dear brother and sister,' to be with her at her Communion on All Saints' Day.

She had written a little letter to Clarence, begging his forgiveness for having cut him, and treated him with the scorn which, I believe, was the chief fault that weighed upon her conscience; and, hearing my father's voice in the house, she sent a message to beg him to come and see her in her mother's dressing-room—that very window where I had first heard her voice, refusing to come down to 'those Winslows.' She had sent for him to entreat him to forgive Griffith and recall the pair to Chantry House. 'Not now,' she said, 'but when I am gone.'

My father could deny her nothing, though he showed that the sight of her made the entreaty all the harder to him; and she pleaded, 'But you know this was not his doing. I never was strong, and it had begun before. Only think how sad it would have been for him.'

My father would have promised anything with that wasted hand on his, those fervent eyes gazing on him, and he told her he would have given his pardon long ago, if it had been sought, as it never had been.

'Ah! perhaps he did not dare!' she said. 'Won't you write when all this is over, and then you will be one family again as you used to be?'

He promised, though he scarcely knew where Griffith was. Clarence, however, did. He had answered Ellen's letter, and it had made him ask for a few days' leave of absence. So he came down on the Saturday, and was

Charlotte M. Yonge

allowed a quarter of an hour beside Ellen's sofa in the Sunday evening twilight. He brought away the calm, rapt expression I had sometimes seen on his face at church, and Ellen made a special entreaty that he might share the morrow's feast.

There are some things that cannot be written of, and that was one. Still we had not thought the end near at hand, though on Tuesday morning a message was sent that Ellen was suffering and exhausted, and could not see Emily. It was a wild, stormy day, with fierce showers of sleet, and we clung to the hope that consideration for my sister had prompted the message. In the afternoon Clarence battled with a severe gale, made his way to Hillside, and heard that the weather affected the patient, and that there was much bodily distress. For one moment he saw her father, who said in broken accents that we could only pray that the spirit might be freed without much more suffering, 'though no doubt it is all right.'

Before daylight, before any one in the house was up, Clarence was mounting the hill in the gusts that had done their work on the trees and were subsiding with the darkness. And just as he was beginning the descent, as the sun tipped the Hillside steeple with light, he heard the knell, and counted the twenty-one for the years of our Ellen—for ours she will always be.

'Somehow,' he told me, 'I could not help taking off my hat and giving thanks for her, and then all the drops on all the boughs began sparkling, and there was a hush on all around as if she were passing among the angels, and a thrush broke out into a regular song of jubilee!'

CHAPTER XXXIV

NOT IN VAIN

'Then cheerly to your work again,
With hearts new braced and set
To run untired love's blessed race,
As meet for those who face to face
Over the grave their Lord have met.'

KEBLE.

That dying request could not but be held sacred, and overtures were made to Griffith, who returned an odd sort of answer, friendly and affectionate, but rather as if my father were the offending party in need of forgiveness. He and his wife were obliged for the invitation, but could not accept it, as they had taken a house near Melton-Mowbray for the hunting season, and were entertaining friends.

In some ways it was disappointing, in others it was a relief, not to have the restraint of Lady Peacock's presence during the last days we were to have with the Fordyces. For a fresh loss came upon us. Beachharbour was a fishing-village on the north-western coast, which, within the previous decade, had sprung into importance, on the one hand as a fashionable resort, on the other as a minor

Charlotte M. Yonge

port for colliers. The living was wretchedly poor, and had been held for many years by one of the old inferior stamp of clergy, scarcely superior in habits or breeding to the farmers, and only outliving the scandals of his youth to fall into a state of indolent carelessness. It was in the gift of a child, for whom Sir Horace Lester was trustee, and that gentleman had written, about a fortnight before Ellen's death, to consult Mr. Fordyce on its disposal, declaring the great difficulties and deficiencies of the place, which made it impossible to offer it to any one without considerable private means, and also able to attract and improve the utterly demoralised population. He ended, almost in joke, by saying, 'In fact, I know no one who could cope with the situation but yourself; I wish you could find me your own counterpart, or come yourself in earnest. It is just the air that suits my sister— bracing sea-breezes; the parsonage, though a wretched place, is well situated, and she would be all the stronger; but in poor Ellen's state there is no use in talking of it, and besides I know you are wedded to your fertile fields and Somersetshire clowns.'

That letter (afterwards shown to us) had worked on Mr. Fordyce's mind during those mournful days. He was still young enough to leave behind him Parson Frank and the 'squarson' habits of Hillside in which he had grown up; and the higher and more spiritual side of his nature had been fostered by the impressions of the last year. He was conscious, as he said, that his talk had been overmuch of bullocks, and that his farm had engrossed him more than he wished should happen again, though a change would be tearing himself up by the roots; and as to his own people at Hillside, the curate, an active young man, had well supplied his place, and, in his TRULY humble opinion, though by no means in theirs, introduced several improvements even in that model parish.

What had moved him most, however, was a conversation he had had with Ellen, with whom during this last year he had often held deep and serious counsel, with a growing reverence on his side. He had read her uncle's letter to her, and to his great surprise found that she looked on it as a call. Devotedly fond as she herself was of Hillside, she could see that her father's abilities were wasted on so small a field, in a manner scarcely good for himself, and she had been struck with the greater force of his sermons when preaching to educated congregations abroad. If no one else could or would take efficient charge of these Beachharbour souls, she could see that it would weigh on his conscience to take comparative ease in his own beloved meadows, among a flock almost his vassals. Moreover, she relieved his mind about her mother. She had discovered, what the good wife kept out of sight, that the north-country woman never could entirely have affinities with the south, and she had come to the conclusion that Mrs. Fordyce's spirits would be heavily tried by settling down at Hillside in the altered state of things.

After this talk, Mr. Fordyce had suggested a possible incumbent to his brother-in-law, but left the matter open; and when Sir Horace came down to the funeral, it was more thoroughly discussed; and, as soon as Mrs. Fordyce saw that departure would not break her husband's heart, she made no secret of the way that both her opinion and her inclinations lay. She told my mother that she had always believed her own ill-health was caused by the southern climate, and that she hoped that Anne would grow up stronger than her sister in the northern breezes.

Poor little Anne! Of all the family, to her the change was the greatest grief. The tour on the Continent had been a dull affair to her; she was of the age to weary of long confinement in the carriage and in strange hotels, and too young to appreciate 'grown-up' sights. Picture-galleries and cathedrals were only a drag to her, and if the experiences that were put into Rosella's mouth for the benefit of her untravelled sisters could have been written down, they would have been as unconventional as Mark Twain's adventures. Rosella went through the whole tour, and left a leg behind in the hinge of a door, but in compensation brought home a Paris bonnet and mantle. She seemed to have been her young mistress's chief comfort, next to an occasional game of play with her father, or a walk, looking in at the shop windows and watching marionettes, or, still better, the wonderful sports of brown-legged street children, without trying to make her speak French or Italian—in her eyes one of the inflictions of the journey, in those of her elders the one benefit she might gain. She had missed the petting to which she had been accustomed from her grandfather and from all of us; and she had absolutely counted the days till she could get home again, and had fallen into dire disgrace for fits of crying when Ellen's weakness caused delays. Martyn's holidays had been a time of rapture to her, for there was no one to attend much to her at home, and she was too young to enter into the weight of anxiety; so the two had run as wild together as a gracious well-trained damsel of ten and a fourteen-year-old boy with tender chivalry awake in him could well do. To be out of the way was all that was asked of her for the time, and all old delights, such as the robbers' cave, were renewed with fresh zest.

'It was the sweetest and the last.'

And though Martyn was gone back to school, the child felt the wrench from home most severely. As she told me on one of those sorrowful days, 'She did think she had come back to live at dear, dear little Hillside all the days of her life.' Poor child, we became convinced that this vehement attachment to Griffith's brothers was one factor in Mrs. Fordyce's desire to make a change that should break off these habits of intimacy and dependence.

Pluralities had not become illegal, and Frank Fordyce, being still the chief landholder in Hillside, and wishing to keep up his connection with his people, did not resign the rectory, though he put the curate into the house, and let the farm. Once or twice a year he came to fulfil some of a landlord's duties, and was as genial and affectionate as ever, but more and more absorbed in the needs of Beachharbour, and unconsciously showing his own growth in devotion and activity; while he brought his splendid health and vigour, his talent, his wealth, and, above all, his winning charm of manner and address, to that magnificent work at Beachharbour, well known to all of you; though, perhaps, you never guessed that the foundation of all those churches and their grand dependent works of piety, mercy, and beneficence was laid in one young girl's grave. I never heard of a fresh achievement there without remembering how the funeral psalm ends with -

'Prosper Thou the work of our hands upon us,
O prosper Thou our handiwork.'

And Emily? Her drooping after the loss of her friend was sad, but it would have been sadder but for the spirit Ellen had infused. We found the herbs to heal our woe round our pathway, though the first joyousness of life had departed. The reports Mr. Henderson and the Hillside curate brought from Oxford were great excitements to us, and we thought and puzzled over church doctrine, and tried to impart it to our scholars. We I say, for Henderson had made me take a lads' class, which has been the chief interest of my life. Even the roughest were good to their helpless teacher, and some men, as gray-headed as myself, still come every Sunday to read with Mr. Edward, and are among the most faithful friends of my life.

Charlotte M. Yonge

CHAPTER XXXV

GRIFF'S BIRD

'Shall such mean little creatures pretend to the fashion?
Cousin Turkey Cock, well may you be in a passion.'

THE PEACOCK AT HOME.

It was not till the second Christmas after dear Ellen
Fordyce's death that my eldest brother brought his wife
and child to Chantry House, after an urgent letter to Lady
Peacock from my mother, who yearned for a sight of
Griffith's boy.

I do not wish to dwell on that visit. Selina, or Griff's bird,
as Martyn chose to term her, was certainly handsome and
stylish; but her complexion had lost freshness and
delicacy, and the ladies said her colour was rouge, and her
fine figure due to other female mysteries. She meant to be
very gracious, and patronised everybody, especially
Emily, who, she said, would be quite striking if not
sacrificed by her dress, and whom she much wished to
take to London, engaging to provide her with a husband
before the season was over, not for a moment believing
my mother's assurance that it would be a trial to us all
whenever we had to resign our Emily. Nay, she tried to

condole with the poor moped family slave, and was received with such hot indignation as made her laugh, for, to do her justice, she was good-natured and easy-tempered. However, I saw less of her than did the others, for I believe she thought the sight of me made her ill. Griff, poor old fellow, was heartily glad to be with us again, but quite under her dominion. He had lost his glow of youth and grace of figure, his complexion had reddened, and no one would have guessed him only a year older than Clarence, whose shoulders did indeed reveal something of the desk, but whose features, though pale, were still fair and youthful. The boy was another Clarence, not so much in compliment to his godfather as because it was the most elegant name in the family, and favoured an interesting belief, current among his mother's friends, that the king had actually stood sponsor to the uncle. Poor little man, his grandmother shut herself into the bookroom and cried, after her first sight of him. He was a wretched, pinched morsel of humanity, though mamma and Emily detected wonderful resemblances; I never saw them, but then he inherited his mother's repulsion towards me, and roared doubly at the sight of me. My mother held that he was the victim of Selina's dissipations and mismanagement of herself and him, and gave many matronly groans at his treatment by the smart, flighty nurse, who waged one continual warfare with the household.

Accustomed to absolute supremacy in domestic matters, it was very hard for my mother to have her counsels and experience set at naught, and, if she appealed to Griff, to find her notions treated with the polite deference he might have shown to a cottage dame.

A course of dinner-parties could not hinder her ladyship from finding Chantry House insufferably dull, 'always like Sunday;' and, when she found that we were given to

Saints' Day services, her pity and astonishment knew no bounds. 'It was all very well for a poor object like Edward,' she held, 'but as to Mr. Winslow and Clarence, did they go for the sake of example? Though, to be sure, Clarence might be a Papist any day.'

Popery, instead of Methodism, was just beginning to be the bugbear set up for those whom the world held to be ultra-religious, and my mother was so far disturbed at our interest in what was termed Oxford theology that the warning would have alarmed her if it had come from any other quarter. However, Lady Peacock was rather fond of Clarence, and entertained him with schemes for improving Chantry House when it should have descended to Griffith. The mullion rooms were her special aversion, and were all to be swept away, together with the vaultings and the ruin—'enough to give one the blues, if there were nothing else,' she averred.

We really felt it to the credit of our country that Sir George Eastwood sent an invitation to an early dance to please his young daughters; and for this our visitors prolonged their stay. My mother made Clarence go, that she might have some one to take care of her and Emily, since Griff was sure to be absorbed by his lady. Emily had not been to a ball since those gay days in London with Ellen. She shrank back from the contrast, and would have begged off; but she was told that she must submit; and though she said she felt immeasurably older than at that happy time, I believe she was not above being pleased with the pale pink satin dress and wreath of white jessamine, which my father presented to her, and in which, according to Martyn, she beat 'Griff's bird all to shivers.'

Clarence had grown much less bashful and embarrassed since the Tooke affair had given him a kind of position and a sense of not being a general disgrace. He really was younger in some ways at five-and-twenty than at eighteen; he enjoyed dancing, and especially enjoyed the compliments upon our sister, whom in our usual fashion we viewed as the belle of the ball. He was standing by my fire, telling me the various humours of the night, when a succession of shrieks ran through the house. He dashed away to see what was the matter, and returned, in a few seconds, saying that Selina had seen some one in the garden, and neither she nor mamma would be satisfied without examination—'though, of course, I know what it must be,' he added, as he drew on his coat.

'Bill, are you coming?' said Griff at the door. 'You needn't, if you don't like it. I bet it is your old friend.'

'I'm coming! I'm coming! I'm sure it is,' shouted Martyn from behind, with the inconsistent addition, 'I've got my gun.'

'Enough to dispose of any amount of robbers or phantoms either,' observed Griff as they went forth by the back door, reinforced by Amos Bell with a lantern in one hand and a poker in the other.

My father was fortunately still asleep, and my mother came down to see whether I was frightened.

She said she had no patience with Selina, and had left her to Emily and her maid; but, before many words had been spoken, they all came creeping down after her, feeling safety in numbers, or perhaps in her entire fearlessness. The report of a gun gave us all a shock, and elicited another scream or two. My mother, hoping that no one was hurt, hastened into the hall, but only to meet Griff, hurrying in laughing to reassure us with the tidings that it was only Martyn, who had shot the old sun-dial by way of a robber; and he was presently followed by the others, Martyn rather crestfallen, but arguing with all his might that the sun-dial was exactly like a man; and my mother hurried every one off upstairs without further discussion.

Clarence was rather white, and when Martyn demanded, 'Do you really think it was the ghost? Fancy her selection of the bird!' he gravely answered, 'Martyn, boy, if it were, it is not a thing to speak of in that tone. You had better go to bed.'

Martyn went off, somewhat awed. Clarence was cold and shivering, and stood warming himself. He was going to wind up his watch, but his hand shook, and I did it for him, noting the hour—twenty minutes past one.

It appeared that Selina, on going upstairs, recollected that she had left her purse in Griff's sitting-room before going to dress, and had gone in quest of it. She heard strange shouts and screams outside, and, going to one of the old windows, where the shutters were less unmanageable than elsewhere, she beheld a woman rushing towards the house pursued by at least a couple of men. Filled with terror she had called out, and nearly fainted in Griff's arms.

'It agrees with all we have heard before,' said Clarence, 'the very day and hour!'

'As Martyn said, the person is strange.'

'Villagers, less concerned, have seen the like,' he said; 'and, indeed, all unconsciously poor Selina has cut away the hope of redress,' he sighed. 'Poor, restless spirit! would that I could do anything for her.'

'Let me ask, do you ever see her now?'

'N-no, I suppose not; but whenever I am anxious or worried, the trouble takes her form in my dreams.'

Lady Peacock had soon extracted the ghost story from her husband, and, though she professed to be above the vulgar folly of belief in it, her nerves were so upset, she said, that nothing would have induced her to sleep another night in the house. The rational theory on this occasion was that one of the maids must have stolen out to join in the Christmas entertainment at the Winslow Arms, and been pursued home by some tipsy revellers; but this explanation was not productive of goodwill between the mother and daughter-in-law, since mamma had from the first so entirely suspected Selina's smart nurse as actually to have gone straight to the nursery on the plea of seeing whether the baby had been frightened. The woman was found asleep—apparently so—said my mother, but all her clothes were in an untidy heap on the floor, which to my mother was proof conclusive that she had slipped into the house in the confusion, and settled herself there. Had not my mother with her own eyes watched from the window her flirtations with the gardener, and was more evidence requisite to convict her? Mamma entertained the hope that her proposal would be adopted of herself taking charge of her grandson, and fattening his poor little cheeks on our cows' milk, while the rest of the party continued their round of visits.

Lady Peacock, however, treated it as a personal imputation that HER nurse should be accused instead of any servant of Mrs. Winslow's own, though, as Griff observed, not only character, but years and features might alike acquit them of any such doings; but even he could not laugh long, for it was no small vexation to him that such offence should have arisen between his mother and wife. Of course there was no open quarrel—my mother had far too much dignity to allow it to come to that—but each said in private bitter things of the other, and my lady's manner of declining to leave her baby at Chantry House was almost offensive.

Poor Griffith, who had been growing more like himself every day, tried in vain to smooth matters, and would have been very glad to leave his child to my mother's management, though, of course, he acquitted the nurse of the midnight adventure. He privately owned to us that he had no opinion of the woman, but he defended her to my mother, in whose eyes this was tantamount to accusing her own respectable maids, since it was incredible that any rational person could accept the phantom theory.

Gladly would he have been on better terms, for he had had to confess that his wife's fortune had turned out to be much less than common report had stated, or than her style of living justified, and that his marriage had involved him in a sea of difficulties, so that he had to beg for a larger allowance, and for assistance in paying off debts.

The surrender of the London house and of some of the chief expenses were made conditions of such favours, and Griffith had assented gratefully when alone with his father; but after an interview with his wife, demonstrations were made that it was highly economical to have a house in town, and horses, carriages, and servants and that any change would be highly derogatory to the heir of Earlscombe and the sacred wishes of the late Sir Henry Peacock.

In fact, it was impressed on us that we were mere homely, countrified beings, who could not presume to dictate to her ladyship, but who had ill requited her condescension in deigning to beam upon us.

CHAPTER XXXVI

SLACK WATER

'O dinna look, ye prideful queen, on a' aneath your ken,
For he wha seems the farthest BUT aft wins the farthest
BEN, And whiles the doubie of the schule tak's lead of a'
the rest: The birdie sure to sing is the gorbal of the nest.

'The cauld, grey, misty morn aft brings a sunny summer
day; The tree wha's buds are latest is longest to decay;
The heart sair tried wi' sorrow still endures the sternest
test: The birdie sure to sing is the gorbal of the nest.

'The wee wee stern that glints in heaven may be a lowin'
sun, Though like a speck of light it seem amid the welkin
dun; The humblest sodger on the field may win a warrior's
crest: The birdie sure to sing is the gorbal of the nest.'

SCOTCH NEWSPAPER.

The wickedness of the nurse was confirmed in my
mother's eyes when the doom on the first-born of the
Winslows was fulfilled, and the poor little baby, Clarence,
succumbed to a cold on the chest caught while his nurse
was gossiping with a guardsman.

Charlotte M. Yonge

He was buried in London. 'It was better for Selina to get those things over as quickly as possible,' said Griff; but Clarence saw that he suffered much more than his wife would let him show to her. 'It is so bad for him to dwell on it,' she said. 'You see. I never let myself give way.'

And she was soon going out, nearly as usual, till their one other infant came to open its eyes only for a few hours on this troublesome world, and owe its baptism to Clarence's exertions. My mother, who was in London just after, attending on the good old Admiral's last illness, was greatly grieved and disgusted with all she heard and saw of the young pair, and that was not much. She felt their disregard of her uncle as heartless, or rather as insulting, on Selina's part, and weak on Griff's; and on all sides she heard of their reckless extravagance, which made her forebode the worst.

All these disappointments much diminished my father's pleasure and interest in his inheritance. He had little heart to build and improve, when his eldest son's wife made no secret of her hatred to the place, or to begin undertakings only to be neglected by those who came after; and thus several favourite schemes were dropped, or prevented by Griffith's applications for advances.

At last there was a crisis. At the end of the second season after their visit to us, Clarence sent a hasty note, begging my father to join him in averting an execution in Griffith's house. I cannot record the particulars, for just at that time I had a long low fever, and did not touch my diary for many weeks; nor indeed did I know much about the circumstances, since my good nurses withheld as much as possible, and would not let me talk about what they believed to make me worse. Nor can I find any letters about it. I believe they were all made away with long ago, and thus I only know that my father hurried up to town, remained for a fortnight, and came back looking ten years older. The house in London had been given up, and he had offered a vacant one of our own, near home, to Griff to retrench in, but Selina would not hear of it, insisting on going abroad.

This was a great grief to him and to us all. There was only one side of our lives that was not saddened. Our old incumbent had died about six months after the Fordyces had gone, and Mr. Henderson had gladly accepted the living where the parsonage had been built. The lady to whom he had been so long engaged was a great acquisition. Her home had been at Oxford; and she was as thoroughly imbued with the spirit that there prevailed as was the Hillside curate. She talked to us of Littlemore, and of the sermons there and at St. Mary's, and Emily and I shared to the full her hero-worship. It was the nearest compensation my sister had had for the loss of Ellen, with this difference, that Mrs. Henderson was older, had read more, and had conversed thoughtfully with some of the leading spirits in religious thought, so that she opened a new world to us.

People would hardly believe in our eagerness and enthusiasm over the revelations of church doctrine; how we debated, consulted our books, and corresponded with Clarence over what now seems so trite; how we viewed the British Critic and Tracts for the Times as our oracles, and worried the poor Wattlesea bookseller to get them for us at the first possible moment.

Church restoration was setting in. Henderson had always objected to christening from a slop-basin on the altar, and had routed out a dilapidated font; and now one, which was termed by the country paper chaste and elegant, was by united efforts, in which Clarence had the lion's share, presented in time for the christening of the first child at the Parsonage. It is that which was sent off to the Mission Chapel as a blot on the rest of Earlscombe Church. Yet what an achievement it was deemed at the time!

The same may be said of most of our doings at that era. We effected them gradually, and have ever since been undoing them, as our architectural and ecclesiastical perceptions have advanced. I wonder how the next generation will deal with our alabaster reredos and our stained windows, with which we are all as well pleased as we were fifty years ago with the plain red cross with a target-like arrangement above and below it in the east window, or as poor Margaret may have been with her livery altar-cloth. Indeed, it seems to me that we got more delight out of our very imperfect work, designed by ourselves and sent to Clarence to be executed by men in back streets in London, costing an immensity of trouble, than can be had now by simply choosing out of a book of figures of cut and dried articles.

What an enthusiastic description Clarence sent of the illuminated commandments in the new Church of St. Katharine in the Regent's Park! How Emily and I gloated over the imitation of them when we replaced the hideous old tables, and how exquisite we thought the initial I, which irreverent youngsters have likened, with some justice, to an enormous overfed caterpillar, enwreathed with red and green cabbage leaves!

My mother was startled at these innovations; but my father, who had kept abreast with the thought of the day, owned to the doctrines as chiming in with his unbroken belief, and transferred to the improvements in the church the interest which he had lost in the estate. The farmers had given up their distrust of him, and accepted him loyally as friend and landlord, submitting to the reseating of the church, and only growling moderately at decorations that cost them nothing. Daily service began as soon as Henderson was his own master, and was better attended than it is now; for the old people to whom it was a novelty took up the habit more freely than their successors, to whom the bell has been familiar through their days of toil. We were too far off to be constant attendants; but evensong made an object for our airings, and my father's head, now quite white, was often seen there. He felt it a great relief amid the cares of his later years.

Perhaps it was with a view to him that Mr. Castleford arranged that Clarence should become manager for the firm at Bristol, with a good salary. The Robsons would not take a fresh lodger—they were getting too old for fresh beginnings; but they kept their rooms ready for him, whenever he had to be in town, and Gooch found him a trustworthy widow as housekeeper. He took a little cottage at Clifton, availing himself of the coach to spend his Sundays with us; and it was an acknowledged joy to every one that I should drive to meet him every Saturday afternoon at the Carpenter's Arms, and bring him home to be my father's aid in all his business, and a most valuable help in Sunday parish work, in which he had an amount of experience which astonished us.

What would have become of the singing without him? The first hint against the remarkable anthems had long ago alienated our tuneful choir placed on high, and they had deserted en masse. Then Emily and the school-mistress had toiled at the school children, whose thin little pipes and provincialisms were a painful infliction, till Mrs. Henderson, backed by Clarence, worked up a few promising men's voices to support them. We thought everything but the New and Old Versions smacked of dissent, except the hymns at the end of the Prayer-book, though we did not go as far as Chapman, who told Emily he understood as how all the tunes was tried over in Doctor's Commons afore they were sent out, and it was not 'liable' to change them. One of Clarence's amusements in his lonely life had been the acquisition of a knowledge of music, and he had a really good voice; while his adherence to our choir encouraged other young men of the farmer and artisan class to join us. Choir, however, did not mean surplices and cassocks, but a collection of our best voices, male and female, in the gallery.

Martyn began to be a great help when at home, never having wavered in his purpose of becoming a clergyman. On going to Oxford, he became imbued with the influences that made Alma Mater the focus of the religious life and progress of that generation which is now the elder one. There might in some be unreality, in others extravagance, in others mere imitation; but there was a truly great work on the minds of the young men of that era—a work which has stood the test of time, made saints and martyrs, and sown the seed whereof we have witnessed a goodly growth, in spite of cruel shocks and disappointments, fightings within and fears without, slanders and follies to provoke them, such as we can now afford to laugh over. With Martyn, rubrical or extra-rubrical observances were the outlet of the exuberance of youth, as chivalry and romance had been to us; and on Frank Fordyce's visits, it was delightful to find that he too was in the full swing of these ideas and habits, partly from his own convictions, partly from his parish needs, and partly carried along by curates fresh from Oxford.

In the first of his summer vacations Martyn joined a reading party, with a tutor of the same calibre, and assured them that if they took up their quarters in a farm-house not many miles by the map from Beachharbour, they would have access to unlimited services, with the extraordinary luxury of a surpliced choir, and intercourse with congenial spirits, which to him meant the Fordyces.

On arriving, however, the bay proved to be so rocky and dangerous that there was no boating across it, as he had confidently expected. The farm depended on a market town in the opposite direction, and though the lights of Beachharbour could be seen at night, there was no way thither except by a six-miles walk along a cliff path, with a considerable detour in order to reach a bridge and cross the rapid river which was an element of danger in the bay, on the north side of the promontory which sheltered the harbour to the south.

So when Martyn started as pioneer on the morning before the others arrived, he descended into Beachharbour later than he intended, but still he was in time to meet Anne Fordyce, a tall, bright-faced girl of fourteen, taking her after-lessons turn on the parade with a governess, who looked amazed as the two met, holding out both hands to one another, with eager joy and welcome.

It was not the same when Anne flew into the Vicarage with the rapturous announcement, 'Here's Martyn!' The vicar was gone to a clerical meeting, and Mrs. Fordyce said nothing about staying to see him. The luncheon was a necessity, but with quiet courtesy Martyn was made to understand that he was regarded as practically out of reach, and 'Oh, mamma, he could come and sleep,' was nipped in the utterance by 'Martyn is busy with his studies; we must not disturb him.' This was a sufficient intimation that Mrs. Fordyce did not intend to have the pupils dropping in on her continually, and making her house their resort; and while Martyn was digesting the rebuff, the governess carried Anne off to prepare for a music lesson, and her mother gave no encouragement to lingering or repeating the visit.

Charlotte M. Yonge

Still Martyn, on his way homewards, based many hopes on the return of Mr. Fordyce; but all that ensued was, three weeks later, a note regretting the not having been able to call, and inviting the whole party to a great school-feast on the anniversary of the dedication of the first of the numerous new churches of Beachharbour. There was no want of cordiality on that occasion, but time was lacking for anything beyond greetings and fleeting exchanges of words. Parson Frank tried to talk to Martyn, bemoaned the not seeing more of him, declared his intentions of coming to the farm, began an invitation, but was called off a hundred ways; and Anne was rushing about with all the children of the place, gentle and simple, on her hands. Whenever Martyn tried to help her, he was called off some other way, and engaged at last in the hopeless task of teaching cricket where these fisher boys had never heard of it.

That was all he saw of our old friends, and he was much hurt by such ingratitude. So were we all, and though we soon acquitted the head of the family of more than the forgetfulness of over occupation, the soreness at his wife's coldness was not so soon passed over. Yet from her own point of view, poor woman, she might be excused for a panic lest her second daughter might go the way of the first.

CHAPTER XXXVII

OUTWARD BOUND

'As slow our ship her foamy track
Against the wind was cleaving,
Her trembling pennant still looked back
To the dear isle 'twas leaving.
So loath we part from all we love,
From all the links that bind us,
So turn our hearts as on we rove
To those we've left behind us.'

T. MOORE.

The first time I saw Clarence's menage was in that same summer of poor Martyn's repulse. My father had come in for a small property in his original county of Shropshire, and this led to his setting forth with my mother to make necessary arrangements, and then to pay visits to old friends; leaving Emily and me to be guests to our brother at Clifton.

We told them it was their harvest honeymoon, and it was funny to see how they enjoyed the scheme when they had once made up their minds to it, and our share in the project was equally new and charming, for Emily and I,

Charlotte M. Yonge

though both some way on in our twenties, were still in many respects home children, nor had I ever been out on a visit on my own account. The yellow chariot began by conveying Emily and me to our destination.

Clifton has grown considerably since those days, and terraces have swallowed up the site of what the post-office knew as Prospect Cottage, but we were apt to term the doll's house, for, as Emily said, our visit there had something the same effect as a picnic or tea drinking at little Anne's famous baby house. In like manner, it was tiny, square, with one sash-window on each side of the door, but it was nearly covered with creepers, odds and ends which Clarence brought from home, and induced to flourish and take root better than their parent stocks. In his nursery days his precision had given him the name of 'the old bachelor,' and he had all a sailor's tidiness. Even his black cat and brown spaniel each had its peculiar basket and mat, and had been taught never to transgress their bounds or interfere with one another; and the effect of his parlour, embellished as it was in our honour, was delightful. The outlook was across the beautiful ravine, into the wooded slopes on the further side, and, on the other side, down the widening cleft to that giddy marvel, the suspension bridge, with vessels passing under it, and the expanse beyond.

Most entirely we enjoyed ourselves, making merry over Clarence's housekeeping, employing ourselves after our wonted semi-student, semi-artist fashion in the morning; and, when our host came home from business, starting on country expeditions, taking a carriage whenever the distance exceeded Emily's powers of walking beside my chair; sketching, botanising, or investigating church architecture, our newest hobby. I sketched, and the other two rambled about, measuring and filling up archaeo-logical papers, with details of orientation, style, and all the rest, deploring barbarisms and dilapidations, making curious and delightful discoveries, pitying those who thought the Dun Cow's rib and Chatterton's loft the most interesting features of St. Mary's Redcliff, and above all rubbing brasses with heel ball, and hanging up their grim effigies wherever there was a vacant space on the walls of our doll's house.

And though we grumbled when Clarence was detained at the office later than we expected, this was qualified by pride at feeling his importance there as a man in authority. It was, however, with much dismay and some inhospitality that we learnt that a young man belonging to the office—in fact, Mr. Frith's great-nephew—was coming to sail for Canton in one of the vessels belonging to the firm, and would have to be 'looked after.' He could not be asked to sleep at Prospect Cottage, for Emily had the only spare bedchamber, and Clarence had squeezed himself into a queer little dressing closet to give me his room; but the housekeeper (a treasure found by Gooch) secured an apartment in the next house, and we were to act hosts, much against our will. Clarence had barely seen the youth, who had been employed in the office at Liverpool, living with his mother, who was in ill-health and had died in the last spring. The only time of seeing him, he had seemed to be a very shy raw lad; but, 'poor fellow, we can make the best of him,' was the sentiment; 'it is only for one night.' However, we were dismayed when, as Emily was in the crisis of washing-in a sky, it was announced that a gentleman was asking for Mr. Winslow. Churlishness bade us despatch him to the office, but humanity prevailed to invite him previously to share our luncheon. Yet we doubted whether it had not been a cruel mercy when he entered, evidently unprepared to stumble on a young lady and a deformed man, and stammering piteously as he hoped there was no mistake—Mr. Winslow—Prospect, etc.

Emily explained, frustrating his desire to flee at once to the office, and pointing out his lodging, close at hand, whence he was invited to return in a few minutes to the meal.

We had time for some amiable exclamations, 'The oaf!' 'What a bore!' 'He has spoilt my sky!' 'I shan't finish this to-day!' 'Shall we order a carriage and take him to the office; we can't have him on our hands all the afternoon?' 'And we might get the new number of Nicholas Nickleby.'

N.B.—Perhaps it was Oliver Twist or The Old Curiosity Shop—I am not certain which was the current excitement just then; but I am quite sure it was Mrs. Nickleby who first disclosed to us that our guest had a splendid pair of dark eyes. Hitherto he had kept them averted in the studious manner I have often noticed in persons who did not wish to excite suspicion of staring at my peculiarities; but that lady's feelings when her neighbour's legs came down her chimney were too much for his self-consciousness, and he gave a glance that disclosed dark liquid depths, sparkling with mirth. He was one number in advance of us, and could enlighten us on the next stage in the coming story; and this went far to reconcile us to the invasion, and to restore him to the proper use of his legs and arms—and very shapely limbs they were, for he was a slim, well-made fellow, with a dark gipsy complexion, and intelligent, honest face, altogether better than we expected.

Yet we could have groaned when in the evening, Clarence brought him back with tidings that something had gone wrong with the ship. If I tried to explain, I might be twitted with,

'The bowsprit got mixed with the rudder sometimes.'

But of course Clarence knew all about it, and he thought it unlikely that the vessel would be in sailing condition for a week at soonest. Great was our dismay! Getting through one evening by the help of walking and then singing was one thing, having the heart of our visit consumed by an interloper was another; though Clarence undertook to take him to the office and find some occupation for him that might keep him out of our way. But it was Clarence's leisure hours that we begrudged; though truly no one could be meeker than this unlucky Lawrence Frith, nor more conscious of being an insufferable burthen. I even detected a tear in his eye when Clarence and Emily were singing 'Sweet Home.'

'Do you know,' said Clarence, on the second evening, when his guest had gone to dress for dinner, 'I am very sorry for that poor lad. It is only six weeks since he lost his mother, and he has not a soul to care for him, either here or where he is going. I had fancied the family were under a cloud, but I find it was only that old Frith quarrelled with the father for taking Holy Orders instead of going into our house. Probably there was some imprudence; for the poor man died a curate and left no provision for his family. The only help the old man would give was to take the boy into the office at Liverpool, stopping his education just as he was old enough to care about it. There were a delicate mother and two sisters then, but they are all gone now; scarlet fever carried off the daughters, and Mrs. Frith never was well again. He seems to have spent his time in waiting on her when off duty, and to have made no friends except one or two contemporaries of hers; and his only belongings are old Frith and Mrs. Stevens, who are packing him off to Canton without caring a rap what becomes of him. I know what Mrs. Stevens is at; she comes up to town much oftener now, and has got her husband's nephew into the office, and is trying to get everything for him; and that's the reason she wants to keep up the old feud, and send this poor Lawrence off to the ends of the earth.'

'Can't you do anything for him?' asked Emily. 'I thought Mr. Frith did attend to you.'

Clarence laughed. 'I know that Mrs. Stevens hates me like poison; but that is the only reason I have for supposing I might have any influence.'

'And can't you speak to Mr. Castleford?'

'Set him to interfere about old Frith's relations! He would know better! Besides, the fellow is too old to get into any other line—four-and-twenty he says, though he does not look it; and he is as innocent as a baby, indifferent just now to what becomes of him, or whither he goes; it is all the same to him, he says; there is no one to care for him anywhere, and I think he is best pleased to go where it is all new. And there, you see, the poor lad will be left to drift to destruction—mother's darling that he has been— just for want of some human being to care about him, and hinder his getting heartless and reckless!'

Clarence's voice trembled, and Emily had tears in her eyes as she asked if absolutely nothing could be done for him. Clarence meant to write to Mr. Castleford, who would no doubt beg the chaplain at the station to show the young man some kindness; also, perhaps, to the resident partner, whom Clarence had looked at once over his desk, but in his rawest and most depressed days. The only clerk out there, whom he knew, would, he thought, be no element of safety, and would not like the youth the better either for bringing his recommendation or bearing old Frith's name.

We were considerably softened towards our guest, though the next time Emily came on him he was standing in the hall, transfixed in contemplation of her greatest achievement in brass-rubbing, a severe and sable knight with the most curly of nostrils, the stiffest and straightest of mouths, hair straight on his brows, pointed toes joined together below, and fingers touching over his breast. There he hung in triumph just within the front door, fluttering and swaying a little on his pins whenever a draught came in; and there stood Lawrence Frith, freshly aware of him, and unable to repress the exclamation, 'I say! isn't he a guy?'

'Sir Guy de Warrenne,' began Emily composedly; 'don't you see his coat of arms? "chequy argent and azure."'

'Does your brother keep him there to scare away the tramps?'

Emily's countenance was a study.

The subject of brasses was unfolded to Lawrence Frith, and before the end of the week he had spent an entire day on his hands and knees, scrubbing away with the waxy black compound at a figure in the Cathedral—the office-work, as we declared, which Clarence gave him to do. In fact he became so thoroughly infected that it was a pity that he was going where there would be no exercise in ecclesiology—rather the reverse. Embarrassment on his side, and hostility on ours, may be said to have vanished under the influence of Sir Guy de Warrenne's austere countenance. The youth seemed to regard 'Mr. Winslow' in the light of a father, and to accept us as kindly beings. He ceased to contort his limbs in our awful presence, looked at me like as an ordinary person, and even ventured on giving me an arm. He listened with unfeigned pleasure to our music, perilled his neck on St. Vincent's rocks in search of plants, and by and by took to hanging back with Emily, while Clarence walked on with me, to talk to her out of his full heart about his mother and sisters.

Three weeks elapsed before the Hoang-ho was ready to sail, and by that time Lawrence knew that there were some who would rejoice in his success, or grieve if things went ill with him. Clarence and I had promised him long home letters, and impressed on him that we should welcome his intelligence of himself. For verily he had made his way into our hearts, as a thoroughly good-hearted, affectionate being, yearning for something to cling to; intelligent and refined, though his recent cultivation had been restricted, soundly principled, and trained in religious feelings and habits, but so utterly inexperienced that there was no guessing how it might be with him when cast adrift, with no object save his own maintenance, and no one to take an interest in him.

Clarence talked to him paternally, and took him to second-hand shops to provide a cheap library of substantial reading, engaging to cater for him for the future, not omitting Dickens; and Emily worked at providing him with the small conveniences and comforts for the voyage that called for a woman's hand. He was so grateful that it was like fitting out a dear friend or younger brother.

'I wonder,' said Clarence, as he walked by my chair on one of the last days, 'whether it was altogether wise to have this young Frith here so much, though it could hardly have been helped.'

To which I rejoined that it could hardly have displeased the uncle, and that if it did, the youth's welfare was worth annoying him for.

'I meant something nearer home,' said Clarence, and proceeded to ask if I did not think Lawrence Frith a good deal smitten with Emily.

To me it seemed an idea not worth consideration. Any youth, especially one who had lived so secluded a life, would naturally be taken by the first pleasing young woman who came in his way, and took a kindly interest in him; but I did not think Emily very susceptible, being entirely wrapped up in home and parish matters; and I reminded Clarence that she had not been loverless. She had rejected the Curate of Hillside; and we all saw, though she did not, that only her evident indifference kept Sir George Eastwood's second son from making further advances.

Clarence was not convinced. He said he had never seen our sister look at either of these as she did when Lawrence came into the room; and there was no denying that there was a soft and embellishing light on her whole countenance, and a fresh sweetness in her voice. But then he seemed such a boy as to make the notion ridiculous; and yet, on reckoning, it proved that their years were equal. All that could be hoped was that the sentiment, if it existed, would not discover itself before they parted, so as to open their eyes to the dreariness of the prospect, and cause our mother to think we had betrayed our trust in the care of our sister. As we could do nothing, we were not sorry that this was the last day. Clarence was to go on board with Frith, see him out of the river, and come back with the pilot; and we all drove down to the wharf together; nobody saying much by the way, except the few jerky remarks we brothers felt bound to originate and reply to.

Emily sat very still, her head bent under her shading bonnet—I think she was trying to keep back tears for the solitary exile; and Lawrence, opposite, was unable to help watching her with wistful eyes, which would have revealed all, if we had not guessed it already. It might be presumptuous, but it made us very sorry for him.

When the moment of parting came, there was a wringing of hands, and, 'Thank you, thank you,' in a low, broken, heartfelt voice, and to Emily, 'You have made life a new thing to me. I shall never forget,' and the showing of a tiny book in his waistcoat pocket.

When the two had disappeared, Emily, no longer restraining her tears, told me that she had exchanged Prayer-books with him, and they were to read the Psalms at the same time every day. 'I thought it might be a help to him,' she said simply.

Nor was there any consciousness in her talk as she related to me what he had told her about his mother and sisters, and his dreary sense of piteous loneliness, till we had adopted him as a brother—in which capacity I trusted that she viewed him.

However, Clarence had been the recipient of all the poor lad's fervent feelings for Miss Winslow, how she had been a new revelation to his desolate spirit, and was to be the guiding star of his life, etc., etc., all from the bottom of his heart, though he durst not dream of requital, and was to live, not on hope, but on memory of the angelic kindness of these three weeks.

It was impossible not to be touched, though we strove to be worldly wise old bachelors, and assured one another that the best and most probable thing that could happen to Lawrence Frith would be to have his dream blown away by the Atlantic breezes, and be left open to the charms of some Chinese merchant's daughter.

CHAPTER XXXVIII

TOO LATE

'Thus Esau-like, our Father's blessing miss,
Then wash with fruitless tears our faded crown.'

KEBLE.

After such a rebuff as Martyn had experienced at Beachharbour, he no longer haunted its neighbourhood, but devoted the long vacation of the ensuing year to a walking tour in Germany, with one or two congenial spirits, who shared his delight in scenery, pictures, and architecture.

By and by he wrote to Clarence from Baden Baden -

'Whom do you think I should find here but Griffith and his bird? I first spotted the old fellow smoking under a tree in the Grand Platz, but he looked so seedy and altered altogether that I was not sure enough of him to speak, especially as he showed no signs of knowing me. (He says it was my whiskers that stumped him.) I made inquiries and found that they figured as "Sir Peacock and lady," but they were entered all right in the book. He is taking the "Kur"—he looks as if he wanted it—and she is

Charlotte M. Yonge

taking rouge et noir. I saw her at the salon, with her neck grown as long as her namesake's, but not as pretty, claws to match, thin and painted, as if the ruling passion was consuming her. Poor old Griff! he was glad enough to see me, but he is wofully shaky, and nearly came to tears when he asked after Ted and all at home. They had an upset of their carriage in Vienna last winter, and he got some twist, or other damage, which he thought nothing of, but it has never righted itself; I am sure he is very ill, and ought to be looked after. He has had only foreign doctoring, and you know he never was strong in languages. I heard of the medico here inquiring what precise symptom der Englander meant by being "down in zie mout!" Poor Griff is that, whatever else he is, and Selina does not see it, nor anything else but her rouge et noir table. I am afraid he plays too, when he is up to it, but he can't stand much of the stuffiness of the place, and he respects my innocence, poor old beggar; so he has kept out of it, since we have been here. He seems glad to have me to look after him, but afraid to let me stay, for fear of my falling a victim to the place. I can't well tell him that there is a perpetual warning to youth in the persons of himself and his Peacock. His mind might be vastly relieved if I were out of it, but scarcely his body; and I shall not leave him till I hear from home. Thomson says I am right. I should like to bring the poor old man home for advice, especially if my lady could be left behind, and by all appearances she would not object. Could not you come, or mamma? Speak to papa about it. It is all so disgusting that I really could not write to him. It is enough to break one's heart to see Griff when he hears about home, and Edward, and Emily. I told him how famously you were getting on, and he said, "It has been all up, up with him, all down, down with me," and then he wanted me to fix my day for leaving Baden, as if it were a sink of infection. I fancy he thinks me a mere infant still, for he won't heed a word of advice about taking care of himself and WILL do the most foolish things imaginable for a man in his state, though I can't make out what is the matter with him. I tried both French and Latin with his doctor, equally in vain.'

There was a great consultation over this letter. Our parents would fain have gone at once to Baden, but my father was far from well; in fact, it was the beginning of the break-up of his constitution. He had been ageing ever since his disappointment in Griffith, and though he had so enjoyed his jaunt with my mother that he had seemed revived for the time, he had been visibly failing ever since the winter, and my mother durst not leave him. Indeed she was only too well aware that her presence was apt to inspire Selina with the spirit of contradiction, and that Clarence would have a better chance alone. He was to go up to London by the mail train, see Mr. Castleford, and cross to Ostend.

A valise from the lumber-room was wanted, and at bedtime he went in quest of it. He came back white and shaken; and I said -

'You have not seen HER?'

'Yes, I have.'

'It is not her time of year.'

'No; I was not even thinking of her. There was none of the wailing, but when I looked up from my rummaging, there was her face as if in a window or mirror on the wall.'

'Don't dwell on it' was all I could entreat, for the apparition at unusual times had been mentioned as a note of doom, and not only did it weigh on me, but it might send Clarence off in a desponding mood. Tidings were

Charlotte M. Yonge

less rapid when telegraphs were not, and railways incomplete. Clarence did not reach Baden till ten days after the despatch of Martyn's letter, and Griffith's condition had in the meantime become much more serious. Low fever had set in, and he was confined to his dreary lodgings, where Martyn was doing his best for him in an inexperienced, helpless sort of way, while Lady Peacock was at the salle, persisting in her belief that the ailment was a temporary matter. Martyn afterwards declared that he had never seen anything more touching than poor Griff's look of intense rest and relief at Clarence's entrance.

On the way through London, by the assistance of Mr. Castleford, Clarence had ascertained how to procure the best medical advice attainable, and he was linguist enough to be an adequate interpreter. Alas! all that was achieved was the discovery that between difficulties of language, Griff's own indifference, and his wife's carelessness, the injury had developed into fatal disease. An operation MIGHT yet save him, if he could rally enough for it, but the fever was rapidly destroying his remaining strength. Selina ascribed it to excitement at meeting Martyn, and indeed he had been subject to such attacks every autumn. Any way, he had no spirits nor wish for improvement. If his brothers told him he was better, he smiled and said it was like a condemned criminal trying to recover enough for the gallows. His only desire was to be let alone and have Clarence with him. He had ceased to be uneasy as to Martyn's exposure to temptation, but he said he could hardly bear to watch that bright, fresh young manhood, and recollect how few years had passed since he had been such another, nor did he like to have any nurse save Clarence. His wife at first acquiesced, holding fast to the theory of the periodical autumnal fever, and then that the operation would restore him to health; and as her presence fretted him, and he received her small attentions peevishly, she persisted in her usual habits, and heard with petulance his brothers' assurances of his being in a critical condition, declaring that it was always thus with these fevers—he was always cross and low-spirited, and no one could tell what she had undergone with him.

Then came days of positive pain, and nights of delirious, dreary murmuring about home and all of us, more especially Ellen Fordyce. Clarence had no time for letters, and Martyn's became a call for mamma, with the old childish trust in her healing and comforting powers, declaring that he would meet her at Cologne, and steer her through the difficulties of foreign travel.

Hesitation was over now. My father was most anxious to send her, and she set forth, secure that she could infuse life, energy, and resolution into her son, when those two poor boys had failed.

It was not, however, Martyn who met her, but his friend Thomson, with the tidings that the suffering had become so severe as to prevent Martyn from leaving Baden, not only on his brother's account, but because Lady Peacock had at last taken alarm, and was so uncontrollable in her distress that he was needed to keep her out of the sickroom, where her presence, poor thing, only did mischief.

She evidently had a certain affection for her husband; and it was the more piteous that in his present state he only regarded her as the tempter who had ruined his life—his false Duessa, who had led him away from Una. On one unhappy evening he had been almost maddened by her insisting on arguing with him; he called her a hag, declared she had been the death of his children, the death of that dear one—could she not let him alone now she had

Charlotte M. Yonge

been the death of himself?

When Martyn took her away, she wept bitterly, and told enough to make the misery of their life apparent, when the gaiety was over, and regrets and recriminations set in.

However, there came a calmer interval, when the suffering passed off, but in the manner which made the German doctor intimate that hope was over. Would life last till his mother came?

His brothers had striven from the first to awaken thoughts of higher things, and turn remorse into repentance; but every attempt resulted in strange, sad wanderings about Esau, the birthright, and the blessing. Indeed, these might not have been entirely wanderings, for once he said, 'It is better this way, Bill. You don't know what you wish in trying to bring me round. Don't be hard on me. She drove me to it. It is all right now. The Jews will be disappointed.'

For even at the crisis in London, he had concealed that he had raised money on post obits, so that, had he outlived my father, Chantry House would have been lost. Lady Peacock's fortune had been undermined when she married him; extravagance and gambling had made short work of the rest.

Why should I speak of such things here, except to mourn over our much-loved brother, with all his fine qualities and powers wasted and overthrown? He clung to Clarence's affection, and submitted to prayers and psalms, but without response. He showed tender recollection of us all, but scarcely durst think of his father, and hardly appeared to wish to see his mother. Clarence's object soon came to be to obtain forgiveness for the wife, since bitterness against her seemed the great obstacle to seeking pardon, peace, or hope; but each attempt only produced such bitterness against her, and such regrets and mourning for Ellen, as fearfully shook the failing frame, while he moaned forth complaints of the blandishments and raillery with which his temptress had beguiled him. Clarence tried in vain to turn away this idea, but nothing had any effect till he bethought himself of Ellen's message, that she knew even this fatal act had been prompted by generosity of spirit. There was truth enough in it to touch Griff, but only so far as to cry, 'What might I not have been with her?' Still, there was no real softening till my mother came. He knew her at once, and all the old childish relations were renewed between them. There was little time left now, but he was wholly hers. Even Clarence was almost set aside, save where strength was needed, and the mother seemed to have equal control of spirit and body. It was she, who, scarcely aware of what had gone before, caused him to admit Selina.

'Tell her not to talk,' he said. 'But we have each much to forgive one another.'

She came in, awed and silent, and he let her kiss him, sit near at hand, and wait on my mother, whose coming had, as it were, insensibly taken the bitterness away and made him as a little child in her hands. He could follow prayers in which she led him, as he could not, or did not seem to do, with any one else, for he was never conscious of the presence of the clergyman whom Thomson hunted up and brought, and who prayed aloud with Martyn while the physical agony claimed both my mother and Clarence.

Once Griff looked about him and called out for our father, then recollecting, muttered, 'No—the birthright gone—no blessing.'

It grieved us much, it grieves me now, that this was his

last distinct utterance. He LOOKED as if the comforting replies and the appeals to the Source of all redemption did awaken a response, but he never spoke articulately again; and only thirty-six hours after my mother's arrival, all was over.

Poor Selina went into passions of hysterics and transports of grief, needing all the firmness of so resolute a woman as my mother to deal with her. She was wild in self-accusation, and became so ill that the care of her was a not unwholesome occupation for my mother, who was one of those with whom sorrow has little immediate outlet, and is therefore the more enduring.

She would not bring our brother's coffin home, thinking the agitation would be hurtful to my father, and anxious to get back to him as soon as possible. So Griff was buried at Baden, and from time to time some of us have visited his grave. Of course she proposed Selina's return to Chantry House with her; but Mr. Clarkson, the brother, had come out to the funeral, and took his sister home with him, certainly much to our relief, though all the sad party at Baden had drawn much nearer together in these latter days.

CHAPTER XXXIX

A PURPOSE

'It then draws near the season
Wherein the spirit held his wont to walk.'

HAMLET.

We had really lost our Griffith long before—our bright, generous, warm-hearted, promising Griff, the brilliance of our home; but his actual death made the first breach in a hitherto unbroken family, and was a new and strange shock. It made my father absolutely an old man; and it also changed Martyn. His first contact with responsibility, suffering, and death had demolished the light-hearted boyishness which had lasted in the youngest of the family through all his high aspirations. Till his return to Oxford, his chief solace was in getting some one of us alone, going through all the scenes at Baden, discussing his new impressions of the trials and perplexities of life, and seeking out passages in the books that were becoming our oracles. What he had admired externally before, he was grasping from within; nor can I describe what the Lyra Apostolica, and the two first volumes of Parochial Sermons preached at Littlemore, became to us.

Charlotte M. Yonge

Mr. Clarkson had been rather dry with my brothers at Baden, evidently considering that poor Griffith had been as fatal to his sister as we thought Selina had been to our brother. It was hardly just, for there had been much more to spoil in him than in her; and though she would hardly have trod a much higher path, there is no saying what he might have been but for her.

Griffith had said nothing about providing for her, not having forgiven her till he was past recollecting the need, but her brother had intimated that something was due from the family, and Clarence had assented—not, indeed, as to her deserts, poor woman, but her claims and her needs—well knowing that my father would never suffer Griff's widow to be in want.

He judged rightly. My father was nervously anxious to arrange for giving her 500 pounds a year, in the manner most likely to prevent her from making away with it, and leaving herself destitute. But there had already been heavy pulls on his funded property, and ways and means had to be considered, making Clarence realise that he had become the heir. Somehow, there still remained, especially with my mother and himself, a sense of his being a failure, and an inferior substitute, although my father had long come to lean upon him, as never had been the case with our poor Griff.

The first idea of raising the amount required was by selling an outlying bit of the estate near the Wattlesea Station, for which an enterprising builder was making offers, either to purchase or take on a building lease. My father had received several letters on the subject, and only hesitated from a feeling against breaking up the estate, especially if this were part of the original Chantry House property, and not a more recent acquisition of the Winslows. Moreover, he would do nothing without

Clarence's participation.

The title-deeds were not in the house, for my father had had too much of the law to meddle more than he could help with his own affairs, and had left them in the hands of the family solicitor at Bristol, where Clarence was to go and look over them. He rejoiced in the opportunity of being able to see whether anything would throw light on the story of the mullion chamber; and the certainty that the Wattlesea property had never been part of the old endowment of the Chantry did not seem nearly so interesting as a packet of yellow letters tied with faded red tape. Mr. Ryder made no difficulty in entrusting these to him, and we read them by our midnight lamp.

Clarence had seen poor Margaret's will, bequeathing her entire property to her husband's son, Philip Winslow, and had noted the date, 1705; also the copy of the decision in the Court of Probate that there was no sufficient evidence of entail on the Fordyce family to bar her power of disposing of it. We eagerly opened the letters, but found them disappointing, as they were mostly offerings of 'Felicitations' to Philip Winslow on having established his 'Just Claim,' and 'refuted the malicious Accusations of Calumny.' They only served to prove the fact that he had been accused of something, and likewise that he had powerful friends, and was thought worth being treated with adulation, according to the fashion of his day. Perhaps it was hardly to be expected that he should have preserved evidence against himself, but it was baffling to sift so little out of such a mass of correspondence. If we could have had access to the Fordyce papers, no doubt they would have given the other phase of the transaction, but they were unattainable. The only public record that Clarence could discover was much abbreviated, and though there was some allusion to intimidation, the decision seemed to have been fixed by the non-existence

Charlotte M. Yonge

of any entail.

Christmas was drawing on, and gathering together what was left of us. Though Griffith had spent only one Christmas at home in nine years, it was wonderful how few we seemed, even when Martyn returned. My father liked to have us about him, and even spoke of Clarence's giving up his post as manager at Bristol, and living entirely at home to attend to the estate; but my mother did not encourage the idea. She could not quite bear to accept any one in Griff's place, and rightly thought there was not occupation enough to justify bringing Clarence home. I was competent to assist my father through all the landlord's business that came to him within doors, and Emily had ridden and walked about enough with him to be an efficient inspector of crops and repairs, besides that Clarence himself was within reach.

'Indeed,' he said to me, 'I cannot loose my hold on Frith and Castleford till I see my way into the future.'

I did not know what he intended either then or when he gave his voice against dismembering the property by selling the Wattlesea estate, but arranged for raising Selina's income otherwise, persuading my father to let him undertake the building of the required cottages out of his own resources, on principles much more wholesome than were likely to be employed by the speculator. Nor did grasp what was in his mind when he made me look out my 'ghost journal,' as we called my record of each apparition reported in the mullion chamber or the lawn, with marks to those about which we had no reasonable doubt. Separately there might be explanation, but conjointly and in connection with the date they had a remarkable force.

'I am resolved,' said Clarence, 'to see whether that figure

can have a purpose. I have thought of it all those years. It has hitherto had no fair play. I was too much upset by the sight, and beaten by the utter incredulity of everybody else; but now I am determined to look into it.'

There was both awe and resolution in his countenance, and I only stipulated that he should not be alone, or with no more locomotive companion than myself. Martyn was as old as I had been at our former vigil, and a person to be relied on.

A few months ago he would have treated the matter as a curious adventurous enterprise—a concession to super-stition or imagination; but now he took it up with much grave earnestness. He had been discussing the evidence for such phenomena with friends at Oxford, and the conclusion had been that they were at times permitted, sometimes as warnings, sometimes to accomplish the redress of a wrong, sometimes to teach us the reality of the spiritual world about us; and, likewise, that some constitutions were more susceptible than others to these influences. Of course he had adduced all that he knew of his domestic haunted chamber, but had found himself uncertain as to the amount of direct or trustworthy evi-dence. So he eagerly read our jottings, and was very anxious to keep watch with Clarence, though there were greater difficulties in the way than when the outer chamber was Griffith's sitting-room, and always had a fire lighted.

To our disappointment, likewise, there came an invitation from the Eastwoods for the evening of the 27th of December, the second of the recurring days of the phantom's appearance. My father could not, and my mother would not go, but they so much wanted my brothers and sister to accept it that it could not well be declined. It was partly a political affair, and my father was anxious to put Clarence forward, and make him take his place as the future squire; and my mother thought depression had lasted long enough with her children, and did not like to see Martyn so grave and preoccupied. 'It was quite right and very nice in him, dear boy, but it was not natural at his age, though he was to be a clergyman.'

As to Emily, her gentle cheerfulness had helped us all through our time of sorrow, and just now we had been gratified by the tidings of young Lawrence Frith. That youth was doing extremely well. There had been golden reports from manager and chaplain, addressed to Mr. Castleford, the latter adding that the young man evidently owed much to Mr. Winslow's influence. Moreover, Lawrence had turned out an excellent correspondent. Long letters, worthy of forming a book of travels, came regularly to Clarence and me, indeed they were thought worth being copied into that fat clasped MS. book in the study. Writing them must have been a real solace to the exile, in his island outside the town, whither all the outer barbarians were relegated. So, no doubt, was the packing of the gifts that were gradually making Prospect Cottage into a Chinese exhibition of nodding mandarins, ivory balls, exquisite little cups, and faggots of tea. Also, a Chinese walking doll was sent humbly as an offering for the amusement of Miss Winslow's school children, whom indeed she astonished beyond measure; and though her wheels are out of order, and her movements uncertain, she is still a stereotyped incident in the Christmas entertainments.

There was no question but that these letters and remembrances gave great pleasure to Emily; but I believe she was not in the least conscious that though greater in degree, it was not of the same quality as that she felt when a runaway scholar who had gone to sea presented her in token of gratitude with a couple of dried sea-horses.

CHAPTER XL

THE MIDNIGHT CHASE

'What human creature in the dead of night
Had coursed, like hunted hare, that cruel distance,
Had sought the door, the window in her flight
Striving for dear existence?'

HOOD.

On the night of the 26th of December, Clarence and
Martyn, well wrapped in greatcoats, stole into the outer
mullion room; but though the usual sounds were heard,
and the mysterious light again appeared, Martyn
perceived nothing else, and even Clarence declared that if
there were anything besides, it was far less distinct to him
than it had been previously. Could it be that his spiritual
perceptions were growing dimmer as he became older,
and outgrew the sensitiveness of nerves and imagination?

We came to the conclusion that it would be best to watch
the outside of the house, rather than within the chamber;
and the dinner-party facilitated this, since it accounted for
being up and about nearer to the hour when the ghost
might be expected. Egress could be had through the little
garden door, and I undertook to sit up and keep up

the fire.

All three came to my room on their return home, for Emily had become aware of our scheme, and entreated to be allowed to watch with us. Clarence had unfastened the alarum bell from my shutters, and taken down the bar after the curtains had been drawn by the housemaid, and he now opened them. It was a frosty moonlight night, and the lawn lay white and crisp, marked with fantastic shadows. The others looked grave and pale, Emily was in a thick white shawl and hood, with a swan's down boa over her black dress, a somewhat ghostly figure herself, but we were in far too serious a mood for light observations.

There was something of a shudder about Clarence as he went to unbolt the back door; Martyn kept close to him. We saw them outside, and then Emily flew after them. From my window I could watch them advancing on the central gravel walk, Emily standing still between her brothers, clasping an arm of each. I saw the light near the ruin, and caught some sounds as of shrieks and of threatening voices, the light flitted towards the gable of the mullion rooms, and then was the concluding scream. All was over, and the three came back much agitated, Emily sinking into an armchair, panting, her hands over her face, and a nervous trembling through her whole frame, Martyn's eyes looking wide and scared, Clarence with the well-known look of terror on his face. He hurried to fetch the tray of wine and water that was always left on the table when anyone went to a party at night, but he shivered too much to prevent the glasses from jingling, and I had to pour out the sherry and administer it to Emily. 'Oh! poor, poor thing,' she gasped out.

'You saw?' I exclaimed.

'They did,' said Martyn; 'I only saw the light, and heard! That was enough!' and he shuddered again.

'Then Emily did,' I began, but Clarence cut me short. 'Don't ask her to-night.'

'Oh! let me tell,' cried Emily; 'I can't go away to bed till I have had it out.'

Then she gave the details, which were the more notable because she had not, like Martyn, been studying our jottings, and had heard comparatively little of the apparition.

'When I joined the boys,' she said, 'I looked toward the mullion rooms; I saw the windows lighted up, and heard a sobbing and crying inside.'

'So did I,' put in Martyn, and Clarence bent his head.

'Then,' added Emily, 'by the moonlight I saw the gable end, not blank, and covered by the magnolia as it is now, but with stone steps up to the bricked-up doorway. The door opened, the light spread, and there came out a lady in black, with a lamp in one hand, and a kind of parcel in the other, and oh, when she turned her face this way, it was Ellen's!'

'So you called out,' whispered Martyn.

'Dear Ellen, not as she used to be,' added Emily, 'but like what she was when last I saw her; no, hardly that either, for this was sad, sad, scared, terrified, with eyes all tears, as Ellen never, never was.'

'I saw,' added Clarence, 'I saw the shape, but not the countenance and expression as I used to do.'

'She came down the steps,' continued Emily, 'looking about her as if making her escape, but, just as she came opposite to us, there was a sound of tipsy laughing and singing from the gate up by the wood.'

'I thought it real,' said Martyn.

'Then,' continued Emily, 'she wavered, then turned and went under an arch in the ruin—I fancied she was hiding something—then came out and fled across to the steps; but there were two dark men rushing after her, and at the stone steps there was a frightful shriek, and then it was all over, the steps gone, all quiet, and the magnolia leaves glistening in the moonshine. Oh! what can it all mean?'

'Went under the arch,' repeated Clarence. 'Is it what she hid there that keeps her from resting?'

'Then you believe it really happened?' said Emily, 'that some terrible scene is being acted over again. Oh! but can it be the real spirits!'

'That is one of the great mysteries,' answered Martyn; 'but I could tell you of other instances.'

'Don't now,' I interposed; 'Emily has had quite enough.'

We reminded her that the ghastly tragedy was over and would not recur again for another year; but she was greatly shaken, and we were very sorry for her, when the clock warned her to go to her own room, whither Martyn escorted her. He lighted every candle he could find, and revived the fire; but she was sadly overcome by what she had witnessed, she lay awake all the rest of the night, and in the morning, looked so unwell, and had so little to tell about the party that my mother thought her spirits had been too much broken for gaieties.

The real cause could not be confessed, for it would have been ascribed to some kind of delirium, and have made a commotion for which my father was unfit. Besides, we had reached an age when, though we would not have disobeyed, liberty of thought and action had become needful. All our private confabulations were on this extraordinary scene. We looked for the arch in the ruin, but there was, as our morning senses told us, nothing of the kind. She tried to sketch her remembrance of both that and the gable of the mullion chamber, and Martyn prowled about in search of some hiding-place. Our antiquarian friend, Mr. Stafford, had made a conjectural drawing of the Chapel restored, and all the portfolios about the house were searched for it, disquieting mamma, who suspected Martyn's Oxford notions of intending to rebuild it, nor would he say that it ought not to be done. However, he with his more advanced ecclesiology, pronounced Mr. Stafford's reconstruction to be absolutely mistaken and impossible, and set to work on a fresh plan, which, by the bye, he derides at present. It afforded, however, an excuse for routing under the ivy and among the stones, but without much profit. From the mouldings on the materials and in the stables and the front porch, it was evident that the chapel had been used as a quarry, and Emily's arch was very probably that of the entrance door. In a dry summer, the foundations of the walls and piers could be traced on the turf, and the stumps of one or two columns remained, but the rest was only a confused heap of fragments within which no one could have entered as in that strange vision.

Another thing became clear. There had once been a wall between the beech wood and the lawn, with a gate or door in it; Chapman could just remember its being taken down, in James Winslow's early married life, when landscape gardening was the fashion. It must have been through this that the Winslow brothers were returning, when poor

Margaret perhaps expected them to enter by the front.

We wished we could have consulted Dame Dearlove, but she had died a few years before, and her school was extinct.

CHAPTER XLI

WILLS OLD AND NEW

'And that to-night thou must watch with me
To win the treasure of the tomb.'

SCOTT.

Some seasons seem to be peculiarly marked, as if Death did indeed walk forth in them.

Old Mr. Frith died in the spring of 1841, and it proved that he had shown his gratitude to Clarence by a legacy of shares in the firm amounting to about 2000 pounds. The rest of his interest therein went to Lawrence Frith, and his funded property to his sister, Mrs. Stevens, a very fair and upright disposition of his wealth.

Only six weeks later, my father had a sudden seizure, and there was only time to summon Clarence from London and Martyn from Oxford, before a second attack closed his righteous and godly career upon earth.

My mother was very still and calm, hardly shedding a tear, but her whole demeanour was as if life were over for her, and she had nothing to do save to wait. She seemed to

Charlotte M. Yonge

care very little for tendernesses or attentions on our part. No doubt she would have been more desolate without them, but we always had a baffled feeling, as though our affection were contrasted with her perfect union with her husband. Yet they had been a singularly undemonstrative couple; I never saw a kiss pass between them, except as greeting or farewell before or after a journey; and if my mother could not use the terms papa or your father, she always said, 'Mr. Winslow.' There was a large gathering at the funeral, including Mr. Fordyce, but he slept at Hillside, and we scarcely saw him—only for a few kind words and squeezes of the hand. Holy Week was begun, and he had to hurry back to Beachharbour that very night.

The will had been made on my father's coming into the inheritance. It provided a jointure of 800 pounds per annum for my mother, and gave each of the younger children 3000 pounds. A codicil had been added shortly after Griffith's death, written in my father's hand, and witnessed by Mr. Henderson and Amos Bell. This put Clarence in the position of heir; secured 500 pounds a year to Griffith's widow, charged on the estate, and likewise an additional 200 pounds a year to Emily and to me, hers till marriage, mine for life, 300 pounds a year to Martyn, until Earlscombe Rectory should be voided, when it was to be offered to him. The executors had originally been Mr. Castleford and my mother, but by this codicil, Clarence was substituted for the former.

The legacies did not come out of the Chantry House property, for my father had, of course, means of his own besides, and bequests had accrued to both him and my mother; but Clarence was inheriting the estate much more burthened than it had been in 1829, having 2000 pounds a year to raise out of its proceeds.

My mother was quite equal to business, with a sort of

outside sense, which she applied to it when needful. Clarence made it at once evident to her that she was still mistress of Chantry House, and that it was still to be our home; and she immediately calculated what each ought to contribute to the housekeeping. She looked rather blank when she found that Clarence did not mean to give up business, nor even to become a sleeping partner; but when she examined into ways and means, she allowed that he was prudent, and that perhaps it was due to Mr. Castleford not to deprive him of an efficient helper under present circumstances. Meantime she was content to do her best for Earlscombe 'for the present,' by which she meant till her son brought home a wife; but we knew that to him the words bore a different meaning, though he was still in doubt and uncertainty how to act, and what might be the wrong to be undone.

He was anxious to persuade her to go from home for a short time, and prevailed on her at last to take Emily and me to Dawlish, while the repairs went on which had been deferred during my father's feebleness; at least that was the excuse. We two, going with great regret, knew that his real reason was to have an opportunity for a search among the ruins.

It was in June, just as Martyn came back from Oxford, eager to share in the quest. Those two brothers would trust no one to help them, but one by one, in the long summer evenings, they moved each of those stones; I believe the servants thought they were crazed, but they could explain with some truth that they wanted to clear up the disputed points as to the architecture, as indeed they succeeded in doing.

They had, however, nearly given up, having reached the original pavement and disinterred the piscina of the side altar, also a beautiful coffin lid with a floriated cross;

when, in a kind of hollow, Martyn lit upon the rotten remains of something silken, knotted together. It seemed to have enclosed a bundle. There were some rags that might have been a change of clothing, also a Prayer-book, decayed completely except the leathern covering, inside which was the startling inscription, 'Margaret Winslow, her booke; Lord, have mercy on a miserable widow woman.' There was also a thick leathern roll, containing needles, pins, and scissors, entirely corroded, and within these a paper, carefully folded, but almost destroyed by the action of damp and the rust of the steel, so that only thus much was visible. 'I, Margaret Winslow, being of sound mind, do hereby give and bequeath—'

Then came stains that defaced every line, till the extreme end, where a seal remained; the date 1707 was legible, and there were some scrawls, probably the poor lady's signature, and perhaps that of witnesses. Clarence and Martyn said very little to one another, but they set out for Dawlish the next day.

'Found' was indicated to us, but no more, for they arrived late, and had to sleep at the hotel, after an evening when we were delighted to hear my mother ask so many questions about household and parish affairs. In the morning she was pleased to send all 'the children' out on the beach, then free from the railway. It was a beautiful day, with the intensely blue South Devon sea dancing in golden ripples, and breaking on the shore with the sound Clarence loved so well, as, in the shade of the dark crimson cliffs, Emily sat at my feet and my brothers unfolded their strange discoveries into her lap. There was a kind of solemnity in the thing; we scarcely spoke, except that Emily said, 'Oh, will she come again,' and, as the tears gathered at sight of the pathetic petition in the old book, 'Was that granted?'

We reconstructed our theory. The poor lady must have repented of the unjust will forced from her by her stepsons, and contrived to make another; but she must have been kept a captive until, during their absence at some Christmas convivialities, she tried to escape; but hearing sounds betokening their return, she had only time to hide the bundle in the ruin before she was detected, and in the scuffle received a fatal blow.

'But why,' I objected, 'did she not remain hidden till her enemies were safe in the house?'

'Terrified beyond the use of her senses,' said Clarence.

'By all accounts,' said Martyn, 'the poor creature must have been rather a silly woman.'

'For shame, Martyn,' cried Emily, 'how can you tell? They might have seen her go in, or she might have feared being missed.'

'Or if you watch next Christmas you may see it all explained.'

To which Emily replied with a shiver that nothing would induce her to go through it again, and indeed she hoped the spirit would rest since the discovery had been made.

'And then?'—one of us said, and there was a silence, and another futile attempt to read the will.

'I shall take it to London and see what an expert can do with it,' said Clarence. 'I have heard of wonderful decipherings in the Record Office; but you will remember that even if it can be made out, it will hardly invalidate our possession after a hundred and thirty years.'

Charlotte M. Yonge

'Clarence!' cried Emily in a horrified voice; and I asked if the date were not later than that by which we inherited.

'Three years,' Clarence said, 'yes; but as things stand, it is absolutely impossible for me to make restitution at present.'

'On account of the burthens on the estate?' I said.

'Oh, but we could give up,' said Emily.

'I dare say!' said Clarence, smiling; 'but to say nothing of poor Selina, my mother would hardly see it in the same light, nor should I deal rightly, even if I could make any alterations; I doubt whether my father would have held himself bound—certainly not while no one can read this document.'

'It would simply outrage his legal mind,' said Martyn.

'Then what is to be done? Is the injustice to be perpetual?' asked Emily.

'This is what I have thought of,' said Clarence. 'We must leave matters as they are till I can realise enough either to pay off all these bequests, or to offer Mr. Fordyce the value of the estate.'

'It is not the whole,' I said.

'Not the Wattlesea part. This means Chantry House and the three farms in the village. 10,000 pounds would cover it.'

'Is it possible?' asked Emily.

'Yes,' returned Clarence, 'God helping me. You know our

concern is bringing in good returns, and Mr. Castleford will put me in the way of doing more with my available capital.'

'We will save so as to help you!' added Emily. At which he smiled.

CHAPTER XLII

ON A SPREE

'Her eyes as stars of twilight fair,
Like twilight too, her dusky hair,
But all things else about her drawn
From May-time and the cheerful dawn,
A dancing shape, an image gay,
To haunt, to startle, and waylay.'

WORDSWORTH.

Clarence went to London according to his determination, and as he had for some time been urgent that I should try some newly-invented mechanical appliances, he took me with him, this being the last expedition of the ancient yellow chariot. One of his objects was that I should see St. Paul's, Knightsbridge, which was then the most distinguished church of our school of thought, and where there was to be some special preaching. The Castlefords had a seat there, and I was settled there in good time, looking at the few bits of stained glass then in the east window, when, as the clergy came in from the vestry, I beheld a familiar face, and recognised the fine countenance and bearing of our dear old friend Frank Fordyce.

Then, looking at the row of ladies in front of me, I beheld for a moment an outline of a profile recalling many things. No doubt, Anne Fordyce was there, though instead of barely emulating my stunted stature, she towered above her companions, looking to my mind most fresh and graceful in her pretty summer dress; and I knew that Clarence saw her too.

I had never heard Mr. Fordyce preach before, as in his flying visits his ministrations were due at Hillside; and I certainly should have been struck with the force and beauty of his sermon if I had never known him before. It was curious that it was on the 49th Psalm, meant perhaps for the fashionable congregation, but remarkably chiming in with the feelings of us, who were conscious of an inheritance of evil from one who had 'done well unto himself;' though, no doubt, that was the last thing honest Parson Frank was thinking of.

When the service was over, and Anne turned, she became aware of us, and her face beamed all over. It was a charming face, with a general likeness to dear Ellen's, but without the fragile ethereal look, and all health, bloom, and enjoyment recalling her father's. She was only moving to let her pew-fellows pass out, and was waiting for him to come for her, as he did in a few moments, and he too was all pleasure and cordiality. He told us when we were outside that he had come up to preach, and 'had brought Miss Anne up for a spree.' They were at a hotel, Mrs. Fordyce was at home, and the Lesters were not in town this season—a matter of rejoicing to us. Could we not come home and dine with them at once? We were too much afraid of disappointing Gooch to do so, but they made an appointment to meet us at the Royal Academy as soon as it was open the next morning.

There was a fortnight of enjoyment. Parson Frank was

like a boy out for a holiday. He had not spent more than a day or two in town for many years; Anne had not been there since early childhood, and they adopted Clarence as their lioniser, going through such a country-cousin course of delights as in that memorable time with Ellen. They even went down to Eton and Windsor, Frank Fordyce being an old Etonian. I doubt whether Clarence ever had a more thoroughly happy time, not even in the north of Devon, for there was no horse on his mind, and he was not suppressed as in those days. Indeed, I believe, it is the experience of others besides ourselves that there is often more unmixed pleasure on casual holidays like this than in those of early youth; for even if spirits are less high (which is not always the case), anticipations are less eager, there is more readiness to accept whatever comes, more matured appreciation, and less fret and friction at contretemps.

I was not much of a drag, for when I could not be with the others, I had old friends, and the museum was as dear to me as ever, in those recesses that had been the paradise of my youth; but there was a good deal in which we could all share, and as usual they were all kind consideration.

Anne overflowed with minute remembrances of her old home, and Clarence so basked in her sunshine that it began to strike me that here might be the solution of all the perplexities especially after the first evening, when he had shown his strange discovery to Mr. Fordyce, who simply laughed and said we need not trouble ourselves about it. Illegible was it? He was heartily glad to hear that it was. Even otherwise, forty years' possession was quite enough, and then he pointed to the grate, and said that was the best place for such things. There was no fire, but Clarence could hardly rescue the paper from being torn up.

As to the ghost, he knew much less than his daughter Ellen had done. He said his old aunt had some stories about Chantry House being haunted, and had thought it incumbent on her to hate the Winslows, but he had thought it all nonsense, and such stories were much better forgotten. 'Would he not see if there were any letters?'

There might be, perhaps in the solicitor's office at Bath, but if he ever got hold of them, he should certainly burn them. What was the use of being Christians, if such quarrels were to be remembered?

Anne knew nothing. Aunt Peggy had died before she could remember, and even Martyn had been discreet. Clarence said no more after that one conversation, and seemed to me engrossed between his necessary business at the office, and the pleasant expeditions with the Fordyces. Only when they were on the point of returning home, did he tell me that the will had been pronounced utterly past deciphering, and that he thought he saw a way of setting all straight. 'So do I,' was my rejoinder, and there must have been a foolishly sagacious expression about me that made him colour up, and say, 'No such thing, Edward. Don't put that into my head.'

'Isn't it there already?'

'It ought not to be. It would be mere treachery in these sweet, fresh, young, innocent, days of hers, knowing too what her mother would think of it and of me. Didn't you observe in old Frank's unguarded way of reading letters aloud, and then trying to suppress bits, that Mrs. Fordyce was not at all happy at our being so much about with them, poor woman. No wonder! the child is too young,' he added, showing how much, after all, he was thinking of it. 'It would be taking a base advantage of them NOW.'

'But by and by?'

'If she should be still free when the great end is achieved and the evil repaired, then I might dare.'

He broke off with a look of glad hope, and I could see it was forbearance rather than constitutional diffidence that withheld him from awakening the maiden's feelings. He was a very fine looking man, in his prime—tall, strong, and well made, with a singularly grave, thoughtful expression, and a rare but most winning smile; and Anne was overflowing with affectionate gladness at intercourse with one who belonged to the golden age of her childhood. I could scarcely believe but that in the friction of the parting the spark would be elicited, and I should even have liked to kindle it for them myself, being tolerably certain that warm-hearted, unguarded Parson Frank would forget all about his lady and blow it with all his might.

We dined with the Fordyces at their hotel, and sat in the twilight with the windows open, and we made Anne and Clarence sing, as both could do without notes, but he would not undertake to remember anything with an atom of sentiment in it, and when Anne did sing, 'Auld lang syne,' with all her heart, he went and got into a dark corner, and barely said, 'Thank you.'

Not a definite answer could be extracted from him in reply to all the warm invitations to Beachharbour that were lavished on us by the father, while the daughter expatiated on its charms; the rocks I might sketch, the waves and the delicious boating, and above all the fisher children and the church. Nothing was wanting but to have us all there! Why had we not brought Mrs. Winslow, and Emily, and Martyn, instead of going to Dawlish?

Good creatures, they little knew the chill that had been cast upon Martyn. They even bemoaned the having seen so little of him. And we knew all the time that they were mice at play in the absence of their excellent and cautious cat.

'Now mind you do come!' said Anne, as we were in the act of taking leave. 'It would be as good as Hillside to have you by my Lion rock. He has a nose just like old Chapman's, and you must sketch it before it crumbles off. Yes, and I want to show you all the dear old things you made for my baby-house after the fire, your dear little wardrobe and all.'

She was coming out with us, oblivious that a London hotel was not like her own free sea-side house. Her father was out at the carriage door, prepared to help me in, Clarence halted a moment -

'Please, pray, go back, Anne,' he said, and his voice trembled. 'This is not home you know.'

She started back, but paused. 'You'll not forget.'

'Oh no; no fear of my forgetting.'

And when seated beside me, he leant back with a sigh.

'How could you help?' I said.

'How? Why the perfect, innocent, childish, unconsciousness of the thing,' he said, and became silent except for one murmur on the way.

'Consequences must be borne—'

CHAPTER XLIII

THE PRICE

'With thee, my bark, I'll swiftly go
Athwart the foaming brine.'

LORD BYRON.

Clarence would not tell me his purpose, he said, till he
had considered it more fully; nor could we have much
conversation on the way home, as my mother had
arranged that we should bring an old friend of hers back
with us to pay her a visit. So I had to sit inside and make
myself agreeable to Mrs. Wrightson, while Clarence had
plenty of leisure for meditation outside on the box seat.
The good lady said much on the desirableness of marriage
for Clarence, and the comfort it would be to my mother to
see Emily settled.

We had heard much in town of railway shares; and the
fortunes of Hudson, the railway king, were under
discussion. I suspected Clarence of cogitating the using
his capital in this manner; and hoped that when he saw his
way, he might not think it dishonourable to come into
further contact with Anne, and reveal his hopes. He
allowed that he was considering of such investments, but

would not say any more.

My mother and Emily had, in the meantime, been escorted home by Martyn. The first thing Clarence did was to bespeak Emily's company in a turn in the garden. What passed then I never knew nor guessed for years after. He consulted her whether, in case he were absent from England for five, seven, or ten years, she would be equal to the care of my mother and me. Martyn, when ordained, would have duties elsewhere, and could only be reckoned upon in emergencies. My mother, though vigorous and practical, had shown symptoms of gout, and if she were ill, I could hardly have done much for her; and on the other hand, though my health and powers of moving were at their best, and I was capable of the headwork of the estate, I was scarcely fit to be the representative member of the family. Moreover, these good creatures took into consideration that poor mamma and I would have been rather at a loss as each other's sole companions. I could sort shades for her Berlin work, and even solve problems of intricate knitting, and I could read to her in the evening; but I could not trot after her to her garden, poultry-yard, and cottages; nor could she enter into the pursuits that Emily had shared with me for so many years. Our connecting link, that dear sister, knew how sorely she would be missed, and she told Clarence that she felt fully competent to undertake, conjointly with us, all that would be incumbent on Chantry House, if he really wanted to be absent. For the rest, Clarence believed my mother would be the happier for being left regent over the estate; and his scheme broke upon me that very forenoon, when my mother and he were settling some executor's business together, and he told her that Mr. Castleford wished him to go out to Hong Kong, which was then newly ceded to the English, and where the firm wished to establish a house of business.

'You can't think of it,' she exclaimed, and the sound fell like a knell on my ears.

'I think I must,' was his answer. 'We shall be cut out if we do not get a footing there, and there is no one who can quite answer the purpose.'

'Not that young Frith—'

'Ten to one but he is on his way home. Besides, if not, he has his own work at Canton. We see our way to very considerable advantages, if—'

'Advantages!' she interrupted. 'I hate speculation. I should have thought you might be contented with your station; but that is the worst of merchants,—they never know when to stop. I suppose your ambition is to make this a great overgrown mansion, so that your father would not know it again.'

'Certainly not that, mamma,' said Clarence smiling; 'it is the last thing I should think of; but stopping would in this case mean going backward.'

'Why can't Mr. Castleford send one of his own sons?'

'Probably Walter may come out by and by, but he has not experience enough for this.'

Clarence had not in the least anticipated my mother's opposition, for he had come to underestimate her affection for and reliance on him. He had us all against him, for not only could we not bear to part with him; but the climate of Hong-Kong was in evil repute, and I had become persuaded that, with his knowledge of business, railway shares and scrip might be made to realise the amount needed, but he said, 'That is what *I* call speculation. The other matter is trade in which, with Heaven's blessing, I can hope to prosper.'

He explained that Mr. Castleford had received him on his coming to London with almost a request that he would undertake this expedition; but with fears whether, in his new position, he could or would do so, although his presence in China would be very important to the firm at this juncture; and there would be opportunities which would probably result in very considerable profits after a few years. If Clarence had been, as before, a mere younger brother, it would have been thought an excellent chance; and he would almost have felt bound by his obligations to Mr. Castleford to undertake the first starting of the enterprise, if it had not been for our recent loss, and the doubt whether he could he spared from home.

He made light of the dangers of climate. He had never suffered in that way in his naval days, and scarcely knew what serious illness meant. Indeed, he had outgrown much of that sensibility of nerve which had made him so curiously open to spiritual or semi-spiritual impressions.

'Any way,' he said, 'the thing is right to be done, provided my mother does not make an absolute point of my giving it up; and whether she does or not depends a good deal on how you others put it to her.'

'Right on Mr. Castleford's account?' I asked.

'That is one side of it. To refuse would put him in a serious difficulty; but I could perhaps come home sooner if it were not for this other matter. I told him so far as that it was an object with me to raise this sum in a few years, and he showed me how there is every likelihood of my being able to do so out there. So now I feel in your hands.

If you all, and Edward chiefly, set to and persuade my mother that this undertaking is a dangerous business, and that I can only be led to it by inordinate love of riches—'

'No, no—'

'That's what she thinks,' pursued Clarence, 'and that I want to be a grander man than my father. That's at the bottom of her mind, I see. Well, if you deplore this, and let her think the place can't do without me, she will come out in her strength and make it my duty to stay at home.'

'It is very tempting,' said Emily.

'We all undertook to give up something.'

'We never thought it would come in this way!'

'We never do,' said Clarence.

'Tell me,' said Martyn, 'is this to content that ghost, poor thing? For it is very hard to believe in her, except in the mullion room in December.'

'Exactly so, Martyn,' he answered. 'Impressions fade, and the intellect fails to accept them. But I do not think that is my motive. We know that a wicked deed was done by our ancestor, and we hardly have the right to pray, "Remember not the sins of our forefathers," unless, now that we know the crime, we attempt what restitution in us lies.'

There was no resisting after this appeal, and after the first shock, my mother was ready to admit that as Clarence owed everything to Mr. Castleford, he could not well desert the firm, if it were really needful for its welfare that he should go out. We got her to look on Mr. Castleford as captain of the ship, and Clarence as first lieutenant; and when she was once convinced that he did not want to aggrandise the family, but to do his duty, she dropped her objections; and we soon saw that the occupations that his absence would impose on her would be a fresh interest in life.

Just as the decision was thus ratified, a packet from Canton arrived for Clarence from Bristol. It was the first reply of young Frith to the tidings of the bequest which had changed the poor clerk to a wealthy man, owning a large proportion of the shares of the prosperous house.

I asked if he were coming home, and Clarence briefly replied that he did not know,—'it depended—'

'Is he going to wed a fair Chinese with lily feet?' asked Martyn, to which the reply was an unusually discourteous 'Bosh,' as Clarence escaped with his letter. He was so reticent about it that I required a solemn assurance that poor Lawrence's head had not been turned by his fortune, and that there was nothing wrong with him. Indeed, there was great stupidity in never guessing the purport of that thick letter, nor that it contained one for Emily, where Lawrence Frith laid himself, and all that he had, at her feet, ascribing to her all the resolution with which he had kept from evil, and entreating permission to come home and endeavour to win her heart. We lived so constantly together that it is surprising that Clarence contrived to give the letter to Emily in private. She implored him to say nothing to us, and brought him the next day her letter of uncompromising refusal.

He asked whether it would have been the same if he had intended to remain at home.

'As if you were a woman, you conceited fellow,' was all

the answer she vouchsafed him.

Nor could he ascertain, nor perhaps would she herself examine, on which side lay her heart of hearts. The proof had come whether she would abide by her pledge to him to accept the care of us in his absence. When he asked it, it had not occurred to him that it might be a renunciation of marriage. Now he perceived that so it had been, but she kept her counsel and so did he. We others never guessed at what was going on between those two.

CHAPTER XLIV

PAYING THE COST

'But oh! the difference to me.'

WORDSWORTH.

So Clarence was gone, and our new life begun in its changed aspect. Emily showed an almost feverish eagerness to make it busy and cheerful, getting up a sewing class in the village, resuming the study of Greek, grappling with the natural system in botany, all of which had been fitfully proposed but hindered by interruptions and my father's feebleness.

On a suggestion of Mr. Stafford's, we set to work on that History of Letter Writing which, what with collecting materials, and making translations, lasted us three years altogether, and was a great resource and pleasure, besides ultimately bringing in a fraction towards the great purpose. Emily has confessed that she worked away a good deal of vague, weary depression, and sense of monotony into those Greek choruses: but to us she was always a sunbeam, with her ever ready attention, and the playfulness which resumed more of genuine mirth after the first effort and strain of spirits were over.

Charlotte M. Yonge

Then journal-letters on either side began to bridge the gulf of separation,—those which, minus all the specially interesting portions, are to be seen in the volume we culled from them, and which had considerable success in its day.

Martyn worked in the parish and read with Mr. Henderson till he was old enough for Ordination, and then took the curacy of St. Wulstan's, under a hardworking London vicar, and thenceforth his holidays were our festivals. Our old London friends pitied us for what they viewed as a fearfully dull life, and in the visits they occasionally paid us thought they were doing us a great favour by bringing us new ideas and shooting our partridges.

We hardly deserved their compassion: our lives were full of interest to ourselves—that interest which comes of doing ever so feeble a stroke of work in one great cause; and there was much keen participation in the general life of the Church in the crisis through which she was passing. We found that, what with drawing pictures, writing little books, preparing lessons for teachers, and much besides which is now ready done by the National Society and Sunday School Institute, we could do a good deal to assist Martyn in his London work, and our own grew upon us.

For the first year of her widowhood, my mother shrank from society, and afterwards had only spasmodic fits of doubt whether it were not her duty to make my sister go out more. So that now and then Emily did go to a party, or to make a visit of some days or weeks from home, and then we knew how valuable she was. It would be hard to say whether my mother were relieved or disappointed when Emily refused James Eastwood, in spite of many persuasions, not only from himself, but his family. I believe mamma thought it selfish to be glad, and that it was a failure in duty not to have performed that weighty matter of marrying her daughter; feeling in some way inferior to ladies who had disposed of a whole flock under five and twenty, whereas she had not been able to get rid of a single one!

Of Clarence's doings in China I need not speak; you have read of them in the book for yourselves, and you know how his work prospered, so that the results more than fulfilled his expectations, and raised the firm to the pitch of greatness and reputation which it has ever since preserved, and this without soiling his hands with the miserable opium traffic. Some of the subordinates were so set on the gains to be thus obtained, that he and Lawrence Frith had a severe struggle with them to prevent it, and were forced conjointly to use all their authority as principals to make it impossible. Those two were the greatest of friends. Their chief relaxation was one another's company, and their earnest aim was to support the Christian mission, and to keep up the tone of their English dependants, a terribly difficult matter, and one that made the time of their return somewhat doubtful, even when Walter Castleford was gone out to relieve them. Their health had kept up so well that we had ceased to be anxious on that point, and it was through the Castlefords that we received the first hint that Clarence might not be as well as his absence of complaint had led us to believe.

In fact he had never been well since a terrible tempest, when he had worked hard and exposed himself to save life. I never could hear the particulars, for Lawrence was away, and Clarence could not write about it himself, having been prostrated by one of those chills so perilous in hot countries; but from all I have heard, no resident in Hong-Kong would have believed that Mr. Winslow's courage could ever have been called in question. He ought to have come home immediately after that attack of fever;

for the five years were over, and his work nearly done; but there was need to consolidate his achievements, and a strong man is only too apt to trifle with his health. We might have guessed something by the languor and brevity of his letters, but we thought the absence of detail owing to his expectation of soon seeing us; and had gone on for months expecting the announcement of a speedy return, when an unexpected shock fell on us. Our dear mother was still an active woman, with few signs of age about her, when, in her sixty-seventh year, she was almost suddenly taken from us by an attack of gout in the stomach.

I feel as if I had not done her justice, and as if she might seem stern, unsympathising, and lacking in tenderness. Yet nothing could be further from the truth. She was an old-fashioned mother, who held it her duty to keep up her authority, and counted over-familiarity and indulgence as sins. To her 'the holy spirit of discipline was the beginning of wisdom,' and to make her children godly, truthful, and honourable was a much greater object than to win their love. And their love she had, and kept to a far higher degree than seems to be the case with those who court affection by caresses and indulgence. We knew that her approval was of a generous kind, we prized enthu-siastically her rare betrayals of her motherly tenderness, and we depended on her in a manner we only realised in the desolation, dreariness, and helplessness that fell upon us, when we knew that she was gone. She had not, nor had any of us, understood that she was dying, and she had uttered only a few words that could imply any such thought. On hearing that there was a letter from Clarence, she said, 'Poor Clarence! I should like to have seen him. He is a good boy after all. I've been hard on him, but it will all be right now. God Almighty bless him!'

That was the only formal blessing she left among us.

Indeed, the last time I saw her was with an ordinary good-night at the foot of the stairs. Emily said she was glad that I had not to carry with me the remembrance of those paroxysms of suffering. My dear Emily had alone the whole force of that trial—or shall I call it privilege? Martyn did not reach home till some hours after all was over, poor boy.

And in the midst of our desolateness, just as we had let the daylight in again upon our diminished numbers round the table, came a letter from Hong-Kong, addressed to me in Lawrence Frith's writing, and the first thing I saw was a scrawl, as follows:-

'DEAREST TED—All is in your hands. You can do IT. God bless you all. W. C. W.'

When I came to myself, and could see and hear, Martyn was impressing on me that where there is life there is hope, though indeed, according to poor Lawrence's letter, there was little of either. He feared our hearing indirectly, and therefore wrote to prepare us.

He had been summoned to Hong-Kong to find Clarence lying desperately ill, for the most part semi-delirious, holding converse with invisible forms, or entreating some one to let him alone—he had done his best. In one of his more lucid intervals he had made Lawrence find that note in a case that lay near him, and promise to send it; and he had tried to send some messages, but they had become confused, and he was too weak to speak further.

The next mail was sure to bring the last tidings of one who had given his life for right and justice. It was only a reprieve that what it actually brought was the intelligence that he was still alive, and more sensible, and had been able to take much pleasure in seeing the friend of his youth, Captain Coles, who was there with his ship, the Douro. Then there had been a relapse. Captain Coles had brought his doctor to see him, and it had been pronounced that the best chance of saving him was a sea-voyage. The Douro had just received orders to return to England, and Coles had offered to take home both the friends as guests, though there was evidently little hope that our brother would reach any earthly home. As we knew afterwards, he had smiled and said it was like rehabilitation to have the chance of dying on board one of H.M. ships. And he was held in such respect, and was so entirely one of the leading men of the little growing colony, and had been known as such a friend to the naval men, and had so gallantly aided a Queen's ship in that hurricane, that his passage home in this manner only seemed a natural tribute of respect. A few last words from Lawrence told us that he was safely on board, all unconscious of the silent, almost weeping, procession that had escorted his litter to the Douro's boat, only too much as if it were his bier. In fact, Captain Coles actually promised him that if he died at sea he should be buried with the old flag.

We could not hope to hear more for at least six weeks, since our letter had come by overland mail, and the Douro would take her time. It was a comfort in this waiting time that Martyn could be with us. His rector had been promoted; there was a general change of curates; and as Martyn had been working up to the utmost limits of his strength, we had no scruple in inducing him to remain with us, and undertake nothing fresh till this crisis was past. Though as to rest, not one Sunday passed without requests for his assistance from one or more of the neighbouring clergy.

CHAPTER XLV

ACHIEVED

'And hopes and fears that kindle hope,
An undistinguishable throng,
And gentle wishes long subdued-
Subdued and cherished long.'

S. T. COLERIDGE.

The first that we did hear of our brother was a letter with
a Falmouth postmark, which we scarcely dared to open.
There was not much in it, but that was enough. 'D. G.- I
shall see you all again. We put in at Portsmouth.'

There was no staying at home after that. We three lost no
time in starting, for railways had become available, and
by the time we had driven from the station at Portsmouth
the Douro had been signalled.

Martyn took a boat and went on board alone, for besides
that Emily did not like to leave me, her dress would have
been a revelation that ALL were no longer there to greet
the arrival. The precaution was, however, unnecessary.
There stood Clarence on deck, and after the first greeting,
he laid his hand on Martyn's arm and said, 'My mother is

Charlotte M. Yonge

gone?' and on the wondering assent, 'I was quite sure of it.'

So they came ashore, Clarence lying in the man-of-war's boat, in which his friend insisted on sending him, able now to give a smiling response and salute to the three cheers with which the crew took leave of him. He was carried up to our hotel on a stretcher by half-a-dozen blue jackets. Indeed he was grievously changed, looking so worn and weak, so hollow-eyed and yellow, and so fearfully wasted, that the very memory is painful; and able to do nothing but lie on the sofa holding Emily's hand, gazing at us with a face full of ineffable peace and gladness. There was a misgiving upon me that he had only come back to finish his work and bid us farewell.

Kindly and considerately they had sent him on before with Martyn. In a quarter of an hour's time his good doctor came in with Lawrence Frith, a considerable contrast to our poor Clarence, for the slim gypsy lad had developed into a strikingly handsome man, still slender and lithe, but with a fine bearing, and his bronzed complexion suiting well with his dark shining hair and beautiful eyes. They had brought some of the luggage, and the doctor insisted that his patient should go to bed directly, and rest completely before trying to talk.

Then we heard that his condition, though still anxious, was far from being hopeless, and that after the tropics had been passed, he had been gradually improving. The kind doctor had got leave to go up to London with us, and talk over the case with L—, and he hoped Clarence might be able to bear the journey by the next afternoon.

Presently after came Captain Coles, whom we had not seen since the short visit when we had idolised the big overgrown midshipman, whom Clarence exhibited to our respectful and distant admiration nearly twenty years ago. My mother used to call him a gentlemanly lad, and that was just what he was still, with a singularly soft gentle manner, gallant officer and post-captain as he was. He cheered me much, for he made no doubt of Clarence's ultimate recovery, and he added that he had found the dear fellow so valued and valuable, so useful in all good works, and so much respected by all the English residents, 'that really,' said the captain, 'I did not know whether to deplore that the service should have lost such a man, or whether to think it had been a good thing for him, though not for us, that—that he got into such a scrape.'

I said something of our thanks.

'To tell you the truth,' said Coles, 'I had my doubts whether it had not been a cruel act, for he had a terrible turn after we got him on board, and all the sounds of a Queen's ship revived the past associations, and always of a painful kind in his delirium, till at last, just as I gave him up, the whole character of his fancies seemed to change, and from that time he has been gaining every day.'

We kept the captain to dinner, and gathered a good deal more understanding of the important position to which Clarence had risen by force of character and rectitude of purpose in that strange little Anglo-Chinese colony; and afterwards, I was allowed to make a long visit to Clarence, who, having eaten and slept, was quite ready to talk.

It seemed that the great distress of his illness had been the recurrence—nay, aggravation—of the strange susceptibility of brain and nerve that had belonged to his earlier days, and with it either imagination or perception of the spirit-world. Much that had seemed delirium had

Charlotte M. Yonge

belonged to that double consciousness, and he perfectly recollected it. As Coles had said, the sights and sounds of the ship had been a renewal of the saddest time in his life; he could not at night divest himself of the impression that he was under arrest, and the sins of his life gathered themselves in fearful and oppressive array, as if to stifle him, and the phantom of poor Margaret with her lamp—which had haunted him from the beginning of his illness—seemed to taunt him with having been too fainthearted and tardy to be worthy to espouse her cause. The faith to which he tried to cling WOULD seem to fail him in those awful hours, when he could only cry out mechanical prayers for mercy. Then there had come a night when he had heard my mother say, 'All right now; God Almighty bless him.' And therewith the clouds cleared from his mind. The power of FEELING, as well as believing in, the blotting out of sin, returned, the sense of pardon and peace calmed him, and from that time he was fully himself again, 'though,' he said, 'I knew I should not see my mother here.'

If she could only have seen him come home under the Union Jack, cheered by sailors, and carried ashore by them, it would have been to her like restoration. Perhaps Clarence in his dreamy weakness had so felt it, for certainly no other mode of return to Portsmouth, the very place of his degradation, could so have soothed him and effaced those memories. The English sounds were a perfect charm to him, as well as to Lawrence, the commonest street cry, the very slices of bread and butter, anything that was not Chinese, was as water to the thirsty! And wasted as was his face, the quiet rest and joy were ineffable.

Still Portsmouth was not the best place for him, and we were glad that he was well enough to go up to London in the afternoon; intensely delighting in the May beauty of the green meadows, and white blossoming hedgerows, and the Church towers, especially the gray massiveness of Winchester Cathedral. 'Christian tokens,' he said, instead of the gay, gilded pagodas and quaint crumpled roofs he had left. The soft haze seemed to be such a rest after the glare of perpetual clearness.

We were all born Londoners, and looked at the blue fog, and the broad, misty river, and the brooding smoke, with the affection of natives, to the amazement of Lawrence, who had never been in town without being browbeaten and miserable. That he hardly was now, as he sat beside Emily all the way up, though they did not say much to one another.

He told us it was quite a new sensation to walk into the office without timidity, and to have no fears of a biting, crushing speech about his parents or himself; but to have the clerks getting up deferentially as soon as he was known for Mr. Frith. He had hardly ever been allowed by his old uncle to come across Mr. Castleford, who was of course cordial and delighted to receive him, and, without loss of time, set forth to see Clarence.

The consultation with the physician had taken place, and it was not concealed from us that Clarence's health was completely shattered, and his state still very precarious, needing the utmost care to give him any chance of recovering the effects of the last two years, when he had persevered, in spite of warning, in his eagerness to complete his undertaking, and then to secure what he had effected. The upshot of the advice given him was to spend the summer by the seaside, and if he had by that time gathered strength, and surmounted the symptoms of disease, to go abroad, as he was not likely to be able as yet to bear English cold. Business and cares were to be avoided, and if he had anything necessary to be done, it had better be got over at once, so as to be off his mind. Martyn and Frith gathered that the case was thought doubtful, and entirely dependent on constitution and rallying power. Clarence himself seemed almost passive, caring only for our presence and the accomplishment of his task.

We had a blessed thanksgiving for mercies received in the Margaret Street Chapel, as we called what is now All Saints; but he and I were unfit for crowds, and on Sunday morning availed ourselves of a friend's seat in our old church, which felt so natural and homelike to us elders that Martyn was scandalised at our taste. But it was the church of our Confirmation and first Communion, and Clarence rejoiced that it was that of his first home-coming Eucharist. What a contrast was he now to the shrinking boy, scarcely tolerated under his stigmatised name. Surely the Angel had led him all his life through!

How happy we two were in the afternoon, while the others conducted Lawrence to some more noteworthy church.

'Now,' said Clarence, 'let us go down to Beachharbour. It must be done at once. I have been trying to write, and I can't do it,' and his face lighted with a quiet smile which I understood.

So we wrote to the principal hotel to secure rooms, and set forth on Tuesday, leaving Frith to finish with Mr. Castleford what could not be settled in the one business interview that had been held with Clarence on the Monday.

CHAPTER XLVI

RESTITUTION

'Ah! well for us all some sweet hope lies
Deeply buried from human eyes.'

WHITTIER.

Things always happen in unexpected ways. During the little hesitation and difficulty that always attend my transits at a station, a voice was heard to say, 'Oh! Papa, isn't that Edward Winslow?' Martyn gave a violent start, and Mr. Fordyce was exclaiming, 'Clarence, my dear fellow, it isn't you! I beg your pardon; you have strength enough left nearly to wring one's hand off!'

'I—I wanted very much to see you, sir,' said Clarence. 'Could you be so good as to appoint a time?'

'See you! We must always be seeing you of course. Let me think. I've got three weddings and a funeral to-morrow, and Simpson coming about the meeting. Come to luncheon—all of you. Mrs. Fordyce will be delighted, and so will somebody else.'

There was no doubt about the somebody else, for Anne's

feet were as nearly dancing round Emily as public propriety allowed, and the radiance of her face was something to rejoice in. Say what people will, English-women in a quiet cheerful life are apt to gain rather than lose in looks up to the borders of middle age. Our Emily at two-and-thirty was fair and pleasant to look on; while as for Anne Fordyce at twenty-three, words will hardly tell how lovely were her delicate features, brown eyes, and carnation cheeks, illuminated by that sunshine brightness of her father's, which made one feel better all day for having been beamed upon by either of them. Clarence certainly did, when the good man turned back to say, 'Which hotel? Eh? That's too far off. You must come nearer. I would see you in, but I've got a woman to see before church time, and I'm short of a curate, so I must be sharp to the hour.'

'Can I be of any use?' eagerly asked Martyn. 'I'll follow you as soon as I have got these fellows to their quarters.'

We had Amos with us, and were soon able to release Martyn, after a few compliments on my not being as usual THE invalid; and by and by he came back to take Emily to inspect a lodging, recommended by our friends, close to the beach, and not a stone's throw from the Rectory built by Mr. Fordyce. As we two useless beings sat opposite to each other, looking over the roofs of houses at the blue expanse and feeling the salt breeze, it was no fancy that Clarence's cheek looked less wan, and his eyes clearer, as a smile of content played on his lips. 'Years sit well on her,' he said gaily; and I thought of rewards in store for him.

Then he took this opportunity of consulting me on the chances for Frith, telling of the original offer, and the quiet constancy of his friend, and asking whether I thought Emily would relent. And I answered that I suspected that she would,—'But you must get well first.'

'I begin to think that more possible,' he answered, and my heart bounded as he added, 'she would be satisfied since you would always have a home with US.'

Oh, how much was implied in that monosyllable. He knew it, for a little faint colour came up, as he, shyly, laughed and hesitated, 'That is—if—'

'If' included Mrs. Fordyce's not being ungracious. Nor was she. Emily had found her as kind as in the old days at Hillside, and perfectly ready to bring us into close vicinity. It was not caprice that had made this change, but all possible doubt and risk of character were over, the old wound was in some measure healed, and the friendship had been brought foremost by our recent sorrow and our present anxiety. Anne was in ecstasies over Emily. 'It is so odd,' she said, 'to have grown as old as you, whom I used to think so very grown up,' and she had all her pet plans to display in the future. Moreover, Martyn had been permitted to relieve the Rector from the funeral—a privilege which seemed to gratify him as much as if it had been the liveliest of services.

We were to lunch at the Rectory, and the move of our goods was to be effected while we were there. We found Mrs. Fordyce looking much older, but far less of an invalid than in old times, and there was something more genial and less exclusive in her ways, owing perhaps to the difference of her life among the many classes with whom she was called on to associate.

Somersetshire, Beachharbour, and China occupied our tongues by turns, and we had to begin luncheon without the Rector, who had been hindered by numerous calls; in fact, as Anne warned us, it was a wonder if he got the

Charlotte M. Yonge

length of the esplanade without being stopped half-a-dozen times.

His welcome was like himself, but he needed a reminder of Clarence's request for an interview. Then we repaired to the study, for Clarence begged that his brothers might be present, and then the beginning was made. 'Do you remember my showing you a will that I found in the ruins at Chantry House?'

'A horrid old scrap that you chose to call one. Yes; I told you to burn it.'

'Sir, we have proved that a great injustice was perpetrated by our ancestor, Philip Winslow, and that the poor lady who made that will was cruelly treated, if not murdered. This is no fancy; I have known it for years past, but it is only now that restitution has become possible.'

'Restitution? What are you talking about? I never wanted the place nor coveted it.'

'No, sir, but the act was our forefather's. You cannot bid us sit down under the consciousness of profiting by a crime. I could not do so before, but I now implore you to let me restore you either Chantry House and the three farms, or their purchase money, according to the valuation made at my father's death. I have it in hand.'

Frank Fordyce walked about the room quite overcome. 'You foolish fellow!' he said, 'Was it for this that you have been toiling and throwing away your health in that pestiferous place? Edward, did you know this?'

'Yes,' I answered. 'Clarence has intended this ever since he found the will.'

'As if that was a will! You consented.'

'We all thought it right.'

He made a gesture of dismay at such folly.

'I do not think you understand how it was, Mr. Fordyce,' said Clarence, who by this time was quivering and trembling as in his boyish days.

'No, nor ever wish to do so. Such matters ought to be forgotten, and you don't look fit to say another word.'

'Edward will tell you,' said Clarence, leaning back.

I had the whole written out, and was about to begin, when the person, with whom there was an appointment, was reported, and we knew that the rest of the day was mapped out.

'Look here,' said Mr. Fordyce, 'leave that with me; I can't give any answer off-hand, except that Don Quixote is come alive again, only too like himself.'

Which was true, for Clarence took long to rally from the effort, and had to be kept quiet for some time in the study where we were left. He examined me on the contents of my paper, and was vexed to hear that I had mentioned the ghost, which he said would discredit the whole. Never was the dear fellow so much inclined to be fretful, and when Martyn restlessly observed that if we did not want him, he might as well go back to the drawing-room, the reply was quite sharp—'Oh yes, by all means.'

No wonder there was pain in the tone; for the next words, after some interval, were, when two happy voices came ringing in from the garden behind, 'You see, Edward.'

Somehow I had never thought of Martyn. He had simply seemed to me a boy, and I had decided that Anne would be the crown of Clarence's labours. I answered 'Nonsense; they are both children together!'

'The nonsense was elsewhere,' he said. 'They always were devoted to each other. I saw how it was the moment he came into the room.'

'Don't give up,' I said; 'it is only the old habit. When she knows all, she must prefer—'

'Hush!' he said. 'An old scarecrow and that beautiful young creature!' and he laughed.

'You won't be an old scarecrow long.'

'No,' he said in an ominous way, and cut short the discussion by going back to Mrs. Fordyce.

He was worn out, had a bad night, and did not get up to breakfast; I was waiting for it in the sitting-room, when Mr. Fordyce came in after matins with Emily and Martyn.

'I feel just like David when they brought him the water of Bethlehem,' he said. 'You know I think this all nonsense, especially this—this ghost business; and yet, such—such doings as your brother's can't go for nothing.'

His face worked, and the tears were in his eyes; then, as he partook of our breakfast, he cross-examined us on my statement, and even tried to persuade us that the phantom in the ruin was Emily; and on her observing that she could not have seen herself, he talked of the Brocken Spectre and fog mirages; but we declared the night was clear, and I told him that all the rational theories I had ever heard were far more improbable than the appearance herself, at which he laughed. Then he scrupulously demanded whether this—this (he failed to find a name for it) would be an impoverishment of our family, and I showed how Clarence had provided that we should be in as easy circumstances as before. In the midst came in Clarence himself, having hastened to dress, on hearing that Mr. Fordyce was in the house, and looking none the better for the exertion.

'Look here, my dear boy,' said Frank, taking his hot trembling hand, 'you have put me in a great fix. You have done the noblest deed at a terrible cost, and whatever I may think, it ought not to be thrown away, nor you be hindered from freeing your soul from this sense of family guilt. But here, my forefathers had as little right to the Chantry as yours, and ever since I began to think about such things, I have been thankful it was none of mine. Let us join in giving it or its value to some good work for God—pour it out to the Lord, as we may say. Bless me! what have I done now.'

For Clarence, muttering 'thank you,' sank out of his grasp on a chair, and as nearly as possible fainted; but he was soon smiling and saying it was all relief, and he felt as if a load he had been bearing had been suddenly removed.

Frank Fordyce durst stay no longer, but laid his hand on Clarence's head and blessed him.

CHAPTER XLVII

THE FORDYCE STORY

'For soon as once the genial plain
Has drunk the life-blood of the slain,
Indelible the spots remain,
And aye for vengeance call.'

EURIPIDES—(Anstice).

Still all was not over, for by the next day our brother was
as ill, or worse, than ever. The doctor who came from
London allowed that he had expected something of the
kind, but thought we must have let him exert himself
perilously. Poor innocent Martyn and Anne, they little
suspected that their bright eyes and happy voices had
something to do with the struggle and disappointment,
which probably was one cause of the collapse. As to poor
Frank Fordyce, I never saw him so distressed; he felt as if
it were all his own fault, or that of his ancestors, and,
whenever he was not required by his duties, was lingering
about for news. I had little hope, though Clarence seemed
to me the very light of my eyes; it was to me as though,
his task being accomplished, and the earthly reward
denied, he must be on his way to the higher one.

His complete quiescence confirmed me in the assurance that he thought so himself. He was too ill for speech, but Lawrence, who could not stay away, was struck with the difference from former times. Not only were there no delusions, but there was no anxiety or uneasiness, as there had always been in the former attacks, when he was evidently eager to live, and still more solicitous to be told if he were in a hopeless state. Now he had plainly resigned himself -

'Content to live, but not afraid to die;'

and perhaps, dear fellow, it was chiefly for my sake that he was willing to live. At least, I know that when the worst was over, he announced it by putting those wasted fingers into mine, and saying -

'Well, dear old fellow, I believe we shall jog on together, after all.'

That attack, though the most severe of all, brought, either owing to skilful treatment or to his own calm, the removal of the mischief, and the beginning of real recovery. Previously he had given himself no time, but had hurried on to exertions which retarded his cure, so as very nearly to be fatal; but he was now perfectly submissive to whatever physicians or nurses desired, and did not seem to find his slow convalescence in the least tedious, since he was amongst us all again.

It was nearly a month before he was disposed to recur to the subject of his old solicitude again, and then he asked what Mr. Fordyce had said or done. Just nothing at all; but on the next visit paid to the sick-room, Parson Frank yielded to his earnest request to send for any documents that might throw light on the subject, and after a few days he brought us a packet of letters from his deed-box. They

Charlotte M. Yonge

were written from Hillside Rectory to the son in the army in Flanders, chiefly by his mother, and were full of hot, angry invective against our family, and pity for poor, foolish 'Madam,' or 'Cousin Winslow,' as she was generally termed, for having put herself in their power.

The one most to the purpose was an account of the examination of Molly Cox, the waiting-woman, who had been in attendance on the unfortunate Margaret, and whose story tallied fairly with Aunt Peggy's tradition. She declared that she was sure that her mistress had met with foul play. She had left her as usual at ten o'clock on the fatal 27th of December 1707, in the inner one of the old chambers; and in the night had heard the tipsy return home of the gentlemen, followed by shrieks. In the morning she (the maid) who usually was the first to go to her room, was met by Mistress Betty Winslow, and told that Madam was ill, and insensible. The old nurse of the Winslows was called in; and Molly was never left alone in the sick-room, scarcely permitted to approach the bed, and never to touch her lady. Once, when emptying out a cup at the garden-door, she saw a mark of blood on the steps, but Mr. Philip came up and swore at her for a prying fool. Doctor Tomkins was sent for, but he barely walked through the room, and 'all know that he is a mere creature of Philip Winslow,' wrote the Mrs. Fordyce of that date to her son. And presently after, 'Justice Eastwood declared there is no case for a Grand Jury; but he is a known Friend and sworn Comrade of the Winslows, and bound to suppress all evidence against them. Nay, James Dearlove swears he saw Edward Winslow slip a golden Guinea into his Clerk's Hand. But as sure as there is a Heaven above us, Francis, poor Cousin Winslow was trying to escape to us of her own Kindred, and met with cruel Usage. Her Blood is on their Heads.'

'There!' said Frank Fordyce. 'This Francis challenged Philip Winslow's eldest son, a mere boy, three days after he joined the army before Lille, and shot him like a dog. I turned over the letter about it in searching for these. I can't boast of my ancestors more than you can. But may God accept this work of yours, and take away the guilt of blood from both of us.'

'And have you thought what is best to be done?' asked Clarence, raising himself on his cushions.

'Have you?' asked the Vicar.

'Oh yes; I have had my dreams.'

They put their castles together, and they turned out to be for an orphanage, or rather asylum, not too much hampered with strict rules, combined with a convalescent home. The battle of sisterhoods was not yet fought out, and we were not quite prepared for them; but Frank Fordyce had, as he said, 'the two best women in the world in his eye' to make a beginning.

There was full time to think and discuss the scheme, for our patient was in no condition to move for many weeks, lying day after day on a couch just within the window of our sitting-room, which was as nearly as possible in the sea, so that he constantly had the freshness of its breezes, the music of its ripple, and the sight of its waves, and seemed to find endless pleasure in watching the red sails, the puffs of steam, and the frolics of the children, simple or gentle, on the beach.

Something else was sometimes to be watched. Martyn, all this time, was doing the work of two curates, and was to be seen walking home with Anne from church or school, carrying her baskets and bags, and, as we were given to

Charlotte M. Yonge

understand, discussing by turns ecclesiastical questions, visionary sisterhoods, and naughty children. At first I wished it were possible to remove Clarence from the perpetual spectacle, but we had one last talk over the matter, and this was quite satisfactory.

'It does me no harm,' he said; 'I like to see it. Yes, it is quite true that I do. What was personal and selfish in my fancies seems to have been worn out in the great lull of my senses under the shadow of death; and now I can revert with real joy and thankfulness to the old delight of looking on our dear Ellen as our sister, and watch those two children as we used when they talked of dolls' fenders instead of the surplice war. I have got you, Edward; and you know there is a love "passing the love of women."'

A lively young couple passed by the window just then, and with untamed voices observed -

'There are those two poor miserable objects! It is enough to make one melancholy only to look at them.'

Whereat we simultaneously burst out laughing; perhaps because a choking, very far from misery, was in our throats.

At any rate, Clarence was prepared to be the cordial, fatherly brother, when Martyn came headlong in upon us with the tidings that utterly indescribable, unimaginable joy had befallen him. A revelation seemed simultaneously to have broken upon him and Anne while they were copying out the Sunday School Registers, that what they had felt for each other all their lives was love—'real, true love,' as Anne said to Emily, 'that never could have cared for anybody else.'

Mrs. Fordyce's sharp eyes had seen what was coming, and

accepted the inevitable, quite as soon as Clarence had. She came and talked it over with us, saying she was perfectly satisfied and happy. Martyn was all that could be wished, and she was sincerely glad of the connection with her old friends. So, in fact, was dear old Frank, but he had been running about with his head full, and his eyes closed, so that it was quite a shock to him to find that his little Anne, his boon companion and playfellow, was actually grown up, and presuming to love and be loved; and he could hardly believe that she was really seven years older than her sister had been when the like had begun with her. But if Anne must be at those tricks, he said, shaking his head at her, he had rather it was with Martyn than anybody else.

There was no difficulty as to money matters. In truth, Martyn was not so good a match as an heiress, such as was Anne Fordyce, might have aspired to, and her Lester kin were sure to be shocked; but even if Clarence married, the Earlscombe living went for something (though, by the bye, he has never held it), and the Fordyces only cared that there should be easy circumstances. The living of Hillside would be resigned in favour of Martyn in the spring, and meantime he would gain more experience at Beachharbour, and this would break the separation to the Fordyces.

After all, however, theirs was not to be our first wedding. I have said little of Emily. The fact was, that after that week of Clarence's danger, we said she lived in a kind of dream. She fulfilled all that was wanted of her, nursing Clarence, waiting on me, ordering dinner, making the tea, and so forth; but it was quite evident that life began for her on the Saturdays, when Lawrence came down, and ended on the Mondays, when he went away. If, in the meantime, she sat down to work, she went off into a trance; if she was sent out for fresh air, she walked quarter-deck on the esplanade, neither seeing nor hearing anything, we averred, but some imaginary Lawrence Frith.

If she had any drawback, good girl, it was the idea of deserting me; but then, as I could honestly tell her, nobody need fear for my happiness, since Clarence was given back to me. And she believed, and was ready to go to China with her Lawrence.

CHAPTER XLVIII

THE LAST DISCOVERY

'Grief will be joy if on its edge
Fall soft that holiest ray,
Joy will be grief, if no faint pledge
Be there of heavenly day.'

KEBLE.

We did not move from Beachharbour till September, and
by that time it had been decided that Chantry House itself
should be given up to the new scheme. It was too large for
us, and Clarence had never lived there enough to have any
strong home feeling for it; but he rather connected it with
disquiet and distress, and had a longing to make actual
restitution thereof, instead of only giving an equivalent, as
he did in the case of the farms. Our feelings about the
desecrated chapel were also considerably changed from
the days when we regarded it merely as a picturesque
ruin, and it was to be at once restored both for the benefit
of the orphanage, and for that of the neighbouring
households. For ourselves, a cottage was to be built,
suited to our idiosyncrasies; but that could wait till after
the yacht voyage, which we were to make together for the
winter.

Charlotte M. Yonge

Thus it came to pass that the last time we inhabited Chantry House was when we gave Emily to Lawrence Frith. We would fain have made it a double wedding, but the Fordyces wished to wait for Easter, when Martyn would have been inducted to Hillside. They came, however, that Mrs. Fordyce might act lady of the house, and Anne be bridesmaid, as well as lay the first stone of St. Cecily's restored chapel.

It was on the day on which they were expected, when the workmen were digging foundations, and clearing away rubbish, that the foreman begged Mr. Winslow to come out to see something they had found. Clarence came back, very grave and awe-struck. It was an old oak chest, and within lay a skeleton, together with a few fragments of female clothing, a wedding ring, and some coins of the later Stewarts, in a rotten leathern purse. This was ghastly confirmation, though there was nothing else to connect the bones with poor Margaret. We had some curiosity as to the coffin in the niche in the family vault which bore her name, but both Clarence and Mr. Fordyce shrank from investigations which could not be carried out without publicity, and might perhaps have disturbed other remains.

So on the ensuing night there was a strange, quiet funeral service at Earlscombe Church. Mr. Henderson officiated, and Chapman acted as clerk. These, with Amos Bell, alone knew the tradition, or understood what the discovery meant to the two Fordyces and three Winslows who stood at the opening of the vault, and prayed that whatever guilt there might be should be put away from the families so soon to be made one. The coins were placed with those of Victoria, which the next day Anne laid beneath the foundation-stone of St. Cecily's. I need not say that no one has ever again heard the wailings, nor seen the lady with the lamp.

What more is there to tell? It was of this first half of our lives that I intended to write, and though many years have since passed, they have not had the same character of romance and would not interest you. Our honeymoon, as Mr. Fordyce called the expedition we two brothers made in the Mediterranean, was a perfect success; and Clarence regained health, and better spirits than had ever been his; while contriving to show me all that I was capable of being carried to see. It was complete enjoyment, and he came home, not as strong as in old times, but with fair comfort and capability for the work of life, so as to be able to take Mr. Castleford's place, when our dear old friend retired from active direction of the firm.

You all know how the two old bachelors have kept house together in London and at Earlscombe cottage, and you are all proud of the honoured name Clarence Winslow has made for himself, foremost in works for the glory of God and the good of men—as one of those merchant princes of England whose merchandise has indeed been Holiness unto the Lord.

Thus you must all have felt a shock on finding that he always looked on that name as blotted, and that one of the last sayings I heard from him was, 'O remember not the sins and offences of my youth, but according to Thy mercy, think upon me, O Lord, for Thy goodness.'

Then he almost smiled, and said, 'Yes, He has so looked on me, and I am thankful.'

Thankful, and so am I, for those thirty-four peaceful years we spent together, or rather for the seventy years of perfect brotherhood that we have been granted, and though he has left me behind him, I am content to wait. It cannot be for long. My brothers and sisters, their children, and my faithful Amos Bell, are very good to me; and in writing up to that mezzo termine of our lives, I have been living it over again with my brother of brothers, through the troubles that have become like joys.

REMARKS.

Uncle Edward has not said half enough about his dear old self. I want to know if he never was unhappy when he was young about being LIKE THAT, though mother says his face was always nearly as beautiful as it is now. And it is not only goodness. It IS beautiful with his sweet smile and snowy white hair. ELLEN WINSLOW.

And I wonder, though perhaps he could not have told, what Aunt Anne would have done if Uncle Clarence had not been so forbearing before he went to China. CLARE FRITH.

The others are highly impertinent questions, but we ought to know what became of Lady Peacock. ED. G. W.

REPLY.

Poor woman, she drifted back to London after about ten years, with an incurable disease. Clarence put her into lodgings near us, and did his best for her as long as she lived. He had a hard task, but she ended by saying he was her only friend.

To question No. 2 I have nothing to say; but as to No. 1, with its extravagant compliment, Nature, or rather God, blessed me with even spirits, a methodical nature that prefers monotony, and very little morbid shyness; nor have I ever been devoid of tender care and love. So that I can only remember three severe fits of depression. One, when I had just begun to be taken out in the Square Gardens, and Selina Clarkson was heard to say I was a hideous little monster. It was a revelation, and must have given frightful pain, for I remember it acutely after sixty-five years.

The second fit was just after Clarence was gone to sea, and some very painful experiments had been tried in vain for making me like other people. For the first time I faced the fact that I was set aside from all possible careers, and should be, as I remember saying, 'no better than a girl.' I must have been a great trial to all my friends. My father tried to reason on resignation, and tell me happiness could be IN myself, till he broke down. My mother attempted bracing by reproof. Miss Newton endeavoured to make me see that this was my cross. Every word was true, and came round again, but they only made me for the time more rebellious and wretched. That attack was ended, of all things in the world, by heraldry. My attention somehow was drawn that way, and the study filled up time and thought till my misfortunes passed into custom, and haunted me no more.

My last was a more serious access, after coming into the country, when improved health and vigour inspired cravings that made me fully sensible of my blighted existence. I had gone the length of my tether and over-done myself; I missed London life and Clarence; and the more I blamed myself, and tried to rouse myself, the more despondent and discontented I grew.

This time my physician was Mr. Stafford; I had deciphered a bit of old French and Latin for him, and he was very much pleased. 'Why, Edward,' he said, 'you are a very clever fellow; you can be a distinguished—or what is better—a useful man.'

Somehow that saying restored the spring of hope, and gave an impulse! I have not been a distinguished man, but

Charlotte M. Yonge

I think in my degree I have been a fairly useful one, and I am sure I have been a happy one. E. W.

'Useful! that you have, dear old fellow. Even if you had done nothing else, and never been an unconscious backbone to Clarence; your influence on me and mine has been unspeakably blest. But pray, Mistress Anne, how about that question of naughty little Clare's?' M. W.

'Don't you think you had better let alone that question, reverend sir? Youngest pets are apt to be saucy, especially in these days, but I didn't expect it of you! It might have been the worse for you if W. C. W. had not held his tongue in those days. Just like himself, but I am heartily glad that so he did. A. W.'

Choose from Thousands of 1stWorldLibrary Classics By

A. M. Barnard
Ada Leverson
Adolphus William Ward
Aesop
Agatha Christie
Alexander Aaronsohn
Alexander Kielland
Alexandre Dumas
Alfred Gatty
Alfred Ollivant
Alice Duer Miller
Alice Turner Curtis
Alice Dunbar
Allen Chapman
Alleyne Ireland
Ambrose Bierce
Amelia E. Barr
Amory H. Bradford
Andrew Lang
Andrew McFarland Davis
Andy Adams
Angela Brazil
Anna Alice Chapin
Anna Sewell
Annie Besant
Annie Hamilton Donnell
Annie Payson Call
Annie Roe Carr
Annonaymous
Anton Chekhov
Archibald Lee Fletcher
Arnold Bennett
Arthur C. Benson
Arthur Conan Doyle
Arthur M. Winfield
Arthur Ransome
Arthur Schnitzler
Arthur Train
Atticus
B.H. Baden-Powell
B. M. Bower
B. C. Chatterjee
Baroness Emmuska Orczy
Baroness Orczy
Basil King
Bayard Taylor
Ben Macomber
Bertha Muzzy Bower
Bjornstjerne Bjornson

Booth Tarkington
Boyd Cable
Bram Stoker
C. Collodi
C. E. Orr
C. M. Ingleby
Carolyn Wells
Catherine Parr Traill
Charles A. Eastman
Charles Amory Beach
Charles Dickens
Charles Dudley Warner
Charles Farrar Browne
Charles Ives
Charles Kingsley
Charles Klein
Charles Hanson Towne
Charles Lathrop Pack
Charles Romyn Dake
Charles Whibley
Charles Willing Beale
Charlotte M. Braeme
Charlotte M. Yonge
Charlotte Perkins Stetson
Clair W. Hayes
Clarence Day Jr.
Clarence E. Mulford
Clemence Housman
Confucius
Coningsby Dawson
Cornelis DeWitt Wilcox
Cyril Burleigh
D. H. Lawrence
Daniel Defoe
David Garnett
Dinah Craik
Don Carlos Janes
Donald Keyhoe
Dorothy Kilner
Dougan Clark
Douglas Fairbanks
E. Nesbit
E. P. Roe
E. Phillips Oppenheim
E. S. Brooks
Earl Barnes
Edgar Rice Burroughs
Edith Van Dyne
Edith Wharton

Edward Everett Hale
Edward J. O'Biren
Edward S. Ellis
Edwin L. Arnold
Eleanor Atkins
Eleanor Hallowell Abbott
Eliot Gregory
Elizabeth Gaskell
Elizabeth McCracken
Elizabeth Von Arnim
Ellem Key
Emerson Hough
Emilie F. Carlen
Emily Bronte
Emily Dickinson
Enid Bagnold
Enilor Macartney Lane
Erasmus W. Jones
Ernie Howard Pie
Ethel May Dell
Ethel Turner
Ethel Watts Mumford
Eugene Sue
Eugenie Foa
Eugene Wood
Eustace Hale Ball
Evelyn Everett-green
Everard Cotes
F. H. Cheley
F. J. Cross
F. Marion Crawford
Fannie E. Newberry
Federick Austin Ogg
Ferdinand Ossendowski
Fergus Hume
Florence A. Kilpatrick
Fremont B. Deering
Francis Bacon
Francis Darwin
Frances Hodgson Burnett
Frances Parkinson Keyes
Frank Gee Patchin
Frank Harris
Frank Jewett Mather
Frank L. Packard
Frank V. Webster
Frederic Stewart Isham
Frederick Trevor Hill
Frederick Winslow Taylor

Friedrich Kerst
Friedrich Nietzsche
Fyodor Dostoyevsky
G.A. Henty
G.K. Chesterton
Gabrielle E. Jackson
Garrett P. Serviss
Gaston Leroux
George A. Warren
George Ade
Geroge Bernard Shaw
George Cary Eggleston
George Durston
George Ebers
George Eliot
George Gissing
George MacDonald
George Meredith
George Orwell
George Sylvester Viereck
George Tucker
George W. Cable
George Wharton James
Gertrude Atherton
Gordon Casserly
Grace E. King
Grace Gallatin
Grace Greenwood
Grant Allen
Guillermo A. Sherwell
Gulielma Zollinger
Gustav Flaubert
H. A. Cody
H. B. Irving
H.C. Bailey
H. G. Wells
H. H. Munro
H. Irving Hancock
H. R. Naylor
H. Rider Haggard
H. W. C. Davis
Haldeman Julius
Hall Caine
Hamilton Wright Mabie
Hans Christian Andersen
Harold Avery
Harold McGrath
Harriet Beecher Stowe
Harry Castlemon
Harry Coghill
Harry Houidini

Hayden Carruth
Helent Hunt Jackson
Helen Nicolay
Hendrik Conscience
Hendy David Thoreau
Henri Barbusse
Henrik Ibsen
Henry Adams
Henry Ford
Henry Frost
Henry James
Henry Jones Ford
Henry Seton Merriman
Henry W Longfellow
Herbert A. Giles
Herbert Carter
Herbert N. Casson
Herman Hesse
Hildegard G. Frey
Homer
Honore De Balzac
Horace B. Day
Horace Walpole
Horatio Alger Jr.
Howard Pyle
Howard R. Garis
Hugh Lofting
Hugh Walpole
Humphry Ward
Ian Maclaren
Inez Haynes Gillmore
Irving Bacheller
Isabel Cecilia Williams
Isabel Hornibrook
Israel Abrahams
Ivan Turgenev
J.G.Austin
J. Henri Fabre
J. M. Barrie
J. M. Walsh
J. Macdonald Oxley
J. R. Miller
J. S. Fletcher
J. S. Knowles
J. Storer Clouston
J. W. Duffield
Jack London
Jacob Abbott
James Allen
James Andrews
James Baldwin

James Branch Cabell
James DeMille
James Joyce
James Lane Allen
James Lane Allen
James Oliver Curwood
James Oppenheim
James Otis
James R. Driscoll
Jane Abbott
Jane Austen
Jane L. Stewart
Janet Aldridge
Jens Peter Jacobsen
Jerome K. Jerome
Jessie Graham Flower
John Buchan
John Burroughs
John Cournos
John F. Kennedy
John Gay
John Glasworthy
John Habberton
John Joy Bell
John Kendrick Bangs
John Milton
John Philip Sousa
John Taintor Foote
Jonas Lauritz Idemil Lie
Jonathan Swift
Joseph A. Altsheler
Joseph Carey
Joseph Conrad
Joseph E. Badger Jr
Joseph Hergesheimer
Joseph Jacobs
Jules Vernes
Julian Hawthrone
Julie A Lippmann
Justin Huntly McCarthy
Kakuzo Okakura
Karle Wilson Baker
Kate Chopin
Kenneth Grahame
Kenneth McGaffey
Kate Langley Bosher
Kate Langley Bosher
Katherine Cecil Thurston
Katherine Stokes
L. A. Abbot
L. T. Meade

L. Frank Baum
Latta Griswold
Laura Dent Crane
Laura Lee Hope
Laurence Housman
Lawrence Beasley
Leo Tolstoy
Leonid Andreyev
Lewis Carroll
Lewis Sperry Chafer
Lilian Bell
Lloyd Osbourne
Louis Hughes
Louis Joseph Vance
Louis Tracy
Louisa May Alcott
Lucy Fitch Perkins
Lucy Maud Montgomery
Luther Benson
Lydia Miller Middleton
Lyndon Orr
M. Corvus
M. H. Adams
Margaret E. Sangster
Margret Howth
Margaret Vandercook
Margaret W. Hungerford
Margret Penrose
Maria Edgeworth
Maria Thompson Daviess
Mariano Azuela
Marion Polk Angellotti
Mark Overton
Mark Twain
Mary Austin
Mary Catherine Crowley
Mary Cole
Mary Hastings Bradley
Mary Roberts Rinehart
Mary Rowlandson
M. Wollstonecraft Shelley
Maud Lindsay
Max Beerbohm
Myra Kelly
Nathaniel Hawthrone
Nicolo Machiavelli
O. F. Walton
Oscar Wilde

Owen Johnson
P.G. Wodehouse
Paul and Mabel Thorne
Paul G. Tomlinson
Paul Severing
Percy Brebner
Percy Keese Fitzhugh
Peter B. Kyne
Plato
Quincy Allen
R. Derby Holmes
R. L. Stevenson
R. S. Ball
Rabindranath Tagore
Rahul Alvares
Ralph Bonehill
Ralph Henry Barbour
Ralph Victor
Ralph Waldo Emmerson
Rene Descartes
Ray Cummings
Rex Beach
Rex E. Beach
Richard Harding Davis
Richard Jefferies
Richard Le Gallienne
Robert Barr
Robert Frost
Robert Gordon Anderson
Robert L. Drake
Robert Lansing
Robert Lynd
Robert Michael Ballantyne
Robert W. Chambers
Rosa Nouchette Carey
Rudyard Kipling
Saint Augustine
Samuel B. Allison
Samuel Hopkins Adams
Sarah Bernhardt
Sarah C. Hallowell
Selma Lagerlof
Sherwood Anderson
Sigmund Freud
Standish O'Grady
Stanley Weyman
Stella Benson
Stella M. Francis

Stephen Crane
Stewart Edward White
Stijn Streuvels
Swami Abhedananda
Swami Parmananda
T. S. Ackland
T. S. Arthur
The Princess Der Ling
Thomas A. Janvier
Thomas A Kempis
Thomas Anderton
Thomas Bailey Aldrich
Thomas Bulfinch
Thomas De Quincey
Thomas Dixon
Thomas H. Huxley
Thomas Hardy
Thomas More
Thornton W. Burgess
U. S. Grant
Upton Sinclair
Valentine Williams
Various Authors
Vaughan Kester
Victor Appleton
Victor G. Durham
Victoria Cross
Virginia Woolf
Wadsworth Camp
Walter Camp
Walter Scott
Washington Irving
Wilbur Lawton
Wilkie Collins
Willa Cather
Willard F. Baker
William Dean Howells
William le Queux
W. Makepeace Thackeray
William W. Walter
William Shakespeare
Winston Churchill
Yei Theodora Ozaki
Yogi Ramacharaka
Young E. Allison
Zane Grey